I0603101

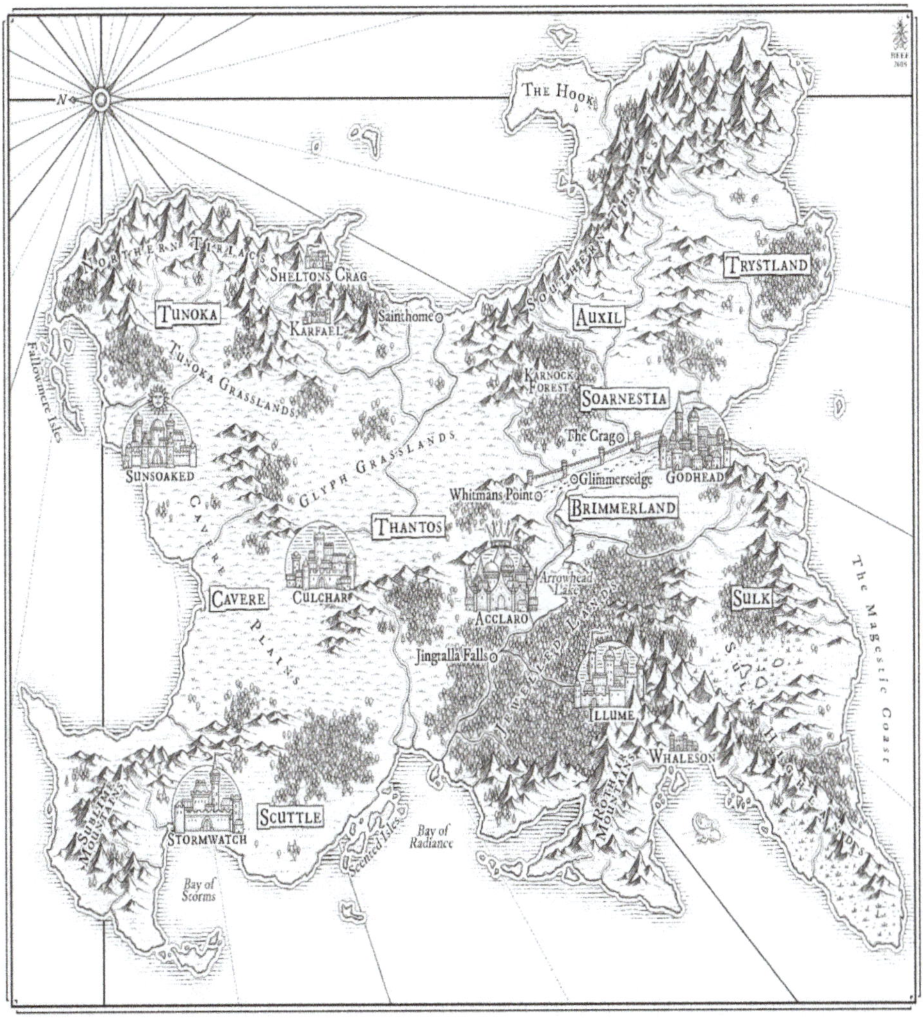

N
The Hook
NORTHERN TIRLACS
SHELTONS CRAG
TUNOKA
KARFAEL
Sainthome
Tunoka Grasslands
SOUTHERN TIRLACS
TRYSTLAND
AUXIL
Karnock Forest
SOARNESTIA
Fallowmere Isle
Glyph Grasslands
The Crag
SUNSOAKED
Glimmersedge
GODHEAD
Whitmans Point
BRIMMERLAND
CAVERE PLAINS
THANTOS
Arrowhead Lake
SULK
CAVERE
CULCHAR
ACCLARO
SEA OF SOUTH
The Magestic Coast
Jingralla Falls
TIRELLED LANDS
ILLUME
SUBLIME MOUNTAINS
SCUTTLE
WHALESON
STORMWATCH
Bay of Radiance
ROTHAR MOUNTAINS
Scented Isle
Bay of Storms

The Elemental Heart

The Elemental Heart by Troy Church
Published by T.A Church Perth Australia 6111

Cover by Justin Randall
Print ISBN: 978-0-6483115-5-3
Ebook ISBN: 978-0-6483115-4-6

Contents

Chapter 1

Nina watched from the guard tower as beside her the flame warrior cursed and spat phlegm in disgust.

'Done my time cleaning pots or emptying bloody chamber pots for my betters, and yet here I am, a fully commissioned flame warrior lugged with looking after an upstart pup while my brethren take the spoils. Bah, what makes you so important anyway, girl?'

Nina would have answered if her mouth hadn't been filled with cloth that kept her on the edge of choking. Just before the attack she had been carried up the tower along with Raul. It was then when her hands had still been free she had seen someone up at the wall above the courtyard peering down, and Nina had waved her arms in warning during that brief moment as the guard climbed up after her. Whoever it was must have seen her since they suddenly disappeared from view.

Nina wished she had of been able to do more to warn the people inside whoever they were. She had watched as Dalwyn's flame warriors swarmed over the remaining guard towers easily dispatching the guards there and then forming up outside the main entrance that opened as if on cue to reveal Katerina. From then on the defenders had no chance as the sounds of merriment turned to shouts of alarm and screams of pain. From beside her Raul sobbed, which earned him a hard kick from their guard. It seemed strange to Nina that the wolfish man was so upset; after all he had been the one to tell Dalwyn where to go.

'Stop your snivelling Raul. What kind of man do you call yourself?' The guard laughed.

It seemed an eternity until Nina and Raul were dragged from the tower and marched into the safe house where flame warriors now dined on the left-overs of the dead and captured defenders who were still being rounded up in the middle of the hall where some sort of celebration had been going on. They were roughly pushed towards the other prisoners when Raul broke free. He managed to pull his gag loose with his tied hands as he charged at Katerina, who calmly stood her ground then tripped him as he attempted to shoulder barge her. When he turned over, blood trickled down the side of his face.

'You said nobody would get hurt, Katerina, that I would be treated well once I led you to the coterie,' said Raul from his prone position.

Katerina knelt by Raul's side then playfully slapped his face.

'Raul, you truly are as stupid as you look. There is something I feel you are entitled to know about me. I am not your new sentinel as I had pretended to be. Caitlyn is dead by my hand, but you will maybe be pleased to know she said your name as I choked the life from her and took her place. Now you have done your bit well and like a snake that you are led us to the rest of the coterie, and as promised I will see you are rewarded. That reward is your life. Now don't be foolish, Raul, you have served your purpose.'

From the other side of the hall the sound of fighting began. Two men ran into the hall then stopped at the sight of the flame warriors and the other prisoners. From behind them, pursuing flame warriors quickly surrounded them. Back to back the two warriors fought, but even Nina knew it was just a matter of time before they fell.

While everyone including her guard were focused on the fight, Nina, who only had her arms tied to the front of her body, ran for the nearest exit. When Nina heard her named shouted, it was too late. She was out the door into a corridor that led to a kitchen area down one way where corpses lay in scarlet puddles. Nina ran the other way, not caring where she went - anywhere would do. When finally her breath was gone, Nina slowed to a walk then hid behind stacked barrels in what appeared to be a store room.

Nina was not sure if she had been pursued. From somewhere close came shouts and screaming, and twice flame warriors passed by the room she hid in as they led more prisoners to the hall. She knew they would come looking for her once Dalwyn heard of her escape. He had referred to her as his trump card, whatever that was, which would get Zacriel to do what he wished. Nina knew Dalwyn well enough by now to know that the old man would never let her escape him.

Nina lost track of time as flame warriors began the search for her, and weariness crept over her muscles. The light of torches were headed for where Nina now hid among piles of stacked weapons leaving her with only one way of escape, a heavy wooden door with metal brackets. Nina managed to lift the bolt, tug the door open, and then slip out into a courtyard area with three pits in the earth and piles of refuse stacked against the stone wall. There was no escape here; the courtyard backed up to the vertical stone of the mountain itself. Realizing the door was still open, Nina moved to shut it. Too late, a figure filled the doorway so thinking quickly Nina lowered herself into a pit of refuse, covering her mouth with a hand to stop from retching.

'Is she out there, Dayne?'

'Can't see her, just pits of refuse here. Looks like this is where they burn all the waste and rubbish, and it smells terrible.'

'Better check anyway, Dayne, I don't feel like having my hide whipped for your incompetence.'

'How was I supposed to know she would run away? The child should be beaten for this.'

'While you check out there, I will try the next room.'

Nina pulled more rubbish over her form, leaving a small gap to breathe from. Something wet seeped into her clothes, and food scraps covered most of her face and chest. Then the guard came outside, his blade out, which he was using to prod around in the first pit. From where she lay Nina could only barely see him, and as she watched he sheathed his blade then undid his trousers to relieve himself. With the other guard gone Nina only had this one between her and safety. Dayne closed his eyes and sighed as a steady stream of piss began, and at that moment Nina lunged up and out of the second pit catching Dayne unawares. Nina reached the man and pushed against him, knocking Dayne into the pit with a cry of alarm. Not waiting to see what happened, Nina slid through the doorway, pulled it shut, then dropped the heavy wooden latch, locking Dayne outside.

From down the corridor came a yell.

'Dayne, have you found her?'

If she waited for the second guard to come she was as good as dead. Nina took off again, losing herself in the corridors until finding an open, unadorned chamber with only one spluttering torch. Nina crawled into an alcove out of sight and began to cry.

The chamber had been meant for so much more. It had been built to showcase the glorious success of how far the Kenzu had come since the King of Scuttle had broken apart the citadel with his catapults and salted the ground so nothing would grow there again. Coming here to the Veiled lands had meant to be a new start for the Kenzu, where they could stay with the coterie safe within their midst until such time as the Mother was ready to receive them from the Kenzu, thus completing the clans sacred duty.

No luxury had been spared with this chamber for Haakon the Kenzu lord. A rack of rare vintages stood against one wall opposite a bed fit for a king complete with real Slaute-hair sheets and goose-feather blankets. A wardrobe complete with the finest of coats, silken shirts and woollen trousers. More shined leather shoes than he would ever need and on the walls a vast array of clan weapons that all told a valuable part of their history forged in blood. Haakon knew them all by name and deed which was one thing he used to pride himself on; now he couldn't care less.

He knelt before a small altar of gold on which sat the most valuable thing of all, the newest volume of the Kenzu clan book that told the complete history of the Kenzu. This twenty eighth volume would continue a tale of the dark and the light times scribed by human hands dedicated to the continuation of clan Kenzu. The first entry would have been one of victory as the clan successfully relocated to their new home, a fortress meant to be impregnable. Now it would open with a tale of betrayal and loss, of Kenzu lives wasted in pointless sacrifice. Haakon dipped the quill in the rare ink as he penned the first of this volume and possibly the last entry for his clan.

On this cold morning I sit chilled not by the cold stone beneath my flesh but the cold bodies of my kin, my people cut down in another act of betrayal. All may be lost, the coterie but one caught by those who would see the Mother destroyed, my love and queen of the ancients who fought her whole life to see this world survive and become a better place now a prisoner again to one who had already broken her spirit and was now free to do so again. Has it all been for nothing? I have a choice to make here and now, knowing that others already are on their way here to their promised refuge of safety. One could take my place and usher in an age of growth no longer bound by the abysmal decisions of the Kenzu's latest master, however, events foretold are coming to pass and to continue in failure is something no true Kenzu could live with. Weighed down by my failures, I know only of one way to restore mine and the Kenzu honour. This, my last deed, will close the history of the finest of clans and like my bones be lost in the dust of ages.

Haakon, Kenzu lord.

Haakon tore his shirt down the middle, popping buttons as he bared his torso. From his side Haakon drew the long knife blade from its sheath, admiring the immaculately made steel that had once taken the lives of three rival clan lords, thus paving way for Kenzu greatness. The point of the blade he placed in the hollow of his throat trying to ignore the slight shaking of his hands and struggling to level out his ragged breaths. Then Haakon rose onto his knees, ready to fall forward onto this most famous of blades that would soon be stained with the blood of four clan lords.

A quiet came over him, an acceptance of what was to come, that he had done all he could in his struggle over a life in which death had touched him many times, taking those he loved while leaving him alive with only their memories. Finally he would be able to rest, to let go of the pain, to forget his failure.

His weight shifted, he exhaled and then a noise came to him, crying- someone was crying, and it sounded like a child. Haakon lowered the blade noticing the bead of blood glittering on the sword point and feel of blood trickling down his chest. With a curse he rose to his feet. He couldn't even kill himself right.

Nina could see the shadows disperse as the two guards searching for her headed in the direction of the chamber where she hid.

'Can't believe you were bested twice by a child, Dayne, and you're covered with your own piss.'

'Put a stop to it, Fen, or I might just take it out on you.'

'Quaking in my boots I am, Dayne.' The sound of laughter carried down to where Nina stood in the alcove. She edged deeper against the wall opposite the doorway through which they would come for her. The time waiting had been spent loosening the ropes that bound her wrists, which seemed easy until she tried it. All that Nina had done was cause stinging wounds to her arms, but she wouldn't give up.

She would never do that.

There came a grating sound to her left that alarmed Nina as the wall seemed to disappear. Before she could scream, a hand covered her mouth roughly; then she was dragged kicking into the space that had opened up.

'Shhhh, quiet, Dayne, did you hear that noise?'

The two guards must have been just outside the chamber, thought Nina as she struggled. Whoever held her lifted her small body off the floor so she banged her heels against their shins repeatedly, but they didn't let go, and she was dragged backwards only able to watch as the wall closed before her.

A voice whispered in her ear, 'Stay quiet unless you want them to find you too.'

They stayed like that as the two guards searched the chamber where Nina had hidden. The sound of the guards searching finally faded away, and the hand over Nina's mouth relaxed just a bit, enough for her to bite down hard. Nina followed it up with another kick against the shins of her enemy. There came a curse and she was free again; scuttling away on all fours, Nina hit the wall where she turned, putting her back against it and listened.

The man's voice came from her left.

'I know you are there, child, and I mean you no harm or I would never have saved your damned life.' There was a pause as whoever it was waited for an answer, but Nina refused to let him know where she was and instead began ever so slowly edging around the wall away from his voice.

'Okay, then, since you won't talk with me I will tell you what will happen now. I am going to start a fire to light a fire.'

Nina stayed where she was as the man rummaged around. Sparks were created as he struck a flint against steel repeatedly. Nina thought it would never light, but then the sparks caught and the man began to blow on the sparks, which soon turned to flames with a small pile of tinder and paper. Nina watched him silently as he continued to feed the flames until a nice little blaze had started on the floor before him.

She took the time to weigh up her rescuer, who was naked from the waist up. Blood had dried at the front of his neck and dripped from a wound to one of his hands. With the uninjured hand he brushed the hair from his eyes, which was beginning to grey at the temples, then he looked up at her.

'There you are. Come warm yourself, I won't hurt you, and it's cold.' The man inspected his hand then tore a strip of cloth from a shirt by his feet to bind the wound.

'You sure know how to bite. It damn well felt like you took my hand off.' He rose then moved to one of the walls where unlit torches sat in sconces and were soon burning.

The chamber was like a temple, thought Nina as she kept one eye warily on the man. There was even a book on a stand made from gold, but maybe that was just her imagination, and what was with all the weapons on the walls? When Nina turned back to look at the man, he in turn was watching her as he squatted by the flames.

'Do you live here?' asked Nina.

'This is as much my home as anywhere, though now it seems to have lost the feeling of safety a home should give. I saw you in the tower when you waved your hands, and I thank you for the warning which is the only reason I'm alive. Unfortunately that cannot be said for my people.'

'You have a picture on your skin like someone I once met.'

'Is that so, and who would that person be then, child?'

'Her name was Zahra, and she was real nice to me.'

The man sat taller, his eyes full of surprise and sudden interest.

'May I ask where you met this Zahra?'

'Illume city, and then Acclaro where I was with bad people who wanted to hurt her and her friends.'

'Tell me, child, is Zahra here also?' asked the man, motioning Nina forward.

Slowly Nina moved to the opposite side of the fire. The heat felt real good.

'No, she isn't. Zahra had a friend she had to help take away, but I don't know where they went.'

'Never mind, child, it may be nothing, but I also know a Zahra who went to Illume. She is very important to me and so is her friend, but maybe they are different people.'

'You seem nice even if you made me bite you, but I am so tired of running away and letting bad people hurt me, so if you too were one of the bad people I would have had to kill you.'

The man's sudden soft laughter made Nina smile.

'Now that we have decided you won't kill me, it is time for introductions, don't you think? I will go first. I am Haakon.'

'My name is Nina. I saw lots of people dead in the hall and others have been taken prisoner by Dalwyn, who is a terrible old man. Are those people your family?'

'Yes, they are family in a way I guess. Who is Dalwyn?'

'Dalwyn is a nasty man who talks a lot about magic and he will hurt anyone to make it come back.'

'Why are you with this nasty Dalwyn then, Nina, and not home with your parents?'

'My parents died a long time ago, but I will have revenge. It is a bit of a long story and I'm hungry. Do you have any food?'

'Only this,' said Haakon as he passed a small pouch holding two strips of dried meat, which Nina began to chew.

'Eat, Nina, then tell me your story while we wait.'

'Wait for what, Haakon?' she replied after swallowing a mouthful.

'We wait for the bad people to rest. Even they must sleep, then we can find out who is still alive and also collect food and supplies for both of us.'

'We are like a team,' grinned Nina over the fire.

'Yes we are a team now, is that okay with you?'

Nina thought a moment then nodded her head. 'I would like that Haakon. Now are you ready for my story?'

Haakon added the last of the paper and thin tinder that he had scavenged outside in the darkness to the fire. From across the fire Nina regarded him with sleepy eyes where she lay huddled using the clan book as a pillow. The clan ancestors would be turning in their graves at this, he thought, amused. The last thing he had wanted was to sit here with the child and hear her story when he had no idea if his clansmen, Latasha and the coterie still lived. The arrival of Nina had actually saved him from taking his life in dishonour, and though that stain still remained on his soul he had made his choice. Now he must see it through.

Haakon slipped out through the hidden door. He would find who still lived and where Dalwyn Trevlon was now, and then he would pay for all the pain he had caused Latasha and Haakon's people. He just hoped he would be in time.

The flame warriors seemed everywhere through the safe house as Haakon ghosted his way through the rooms, using the secret inner passages when he was able to get an idea of what he was up against. Keeping his sword sheathed was the hardest thing for Haakon, who ached to kill those who dared harm his kin, clan, family, but those urges were beaten down by that inner voice warning him not to overreact lest he also become one of the captives.

Dalwyn and his men wouldn't know if he still lived or was even here, and that element of surprise could serve him well in the days to come.

Haakon watched as the survivors of the attack were herded into the cells that had before tonight never been used, and he would never had thought his people would be the first to grace that cold unforgiving place. As he watched he gained some relief to see the coterie members still lived, though he longed to know whether the one he only truly cared for was also alive.

Haakon stayed hidden in that place long after the last prisoners were put in the cells. The two, twin ancients were imprisoned here, but there was no sign of Latasha, and he steeled himself to the possibility she might truly be dead. Until he saw her with his own eyes he would not believe that to be true. It was possible that Dalwyn had Latasha in another part of the safe house.

Just when he was ready to leave and continue the search for Latasha, the door to the corridor that led to the cells banged open and then he saw her being carried in the arms of a large soldier, her dress torn, long pale hair partially covering her face. Latasha looked so small in the arms of that warrior, and it broke Haakon's heart all over again to see his lover endure more pain when she had suffered enough already. Latasha was dumped inside the cell, where she lay unmoving as the guard locked the door then joined two more flame warriors at a table where one man produced a set of playing cards with a smile and began to deal.

Saving Latasha or the coterie was not a task for this night that was nearly done. He needed to return to Nina before she woke again, and as he made his way back to her only stopping to claim an array of food and a water skin, he couldn't help but worry that when he got there she too would be gone or lying broken like his Latasha.

Back in the clan room Haakon stoked the fire again and covered Nina with a blanket. Tired beyond belief, he lay down searching for the relief sleep would bring from reality and silently praying to whatever forces might be listening that a chance to redeem the deaths of his clansmen would be coming soon.

Nina pretended to still be sleeping as Haakon covered her with a blanket then lay down himself. The truth was Haakon scared her with those intense eyes of his and his quick movements. Knowing that he was friends with Zahra made Nina feel better, and as she drifted off again feeling safe for the first time in a long while she wondered if she would ever see Zahra again.

Nina awoke the next day to the sight of Haakon readying his weapons. As she watched he oiled a long, curved blade then filled a quiver with crossbow bolts.

'Now you are awake, you need to eat some food. We have a big day ahead and it's already four chimes after dawn.'

'Big day, how?'

'Nina. Today we go to war. We will make those flame warriors regret the moment they entered this place and we will drive Dalwyn crazy with the problems we create for him.'

'But, Haakon, there is only us two, not an army.'

'Precisely, Nina, and that is why we can be so dangerous. Nobody will expect that we can cause so much trouble.'

Chapter 2

Dalwyn Trevlon stood by the fire warming his hands as he picked at the trays of untouched food that were found in the kitchen, presumably for the Kenzu celebrations that had been well under way when his men attacked the safe house. The Kenzu had fought like men possessed as they battled his flame warriors through the hallways. That had cost Dalwyn over three score of men, and their only mistake had been not barring the doors to the safe house or posting enough sentries which ultimately allowed Dalwyn's flame warriors to breach the defences.

Though he hated to put any trust in Infernals, the other three lords excluding Zacriel had been true to their word and had allowed Dalwyn safe passage out of Acclaro as well as providing transport to get Dalwyn safely across the Tiriacs to the Veiled lands. The trip had been terrifying, and the act of just recalling the traumatic event made Dalwyn shiver despite the heat radiating from the flames beside him. On steeds of deathly horses like the legendary beasts of Cavere without the blood flowing through their veins, Dalwyn and his men had ridden the winds holding on for their dear lives amidst the keening cries of the beasts and their soulless rolling eyes. Given the choice Dalwyn had silently promised himself he would never ride the beasts again, and he had in fact already thought of alternative travel to leave here when he headed back to Acclaro victorious with the coterie.

His second in command, Flint, a capable warrior trained in the Cavere legions before fleeing after killing a high ranking officer, approached Dalwyn and waited silently to be noticed.

'Is the safe house secure, Flint?'

'Yes. Lord Dalwyn, although we have a few minor troubles to deal with still.'

Dalwyn poured himself wine then turned his chair to face Flint. 'Minor, how?'

'Nothing you need to be so worried about, Lord Dalwyn,' said the man as a twitch of muscles below his right eye betrayed his nervousness.

Dalwyn raised his goblet to drink, his hand wavering slightly with the shakes that lately had become more prominent. This cursed body was failing him ever so slowly.

'Tell me about these minor troubles that are worrying you.'

'The lord Kenzu, Haakon, has not been found. We have searched the dead and the whole of the safe house. Some of our men say that the place is riddled with secret passages.'

'Is that it?'

'Unfortunately, no, it isn't Lord Dalwyn. One of the coterie named Ishmael Shantari isn't here at the safe house. I had the coterie members questioned, and they proved less than cooperative.'

'Raul had told us they would all be here, so how is it that we have missed one? If he has betrayed us I will skin him like I did Brianna Dusk.'

Dalwyn surveyed the array of food on the table then shook his head in dismay.

'I seem have lost my appetite. Pass that wine decanter then leave me.'

Dalwyn poured the last of the wine then smashed the crystal decanter on the stone floor before noticing Flint was still beside him.

'I told you to leave me, and yet you are still here Flint, why?'

'There is one other matter you should know of, my lord.'

'Then enlighten me already.' Dalwyn growled.

'Nina escaped her guard and is somewhere in the safe house.'

The goblet bounced off Flint's chest, showering the man with wine. If Dalwyn had hoped for some sort of reaction like a flinch, he was left disappointed. Flint still stood stone still as wine rivulets dripped down his face.

Dalwyn was on his feet now. How could his men continue to be so incompetent?

'Rather than just standing here, don't you think you all should be once again covering every stone of this damn place until you find that damn Kenzu leader and Nina?'

Flint saluted then spun on his heels, indicating to a group of nearby flame warriors.

'C'mon, you heard Lord Dalwyn, find them. And until you do none of us rest!'

Dalwyn sat in the hall long into the night sipping the fine wines of the Kenzu as he pondered his next move. Already he had sent word to his brother asking for aid in transporting him, his men, and the prisoners out of here and also requesting extra troops. Whether or not his younger brother took him seriously was yet to be seen.

From behind him Katerina arrived with a full bottle in hand and with a clever little grin plastered on her face that made him want to slap it off.

'The prisoners have been locked away in the cells. Care if I join you, Dalwyn?'

'By all means, Katerina, come sit beside me and tell me how it is that Raul failed to tell us one of the coterie wasn't present here at the safe house.'

He watched in amusement as the woman paused ever so slightly then recovered her composure and sat beside him. She filled his mug then raised her own in toast.

'To you, Lord Dalwyn, and this small victory.'

Dalwyn didn't honour her toast by drinking and instead he just glared at her, waiting for an explanation.

'The coterie have abilities that are surfacing since they have been recovering the crystals that the Mother has tasked them with finding. Ishmael Shantari was supposed to meet the other coterie members here, but instead chose to ignore their shared task in order to chase his faith at the godhead. This information was kept from Raul and the coterie until it was too late to do anything about it.'

'Where is this Ishmael now?'

'That as yet is unknown, Lord Dalwyn. Raul has spoken of the coterie needing to be joined to complete their task with the crystals, but as yet he says none of them know what they are to be used for.'

Dalwyn rose on legs that were becoming unsteady. 'We will return to Acclaro with the coterie, and it makes sense that if magic is to return to this world then this Ishmael will be wanting to reunite with them. Acclaro is just the place for us to return so that he can surrender to us. Then, Kaitlin, we can control what they do.' He stood before her.

Looking up at him, Kaitlin smiled coyly and let one hand glide up Dalwyn's thigh. He stood staring down as she loosened his belt.

'No, leave that, I have no interest.' But his words were cut off by the warm caress of her hand, and when their eyes met he could see the leer clearly in her features.

'Kaitlin, enough of this.'

'Shhhhh, my lord, you are so tense, and even you need a little release. After all, you a still a man.'

Dalwyn felt himself begin to harden and then a thought came to him that shattered the moment and the pleasure that surely would have come. *She pities me, he realized,* and with that any chance of that release turned to softness as below him Katerina doubled her efforts then put down her goblet, pulled her long auburn hair to the side and lowered her head.

Dalwyn pushed her away. Her look of surprise only angered him more.

'I said enough of that! I don't need your pity, Katerina,' said Dalwyn, stepping away and relacing his trousers.

'You don't need to be embarrassed, Dalwyn, there are ways of dealing with it if you have problems. Maybe it was the wine.'

'Shut up, woman, I have no problem rising to the occasion if that is what you are implying. I just don't want you or your dreary company. If I want a whore I will pay for one.'

Katerina rose to her feet and began to walk away before Dalwyn stopped her with a hand on her shoulder. She stopped but didn't turn around.

'Tomorrow you will leave us. I will pay you the full amount owed, but I have no further use for your services. Now leave me alone.'

Dalwyn watched Katerina stride away with a straight back. She was a strong woman and had to be in her profession, attractive too, but he would never allow a woman to bed him in pity. Half a bottle left now, and drinking straight from the neck Dalwyn wound his way through the unfamiliar building to his new room where the one and only lord of the Kenzu should have been sleeping.

He posted a guard by the open door in case the Kenzu fool had any inkling of attacking him then he fell onto the thick bed and sighed. He had missed the pleasure of a decent bed. In the morning he would visit the coterie and find out the answers he still needed.

Chapter 3

The next morning Dalwyn waved away his guards attempts to give him breakfast. He had slept late and only rose when Katerina arrived to take her leave. One of his men bought his money chest from which Dalwyn counted out the cetas he had promised the assassin then without a second thought dismissed her. Dalwyn wanted to see the prisoners they had captured. He took Flint with him, though the man looked exhausted from searching all night for Nina and the Kenzu lord. Already knowing the answer, Dalwyn asked anyway.

'Did you manage to find the Kenzu lord or that upstart child?'

'No my lord, we have failed you.'

'Flint, I am unused to failure and simply won't allow it again.'

They were at the cells now. Dalwyn looked over the Kenzu survivors in the first two cells before stopping at the cell with Raul and two other women who were sitting discussing something in hushed tones. Someone lay on a pallet behind them, but Dalwyn couldn't make out their features.

'In the days to come, Flint I am going to need to have beside me the most capable warriors. You have impressed me up to this point, and it disappoints me deeply to know of this failure that may just prove to be our undoing.' Dalwyn stopped and watched the three prisoners who had not even noticed him.

Raul stood and approached the bars when he saw Dalwyn, and that was when Dalwyn saw the figure on the pallet ever so slight and petite with skin of palest moon and long silver hair. *Could it be?* he thought to himself. Surely not, she would have died from those wounds, and yet…

'Lord Dalwyn, is this truly necessary to keep us locked up here? We have agreed not to flee, and it is important that we all unite to complete our task with the magic.'

'Move aside, Raul.'

'What, why?'

'Flint, bring that one on the pallet here for me to see, I would look upon them.'

Two warriors opened the cell, their drawn blades enough to make the other three prisoners back away as they dragged the pallet over to the bars. The figure lying on the pallet awoke and sat up, waves of silver tresses spilling down around her face, a face that Dalwyn knew well from the time he spent cutting the answers from her with his blades.

Latasha looked up, her eyes going wide as she saw Dalwyn. She shook her head twice as if to shake away the remnants of sleep and the image that must be the fading reminder of a terrifying nightmare she had thought left behind. He smiled at her.

'Hello, Latasha Meldoriel, have you missed me?'

'No, it can't be, no, please don't let it be real!' Then the screaming began.

Later when Dalwyn had recovered from the effects of the wine he sent for his men to bring Latasha to him in the dining hall. Earlier he had his men prepare two meals before the fire. As he waited for her arrival, Dalwyn gazed into the fire, which gave him a similar feeling to when he was accessing the astral world in those first moments of each journey where everything bled together before sorting themselves out into the amber landscape. If his men didn't find Nina soon, Dalwyn would enter the astral to hunt and find her himself. In their time together Raul had taught Dalwyn some useful tricks to use while in the astral that he was looking forward to trying.

Dalwyn turned when he heard his men approaching. One carried Latasha in his arms, and even there she managed to look regal and unbothered by her current situation. Dalwyn knew this was only some strong, pointless act of bravado she could never hope to keep up as she had shown this morning when coming face to face with him for the first time since he had found her.

There was an awkward moment as the men placed Latasha on the chair opposite Dalwyn, not sure how to place her legs, but she managed to sit normally even with the useless things dangling below her wasted from disuse.

Dalwyn regarded her challenging glare a moment then grasped a jug and rose to his feet.

'I found a bottle of your people's winter wine; would you care for some?'

Latasha just nodded in reply, so Dalwyn waited eyebrows raised in question until she answered him.

'Yes I would like to once again taste that,' she said as if every word hurt her. Dalwyn poured himself wine then purposefully left Latasha's glass empty.

'Come now Latasha, we know each other well enough by now to put all pretence aside and share a meal as we discuss what is going to happen now.'

'Dalwyn, why should I give you that satisfaction? You are no better off than last time we met at my home or any closer to succeeding in your blind aspiration of attaining magical skill.'

'If I am no better off, then you are definitely worse off, Latasha, though I must say you have recovered from the injuries you sustained incredibly well. I was truly surprised to see you in the cells like a common criminal.'

'You may have broken my body, Dalwyn, but my mind is my own and you can never take that from me.'

'Are you so sure? Because given the time I could tear every secret from you, or have you forgotten that day in your home when you shared the names of the coterie with me just to escape the attentions of my knives? A second time and you would break before the first cut. But enough of that,' said Dalwyn, standing suddenly, which caused Latasha to flinch.

'Now let's toast to the one thing we both want, the return of magic.'

Latasha could only watch as Dalwyn drank down the sweet, light, bubbled wine that from its aroma hinted at strawberries and plum.

'Now you can choose to ignore this fine meal or my company all you want, Latasha. There are questions I need answered, and if you refuse to play along then I will have to start taking out my frustrations on the other prisoners. So play nice and share a meal since it may even be your last.'

Dalwyn took it upon himself to serve Latasha a plate of cheese, fresh vegetables and roast fowl drizzled with thick gravy. With a second thought he added sugared pastries as a dessert. They sat a while eating while silently scrutinizing each other until Latasha wiped her mouth with a napkin and lay down her cutlery.

'Dalwyn, do you even realize how dangerously close you came to destroying everything when you killed poor Brianna Dusk?'

'Trial and error was all I was given to work with. Had you informed me that killing her would not have the desired effect, then the poor woman might be still alive. I blame you for that, because I gave you every chance to tell me what you knew, but you didn't and look where we are now.'

Latasha laughed as she shook her head slowly.

'I told you that the magic must return at the right time, ushered in when the Mother is ready to receive it once again. But you just couldn't wait, Dalwyn, you had to force the situation because you are losing the final battle, which is old age, and you cannot bear to face the death that gains on you day by day. Even if you were to gain some power when it returns, it will consume you.'

'That is one risk I am willing to take, Dalwyn said. 'I will not die in this forsaken, wreck of a body, and I only want was is rightfully mine like it was my ancestors'. I will see my family returned to our birth city, Karfael, or die trying.'

'It seems you are content to drag us down into the Infernal lands with you. For what, your ego?' Latasha asked. 'The return of magic may be so different to what it once was since nobody can hope to guess what the Mother has in mind. If we cannot usher the magic back to our world under the correct circumstances, nothing will have changed. The time of upheaval is supposed to be over, while the return of magic is a time of change, new beginnings, and a chance to make things right and restore the right relationship with the Mother.'

'If you are so intent on seeing this come to pass, Latasha then share your knowledge with me. You can start with the crystals.'

'I don't know what you are even talking about,' said Latasha, reaching for the wine and pouring herself a glass.

Dalwyn called over one of his men who held a small sack, then emptied the contents onto the table among the dishes revealing a deep, red rock that flared with some inner light every few moments and a dark green one that seemed to drink in the very light around it.

'Two of the prisoners you shared the cell with had these crystals with them. Does that refresh your memory now, Latasha, or must I execute one of the prisoners to make you speak?'

'You already had many innocents executed for no reason other than your lust for blood, Dalwyn, so I hardly think you will stop killing anyone else even if I tell you.'

'Well, yes, but the deaths of those of the Kenzu clan are not on your conscience, while the next ones will be. Must I sour our meal with the death of one of the coterie? After Brianna was killed I witnessed with my own eyes the magic leave her then shoot off in different directions. For a long time I pondered what that meant, and it was only recently I realized that the magic released with her death sought out the magic within each of the coterie, so that means we can kill one and it will do nothing but strengthen the others who remain.'

Latasha banged a tiny fist down on the table, making her glass fall over and utensils clatter to the ground.

'That is not so, Dalwyn. The coterie were all chosen by the Mother when the magic passed to them. All five were needed to be sure when the magic is returned it happens in the correct way thus avoiding as much upheaval as possible.'

'Where will these crystals go then?'

'The crystals will combine and be protected within a great elemental tower where they must be kept in balance. This balance will affect our world, and it gives the Mother the power over us and our world that she never had while ensuring those who live there fight to maintain that balance or suffer the effects of their negligence.'

'So suddenly you choose to open up to me. Why, Latasha?'

'In the slight hope of clearing your muddled head enough so you realize there is a path that must be followed as we strive to return the magic in as safer way as possible.'

'But what will that mean for us individuals?'

'It will mean power can still be accessed and yet the Mother will not allow herself to be at the mercy of power hungry individuals that threaten her existence ever again. Yes, you can learn magic if you live by the laws that exist.'

'What laws, Latasha? I want details!'

'Now that is the one thing I will never share with you,' snarled Latasha, leaning forward.

'You may do as you will with me or anybody else, but it will change nothing except the final outcome. Mess with the coterie anymore and I can promise you that the Mother will take vengeance upon you like you could never believe. The Mother is so filled with anger at how the races betrayed her once before that should it happen again that her only chance at restoring balance is thwarted then all of us will suffer and your precious magic that will restore your lost youth will never happen.'

Dalwyn smashed the dishes before him to the ground. 'You lie, Latasha. Why would the Mother destroy us all? We are her children, or so your kind have always preached, haven't they?

'Every Mother has the ability to punish her children. When I first was made aware of the damage that had been done to the Mother and shared it with the council, we begged the Mother for a second chance. That chance was the Severing, and now the Mother has healed and is ready to restore this world to its former state. I have seen the results of that failure should the coterie fail in its chance to make sure this happens. The Mother will turn her full fury upon the world, and where once we have enjoyed the bountiful plains, lush forests, calm seas, they will all be turned against us mortals. Is that the sort of world you want to live in, Dalwyn?'

Dalwyn, sat regarding this thin creature before him who sat shaking with emotion and anger, and as much as he wanted to deny it, he believed her. His silence only made her bolder, it seemed.

'Dalwyn you and I and a great many others are fighting for the same thing. If we just work to together, imagine what we can accomplish as well as keeping our world whole.'

Dalwyn stood again. Grasping the crystal decanter in one hand, he slugged down some of its contents then dashed the crystal against the fireplace, the wine hissing as it snuffed out most of the flames. With the shadows dancing behind him he turned to look at the twisted ancient before him that sickened him with her weakness and lies.

'You say we can achieve this transition together, and yet the Severing was the greatest example to show that this will never happen. Mankind is unable to work together on such a vast scale, add into that the secrecy and arrogance of your race who never would have dreamed of sharing their knowledge with man you have a major problem. What was lawfully mine was taken away before I could claim it, now it's time I take that back. And you, Latasha Meldoriel, will not be able to stop me.'

Chapter 4

Rapture climbed the stairs and came to a stop in front of the double doors to the Zacriel's chamber. Two hulking Infernals in blackened armour that leaked slime from the joints barred his path with their halberds.

'The Bone Lord has instructed us that nobody is to enter. He wishes to be alone.'

Rapture untied the thick whip coiled at his belt, letting it fall into his palm with exaggerated slowness. The two guards tracked his movement. They too had heard the tales of Rapture and the weapon that had torn the life from so many souls.

'Rapture, we are bound by our oath to Zacriel. I repeat, we cannot let you pass…'

The whip flicked out and entwined itself around the armoured hulks neck, then he was tugged forward falling to his knees. Rapture stuck the point of his stiletto blade into the gap of the guard's helmet visor.

'I am his advisor you fools, and if you wish me to inform the, Bone Lord, that the news I withheld from him was due to his personal guards refusal of entry, then you are braver than I. If it wasn't important I wouldn't even bother trying to gain entry, you morons.'

Rapture uncoiled his whip and kicked the kneeling guard in the backside, sending him clattering down the stairs in a heap. The remaining guard moved to point his halberd at Rapture then decided against it and stood aside.

The chamber beyond was drenched in shadow as the dying embers in the fire grate fought to stave of the darkness. Rapture's night vision adapted to the chamber, which now had been refurnished with the finest pieces even though they would never get much use. Even now he could see the thin layer of dust and spider webs that coated everything, showing the Bone Lords dislike of the royal chamber.

Rapture knew he would find Zacriel on the balcony where his lord would sit for chimes at a time looking out over the city as if it was something to behold only and not partake. His lord felt trapped here in the capital of the mortals, and Rapture worried that the loss of the human child, Nina, would make him shy away from his duties more and more. He paused to listen at the balcony door, but there was nothing except the soft keening of the early morning wind. Rapture took in a deep breath and turned the handle.

Zacriel sat staring at the canvas board leaning against the balcony. It had been painted in his likeness, and he had to admit that the artist had managed to capture his image almost perfectly. From the missing nose and disgusting burn wounds that had twisted the tissue of his face, neck and arms, to the regal pose he often adopted when looking down over Acclaro from this very place, it was a masterpiece. However, the artist had managed to get one thing wrong. The image of Zacriel was smiling.

That smile took away from the imposing figure that he had wanted painted, and replaced it with a phony double that seemed content with its place in the world, lost in a memory or sight that warmed the heart. Zacriel had planned to tear the painting to shreds. He even toyed with the idea of throwing the painter from the balcony, and yet he found himself repeatedly drawn to the image. As he sat once again studying the fine piece of art he realized the sight of that captured moment of happiness evoked a vivid memory from a lifetime ago.

The streets had already been steeped in shadows when Zacriel stopped playing street shot with the other children. They had lost both the games, but he was just happy to be asked to play since he had no real friends, until now that was. When he left the playing area the sun sat just above the city. His father would kill him. Zacriel set off at a sprint. He barrelled around a corner straight into a man who was carrying a parcel.

'Whoa, lad, you nearly killed me. Why are you in such a hurry?'

'Sorry sir. I meant no offence, please forgive me. I'm late to get home and my father will be ever so angry.'

The man was dressed like one of those well to do types with shiny black high boots, and crimson pantaloons held up by a broad belt that showed a wolf head buckle. His shirt was a lighter shade of his pants, and his facial features were unclear in the dappled shadows of the alley. Zacriel noticed he had knocked the parcel from the man's arms when they had collided. The parcel had fallen open to reveal a fine set of leather shoes. Bending, Zacriel repacked the shoes, then handed the damaged parcel out to the stranger.

'Sir, you dropped these.'

'Boy, I think it is fate that we should meet on such an important night. Do you know what night this is?'

'No, Sir, I don't. I have never been to school.'

'Never mind,' said the man tapping the lid of the parcel with a long finger. 'These shoes were for my son who is just around about your size, but he won't wear these shoes no matter how much we coax him to do so. He says they are ugly.'

'Sir, they are very fine. I have never seen their like before.'

'Try them on. I think they might fit you.'

'No, I can't do that, my father is waiting for me to get home.'

'It will take just a moment, lad. Please. I insist, since you nearly bowled me over.'

Zacriel looked at the fine shoes then sat and placed them on. They fit his dirty feet very well, and they looked and felt great. He moved to take them off, but a hand patted his shoulder.

'Leave them on. They suit you, and should you ever tire of your father treating you badly then remember this address.' The man passed him a card with some writing on that Zacriel didn't understand then walked away with the clacking of his boots fading with him.

Zacriel took off again at a sprint. The shoes at first felt awkward, but then he began to get used to them. At the bakery near his home, Zacriel stopped to look at his reflection in the big windows, which were lit by a street lamp revealing all the yummy goodies inside. Zacriel wasn't interested in the goodies this time though, he just wanted to see how his new shoes looked on him. His reflection broke into a huge grin at the sight of the shoes, and for a moment he forgot the terror that awaited him at home in the small house he shared with his father.

Zacriel wiped the sweat from his face with his holey shirt. He placed one hand over his eyes and the other over his mouth in the sign of Churl the keeper of secrets. With any luck his father would be asleep by now, then he could slip up to his bed and the warm blankets that lay there awaiting him.

Before Zacriel could reach the door to his home it swung open with its customary grating on the stone beneath it to reveal the considerable size of his father, shirtless, his large gut hanging before him. Zacriel stood looking at the ground, unwilling to meet his father's gaze as to do so would earn him a beating.

'Finally decided to come home then, Zac?'

When Zacriel stayed silent his father cuffed him hard across the head.

'Not even any smart replies tonight, Zac? Well, maybe you're finally learning. Now the only reason I could think off as to why my son had stayed out so late is that he has returned with a considerable trove of loot. Come in, Zac, show me what you have found for me.'

Zacriel could taste the coppery blood in his mouth where he had bitten down on his tongue to avoid crying in front of his father. He emptied the days finding onto the table while his father sat waiting expectantly.

'Not much here boy, unless you call two coppers, an iron hairpin, and a gold ring an acceptable find.'

His father picked up the ring then used the point of a sharp knife to scratch its surface. Flakes of gold peeled away, then the ring bounced off Zacriel's face before spinning away to the floor.

'Fake shit, boy! Can't you steal anything valuable? Since I was unable to locate you tonight there is no dinner. To bed with you now, and by the gods if you don't improve tomorrow you will get a whipping.'

Then Zacriel's father seemed to notice the shoes for the first time.

'Where did you get those shoes, Zac?'

'A man gave them to me. Can I please keep them? They will help me to do my work better, and they fit me well.'

'Bring them here so I can look at them. You can have them in the morning.'

Zacriel reluctantly removed the shoes. He knew he would never see them again.'

'Off with you now, Zac.'

Zacriel turned to go. Something hit him in the back of the head making him stumble. He heard his father walk over to him, and then something hard crashed into the back of his head until he fell to the ground. He tried to roll into a ball and protect his head with his arms, and saw his father had been using one of the shoes to beat him with. The next strike slammed into Zacriel's cheek, then more blows rained down on his back until with loud wheezing breath his father stopped, leaving Zacriel to crawl away to his bed.

The recollection of this event unnerved Zacriel. It reflected the way he had treated not only Nina, but many people during his life on the path of power. As he now sat looking upon the painting of himself once more, Zacriel realized he hated the twisted, ugly creature he had become. He was just like his father.

Banishing the memories of the past, Zacriel gazed down on Acclaro, the last remaining city of the Thantosian Empire that was now under his rule. The once majestic city now lay in ruins with the castle the only remaining untouched structure left standing. Arrowhead Lake no longer shimmered beneath the sun's rays. It had been turned into a sludge ridden diseased waterhole in which strange Infernals were being birthed from Lilith's experiments. Whatever Lilith had put into the lake had turned it into a cesspit of bubbling evil that now leaked its poison into the river too.

The Infernal forces of Acclaro had not stagnated since Zacriel had captured the city. He had been organizing the city's defences. He had ordered a great chain curtain made by human slaves, then attached it to the castle sky walk. To finish off the aerial defences, Zacriel had ordered ballista's placed upon the sky walk.

The frenetic, flow of Infernals, cultists, and mercenaries had continued over the last month, and now a town for these newcomers had formed around the northern and western side of the city.

The other Infernal lords still hated that Zacriel held the power here, and in succeeding the Lady of Whispers, Zacriel had inherited the great army that the Lady of Whispers had built up to complete her nefarious plans. Zacriel knew the lords had tried to undermine him to his new army, but he managed to stay one step ahead by making sure his Infernals were given the best of everything in order to secure their loyalty.

Though he made sure he was always busy, Zacriel hated the way his attention always returned to Nina, who Dalwyn had whisked away from him at the orders of Lilith. If he ever saw the old meddling fool again, Zacriel would have his revenge, and Lilith would also pay for her part in it. He knew Dalwyn had taken Nina with him to the safe house, where he expected to capture the Coterie of the Heart. Even though his relationship with Nina was a strange one, Zacriel realized how much he had enjoyed having Nina around. There was a kinship between them that had grown into more of a bond during the flight from Acclaro, and the failed uprising beneath the mountain. Zacriel had begun to question this bond. He had come to the conclusion that Nina was better off far away from him and this cesspit of vipers. This was not the place for a child, and he just hoped she could escape Dalwyn who harboured a special hatred for the girl.

Behind him, Zacriel heard the doors to the balcony open. Only one would dare to interrupt him when he was up here, Rapture.

'It appears, I would need to start looking for better guards to protect what meagre privacy I still have,' called out Zacriel without turning.

'You are one of the Infernal lords. You gave up that luxury when you assumed the mantle of Bone Lord,' muttered Rapture from behind him.

Zacriel turned around. 'I tire of it already, Rapture, here, take the rod and pin, they're yours.'

Rapture held his hands up in defence. 'No, Zacriel. I have no desire to replace you.'

'Well since I can't give away my title to you, then what have you dragged me away from my musings for?'

'There is something strange that you need to come see, Bone Lord. Something that I cannot make sense of.'

'Sounds interesting, but I will just stay here. How goes the rebuilding now that the curtain is in place?'

'The rebuilding is going as planned Zacriel, but what I need you to see isn't in Acclaro. Its north west from here towards Jingtalla falls.'

Zacriel reached for a silver mug that held wine, or so he thought. Now it was empty, and he placed it down with disgust. 'Is this truly necessary, or just a ploy to wrest me away from my doubting mind?'

'Both, it's better if your army actually sees you occasionally my lord, and this will do that as well as giving you a chance to escape Acclaro for a time. I have taken the liberty of having the servants bring up the necessary clothes. Maybe you could even take the time to bathe since it will be hard to conceal ourselves with the stench emanating from your venerable self. Midnight will be saddled and ready once you are finished. Just call me when you are ready to summon her, meanwhile I will ready myself and be back in one chime.'

Now that Zacriel thought about it, escaping the city did sound appealing. Rapture was right, an adventure away from here would do him the world of good. There was little he could do about Nina now except move on.

As Zacriel bathed he read the many scrolls that Rapture had so thoughtfully placed beside the iron bath for him to peruse while he soaked. It appeared that he couldn't even enjoy a quiet bath anymore.

By all reports the unrest across the world was reaching levels where war would soon be unavoidable. It surprised him that the other nations had allowed the capital to continue growing in power after its fall, right under their noses. The fact that the former king of Thantos had lost all his allies had been a major reason why the old empire had finally collapsed. With no allies to call on, Thantos was left to its own struggle from within as the nations of Cavere, Brimmerland, and Scuttle chose to strengthen their own borders and leave Thantos to rot.

Zacriel couldn't deny it. The Lady of Whispers had refused to sit pining for her homeland like so many others of her kind, and instead had masterminded a glorious plan that concluded with the downfall of the Thantosian Empire. And yet, in the end she had died as easy as any mortal

Zacriel followed Rapture up out of the tower and onto the sky walk. The door was barred behind them by the recently added guards who now manned the points of aerial weakness. With the great chain added to the curtain wall these guards would be used to deploy the defensive tool during the aerial attack that would no doubt come in the near future.

Zacriel blew the whistle that summoned his lunar mount, Midnight. As he waited the excitement built within him at the thought of flying again, and leaving behind the constricting problems that now assailed him with his new level of power. There came a flash of black, and then Midnight circled lazily downwards to land before Zacriel. He scratched the mount between the wings, noticing that Midnight thrummed with barely contained energy as if the beast was also impatient to get going. Once saddled, Zacriel led Midnight up into the thermals above the city, where they circled before banking off to in the direction of Jingtalla Falls.

Zacriel had been a man ready to ascend to the ranks of the Infernals. Chosen to go beyond the mortal realm to the hells, where the death and carnage he had wrought on the world would be recognized and celebrated. The Severing had taken away that chance, and now that he had received the power thrust upon him from the death of the Lady of Whispers he was not so sure it was what he wanted.

All the time with Nina had changed him, and where once he would have seen those changes as weakness he now saw it as growth. He had been sorely out of balance and concerned with only destruction, which had nearly backfired and ended with his own demise. He still wanted revenge against those who had crossed him, but it was no longer an all-consuming necessity. Nina had been an unwilling student, but now as Zacriel drifted on the wind again he wondered who had been the teacher? Nina had uncovered many memories for Zacriel, unlocking something within his mind that until now had stayed hidden away. Those memories had begun seeping out into his conscious daily life where he would find himself lost in a fugue state, like earlier this morning with the painting. This usually happened out on the balcony, the one place at the castle where he felt some sort of balance. Maybe it was the fact that the balcony offered a means of escape should he ever wish to take it. This opportunity was dwindling away fast as Zacriel became mired in the commitment that the role of an Infernal lord brought with it.

Rapture turned then spread his wings to glide in a circle. As Zacriel caught up, Rapture indicated an area ahead where the Winding River met Jingtalla Falls before turning into the Devouring River. The typical crystal that covered the trees like moss in the Jewelled Land was not apparent near the falls at the moment. Instead Zacriel saw that the river itself flowed in an ever changing hue of colors as it continued down the falls, and over the bank where it bled out to the western part of the Glyph plains. It was this that Zacriel thought

Rapture was trying to draw his attention to. He had to admit as he turned Midnight for another pass that it was strange, but as he caught Rapture waving to get his attention once again he realized his general wanted them to go in lower to see something else. Zacriel sped down behind Rapture, coming in low just above the height of the trees themselves near the river. He saw in amazement that where the liquid crystal hit the land as it flowed over the river bank the crystal it gathered in places, changing form. To his further amazement as he slowed and flew onwards the change in form showed itself to be human- like crystal figures. Zacriel realized they were the Harlequin.

They flew two more circuits of the strange phenomenon as Zacriel attempted to piece together what was going on. It had been taught by scholars that the Harlequin could only live in the Jewelled Land due to their reliance on the regular rain fall, and it was believed that the crystal deposits there kept them alive. This now shattered that idea, and the question Zacriel ached to know was where were they going?

As Zacriel and Rapture headed back towards Acclaro, Zacriel's keen eyes picked out a dust cloud far below to the north of where they were. He indicated he was going in for a closer look, and swept down over what he saw was human slaves, and herds of cattle. The Glyph had no cattle, so where had they come from? He saw the insignia worn by many of the Infernals below was of an eyeless skull. They were the Unseeing lords troops heading back from a raid on the land of Scuttle. At least the other infernal lords had taken to their tasks with fervour. How long before the other nations began striking back? They could no longer ignore the nest of Infernals that dared threaten their own lands, and not just that of rotting Thantos.

Before returning to the castle Zacriel did a circuit around the city. He flew low enough to be seen by the inhabitants and newcomers in the town that had sprung up outside the gates. Roars and cheering followed his movement, and he faintly heard chants of, 'Bone Lord', as he passed. Midnight landed on the sky walk and Zacriel climbed off as Rapture landed beside him.

'See, Bone Lord, your army adores you. They believe you will deliver the bloodshed they have only dreamed of while they lay hidden away in the cracks of this world for the Infernal gates of hell to reopen.'

Rapture slapped Zacriel on the back and roared at the sky.

'This world will quiver at the thought of you Bone Lord, and what you will achieve for us Infernals.'

Zacriel grinned at his general, but inside he worried that he just might not live up to the expectations of the infernal forces. As soon as Zacriel entered his chambers he was swamped with messages from couriers and invitations to dine with this or that important Infernal. Zacriel had reached the limit of his impatience.

'Rapture before you go I need you to appoint some of your men to deal with these tasks. Choose your best, the ones who can think for themselves and get them working on the problems we face with the ever increasing army we have. There are many forces gathering under our banners now, and I wish to know who they all are, and who leads them so I can familiarize myself with the different factions.'

'As you command, my lord. What shall we do regarding the Harlequin?'

'Monitor their progress. We need to clarify whether they are marching on us as enemies or allies. If they keep their current direction we may need to approach them to find out. I also want updates on the situation at Whitman's point and Culchar.

Chapter 5

The sunset behind the Godhead stained the sky a sickly yellow that bled to orange fire. A fey wind swirled around the small campsite huddled against the rock outcrop, attempting to snuff the life from the fire that Aeon, the god of time, had painstakingly spent lighting. Ishmael sat with his knees hugged to his chest, shivering. He felt a blanket being draped around his shoulders a moment before Zahra squatted beside him, concern evident in her eyes.

'Just rest now, Ishmael, and when you are ready tell me exactly what you saw. In no time Aeon will have some hot food for us all, hey.' She punched him softly in the shoulder, smiling, but Ishmael had no smile to give back.

He had come to the Godhead in Trystland to see the gods themselves, and now one, the last one, sat before him cooking some sort of broth that Ishmael had to admit was causing his mouth to water in anticipation of filling his empty belly. Aeon's eyes looked up meeting Ishmael's then winked at him with the light one.

'This will be the best broth you ever tasted, Ishmael, I learned this recipe not long after we were cast out from the Celestial lands. It's a strange thing that I never had any interest in food until the Severing. I am the only living god that has retained their power, and yet I have taken on many of the mortal trappings my kin have also. In the Celestial lands you never go hungry so sustenance is never an issue, but nowadays I can't imagine not having the delights of food in my life.'

Ishmael had many questions he wished to ask Aeon, but his body had suffered too much trauma and it was all he could do to keep awake. As if reading his mind, Aeon spoke again without looking up this time.

'After our meal I shall tell a story of our two moons and the gods. I think that you will find it most enlightening.'

'I don't care much for stories at the moment, Aeon. It seems that each time I trust in something that it turns out to be nothing but another lie. My family, my faith, all gone, and for what?'

'Things change and constantly evolve, Ishmael, and you are not the only one whose existence has been proven to be based on falsehoods, nor will you be the last,' said Aeon.

'Yes, but…'

Aeon's strange eyes seemed to glow from within as he looked up at Ishmael and Zahra.

'This is not the time for indulging yourself in self-importance, Ishmael. There are larger things at stake here now, like this world, and like it or not the Mother has selected you to step up as the mortal representation of her.'

Ishmael looked away from Aeon's eyes still peering at him over the small flames. He knew he was being petty, and yet he felt he had a right to be pissed off. All he wanted was things to be easy. He was sick of putting faith into something to only see it collapse before him when it mattered the most.

Ishmael shrugged off the blanket and stalked over to the top of the rough stairs they had climbed to reach the Sulk highland. He sat and looked down over the Godhead. Fajira and Fausto came to mind, and Ishmael couldn't help but wonder if they managed to get to safety away from the rioting that had overtaken the great sprawling cityscape. He could hear Zahra get up and begin to follow him, but then Aeon called out.

'Zahra, let him go. Ishmael needs to sort his head out and get some clarity, alone.'

Ishmael wanted to call out to ask Aeon what he could know of suffering when you knew your death would only occur at the end of time and not before, but he didn't and instead stayed where he was, letting the wind tousle his short hair and whip against his clothes. It was chilly, but Ishmael welcomed the sensation that bordered on pain that took his mind off the problems that loomed over him. Trying to regain what little composure he could, Ishmael slowed his breathing and drew the deep breaths into his body, feeling their calming effect almost immediately. When the sunset had fallen behind the horizon and the only light was the flames from the Godshead far below, Ishmael now feeling more himself, rose and made his way back to the sheltered campsite and fire, his stomach leading the way to the origin of the mouth-watering smelling broth.

'Just in time, Ishmael,' said Aeon over a spoonful of steaming broth. 'If you had taken much longer I think Zahra would have eaten your bowl as well as hers. I was lucky to keep my own.'

Zahra smiled through a mouthful of food and moved along so Ishmael could sit beside her out of the chill wind. Aeon passed him a bowl and twig to use as a fork, and Ishmael became lost in the tasteful hot food that his body welcomed eagerly.

Aeon emptied his bowl then scooped some out, which he poured onto the bare soil behind him before unstoppering a wineskin and pouring wine onto the same spot before coming back to the fire. He saw Ishmael watching him and answered his question before it was voiced.

'For the Mother, she who provides us with sustenance we return to her and like life it completes the circle. I learnt that from the Sulk, whom soon you will meet face to face. They believe that the Mother must be honoured at meal times as well as their own bodies to give thanks for the sustenance she provides us all. Now are you both ready for a story?'

Aeon placed a small pot of water on the fire and began his tale.

'Following the Severing, it was not just the mortal world that was rocked by the cataclysmic event. The gods, Infernals, and all Celestials were deeply affected as well as the mortals, but what most do not know is that the moons were affected too.

'Since day one of this world and my existence, the red moon, Tamul has chased his sister moon, Aspre across the sky. When the Severing came and the world was plunged into darkness, the Mother called on her daughter Aspre for aid. Aspre stopped to listen to her Mother, who explained the gods were to be cast out of the Celestial and Infernal realms and dumped into the strange mortal world where they, like any man, could be killed. The gods would now be weak and vulnerable, and it was the Mother's wish that Aspre help the gods survive until the time of magic returned to the world. While Aspre had stopped her heavenly circuit, Tamul, who had chased his sister across the skies, finally caught up. That collision caused parts of Aspre to shower down onto the world, and these were the children of Aspre chosen by the Mother herself to protect the fallen gods.'

'Protect the gods from whom?' asked Ishmael.

'I see I have your attention, Ishmael, and that is good because this is especially pertinent to your achievement of returns the magic to our world.

'Now when that collision occurred, it wasn't just Aspre's children that fell to our world but also the children of Tamul, whose sole aim was to destroy these gods made mortal so that their knowledge could not be used to usher in a new world of peace where all the races respect the Mother and live in harmony. Tamul's children have come to be called the life quenchers, and they hunger for the god's life-force, which will give the Quenchers the energy to assault the Mother directly and destroy this world.'

'But why does it have to be like this, I mean what does that achieve if Tamul and his children destroy the Mother, our world? asked Ishmael.

'I can only say that since the birth of the universe around us and our world among all others that these forces of creation and destruction continue the cycle of life of everything we know. We are born and we die, and so do worlds.'

Zahra snapped a twig she was holding and added it to the flames. 'This all sounds kind of hopeless if we are fighting a doomed cause.'

'That is one way of looking at it, Zahra but what else do we have except to fight for our existence and make the most of what little time we are blessed with in this world.'

Ishmael leaned forwards, his interest piqued now. 'At the monastery we learned briefly about the small chance that Aspre would defeat Tamul and our world, the Mother would be free of this circle of destruction to become a place of paradise bathed with the holy light of Aspre. Does this have anything to do with us, the Coterie of the Heart?'

Aeon smiled and his eyes seemed to light up from within then fade again.

'Very astute Ishmael. The one chance of that happening is the return of magic in such a way that the world stays balanced and that means you four of the coterie that remain will be needed to usher in the age of this new world by protecting the great power you hold until you are reunited. That is when you shall truly know the power that has shaped your life.'

Aeon removed the boiling water then poured tea with honey for the three of them.

Ishmael interrupted the short silence with a curse and digging at the coals with a stick.

'I never asked for this power or the responsibility it brings with it. It has never even been useful to me!'

Aeon burst out laughing and slapped his knees in joy as moments later Zahra joined in and then Ishmael too. When their merriment subsided, Ishmael felt embarrassed.

'Nobody has control of all the cards they are dealt in life, Ishmael. I didn't ask to be a god, and some days I'm so tired of all that role brings with it. Zahra, did you ask for your family to be killed by your village or to be stuck with such an self-absorbed ass like Ishmael to protect?'

'By the Infernal lands, no!' Zahra replied, rolling her eyes comically, making them all laugh again.

'The challenge we all have then is to choose how we deal with those things we cannot change and take back some of that lost control, which can be harder than wallowing in pity while our lives pass us by.'

A strange trumpet-like sound came from the night, and Aeon stood suddenly alert then he visibly relaxed before excusing himself and vanishing into the night, leaving Ishmael and Zahra alone.

Chapter 6

Ishmael sat silently beside Zahra, waiting for her to say something. But she stayed silent, staring into the fire, and as he watched her he thought this was the most relaxed he had ever seen her.

'Zahra, I just wanted to apologize for, you know…'

'No, I don't know, Ishmael, enlighten me, 'said Zahra still looking into the flames.

'For drugging your wine at the mill after we did what we did.'

Zahra turned to look at Ishmael with an incredulous look of disbelief. 'Just say it Ishmael! We fucked, and that was all. It meant nothing to me and was just a way to escape from all the death and destruction we had endured.'

'I didn't mean to hurt you. Moving ahead, I hope you will forgive me.'

Zahra met his eyes with hers filled with hardness now. 'You just don't get it, do you? I'm not mad that we slept with each other. You made those vows just like you chose to break them, and as I remember you were hardly trying to stop me that night. The thing I can't and won't forgive you for was abandoning me and leaving me in danger when you knew the Infernals would be seeking us. I could have died and most likely you too.'

'Zahra, don't you think you are overreacting?'

'If it wasn't my duty to protect you, Ishmael, I would throw you from this cliff and be done with your idiotic tendencies. I am your sentinel and that is all. I will continue to protect you but that is all, so stop fawning around like a love-struck idiot. You will never have any idea how much distress you caused me and how it made me feel when you left me there unable to defend myself. It was as if you didn't trust me to protect you.'

'Zahra, all that happened was I tried to stop you from getting hurt. Everyone I get close to ends up getting hurt or killed, and I didn't want that for you and still don't.'

'Ishmael! I am your sentinel sent to keep you safe and yet you insist on protecting me. It doesn't matter if I die, just that you survive to return the magic. It is as simple as that.'

Ishmael put his hand on Zahra's knee which she brushed away while shaking her head in disbelief then got up and stalked away.

Two companions and you manage to upset them both thought Ishmael as he threw more timber on the fire before sitting back to watch it burn. There was something about fire that had always fascinated him since he had learned of the art of scrying from brother Torvald back in the monastery.

'Fire and water are the two best mediums for scrying, but mark my words, this is not for the fainthearted. Be sure to anchor yourself before experimenting or risk madness at least and attack from entities at worst.'

Ishmael felt suddenly nauseous as if by vertigo and had to steady himself with his hands as a voice buffeted himself into his mind. 'Ishmael, use the fire, there is something you need to witness.' Ishmael closed his eyes and began to deepen his breathing as he sought to recreate the little campsite in his mind the rock wall behind him was the easiest feature to focus on, and so he anchored himself on that feature even to the feel of the cool rock on his back.

Ishmael gazed into the embers, allowing them to draw his awareness deeper. The scene he was focused on cleared and Ishmael was looking through Raul, who he knew had acquired the fire crystal. Almost instantly he felt himself connect to the wolfish man, becoming aware of Raul's resistance and then the grudgingly opening of his vision.

Raul was sitting beside Selene and Jona, who were shouting as two men were dragged out before them. Their hands were bound behind their backs, and they had been gagged. The two had suffered quite a beating evident from the swelling and cuts on their faces.

'What's going on, Raul, and who are the two men?'

'They are the sentinels of Jona and Selene, and they are about to be executed. I am sorry, Ishmael. This is all my fault. They told me nobody would be hurt and I believed them.'

'What about your sentinel, can she help?'

'My sentinel died in an accident and a new one was sent but it turns out this one was murdered by Katerina who took that role. She betrayed me and now we are in great danger. Thank the gods you are not here Ishmael otherwise it would be the end of all of us.'

Ishmael reeled under the information and had to focus to stay in the vision. The two men were kneeling now and without any words soldiers came into view, their uniforms marked with a flame showing their allegiance to Dalwyn Trevlon. The soldiers made a ring around the two kneeling men, then the order was issued to cut them down. Ishmael closed his eyes as the soldiers fell upon the two harmless prisoners, not wanting to see the slaughter. He felt his connection fading now and could barely make out Raul's next words.

'We need you, Ishmael, you are now the only hope for the coterie. Don't forget us. We will meet you in the tree chamber!'

Ishmael found himself back at the fire opposite Aeon, who had returned and was watching him closely. Ishmael tried to stand, swooned then toppled towards the fire, but Aeon seized his shoulders and pulled him back out of harm's way.

'You had me worried, Ishmael. When I returned you were in a trance staring at the fire as if scrying. Are you okay?'

'I was drawn into it by the coterie. Dalwyn Trevlon has executed two of the sentinels.' Ishmael looked around the site. Where is Zahra? She must be told. '

Zahra stepped into the firelight holding a load of wood. She stopped to stare at Ishmael.

'Ish, what is it, why are you looking at me like that?'

I saw it with my own eyes, Zahra, two of the sentinels are dead, executed!'

Zahra dropped the timber, and her hands went to her mouth.

'No, you must be wrong, it can't be,' she said, shaking her head in disbelief.

'I'm sorry, Zahra, but I saw it happen through Raul's eyes.'

Aeon stood and wrapped his arm around Zahra's shoulder then guided her to a seat, where he wrapped her in his embrace as she sobbed into his chest.

Even though he knew he was being pathetic, Ishmael felt hurt by seeing Zahra in Aeon's arms. Was he jealous? Not knowing what else to do, he lay down and curled up beside the fire.

✦

Chapter 7

When Haakon became bored watching the shadows dance across the walls, he rose from his makeshift bed. He realized sleep was not going to come this night. He made sure Nina was warm before activating the side passage from the clan chamber to his hidden terrarium. The chamber had been set up for him by one of the cunning folk who travelled the lands selling herbs and medicine. As the wall grated inwards he stepped through into a short tunnel that stopped before a chamber made entirely from crystal with a small door before him fitted expertly with steel hinges. The crystal for this secret chamber had cost a fortune and had been cut in the Sunsoaked city then carted here by the clan. It was the first time he had ever entered it since designing this place, and he had been unaware of what to expect.

The sight before him took his breath away. The cunning man, as he preferred to be called, had done well with filling the chamber with an array of plants that would cause animals or people to suffer instant illness if any of the flora were consumed in minute quantities and fatal in higher doses.

Haakon retrieved a pair of chain metal gloves, a bowl, and a small slashing blade from a table against the wall, then he carefully opened the chamber and stepped in. From inside when he looked up he could see the night sky some way above. Carefully moving through the colourful but deadly terrarium, Haakon stopped by the purple wolfs bane that contained aconite, a dangerous poison. He pulled up three plants, carefully digging free the roots which was where the poison was most formidable. Back at the table Haakon used a mortar and pestle to mash the plant roots then he placed the result into a jar only keeping a small amount that he scraped into a vial. The garden relaxed Haakon, and he set about noting the different specimens the glass house held before leaving. When he returned to Nina, she was already up and about and sat reading a thick tome by candlelight.

'What is in the vial, Haakon, and where have you been?'

'Just getting some herbs for our little outing, Nina, now put your boots on. We have a little visit to make to the kitchen before dawn.'

As the faint winter rays of sun began filtering through the gathering clouds outside, two shadows prowled the dark corridors of the Kenzu safe house. They ghosted easily past two flame warriors who guarded the corridor to the kitchens. Voices could be heard in the kitchen so Haakon activated another hidden passage that took them into a storeroom where herbs hung in bundles among containers of sauces, trays of meat and piles of vegetables. Outside this room was the main kitchen area where two men stood chopping food in between lubricating themselves with wine.

'By the jester's death, Nial stop drinking the damn wine. If Flint, or worse Dalwyn, finds out he will not only flay the skin from your back but also mine. Now this plate I have nearly finished now is for Dalwyn's breakfast, while the bowls already on the trays are for the prisoners and our own men to be filled from the pot. Once the bacon is finished frying you must take it. Dalwyn hates his food cold.'

'Blah, blah, blah, Liam, you worry too much. I was sent to watch you, not be your servant.' the man lurched back then as Liam chopped down at the table with a cleaver, slicing through the wine bladder and spilling ruby rivulets across the bench and floor.

'Now see what you have done! There was no need for that, was there?'

'I told you I am in charge of the kitchen, so if you think I'm going to let you get Dalwyn's attention by messing up his meal then you need to leave, Nial.' Now clean this up. I'm going to show the gods my hairy ass, and when I get back you had better be gone to deliver the food,' said Liam as he unfastened his apron and slung it on a bench before stomping out of the kitchen.

As the man named Nial began sluicing the floor down with a bucket of water, Haakon glided up behind him, slipped a wire garrotte over his head and pulled tight, then half dragged the struggling Nial back into the store room. The bucket dropped with a clatter that made Haakon curse, but no guards came running. Haakon saw Nina watching with wide eyes as Nial's struggles grew weaker.

'Turn away, Nina; you don't need to watch this.'

'Yes, I do,' replied Nina in a wavering voice. 'My parents told me the world is a good place, now I know it isn't, and Zacriel taught me to face what scares me so it loses its power to make me weak.' She trailed off at his look then, and Haakon wondered who this Zacriel was.

The gurgling sound Nial made as he died soon ceased entirely, and Haakon lowered the man's body to the floor. With Nina's help they dragged him deeper into the storeroom, stripped off his uniform, and covered his body in sacks of potatoes and other vegetables to hide it.

Haakon changed into the uniform of the dead flame warrior. It was too big in places, but there was no time to worry about that now. Hopefully he would pass any casual meetings with the intruders in his clan house. He returned to the trays of food and dished up bowls for the prisoners. Once done he removed the stopper from the vial of wolfs bane root then added some to each plate of porridge and the bacon and eggs for this Dalwyn Trevlon.

'Nina, go back to our room. I will be back as soon as I can.'

'Let me come too. I can help.'

'No, you must stay hidden, Nina. They are looking for a child and you will be caught. Do you want that?'

Nina shook her head. To be under the power of Dalwyn again would be terrible, and yet she was more scared of Haakon not coming back to her.

'I'm scared,' she said, looking down at her feet.

Haakon knelt before Nina, placing his hands on her cheeks. 'You are so brave and smart, so you know like I do that this is very dangerous and must be done only by me. I will return as soon as I can.'

Nina nodded and a tear slowly wound its way down one of her cheeks, which Haakon wiped away.

'Now go, Nina, back through the secret doors like I showed you, and wait for me there.'

He waited until Nina activated the door, then Haakon took the trays and walked out into the corridor down towards his own chambers where Dalwyn Trevlon hopefully waited.

Haakon forced himself to move at a leisurely place and maintain a bored countenance as two guards watched his approach. The one thing he had in his favour he realized was that he had managed to elude the flame warriors when they attacked, which meant they had no real idea of his appearance. Hopefully this would save him from any close attention, and as well as the early time of the day when he knew the guards would be weary. His earlier scouting had showed him that the flame warriors had taken many casualties at the hands of his men, which gave Haakon hope that nobody would be coming to change over the watch duty.

'I would wager a gold ceta for each of you that you are both famished,' said Haakon smiling, as he stopped before the two flame warriors with the push cart laden with food.

'Not for any of that slop,' said one guard through a yawn.

'It's not that bad. I even managed to find some honey to sweeten it for you.' Haakon scooped honey from a bowl onto two wooden plates for the guards, who took it hesitantly, one sniffing it then dipping in a finger to taste.

'Actually not so bad with the honey,' he said, taking the two spoons Haakon handed him as he continued moving on with the hand cart.

So far so good, he thought as he turned into the mess hall where the other warriors would soon be gathering to eat. He lifted the heavy pot of porridge onto the centre most table then a bowl of honey, the plates and spoons. Through the opposite side of the mess hall he exited towards the clan masters chamber where two more guards waited.

One of the guards, whose face was all sharp angles, hard as chiselled stone with deep brown eyes, motioned for Haakon to stop when he reached them.

'I tasked Nial with bringing Dalwyn's food, where is he?'

Haakon bought his hands up in the prayer position and bobbed his head in defence. 'Nial has once again imbibed too much wine, which Liam the cook knew would anger you, so I was made to bring the food.'

'I will deal with Nial later,' replied the guard, taking the proffered tray from Haakon and entering the chamber behind him.

Haakon moved on to the cells, praying as he went to the Death jester that Dalwyn would eat the food. He nodded to the two guards who, once satisfied he was here to feed the prisoners, opened the door. As he counted out enough bowls for the prisoners Haakon listened to the guards rambling.

'If Flint keeps us doing these double shifts there will be trouble, I tell you. We should be drinking and eating in that fine hall like kings after the great work we did.'

'Shut your damn yapping already. You heard Flint. The messenger has been sent to Dalwyn's brother for reinforcements, and they should be arriving any day now.'

Haakon slid in four bowls for Latasha, Raul, Jona, and Selene. When Jona bent to take them, he grasped her wrist. To her credit Jona didn't cry out, and he leant close.

'Whatever you do don't eat any food from bowls other than these four. We are trying to get you out of here.' Then he rose and turned away before she could speak.

'Hey, did you bring some of that porridge for us?' asked one of the guards as Haakon turned to leave.

'Most of the food I already put in the mess hall, although I have extra bowls here if you want them now.'

'It doesn't look like we are getting rest any time soon, so pass them here.'

Haakon heaped honey on two of the steaming bowls of porridge, which the guards took eagerly.

'Smells just like my ma used to make when I was a littlin,' said one stirring through the liberal amount of honey Haakon had added to mask the smell of the poison.

Haakon hurried back the way he had come. From where Dalwyn was he could hear a heated discussion then he was past and looking in the hall where a group of flame warriors were dishing up the hot breakfast and talking happily which soon they wouldn't be. The first two guards were already on the ground, one holding his stomach and vomiting up the food while the other grasped his throat and stumbled around as if blind. He made short work of the two of them with his dagger and using the blood scrawled a message for Dalwyn Trevlon on the wall before leaving.

Chapter 8

Someone shook Ishmael awake and covered his mouth as he tried to talk. He panicked and bucked his body, trying to dislodge his attacker.

'Ishmael, it's me, Aeon. Stop it, you're safe,' hissed Aeon into his ear.

Ishmael lay there trying to regain his senses.

'The Sulk will be here soon, now awaken yourself and there is hot tea and leftovers by the fire so make use of it.'

When Ishmael made his way to the fire, Zahra was sitting sipping tea. She moved along to give him room, and he slumped down beside her.

'Are you okay, Zahra?'

'No, but I will be. Thanks for asking.'

Ishmael ate some broth and would have done anything for some fresh baked bread to dip with or some sugar for the tea but was just grateful for something hot.

'Did you know the sentinels well?' asked Ishmael.

'Their names were Benjani Dutoolo and Ansar Pel. Benjani came from the Sunsoaked city where his family fled to from over the oceans. Ansar Pel grew up a sailor's son in Sainthome where his family traded with the sea gypsies. We survived together through many trials, but that was lifetimes ago before we were tasked with the coterie. Of course I knew this might happen, but it makes it no easier when it does. Huh, you would think someone that has been touched by death would be immune to such sentiment, but it would seem I still hold a semblance of empathy.'

A series of hoots cut through the night carried on the wings of darkness, and Aeon came hurrying back to the fire.

'The Sulk are almost here. They are a shy folk, so stay away from your weapons and prepare to be amazed by these creatures.'

'Why are they here Aeon? You mentioned we would meet them, but to what purpose?' Ishmael asked.

Aeon tilted his head to one side and smiled. 'No I cannot tell you. If they are here, they should be the ones to share their purpose with you.' His one light eye seemed to flare in the firelight.

'Come on, both of you, this is something you won't want to miss.'

Ishmael followed Aeon and Zahra out around the wall that had sheltered their campsite onto the rocky clearing still within sight of the cliff they had laboured up the day before. The wind was stronger here and whipped up flurries of sand that stung Ishmael's face and hands. Aspre had brightened the night with its glow and sat swollen in the sky.

Following Aeon's instruction, he peered down the sloping hill leading to their current position where rough stone steps had been worn away by time and weather. A procession of hooded, robed figures slowly made their way up the steps. Ishmael counted nine of them. Farther down the incline he also noted more of the figures appearing as they uncovered some sort of light source that gave off a yellow hued glimmer. The figures down the hill were spaced in such a way that the lights they had placed met one another's circle of illumination and left a trail of light illuminating the whole perimeter they appeared to be guarding. The question Ishmael had was what were they guarding from?'

The nine Sulk made it to where the three companions waited, and when they arrived the first thing that struck Ishmael was the size of them. They easily stood eight feet tall. Ishmael looked sideways to Zahra who stood totally absorbed by the visitors. The lead Sulk walked forward and stopped before Aeon, who brought both his hands together before his face then up above his head around before the hands came apart and the arms circled down along the side of his body to rest upon his abdomen.

Aeon stepped forward. 'You have come, my brothers. The light of Aspre shines on us and we are fortunate to meet with you on such a hallowed night. My companions you will soon know, they are Ishmael Shantari of Illume and coterie of the heart. Beside him stands his sentinel, Zahra from clan Kenzu. They are friends that I vouch for.'

The Sulk formed a semi-circle facing the three of them, and Ishmael noticed Zahra's hand move to rest on the hilt of a dagger at her back.

One of the Sulk stepped forward and bowed low to Ishmael and Zahra. Ishmael tried to catch a glimpse of what lay under the hood but only saw large, listless, opaque eyes looking back at him. Ishmael returned the gesture, then the Sulk moved forward, stooped and embraced Aeon heartily one by one with the last, placing a palm onto Aeon's chest. Something passed through the two of them, but Ishmael couldn't see how.

Aeon turned to Ishmael and Zahra. 'The Sulk cannot speak and communicate only through touch, this is what they said to me. It is good that you are here, your presence bodes well for this night, and your companionship is always a welcome thing, counter of time. Now the time we have till dawn is short, and we need healing. Please ensure your companions don't disturb us until we approach you again.'

The Sulk filed away and took up positions in a circle facing outwards. The leader emitted a low, warbled whistle, and as one the nine Sulk let their robes and hoods fall away to pool at their feet.

Ishmael heard Zahra gasp. The Sulk had grey skinned stippled with sores that was transparent enough that their shrivelled internal organs could be seen. The eyes were bleak, washed out white, with no apparent pupils or eyelids. Where their nose would be was only a bony ridge, and the mouth was vertical and narrow. They looked sick, thought Ishmael as he looked on, expecting something to happen.

The nine Sulk began to glow from the inside, and as light swelled within them the blemishes on their skin faded away and those large eyes cleared until gleaming pearl that shone with intelligence. The sight was beautiful, and Ishmael felt the answering call of life thrumming through his own veins in response. He felt another presence with him then and realized it had been within for so long he no longer took notice.

It was the Mother with whom he had connected to help his dreaming skills, and that pure energy had then saved him from death not once but twice. Ishmael thought the Mother had deserted him, but now, filled with her love, he knew she would always be within him, that was a connection that could never be broken. As the Sulk filled with the light of Aspre they began to change colour, a band of energy that rolled up then down their bodies, changing through the hues of the rainbow and coming to stop on white that in moments changed briefly to other hues, maybe reflecting their emotions, thought Ishmael, still speechless. The Sulk, now transformed and brimming with life, began to dance long loping steps as they twirled. The nine Sulk kept dancing until as one they collapsed to the ground where their robes had dropped.

From somewhere, high guttural screams rolled up to them from far below. That took some of the joy out of what Ishmael had watched, and he felt that primal urge to flee. What was out there? Zahra moved to the edge of the rise they were, on and Ishmael followed her. They knelt at the rock ledge where the lanterns below shone their protection. The farthest lantern was suddenly snuffed out with a cry, and Ishmael heard the breaking of glass. The bearer of that lantern still slightly visible was snatched out of the faded glow of the next lantern by long, spiked limbs. Then the screaming began.

One of the Sulk moved quickly to Ishmael and Zahra, pulling them away from the edge. The mere contact with the strange creature showed Ishmael a burst of images of many Sulk running as creatures bigger than they with triangular heads and bulging eyes on each side and elongated bodies sprung after them on segmented, long limbs. They seemed like the small mantis that the younger monks at the monastery used to bet on.

The images changed to a glittering town with high, sharpened walls where the Sulk stood staring down to many of the mantis creatures and five other beings in some type of jet- black armor, sleek and like slivers of night. Then Ishmael was back and realized their touch was broken. Looking to Zahra, he knew she had seen the exact thing he had.

The Sulk placed a palm on Ishmael and Zahra's chest, and then Ishmael knew its name, which couldn't be pronounced but was more like a feeling of joy. Ishmael knew things about this creature and how it was directly from Aspre, the white moon that they had been sent to protect something very important from the children of their uncle, Tamul the red. This had started when the Severing undid the balance of the world by taking away magic. Tamul saw great opportunity when the Severing happened and sent his own children torn from his body. These became terrible warriors and their aim was to destroy the gods and gain their knowledge to take their places.

'The gods are dead,' thought Ishmael.

'No, not dead Ishmael, just mortal now and of great use to the races of our world in guiding them back into the time of magic. If we can save them, then this world stands a chance, but if we fail then Tamul wins and that is the end of the Mother, our world,' came back the thoughts of the Sulk.

Then Ishmael was back in the clearing with the wind whipping around them. Zahra stumbled into him, and her eyes were fierce. She grabbed Ishmael's shirt then pulled him close. 'They're alive, Ish, now you can see Shail for yourself!'

Ishmael didn't know how to react about the news of Shail. He had believed the gods dead but understood why Aeon had kept it from him. It gave him someone to help the Sulk as well as allowing Ishmael to meet the god he had spent his life worshipping.

'Where are the gods now if they're so important?' asked Ishmael, overwhelmed at everything that was happening. He could feel the crystals in his pack burst to life just a moment before blue and white light began to emit from the pack beside him. The Sulk immediately all turned to him and began crowding around him as their bodies turned to bands of orange and yellow.

Ishmael knelt and removed the two crystals from their coverings for the Sulk to see then he stood back beside Zahra and watched.

Zahra leant in to him. 'Are you sure this is a good idea, Ishmael?'

'I don't really know, but the crystals themselves lit up, so I thought maybe this is meant to happen.' As they watched, two of the Sulk held a crystal each above them and the others crowded in close, their reaching hands all touching. The light of their bodies merged and swelled further with that emanating from the crystals until Ishmael and Zahra were forced to turn away. From close by Ishmael heard laughing and saw Aeon clapping his hands in glee, then the clearing seemed to explode with light and everything went dark but the light of Aspre.

When Ishmael looked up, energy crackled in blue lines over the Sulk and the two crystals sat suspended, pulsing and hovering in mid-air as the Sulk stood transfixed and staring at them.

'They are communicating with the crystals,' muttered Zahra in a low voice tinged with wonder.

'No, they are merely seeing what purpose the crystals serve and learning the role that Ishmael and the coterie play. For you, Ishmael, are more important than the gods now, and it is the Mother's will that the Sulk help you to return magic.'

Before Ishmael could ask Aeon a question, another scream came from down the hill. Ishmael went to look. Far below him stood a figure bathed in the glow of the final lantern that now lay on the ground alongside that of the Sulk who had held it.

Ishmael felt the figure's eyes on him even though they were masked behind what appeared an iron helm, The figure extended a finger to point at him then curled it into a fist, relaying the simple message easily enough. He realized Zahra was standing alongside him as she raised a hand with the index finger straight then curled it downwards as if to indicate the creatures manhood, if indeed it had a sex was small. When Zahra looked at him they both grinned as the black figure stood still, regarding them in his night armor with his cape flapping around behind him. As they watched, it reached down to the fallen Sulk at its feet then pulled it up by the throat.

Weak hands beat at the arms that held it, and Ishmael realized with horror that the Sulk was still alive, then they watched as it fell still and the figure tossed it away as if a gnawed chicken bone. It gave them a final look then screamed with such fury and hatred and stomped on the lantern, killing the light.

'That was one of the Life Quenchers,' said Aeon his hand squeezing Ishmael's shoulder. See the sacrifice they make for us? Our arrival and the healing of the Sulk beneath the moon and crystal will have given them something to think about this night. Mark my words, this won't be the last we see of them.'

'What do we do now, Aeon?' asked Ishmael.

'We get to safety while the Sulk are infused with light. Most of the travel is below ground, and we are safer there.'

Ishmael rewrapped the crystals then returned them to his pack, and they left marching within a protective circle of iridescent Sulk warriors.

Chapter 9

Dalwyn, who was up early meditating, was hungry by the time his breakfast was bought to him by Flint, who had stood guard at his chamber all night. He had been pleasantly surprised to find out the food stores had bacon, which had been scarce since he left Shelton's Crag. He sat and cut into the meat, and then he dunked it into the thick egg yolk. He then raised to his mouth and stopped.

There was a bitter smell to the food that Dalwyn had not noticed yesterday. He lowered the fork then looked closely at his plate, noticing now the very fine dots of brown that stuck to the bacon pieces and some on the egg whites. He sniffed the plate of food and knew something wasn't right.

'Flint,' he yelled and immediately Flint along with another flame warrior rushed into the chamber.

'This food has been poisoned. Where is the one who delivered it here?'

'He passed me on the way back to the kitchen not long after delivering food to the hall and cells.' The guard and Flint looked at each other then exploded into motion.

'Find that man,' yelled Dalwyn after them, his mood now spoiled. Dalwyn took his time in the adjoining bath, making sure one of his trusted men carried the hot water personally to his chamber.

Once dressed he emerged from his chambers to chaos. The two guards at the cells had been found paralysed, foaming at the mouth and convulsing while five more men who had eaten the poisoned porridge in the hall had fallen ill with severe abdominal pain and weakness. Worse yet two more guards had been found with their throats slashed and a personal message had been left scrawled on the walls in blood, for him.

'Don't eat, don't sleep. I am coming for you, Dalwyn Trevlon.'

Dalwyn cursed and kicked one of the dead guards. With these two dead and many others incapacitated with illness, Dalwyn was left with fewer than a score of able warriors.

He turned to Flint. 'Double the guard on my chamber as well as the cells. From now on we stay together, especially at night. Stock up with food and make sure the weapons are destroyed or stored with us so they can't be used against us while we wait for my brother to arrive. Let's see how brave this fool Kenzu lord is now. Find them, Flint, I don't care how, but find them before I lose all my men.'

Zahra easily kept up with the steady pace of the Sulk, but more than once she reached out to steady Ishmael from falling as he began to tire. She could ignore the physical exhaustion like she was taught easy enough but not the new developments in her mission. Things were moving too fast for her to manage. The Sulk, Life Quenchers, and the gods, what was next? Zahra knew she needed to get the coterie together if any besides Ishmael were still alive, and now she was the last living sentinel.

She needed Haakon, the clan leader. He would know what to make of all this. But Haakon wasn't here, and Zahra didn't want to attempt contact across the astral with all the storms there.

They walked for the rest of the night, reaching a low entrance to a cavern that they had to crawl to get to, and when they climbed out the other end the Sulk closed it with a barricade of wood and stones. The Sulk lit the cavern as they moved with the area, soon changing to signs of habitation with arrows showing directions and also messages scrawled on the stone walls with chalk. They entered a large cavern decorated with colored cloth hanging from stalactites above a clear pool with some kind of light beneath its surface. On the opposite bank of the pool, an area of the cavern was hung with heavy rugs, forming a sort of shelter. Torches lit a path farther into the darkness from the pool around a bend, and Zahra helped Ishmael sit on a rock beside the pool alongside Aeon.

'Why are we waiting? Do they have food or somewhere for us to rest? she asked, looking at Aeon.'

'Yes, they do and will give them to us freely but first must tend to their own.'

From within the blankets figures began emerging, dull and grey like the other Sulk had been before bathing in Aspre's light. As they met and embraced, light transferred into their bodies, healing them and the light of the givers faded with each transference. When they were done, the chamber was crowded with glowing Sulk who all turned to the three newcomers then knelt and lowered their heads.

'Why are they doing that?' said Ishmael sounding nervous.

'They are showing their respect to you I think. Is that right Aeon?'

'Yes, Aeon replied to Zahra. You see, Ishmael, try as you want to throw aside this momentous task that has befallen you, it will not stop those who know you from knowing your importance. The Sulk have agreed to aid you and in return we will help them get the gods to safety, since both of these serve the Mother.

'I have been shown that we must rest now while the Sulk here make the necessary preparations for our departure.'

'We just got here, and where are these gods then?' asked Ishmael.

'This is a temporary hideout. The Sulk have many of them hidden away in these hills and use them to emerge for Aspre's appearance as well as hiding from the Life Quenchers. To get to where my brothers and sisters are we must go deeper. Now there is much to be planned, and I am to be included in this planning, so I must leave you for a time. I can tell you from experience that the pool you see is for bathing and has been laden with salves and herbs that will leave you feeling refreshed. There are clean robes over there for you both and food also. We leave in four chimes, so rest while you can.'

Zahra stripped off her clothes that had acquired quite a stench and knelt at the water's edge. She soaked her clothes then placed them on the floor nearby to wash before getting out since the robes that had been put out for her and Ishmael seemed too bulky and warm, which would also hamper her movement in combat. The water was neither warm nor cold. Now she was in it she could see the minute pieces of jelly-like substance that coated the surface. Below it was lit by light that broke apart when Zahra entered the water, and she realized the light was actually fish-like creatures that now swarmed over her skin. She began to panic.

'Zahra, just relax. They aren't dangerous; they will clean your skin, that's all,' reassured Aeon.

Zahra lay back against the rim of the pool trying to ignore the strange feeling on her skin, watching as Ishmael approached, undressed, and entered the water. He dunked his head under the water then came up as she watched, noticing a difference about him.

'What are you staring at?' he said, splashing water at Zahra.

'You have new scars. The one on your arm, what was that from?'

'A hound that I tried to steal food from. In Brimmerland I unknowingly insulted an important man by ignoring his offer of food and shelter. I became his property, which is why I took so long to reach the Godhead.'

'So taking off by yourself without my protection didn't turn out so good for you after all?'

Ishmael sighed. 'No, it didn't. Is that what you wanted, to hear me say it?'

'I just need to know that if I continue to put my life in danger to protect you that you will actually let me do what I am trained to do, protect you.'

'Zahra, do we have to do this again?'

'Yes, we do, Ishmael. If I don't hear you say it then I'm done, gone out of here, because I refuse to die for an idiot.'

'Well, what was I supposed to do then? I had already put you through that mess with my family.'

'We could have talked about it, Ishmael.'

'Would you have come with me?'

'No, but that's not the point. Your actions have put the coterie in danger now and though we may never have been able to avoid this situation is something we will never know.'

'I'm sorry. I didn't cope well with what happened with my family and the attack at the monastery. I turned to the one thing I always had, Lady Shail of Illume. I had to know if the gods were truly dead or not.'

'And now you know.'

'Yes, now I know, and I agree to do the right thing and let you do what you must to keep me safe.'

'No running off?'

'No, not this time. Both of you were right. I cannot hide and run anymore. Actually I don't want to run either, Zahra.'

Zahra shrugged. 'That's a step in the right direction, Ishmael. With the rest of the coterie and their sentinels being captured, you are the last chance for us to redeem anything from this situation. We need to reunite you with the coterie, and soon.'

The strange pool with its herbs and sucker fish drained the tension from their bodies, eased the soreness in their muscles, and soothed their injuries, leaving them relaxed yet tired. As they emerged from the water two Sulk children, or what Zahra assumed to be children due to their shorter stature brought towels to wipe them down. Then the two of them were led to a darker area of the cave to sleep.

Chapter 10

Haakon was stone sober and cold to the bone with a chill that wouldn't thaw. He stood watching from a spyhole that overlooked the cells. Dalwyn had moved his remaining men between the cells and Haakon's private rooms by night while during the day they moved around but never alone. With Nina as his only support he was constantly aware of the need for her safety, which stopped him from fully unloading his rage. The time observing the cells had left him feeling like he was missing something, and as it had turned out he had missed someone, not something.

The two brothers Dre and Lim were not in the cells, which could only mean they had been killed or had escaped capture. Now he thought of it he had seen neither of the younger ancients since arriving at the safe house. Even amongst the celebrations he couldn't recall them being involved. By nature Latasha had told him her kin were very shy and wary of man, who looked upon their race with mistrust. The change in the brothers had been nothing short of miraculous when they had been reunited with Latasha after her trial. They had believed the race of ancients was ebbing away towards its doom and that they had been the only survivors, and in the short time they had been together it had been hard to keep them apart. Haakon hadn't minded that much since it meant Latasha was also protected when he wasn't about.

Haakon thought back to the evening of the attack when he had dismissed the servants to their beds or to join in the feast and now the only other sober people he spotted were the unlucky guards who had been given the late shift.

The construction of turning the house into a fortress was well under way, and work had also begun on the second level of the building. The location was close to a stone quarry used for this very purpose. As he had seen when arriving, the fields had begun providing an abundance of fresh food while livestock thrived in small fields surrounding it. The safe house backed up to the mountain, where three unfinished watch towers stood. Their placement would make surprise a tough thing indeed once they were completed. The work had been of the highest quality so far, and Haakon had been impressed that his instructions of allowing for the construction of a secret chamber with an escape passage had been followed to the letter.

From a side entrance to the safe house Haakon climbed up a ramp alongside a rope pulley system and square-cut stone cubes for the second level. He climbed up and stared up through the night tinged with crimson light Tamul, inspecting the three watch towers high above. Three layers of stone blocks had been fitted at the front of the house for the second story, and he made his way to that wall which looked down on the courtyard in front. The heavy wooden gates were open, he realized, and looking to the watch tower on each side of the gate he expected to see one of his men, but there were none. Then came a movement on one of the towers as a head peeked out. It was a young girl with blonde hair waving her hands as if trying to get his attention, which she surely had done. The girl pointed to her right, and following her direction Haakon saw that the courtyard wall was steeped in shadows without the glow of any lit torches. As he peered down, movement caught his eyes; a group of ten armoured figures emerged from the darkness and ran crouched over with blackened weapon towards the undefended entrance of the safe house.

Now he knew the girl was Nina. The brave little girl had really grown on him over the last two days, but she was also a hindrance, and Haakon had no inclination to have her death on his conscience. He left his hiding spot and signing to Nina to leave hers they crept from between the walls to a narrow staircase that led up to the roof level of the ground floor. Not needing to watch for sentries since Dalwyn's men were largely occupied with recovering from the poison, they climbed out among the still night, bathed in half of Aspre's regal form. Soft flakes of snow drifted down, and the child beside him couldn't help herself but leapt to snatch them from the air, smiling as they melted in her hands.

Haakon moved to the buildings edge where he had first seen Nina at the tower and the men rushing his new clan house. He stood there making sure he would be seen by any observers and hoping the two twins would be the ones watching. They stayed that way for half a chime, only leaving when Nina became bored and Haakon began to think this was a waste of time and energy since the twins may have just left the area all together.

At the time of early morning when most people are at their least attentive Haakon and Nina next struck at their foes. Haakon had located some empty fire pots made of clay, which they heated by fire then filled with oil. Painstakingly slowly they moved the fire pots through the hidden corridors to the escape point closest to the cell block. While Haakon stayed hidden, Nina walked out into view of the guards, who initially didn't see her. When they did, they became alarmed at seeing the young girl who had used ash to colour her face and wore a long white dress she had also acquired that made her appear an apparition. Nina ran towards them carrying a fire pot then with a scream tossed the fire pot at them as they looked on in horror. The clay fire pot shattered on the stone spreading oil over the flagstones and up the wall without harming the guards.

'Awake! We are under attack!' one of them bellowed, then the two gave chase after Nina, who raced back to Haakon and into the false corridor.

Haakon stepped out then scattered a bag of caltrops across the ground towards the guards. One managed to skid to a halt, though the other stepped on one of the twisted, sharp iron caltrops with a scream. He hopped about, stepping on another, and fell, which only made things worse as he landed on multiple caltrops.

Haakon and Nina were already on their way with another fire pot that Haakon carried. They didn't bother to move quietly, as the guard's shrieks and excited shouts of his comrades easily hid their movements. They arrived at Haakon's private chamber, where he checked through a spyhole for inhabitants.

The bedding was crumpled but no one was in the chamber, so Nina activated the hidden door to open and Haakon launched the fire pot onto the bed. They retreated and ran back the way they had come, giggling together at their mischievous attack. Even though Dalwyn would not be hurt, his comfortable bed was now ruined, which would make rest harder for him. Haakon thought this was only fair since it was actually his bed and not the old man's.

Dalwyn was quickly out of bed and into the corridor outside when the disturbance began. He had his sword in hand and couldn't remember even grabbing it. Flint was already running towards the cells and the corridor that met this one, leaving one guard with Dalwyn.

'With me,' he ordered as he stalked past bare foot and turned the corner. Up ahead he could see that the corridor near the cells was on fire. Two of his flame warriors used blankets to try to smother the flames which smelled of burning oil. Flint was crouching over a guard who lay in the corridor shrieking.

'Shut him up or by the gods I will cut his tongue out,' yelled Dalwyn as he hurried over.

Flint turned towards Dalwyn from where he knelt and yelled something, but it was lost in the screams of the guard. Something sharp punctured Dalwyn's foot, bringing him instantly awake as he hopped about back the way he had come.. Now on the ground he could see sharp caltrops scattered over the corridor. The pain was immense, and Dalwyn bent then tore the caltrop free from his foot nearly passing out from the pain it caused. He leant against the wall panting, pushing aside the guard who accompanied him as he attempted to offer assistance.

'Haakon, hear me now. If you value the lives of your bitch and her damn coterie, hand yourself over to me or I will begin killing them one by one. You have until nightfall tomorrow or someone dies.'

The shrieking guard fell silent, either dead or passed out, and as other guards carefully removed the remaining caltrops Flint helped Dalwyn up and towards his chamber. When they hobbled around the corner, the smell of burning was as thick as the smoke that billowed from the chamber.

'Bring water, buckets of water,' called back Flint as he sat Dalwyn up against the wall, drew steel, masked his face with his shirt which he tied over his face then entered the chamber.

Dalwyn was shaking with anger now. This Haakon was making him look a fool, and he had overheard the other guard saying it had started with the girl Nina whom they thought was a ghost.

They would both pay for this, and Nina, little Nina… he had a surprise for her when she slept next.

When Flint hurried from the smoke Dalwyn flinched. Flint ignored it, squatting beside his lord.

'It was the bed, Dalwyn. They torched the bed but nothing else. That Kenzu bastard is intent on unsettling us while disrupting any rest or plans we have.'

'Take me to the cells, bring clean water and bandages, and have pallets made for us all. We sleep together from now on, and tonight I must be comfortable and well-guarded,' Dalwyn said. 'I have a surprise for our little ghost.'

Chapter 11

When Ishmael awoke, Zahra wasn't there. He stayed in his robes since his clothes had also gone. Back in the main chamber Zahra sat by a fire where he saw his clothes hanging to dry. He smiled at the sight of her, and though he would never admit it to her, he realized he had missed Zahra's company. Ishmael felt great, light on his feet and alert, a feeling that had been absent lately.

Zahra sat eyes closed, maybe meditating or travelling as Ishmael approached and checked his clothes that were dry. He dressed while thinking about the astral plane and the need to try contacting one of the coterie. The need for knowledge of each other's situation was paramount now as they tried to unite.

They filed out of the camp with their party in the middle, surrounded in the glow of the Sulk's illumination as they moved deeper into the cavern system. The weathered rock led them steadily down through the steep tunnel into an active cave where a steady trickle of water bubbled up through the rock to run away into a small stream that flowed along one of the many exit passages. They stopped here for a time, watching as the Sulk gathered together in a group with their forms changing in colour that continued to pulse up and down their bodies. Aeon had said the colors were emotionally driven, and looking at them now with purple, red-orange bands interspersed with bands of white rolled over their forms Ishmael could feel their fear and confusion. Something bad was going to happen.

Beside him he heard Zahra's weapon Moonblade slide free of its sheath, and she pushed him behind her with an arm. 'Stay close to me no matter what happens.'

Aeon came hurrying over. 'We are being pursued through the caverns by the Life Quenchers, who have already been at our old camp and are gaining on us now.'

'The corridors are narrow enough to choke their attempts although if we do that they might find side passages where they branch and get in to flank us,' said Zahra to Aeon.

'My thoughts are the same,' Aeon said. 'We need to press on with more pace to find a defensible location. The Sulk will hold them off as long as possible.'

'How far to our destination and the gods?' asked Zahra.

'A chime or close to it to get to the gods, but at least a full day to leave the cavern, and that's if we dare our luck to move through the territory of the Shingle people, who are never happy to see outsiders.'

'The Shingle are also called children of stone and worshipped the god Melde, Ishmael said.'

'Yes, that right, Ishmael. Melde is the deity of stone and earth. I of course know Melde, he is one of my brothers; and like the things he signifies he is hard, tough and stubborn. I have no idea how he has taken his loss of power and have not met him since before the Severing, when even then he stayed here among his people instead of with the other gods.'

The Sulk finished their discussion and now were urging them onwards at a slow jog. It felt good to Ishmael to stretch his legs; the repetitive stomp of boots on the stone that echoed around them had a hypnotic effect on him after some time, and he was surprised when they came to a halt at a portcullis which was winched up to allow them passage. As the portcullis was released and crashed into the stone, Ishmael looked back to see the Sulk who had raised it twitch spasmodically, his form turning to orange into which black seeped into slowly drowning out the colour.

Ishmael raced to help the Sulk, but was cut off by Zahra who dragged him back standing between him and the portcullis. The darkness thickened around the stricken Sulk, and as its form faded, hatred coiled in the darkness around it. A dark, ropey tendril shot out towards Zahra that was sliced by Moonbite who flared at the wet contact, bathing the area in incandescent light. The dark creature shrieked then sprang back into the safety of the darkness.

'Go, Ishmael. Next time don't stop to help anyone.'

'Sorry. It was just a natural instinct, Zahra.'

'Yes, a natural instinct you must replace if you want to live,' she replied, pushing him before her.

The Sulk closed back around them, leading the party along a path that took them down the inside of an open cavern.

'Come on Ishmael,' Zahra said, practically dragging him with her.

That portcullis will only stop them for a while, then they will be after us again. The Sulk are not warriors so remember that if you are to stay alive then stay beside me.'

As Aeon hurried by, Zahra reached and caught him by the shirt sleeve.

'I don't like this, Aeon. These Sulk are not warriors and I get the feeling we are being flanked as we move. If it comes to a battle we are in serious trouble,' Zahra hissed.

'While I agree with everything you have said, Zahra, there is no option other than fleeing as fast as we can. I will lead the way, and if we hurry then we reach safety before another attack comes, so let's move.'

⚜

Chapter 12

Dalwyn's solution to stop the coterie from travelling the astral was simple: don't allow them enough rest. Through the nights and days his men would run their blades against the iron bars of the cells, bang the doors, even throw water over them. It was crude and cruel, but it worked. Now he would enter the amber realm for the first time since taking the Kenzu stronghold. Safely surrounded by his remaining men who guarded the only entrance to the cell block, Dalwyn loosened his clothes, removed his one boot since the injured one hurt too much to be covered, then lay down on his pallet with the only light coming from two hooded lanterns.

He focused on the image of a water drop falling into a pool, sending out a rippling ring radiating from the center then deepened his breathing until he sensed his body sink down through the floor connecting him to the Mother, the energy of the feminine, life. Surrounded now in a world tinged red, Dalwyn began his rising breath that would warm the vortices in preparation for his astral journey. In the volumes of books Dalwyn had poured over he had read that unless the traveller defeats the ego at the first vortice and stops acting and thinking as if the world owes them something, they will fail to move onto any of the further vortices. His many successful travels defied that knowledge and he was unsure why until he had spoken to Raul. There was another way to move through the vortices that was dangerous and highly energy consuming that involved certain practices to cause the energy vortices to spin in reverse, which would allow the traveller if they harboured enough energy to shoot through the lower vortices with the ego intact. The downside to this was the vortices becoming locked in that unnatural position, causing the traveller to suffer a form of mental illness or, worse, to become trapped in the astral world.

Dalwyn locked the first vortex closed then felt the astral cord loosen and his body float out of its material prison. In this state as he glanced down at his body he could see the foundation vortex at the base of his spine, where it was spinning slowly in reverse. The vortex was black and crusted around the edge and at one point in its spin it would lose its shape before correcting itself. This change to the pure red energy of the foundation vortex was caused by his ego, or so Raul had taught him.

With an explosive exhale Dalwyn flung his astral form up through this red world towards the second vortex, a spinning orange light far above him that was known as the home of the self. The deep well of energy Dalwyn had built up through regular training allowed Dalwyn to shoot up through the orange vortex. He ignored the overwhelming fear that came over him, put aside thoughts of failure long enough to continue upwards towards the third vortex, a blinding yellow that tinged with a sickly mucus green around its edges.

He surged through into a tunnel that further infused him with a jolt of energy, shooting him out to fall down into the golden astral river. Now came the hard part, to access the fourth vortex of green called the Unbound, which if successful would allow him to choose a destination, and even though his strength was of that of a child, now he could reach where he wanted, which was the present time in the very Kenzu stronghold where his body rested but without the shortcomings of the physical body to restrict him.

The fourth vortex loomed before Dalwyn as he was swept along on the astral river and into that green energy where he knew travellers would need to surrender to the pure love of creation or risk unhealthy infatuation with the self. Dalwyn had no idea of the risk or problems this would present him. All he knew was the desperation of striking back at his enemies before they undid his plans, and any problems this caused him he would deal with later.

Chimes of visualization of where his body rested over the last day allowed him to grasp that image and hold tight as he was spat out of the astral river back into the Kenzu stronghold. His sight was enhanced now allowing him to see the heat trails of the living as well as their auras. Dalwyn flexed the fingers of his astral hands, rolled his neck, and squatted down on his haunches, revelling in the absence of pain this astral form gave him. Looking back at his material body. Dalwyn thought it looked pathetic and weak, he could see the death in his body. The mustard colour gathered around his lungs or the cloudy red pooling at all his joints. Worst was the darkness around his skull area, and though not a healer he knew none of these were good. He was dying, and the time left to save himself was dwindling fast.

Dalwyn felt as if he were being watched and turned to see Latasha at the bars of the nearest cell, hands white around the knuckles as she gripped them hard while she watched him. Dalwyn glided forward to stand before her out of reach.

'You can see me,' he said to himself rather than Latasha.

'My kind have always been able to do so, Dalwyn. I saw you watching your body. Did you see the death there?'

Although he didn't answer, Dalwyn knew Latasha saw it too.

'Dalwyn, we can stop this foolishness now, get you help, and when the coterie brings back magic you can be healed. The Mother will forgive you, but if you continue to defy her wishes and fight against her coterie, you are ruined.'

'Tell me one thing, Latasha. Do your legs work here in the astral?'

Latasha refused to meet his gaze, and Dalwyn knew he had hit a nerve.

'They do, don't they?'

'I don't know,' hissed back Latasha. 'It is too dangerous for me to enter the astral world now, I am too weak!'

'Such a shame, Latasha, that you have no way of saying your goodbyes to that snake Haakon, or Nina. Without you being able to meddle it will make killing them so much easier.'

Dalwyn turned and began to run down the corridor past the two flame warriors who were watching Latasha talk to nobody. As he rushed past them they looked about nervously; then he was focused on the hunt and nothing more.

Nina held a little celebration that night after their successful attack with the fire pots. The highlight had easily been when she and Haakon had watched through spyholes as Dalwyn stepped on one of the caltrops and had what mother used to call a hissy fit. Trying to contain her laughter had been one of the hardest things Nina had ever done, and if Haakon had not have covered her mouth with his hand she may have betrayed their location to Dalwyn or his flame warriors. Afterwards while their enemies were licking their wounds, Nina had snuck into the kitchens to search for something sweet and had found a cake covered all in chocolate icing along with tea leaves, which would make Haakon happy since it was his favourite drink- just like a lot of adults, she thought.

While Haakon was once again showing himself from the top of the unfinished rooftop in the hope of the twin ancients seeing him, Nina boiled the water for tea near the small, natural chimney at the back of the secret clan room where it wouldn't alert the sentries, then she cut cake for the two of them and impatiently awaited his return.

Soon she could hear him moving through the hidden corridor that led to the clan room, and he entered with the tip of his nose red from the cold with snowflakes decorating his long coat. His blank face told her that the ancients had not seen him or didn't want to, and she passed him hot tea with cake, which finally made him smile.

'Cake? You certainly have a talent for finding the best foods, Nina. One day you will make somebody a great, fat wife.'

'I don't want to be fat or be a wife, where you must do what a man wants of you all the time. I'm going to be an assassin just like Zahra.'

Haakon raised his eyebrows at this as he shovelled cake into his mouth, which was stale but still tasty.

'Fat people don't make great assassins, so how are you going to do that then, Nina?'

'You will teach me, silly.'

'Oh will I? Okay I will make you a deal. If we get out of here alive you can come live with me here and be the cook and cleaner in return for your assassin lessons.'

'That is not a good deal, Haakon. This place is too cold and has ghosts.'

'I will supply you with all the cake you want. The only ghost is a very scary- looking one of a little girl so white because she hasn't seen the sun in a very long time. She haunts the corridors constantly looking for cake and asking every living person she encounters if they have seen one.'

Nina laughed. 'You are just as silly as my father always was.' She curled up in blankets beside the fire, and Haakon came over to lay beside her. Haakon brushed the hair from Nina's eyes. 'Your parents would be so proud of you, and I bet somewhere in the Celestial lands they are looking down on you smiling right now.'

'Well I think they would be so happy to know that a very nice man is here to protect me from the bad people,' replied Nina, yawning.

'Nina, you need to remember what I told you about what you are trying to achieve tonight. Learn the limitations of the astral cord so you know how far you can move from here. First try the flames and other potential scrying surfaces, and if you get the chance before you run out of energy, attempt to contact Latasha or the coterie.'

Nina turned to face Haakon. She realized she was biting her lower lip and made herself stop. She could do this. I wish you could come with me, Haakon, this place is scary and I feel lonely in the astral here.'

'You know I would if possible, dear Nina.'

And Nina did know that he would but couldn't since he had been hurt so badly in the astral that his energy body was too damaged to risk it. Nina squeezed Haakon's hand then closed her eyes.

Within a short time the two of them were dozing as the wind outside grew stronger, whistling down the chimney and howling outside the stronghold as if a terrible beast was attempting to force its way in.

Chapter 13

The way onwards became perilous due to the uneven and crumbling floor they began to descend along. After a brief consultation they placed one of the Sulk at the front of the party alongside Aeon. Its form flared with white light making it easier to traverse the difficult route and reduced any chance of injury for the three companions. All Zahra could think about was if the Sulk were killed, then they would be effectively blinded. There were too many possibilities for this to go wrong, and Zahra knew that this fear was mainly because of what had happened to the other sentinels and the coterie for which she partially blamed herself. Though she realised it was not her fault, Zahra couldn't help thinking she should have been tougher on Ishmael. If they had avoided Acclaro, then they would have been with the rest of the coterie and maybe just maybe been able to help fight off Dalwyn and his flame warriors. Zahra knew although she would never admit it to anyone else that the death of the sentinels had rocked her to the core. And what of her clan leader, Haakon? Was he also dead?

Pushing these thoughts from her mind, Zahra hurried along with Moonbite held ready in one hand, the other on Ishmael's shoulder in front of her. They made great time and arrived at a fortified corridor with an iron door. At Aeon's call a viewing hatch grated open. Whoever manned the door recognised the Sulk and the door opened allowing them entry. Four men lean yet strong looking stood in armour that had been scavenged to create what protection they could find and they returned Zahra's stare silently. The lead Sulk placed his hand on one man's chest to communicate. Once the door was bolted shut they were led onwards past a warrior who stood by a large bell which he struck to warn those ahead of the groups approach. They passed a group of eight warriors who hurried past them to help defend the door they had entered through.

They were ushered through another two doors like the first one then into a cavern where a high stone wall like a castle stretched across its width above a thick iron studded door behind a raised portculis. Above this the walls were more barricades fitted with archery towers, and along the wall tops huge iron pots bubbled away, giving off the stench of oil. Those atop the wall called out greetings to their guide and bowed to the Sulk as the gates slowly were wound open to allow them through. Their guide took them to a chamber with chairs and a number of long tables where women bustled around in bright dresses, busily cooking and bringing food as they saw the newcomers arrive. The men gathered here in groups smoking and drinking ale at a bar, regarded them with serious stares over whispered conversation.

Aeon sat beside Ishmael grinning.

'Zahra, sit with us,' said the god.

'I need a drink,' said Zahra, squeezing Ishmael's shoulder, then she joined the men at the bar who looked surprised as she approached them.

'What we drink here is only for men, lass. Maybe you should go back and drink tea with the ladies,' said one, which was followed by the clanking of steins and laughter.

Zahra grabbed the man's drink, guzzled the ale down, wiped her chin, and belched loudly. 'I bet not only can I better you in drinking the piss that passes for ale here but that I am more man than you will ever be,' she replied, sitting down amongst them as the other men burst out laughing and slapping their knees.

Ishmael smiled at Zahra's actions then turned back to Aeon.

'We eat, then we must bathe to enter the presence of the gods, who are susceptible to disease from the outside world. The Sulk are already carrying news of our arrival.'

'Who are these people?' asked Ishmael. 'And can we trust them?'

These people are stout worshippers who chose to come here and protect the gods who survived. They are volunteers and very capable of surviving here beneath the ground. The Life Quenchers know the gods are down here somewhere from the prisoners they have captured and tortured, they just don't know where.'

'They were right behind us earlier, Aeon. Is it too dangerous coming here then?'

'Ishmael, we had little choice, outside the Sulk and yourselves are easy targets. At least here we have allies and a fighting chance to get both you and the gods to safety.'

'Where exactly is that, Aeon?' asked Ishmael exasperatedly.

'I was hoping that was something you could tell us, Ishmael, since you are one of the coterie of the heart. Maybe the gods have knowledge they can share with you, but the sooner you realize we are all just trying to help you the better and easier it will be for all of us.'

Ishmael sighed and rubbed his forehead. 'I apologize I just find this all too much after the events of the Godhead, then believing Shail was dead only to find out in fact she along with most of the other gods are alive and well.'

'The blame for that lies on my shoulders, Ishmael, and I chose to withhold the fact that Shail lived from you to be sure we destroyed the Vorm's hold over the people, otherwise it would have distracted you from that cause. I could no longer watch on and be a part of the cruel deception that mocked the faith of all the pilgrims while keeping the plight of the gods a secret.'

'So how do I approach her, them, all of them? asked Ishmael.'

'That, my friend, is up to you. Shail is still your deity and yet now as mortal as you. Some of my kin have changed with what has happened and refuse to be treated as anything special, while others have been stuck in the past unable to adapt and still feel as if they are better than you mortals.'

'Which one is Shail?'

'Nice try,' said Aeon, laughing. 'The simple fact that you are a true follower of Shail gives you a chance to persuade the gods to help us and let us get them to safety.'

They dined on a tasty vegetable broth with thick, dark bread, then Ishmael along with Aeon joined Zahra and her new friends for a mug of ale to settle Ishmael's anxiety around meeting the gods, especially Shail.

When it was time one of the Sulk came to guide them. It stopped before Ishmael then placed a hand on his shoulder. Through images he saw there was no need to be afraid or anxious, that they were safe here and that Shail not only knew of his arrival but looked forward to meeting him. This actually did little to put Ishmael at ease, though the touch of the Sulk seemed to relax him, and the tension he felt in his muscles faded away.

They were led outside into the cavern where a town spread out before them. The rooftops were covered in brightly coloured fungi that lit the town that spread out from a large rectangle temple made of white stone around which a garden of strange plants thrived. From this vantage point they could see many Sulk gathered at the temple.

The temple was warm when they entered by the stairs into a hall that held many alcoves as well as a stairway winding up another three levels that Ishmael could see. In the middle of the hall were lounging beds and tables. Soft music played and entertainers performed before those seated.

❧❦❧

Chapter 14

Since Raul had made Nina enter her astral body by feeding her salty foods without water while back in Acclaro, Nina had realized there were other ways to enter the astral world, each with its own good and bad points.

The ways to make someone enter their astral body were far more restrictive for the traveller than if you entered voluntarily through the vortices, and now Nina knew thirst, extreme hunger or exhaustion could force you out also. Except in these states you would be severely at a disadvantage and unable to move far from your material body. For one and a half days Nina had restrained from resting or sleeping, which had been helped by the use of some char, an evil tasting drink that stopped the user getting tired. Now she would use that exhaustion to force herself out of her body.

Haakon wanted her to learn to defend herself first when not in a prime astral state which was what you were if you entered through the vortices. It seemed that no sooner than she lay down that she became aware of the strange realm around her, and she rose to see her astral cord shimmering down to her sleeping form beside Haakon. Nina glanced at the fire beside them, which was the only truly colourful thing, while the walls and the rest of the clan rooms' colours were fading. When she squatted beside the fire and focused on its flames, it flared to life, making her gasp as she saw something obscured there in the flames. Breathing deeply Nina exhaled in a rush, expelling all her air, which was called the dragon breath, and amazingly for the first time after many attempts Nina found herself near the fire in the main hall of the stronghold. The fire in the hall had absorbed the colour, leaving her surroundings with an ashen tint.

Nina was already in the hall, so she ran over to the entrance of the stronghold to see how far the astral cord would let her go. The doors were currently shut, however, the window to its left was missing a shutter that had been damaged during the attack Nina climbed through it to stand outside where everything was covered in a thin, white cover of snow. Outside she could see the amber sky overhead that made the world look so much weirder than normal. A part of her worried about her feet and getting that horrible frostbite thing that turned fingers and toes black until they fell off. It was a silly thing, though, because Nina had learnt the weather had no effect on the astral body; only weather within the astral like a storm could hurt her here. Nina kept walking away from the stronghold until with a tug in her abdomen letting her know she could go no farther, then she ran back to the window where she used the astral cord like a rope to climb back inside.

Dalwyn moved swiftly through the stronghold to the kitchens where he assumed Nina or Haakon had been since they had poisoned the food the day before. He would now attempt to gain the service of one of the astral entities, which he had never done before. Once there Dalwyn grasped his astral cord, through which he could feel the pulsing of his heart way back to his physical body. With his teeth he punctured the cord then used the drizzle of silver fluid that oozed out to form a protective circle around himself. Once finished Dalwyn let the precious astral fluid in the cord drip down to form a puddle just outside the circle, then he blocked the puncture wound with his fingers, holding it closed as he waited for one of the astral entities to come.

With the loss of astral energy he felt faint for a long moment and when he became aware of his surroundings again he heard the faint lapping near his feet just outside the circle. A sinuous creature with many legs and a long, narrow body lay there, its swollen, purple tongue lapping the precious fluid off the ground at his feet. Dalwyn scuffed his circle with one foot to break it then swiftly surrounded the drinking creature with more of his astral life, trapping it. When it had cleaned the floor of the precious fluid, the creature attempted to move closer to him. The barrier of the circle around it burst into white light at its touch, making it scuttle backwards only to hit the other side. With a scream the entity rose up on its four back feet to observe Dalwyn.

'Give me your name and I will give you sustenance,' said Dalwyn, whose legs felt like they were shaking from fright. To show fear to this being would end in it hunting him every time he entered this astral realm since it had the taste and scent of his being.

'More energy, I am weak. Then I will tell you what you want,' said the creature as it licked its clawed feet, trying to find any missed astral fluid.

'You don't get to make demands of me here. You are trapped in my circle and at my mercy. The only way out is for you to take my offer, otherwise you will die here.'

'I will do your bidding, great man, but not as a slave as an equal. Break the circle and I promise you no harm.'

'I know of your lies and flattery, entity, and am immune to both of them.'

The creature flung itself at Dalwyn, colliding with the energy circle again, which sent white sparks flying upwards, obscuring it from Dalwyn's vision for a moment. Every time it cleared its twisted malevolent gaze fixed on his and it tried to break the circle again. This kept on until with another scream it sat on its haunches, panting and observing him.

'Your name and live or rot here and die,' yelled Dalwyn.

'Screareed,' hissed the entity.

'I submit to you, sorcerer.'

Dalwyn had a moment of satisfaction at being referred to as a sorcerer. He stepped to the circle. This next step was by far the most dangerous, but now he had the entity's name he could force it to submit again.

The creature watched him intently with eyes full of need or was it greed as Dalwyn let some of his life fluid fill the palm of his opposite hand then passed it through the protective circle.

The entity grabbed his wrist then drank the viscous silver fluid as if sucking his palm and that's what happened once the liquid was gone, it kept sucking, making Dalwyn feel dizzy again and weaker while his arm before him became more transparent.

'Screareed, enough!' said Dalwyn simply, and the entity reluctantly let go of his palm, which he withdrew from the circle. There was swelling to his palm where a lump had grown. When he touched the wound to his astral cord it closed up; however he saw the lump in his palm remained.

'The entity sat watching him lazily now, sated with power, and its form changed to one Dalwyn knew well, his father. Of course the books had warned him of this, so had Raul who had been taught the astral craft by his grandfather. Once the entities drink from your astral life's well they will have knowledge about you, people of past events in your life, and will attempt to use this to their advantage. 'I have a task for you, Screareed, with a great reward should you succeed.'

'I won't let you control me,' it replied, belching loudly as long claws at the ends of it legs dug deep furrows into the stone.

'A chance for a body that will allow you release from this world to the world of man. All you have to do is listen.'

'A body, say you? I have great need of one of those.'

Dalwyn grinned, and Screareed mirrored it back at him.

Chapter 15

The Sulk guide grasped Ishmael's hand and led him away from the others. Zahra moved to follow, but Aeon stopped her and Ishmael heard him say, 'He is in no danger, Zahra, and will be in easy sight of you.'

Ishmael felt his mouth go dry as he walked towards the alcove following the Sulk, who gestured to him as a mixture of pink and white rolled over its body. The alcove was in semi-darkness, only lit by candles that illuminated a long lounge with a table on which sat a decanter of sapphire wine. A figure, with her back to him, knelt on the wooden boards with a long piece of parchment rolled out before her, ink wells and quills beside her on a tray, and it seemed she hadn't even noticed Ishmael standing at the opening watching her.

He turned to ask the Sulk if he should enter only to find the Sulk had abandoned him. Aeon stood farther back waving him onward. Quietly so as not to disturb her, Ishmael removed his sandals then entered and sat on the lounge waiting.

He didn't have to wait long.

'Don't just sit there, Ishmael, pour us both some wine.'

When he didn't do it straight away, Shail turned to look at him, and he couldn't help but smile at the ink that left a smear above one eye then down the cheek below.

'It will calm your nerves.' She then cocked her head curiously. 'What do you find so amusing, then?'

'You have, ah, ink on your face, and, well, I just assumed that Lady Shail would be immaculately presented, which I of course know is silly. I'm rambling now, so I will just get the wine.'

'Wise choice. While you do that I will make myself more immaculately presentable for you,' said Shail with a small laugh.

When Shail returned from a small adjoining bathing room, she still had ink on her face, which also stained her hands. The only change was a long, flowing, green dress, and her hair now sat loose, long blonde hair flowing over her shoulders and down her back.

'The ink won't come off easily so you can just deal with your imperfect goddess. Maybe it will help you realise we are not so unlike you, especially now that we share the common curse of mortality.'

Shail came around the table to sit beside Ishmael on the chaise lounge where he passed her a flute of the sparkling wine. They chinked glasses, then Ishmael drank half the glass with one gulp before looking embarrassed as Shail regarded him.

'It must be quite a shock for you to find out that I am still alive, as well as most of my brothers and sisters.'

'I was told you were nothing but dust and bones in the tower of Illume. Deep down I had never believed that, though which is what led me to travel the Seekers road to the Godhead. I just had to know.'

'The body in the tower was my closest keeper, a wonderful lady who knew she was dying and helped me to realize it could be used as a necessary deception so all hope for my followers wasn't lost. My brother, Aeon, said you would come. I hardly believed it would happen and often forget that unlike us other gods, Aeon has retained all his powers, which allows him to glimpse events involving people who can alter reality.'

'I can't alter reality any more than the average person,' replied Ishmael, draining the remainder of his wine.

'Still in denial then, Ishmael?'

'No, I realize the responsibility I have now, just that I have done nothing out of the ordinary that anyone else with my knowledge would have done.'

'That is wrong and you know it, Ishmael. Wherever you go things change and many lives are affected without you even being aware of what comes after you have continued on your way. You are the catalyst of the Coterie of the Heart, which is why the great event of returning magic cannot occur until you are united with the other members. Otherwise why would the Mother toil so hard to keep you alive?'

'That only happened because I connected to her with my dreaming body like I was taught to do,' he replied. He paced along the chamber, being careful not to step on the parchment on which the beautiful flowing writing that covered it was still drying.

'Actually it was the Mother who connected to you knowing that you were her catalyst. I am sure that connection has kept you alive more than once in the near past. Now is the time the Mother must ready herself for the return of power to come, and you will be susceptible to injury and death like the rest of us. From this time onward you are in greater danger than ever before.'

'I thought you had lost your powers, so how do you know all this, Shail?'

'Dreams,' she replied then gave a girlish laugh and placed her hand on his wrist momentarily.

'I know you have dreams of the Mother too, Ishmael, and we gods are no different. We were her first children who would help sculpt the world around the Mother. When we failed her and lost our power, thrown out from our homes in the Celestial realms and Infernal realms, the Mother bombarded us with visions of what was to come with tasks to be completed, a chance to make amends for our shortcomings and prepare for a new world where harmony with the Mother will be the basis of the magic here.'

'Can you tell me then what I should do once we have all the crystals? The rest of the coterie are captured by my enemies, as are the two crystals they found.'

'You don't need my help, Ishmael. You already have the ability to find those answers in what you have now, but I cannot lead you to this. There is an invitation that must be followed to unlock that which you must know before the future will clear for you.'

'And here I was thinking I would meet Shail, the lady of Illume, who would illuminate the way onward and provide me with the knowledge to do so,' said Ishmael, laughing drily as he refilled their glasses.

'It's rarely that easy in the realms of power, Ishmael.'

As he sipped more wine, which now was making him bolder, he indicated the parchment on the ground.

'What is this, anyway?'

'It is a guide to a new world that all of us gods have a part to create, a legacy we will leave behind us after all we have caused. It the last act we will be forced to do.'

'Why do you keep talking like you won't be here and this being the last act and chance to atone for the last failure, Shail?'

'Because this is to be our last act. Now your arrival tells me that our time hiding away from the Life Quenchers is almost at its end. Our life force is so strong that when we return to the Mother it will usher in this new world, providing the power to unlock the crystals you of the coterie have collected.'

'I still don't understand what you mean by returning to the Mother, Shail.'

'Death, Ishmael. I mean that we will be absorbed into the Mother and then Shail of Illume or any of the gods except Aeon and the Jester will cease to exist.'

'So what will exist then if no gods?'

'I don't know,' Shail said. That topic is often a choice for debate, though, with the consensus being that there will be no more of us and that we have served our purpose already. Before us gods there was only the three true powers; The Mother, who represents the cycle of life and death; Aspre, or everything good; and Tamul, or everything evil.'

'Can't you fight it? I mean going to your death like livestock goes to slaughter. Why would you choose this?'

'It is far from being like that. It is about returning home to peace while knowing a part of us has served to restore the Mother to her full power. It is why you must lead us back home, Ishmael, and no great surprise too since you are her catalyst .The coterie need to learn from one another. You used to meet in the tree chamber, which is a place you will be safe from attack while in that state, then teach one another the different knowledge you have.'

'I have made things hard by insisting on departures from meeting with them, which I realise now has caused a rift that made us all vulnerable. Now I will fix that problem, and you are right,' said Ishmael excitedly. 'It doesn't matter that I am separate from them.'

'You are weak in the astral, Ishmael, using it rarely if at all and prefer the dreams to travelling the vortices. The astral is where you can come together, and you are the catalyst but don't be fooled into thinking that they have no role or that you are more important than they. Your role is in bringing them together now and seeing us gods returned safely back home.'

'I had thought of so many questions to ask you when I knew this meeting could happen, and yet now I'm here I can't remember them. Can you tell me if my mother will ever forgive me or if my friends in the monastery still live, Shail?'

'I wish I could do that for you, Ishmael Shantari, but I can't. It doesn't work like that. We, the gods, got our power through our followers, which then gave us influence to allow us in helping achieve our own ambitions while also changing the lives of our followers. Now we don't have that connection.'

'So what happens now then, Shail?'

'My brothers and sisters are preparing to leave this place, and there are some that refuse to do so. I am one in favour of returning to the Mother, but the others still fear such a thing and will not give up what little life remains to them. Soon I will leave you to try once again in swaying them to my view, but before I do that there is one of my brothers who wishes to meet you.'

'Which god would want that and why?' Ishmael asked, feeling once again the familiar anxiety welling within his stomach.

'Ishmael, there is no need to fear any of us. This god has been with you since birth and throughout your life even if you were not aware of his presence. Now follow me and put aside fear and worry, it has no place here.'

⸎

Chapter 16

Back in the hall now, Nina began to return to her body. Off to her left in the corridor something moved, and she only caught sight of a glimpse of black material, a cloak, before it vanished. Curious, Nina ran to the corridor to peer around the corner, cursing that she couldn't just move through the walls like normal when she entered the astral.

There was no sign of the shadow in the corridor. Nina wasn't even sure it hadn't just been her imagination. Then as she went to move away she saw something again towards the cell block. In the middle of the corridor something furred lay moving or shivering, she thought. It looked like a cat.

Nina moved forward cautiously then stopped to watch again. It mewled, and Nina relaxed; it was a cat. She ran forward. When Nina was only about ten feet away the cat morphed into something terrible with many legs on a segmented body with razor claws and a head with wide, curving lips through which protruded its tongue. It leapt at Nina, who threw herself to the floor then turned to see the creature hunched ready to leap again. This time it was between herself and safety.

As she had been taught by Haakon, Nina attempted to force away her fear and concentrate on memories of her parents in happier times, to project an aura of good. She let the images of her happiness wash over her drawing from memories of love and happiness, feeling her vortices open to emit a white glow emanating from first the foundation then the home of the self vortex before the creature that wasn't a cat collided with her, knocking Nina to the floor. Its back legs held her pinned to the stone, and she could feel her flesh tear as its claws raked her body.

Nina screamed but could do no more since her training wasn't advanced enough to protect herself. Her head was struck, knocking it to the side where incredibly she saw three figures walking towards her, clothed in the brightest glare of golden light. She recognized the three prisoners, the coterie, or so Haakon had told her. The man whom she did know, Raul, was mouthing something then traced a pentacle of light before him that shot down at Nina and her attacker, who was dragged off her, now caught in a web of light which was already fading until the two women held hands with Raul. With the three of them linked he web grew brighter and brighter, exploding with a flash of light and an unearthly howling.

Nina managed to climb to her feet, silver energy dripping from her wounds. From behind her three rescuers Nina saw energy begin to build. At the far end of the corridor stood Dalwyn, who charged at them. The short woman was the slowest, and Dalwyn struck her with a sword of energy that had formed in his hands. Red fire spattered over her astral form before she was dragged back to her body as her astral cord retracted.

The second woman turned back to Nina. 'Go, girl, or you will die. Don't let this be for nothing!'

Nina ran faster than she thought possible as her strength began leaking away. She knew it was too far to the clan room and headed for the hall and its fire. Through the flames she went back into her body and sat upright, startling Haakon, who was sat beside her.

'Nina, are you okay?' he said, and she began to cry. Haakon cradled her in his arms until she was done crying then ordered her to lie down so he could tend her wounds.

'I don't have any wounds, only astral ones,' she began to reply, then following Haakon's gaze she saw the welts and bruise begin to appear on the flesh of her thighs and her shirt turn red. Beneath her shirt scratches ran from her lower tummy to her chest from the astral creature's claws.

'This is the worst disadvantage of entering the astral through exhaustion, extreme hunger, or thirst. Wounds sustained in the astral directly affect the physical body,' said Haakon, but Nina didn't hear, she had mercifully passed out.

When Nina awoke she found Haakon still by her side. She reached for his hand and he took it in his, smiling down on her.

'I thought you were going to sleep all day and was worried who would get my dinner,' he said with a twinkle in his eyes.'

'Am I going to die?'

'Not today, Nina, your wounds were shallow. You were so lucky. Now tell me what happened.'

Nina explained in detail the events of her adventure. Haakon praised her when she told how she had successfully travelled through the flames twice and tested the distance of her astral cord. He listened carefully, asking many questions about the astral creature that had hurt her and stayed quiet when she finished her tale with her saviours, the coterie.

Nina watched Haakon redress her wounds. He also gave her some seeds to chew that would help with the pain. She kept quiet as he worked.

'Haakon, did I do well?'

'Yes, Nina, you were so brave and now have some valuable lessons to learn from.'

'It's just that you were so quiet and I thought…'

'You did great, Nina. Don't make my silence mean I am not proud of you or that you did poorly, because you have managed something most people never do, and that is astral travel. I am worried because Dalwyn seems to know more than I hoped, and if he has made a pact with one of the astral creatures he will most likely do so again, which makes our situation very dangerous.'

'The books I read all warn about the danger of dealing with astral beings. The one that attacked me was the first one I have ever met, and I didn't know you could get them to help you.'

'It is very dangerous to deal with these creatures. They will tell you how wonderful you are and make all kinds of promises they can't keep. It is better to stay away from them, Nina, because the cost you must pay for their help is too much and the more you use their help the stronger they become.'

'So how come Dalwyn can get to these creatures if I can't?'

'Nina, there are two paths to take in the realm of power, good and evil. The one Dalwyn sent against you is evil and shows he has chosen that path that is easier but ultimately more dangerous. You have chosen the path of good and have no doubt, astral celestial beings will have been watching you, but they are harder to convince to help you and very careful whom they reveal themselves to.'

'Are they angels?' she asked.

'Some people call them that, but I personally don't think so. Now rest some more while I plan what we do next,' he said and kissed Nina on the forehead.

'Will you wait with me while I fall asleep?'

'Yes. I give you my word that I won't move from this very spot until you are snoring like a pig.'

It took a long time, but eventually Nina's eyes closed and her breathing deepened. Haakon covered her in another blanket then began to pace around the chamber, worried. If Dalwyn had learnt to use the dark path in the astral world and was bargaining with its denizens, then he could use those resources to find him and Nina. The time to get Latasha and the coterie to safety was running out.

Haakon pulled on a thick coat and extra trousers as he prepared to go outside and try one more time to find the twin ancients. If they didn't show then he would be forced to act on his own, which was going to be very dangerous. Dalwyn had the advantage over him and knew Haakon would have to come to him soon.

The wind had died down when he made his way over the roof top to the ledge looking down over the courtyard. The visibility was almost non-existent below him as wind threw up flurries of snow, which helped to settle his mind to the task ahead of him, one in which he would succeed or die.

When Haakon could take the cold no more he battled against the wind to return to his bolthole. He reached the ladder down the back of this roof section and dropped to the ground, he realized he was not alone. Two figures stood huddling against the door using the little shelter provided to keep out of the snow, and Haakon stood there staring, not quite believing he had found them. Or had they found him?.

'Don't just stand there, stupid man, we're freezing here.'

Haakon stumbled forward, fumbling for the iron key with his mittens, and finally they were in the corridor away from the weather. He locked then placed the timber blocks against the door then turned and embraced Dre and Lim, who were shivering.

'Come, friends I have a fire but also a sick child so, we must respect her position. By the gods it's good to see friendly faces,' Haakon said, leading them back to the Kenzu clan room. Haakon busied himself stoking up the fire with his small pile of tinder before making tea for the three of them. The twins huddled around the fire. It was a pleasant reunion that required no words, just enough to be in each other's presence and though he had many questions Haakon was happy to leave them unanswered for now, as were the two twins.

Chapter 17

Ishmael followed Shail out of the alcove and up a set of winding stairs, where a crystal column glittered with light from within. In front of it kneeled a figure hidden within a long, dark-blue-almost, black hooded robe. Shail squeezed his shoulder and retreated back down the stairs.

'Come sit beside me, Ishmael Shantari. I would look upon the one who will change this world for the better,' the figure said in a low yet clear voice.

Ishmael did as the figure bade him, and when he was seated the figure turned to him, and he found himself looking upon the mask of a jester and gasped. It was the Death Jester.

'Sorry, I forgot I still wore the mask. It has become a part of me now and protects others from my true visage, which truly lends a touch of anxiety to those who see it.'

'Will you remove it for me?' Ishmael asked in a voice he was sure wavered with the fear that crept through his veins.

The Death Jester reached up and removed the mask in one quick motion while keeping its head bowed, and in that position Ishmael saw a curious thing. Its hair was changing between all different types, even to no hair, and when it finally looked up Ishmael gasped once again. He sat looking upon the face of his father, then almost immediately it morphed into that of his sister then his mother before settling into that of the abbot who had presided over the monastery of Illume.

'Don't be alarmed. My face and features will change between those whom you have met in this life and may even take on yours from an earlier point or future part in your life.'

'Why does that happen?'

Nobody, not even I truly knows, Ishmael, and it is why you may have heard me referred to as the many-faced god,' the Jester explained.

'Now before we can continue there is something that must be seen.'

'What do you mean?'

Before the Jester answered he reached across and grabbed Ishmael by the forearm, and Ishmael found himself within vision.

Ishmael saw his sister Christine sitting in a chair, and Dalwyn knelt before her holding her chin up, forcing her to watch something he couldn't see. She was crying hysterically

As Dalwyn stood up and walked away to be replace by the figure of a huge man whom Ishmael knew to be his brute Knuckles. A hand covered his sister's mouth and the other grabbed her by the throat and hefted her up into the air. Ishmael watched her slow death as Knuckled throttled her, and he could feel the tears washing down his cheeks. He and Christine had rarely seen eye to eye, and yet she didn't deserve this death.

The scene changed now to the rolling green grounds of the asylum where his mother was kept and then narrowed into a barred window to a plain cell, where Ishmael saw his mother crouched on the floor looking gaunt in a soiled, white shift. He could hear others crying to be let out, and he realized they had all been left there to rot. His mother stared off somewhere above her and was talking nonsense and clapping her hands together. As he watched she tried to rise but was too weak and slumped back onto the stone floor repeating his father's name over and over until mercilessly she fell still and her eyes closed.

Ishmael found himself back beside the Jester, who looked at him from the features of Manu. 'I'm sorry I had to show you this. There was no other way if you are to be clear and free from the wondering of what happened to them.'

Ishmael did the only thing he could, nod as he cried.

'How do you put up with all the knowledge of the deaths you see?' he blurted out.

When I was younger it caused me great pain. Now I only cling to the peace I finally bring to them, to free them from all the suffering they endured in their mortal forms. Though it's not all bad. I also see the good things they had happen, sort of like a life review, if I must name it.

'Where do the dead go now that the Infernal and Celestial realms are closed?'

'We are all energy, Ishmael, and that is what we return to. Each life and death makes up the history of our world, and the dead stay alive within us as memories. That is the simplest way I can explain it.'

Ishmael nodded. He felt drained now, and as if reading his thoughts the Jester once again put on his mask.

'Return to your friends, Ishmael. Now more than ever you need to be with them.' The Death Jester turned back to the crystal column, and Ishmael rose and made his way downstairs.

When Ishmael found Zahra and Aeon, he couldn't meet their eyes, especially Aeon's. They reminded him of his mortality now more than ever, the passing of time that he was so consciously aware of in this moment.

'Ishmael, are you okay?' asked Zahra, rising to face him.

He grabbed her and hugged her tightly, and after a moment she returned the hug.

'I'm just tired. I have seen upsetting things that will take some time for me to digest, and right now I have few words and no desire to talk about them. Will you sit beside me, Zahra?'

'Of course I will. Come and sit here. There is water and food should you want them,' she said, looking concerned.

Ishmael wanted nothing more than the restful peace of deep sleep before he mulled over what the two gods had shared with him, and yet as he began to drift off with the changing face of the Jester in his mind he knew that would be denied him. He could feel the pull of the summoning already. It seemed his meetings with power this day had not ended after all.

Chapter 18

Dalwyn Trevlon shivered and coughed through the whole morning. He had expended too much energy fighting the coterie as he attempted to catch Nina, and now his immune system was at its lowest ebb. He coughed again, a, long, hacking wheeze that caused his ribs to ache, then fell back against the pallet as Flint guarded him. He moved on to his side so he could see across into the cell next to him where Latasha and the coterie were locked and saw Latasha busy attending to the coterie. As she worked she sang in a low, melodic voice that Dalwyn found annoying rather than soothing.

Flint followed Dalwyn's glance at Latasha.

'I can get her to attend to you instead of them, my lord, she knows how to treat these things, I heard her say so.'

Dalwyn could only nod.

Flint went to the bars, which got Latasha's attention.

'Lord Dalwyn needs your attention. I will unlock the cell and you will come to assist him. Do I make myself clear?'

Latasha stared at the hard-faced man as Dalwyn watched on through a particularly rough bout of shivering.

'Your precious lord Dalwyn caused all the injuries to himself as well as the coterie, so he can suffer and hopefully die for all I care,' she said, spitting at the floor before Dalwyn and turning back to her work.

'If you refuse to do this I will make sure you suffer,' retorted Flint, causing Latasha to turn around again.

'Or what, you will kill me? I am truly starting to think that would be the best option,' she replied, turning away.

Dalwyn dozed again but only flirted with sleep as he thought about the events the night before. The bonding with the astral entity had gone well, and it was still out there somewhere to continue his bidding. The coterie rescued Nina but failed to destroy the entity after Dalwyn attacked them. The battle had been short but vicious, with the all three of the coterie as well as Dalwyn being returned to their material bodies with injuries. Now it would take at least a day to ride the effects of that energy spent in the astral and the healing of the astral body, time he didn't have.

He called out weakly, and Flint hurried over like the good obedient hound he was.

'Get me char to keep alert and also some wraith flower to allow me to enter the astral plane. I have unfinished business to attend to.'

'My lord, you are too weak to do this.'

'I am not asking for your opinion, Flint, just do it!'

When Flint woke him again he had the char and wraith flower like Dalwyn had requested. His body shook with the effort of sitting up as he chewed the char then used the pipe of one of the flame warriors to smoke a small bowl of the wraith flower. The dangers of wraith flower were well documented since it had become a crop that nations like Brimmerland started to cultivate, and Dalwyn knew it was a risk that could go wrong. However, as he saw it, he had little choice. He needed to find the rats in the cellar, he thought and laughed at his own analogy as a concerned Flint looked on.

It started with a tingling that crept over him that became the steps of thousands of ants that made him want to cry out, then when Dalwyn thought he couldn't stand it anymore the sensation disappeared and he broke into a full body sweat. He wiped his face with the back of a hand that had turned semitransparent then faded away as the sound of a wind around him grew and Dalwyn stepped away from his body. He turned to regard the coterie, which showed their auras speckled red where they were injured, and met the glare of Latasha for the second time in the astral world in two nights. The witch was talking rapidly in the language of ancients, a dialect that Dalwyn had always thought of as crude, even savage like.

Before her she raised a hand, tracing a pulsing star between herself and Dalwyn that hurt him to look at. Dalwyn smiled then turned away. The coterie were out of action for now, and Latasha was unable to access the astral for travelling; even the energy she expended using a ward would tire her deeply.

He was focused on one other thing, finding Nina and Haakon since Nina wouldn't be going anywhere soon after the attack she endured from Screareed who had fled the coterie before taking too much damage. Dalwyn only hoped the astral entity had enough power to answer his summons. He walked to the exact spot where he had fought last night then bit into the cord, allowing the silver life to fill his palm where the lump was.

'Screareed I command you to show before me, as the astral lords are my witness I bind you in the amber rings of rites as old as time.'

Screareed seemed to seep out of a wall up ahead, dragging itself along the stones with burn wounds visible on its skin and scales while two of its thick legs dragged uselessly behind it. Dalwyn traced a circle around himself with the viscous astral fluid. He choked down his revulsion since dealing with the entity was necessary and held out his palm to Screareed watching as it drank from his palm. It suckled on the lump there which he could no longer consider a lump when he knew it was a nipple. Even when the suckling made him want to tear his hand away, he kept it there knowing that Screareed would need to be stronger to do his bidding.

As Dalwyn watched, the burn wounds scabbed over then healed, the legs that were useless only moments ago twitched then took on full motion, and his entity Screareed now strong again, fought him when he tried to pull away, mewling as he was disconnected from Dalwyn's life force.

The entity sat there drunk on energy with its tongue lolling to the side, yet it was its eyes glittering with hate and intelligence that caught Dalwyn's attention, and he knew it would attempt to turn any situation to its advantage in attempting to get Dalwyn to make a fatal error.

'Screareed it is time to complete the task I gave to you.'

'You promised me a body, sorcerer!'

'Yes and you shall have it now that you have tasted the astral force of the girl, Nina, who you attacked last night. You have her scent.'

'As I have yours, sorcerer?'

'I can just as easy break the bond between us. There are many of your kind willing to serve me, Screareed. If you attack me now then our agreement is ended and I will destroy you.'

The entity started toward him then stopped just shy of the circle, its muscles quivering, face contorted with hate. It stomped its legs, hissed and spat, then stopped and sat meekly regarding him.

'That is better. Now find the girl and kill her!'

Chapter 19

Ishmael found himself in the tree chamber, a place where he and his coterie had not been together since the death of Brianna Dusk. The tree was the biggest change. Gone now were the weeping sores and pale bark with cracked, dry soil around its base. Now it radiated the presence of the Mother, and Ishmael now knew the tree in this chamber actually was her true form. The bark was now healthy, and from its trunk new branches had started sprouting while the dead ones had fallen to gather at her base. The stone chairs remained, and as he began to fully materialize in his own he could see the others doing likewise.

Small plump Jona with her immaculate hair in a bun sat regal as a queen; and beside her sat Selene, tall and lithe still with challenge in her striking eyes; and finally Raul slumped in his own chair, his handsome, wolfish features looking grim.

It didn't need saying, and Ishmael knew without a doubt once he was fully in the chamber that the power of the coterie had grown considerably. None of the surroundings faltered and began to break up, and the four of the coterie that were left regarded each other silently.

'It gladdens my heart that the three of you are still safe,' Ishmael said, breaking the peace.

'We don't need to talk like this you know, Ishmael. We can easily communicate telepathically now,' replied Raul flippantly.

'Don't mind him, Ishmael,' Selene said, laughing afterwards. 'I for one propose we all speak normally while in this sacred chamber. The normalcy of it offers some comfort.'

'I hardly think Raul should have any input on what happens with us after his betrayal,' snapped Jona, turning a dark look on Raul beside her.

'What is important is that we have been summoned here by the Mother and that we are all safe for the time being and free to move forward with the necessary plans for the return of the magic,' replied Ishmael, trying to diffuse any forming conflict.

Raul stood and walked over to Ishmael. He then knelt and bowed his head before looking up again.

'For my part in all this mess I am truly sorry, and I don't expect forgiveness from Jona or any of you for my stupidity. I was tricked and thought I had been sent a new sentinel in Katerina. Of course I was wrong and if it wasn't for your stubbornness, Ishmael, in continuing onto the Seekers Road then we all would have been captured. What I can offer going forwards is complete loyalty. I have seen the error of my ways and know we together can end this the right way, but divided then all will perish from the Mother's anger.' Then Raul sat down leaving the other three looking around in amazement.

They all turned towards the tree at the sound of slow clapping to see a figure leaning against the tree. She was wild looking with long, unkempt hair and the pale skin from which small tendrils of new born plants and flowers grew the green of meadows in spring, and her warm smile filled them with love.

'Finally I see some dialogue between you and none of the self-pity or bitching that has kept you all so apart. Events are moving forward and between you four of five crystals have all been found, even if they are not directly in your possession. You will be brought together by circumstances, and yet one of you must choose to make sure that at the pivotal time when you need to merge your power that you are all together in the one place. The Harlequin build what will not only be my new home but the center of the known world from where the magic will radiate out over the lands. It is the temple of the Elemental Heart.'

How will we find this place?' asked Jona.

'You will be taken to a place nearby, either by your own actions or the actions of others, because this is where this age ends and the new world will begin. Power unseen will amass there and witness what I have wrought.'

Ishmael was confused. 'You mentioned we have found the crystals and yet you spoke of another, a fifth crystal?'

'Very observant, Ishmael, and yes, you are correct. The fifth is the crystal of spirit that binds the other four together. One of my original children has that one and will give it to the one who will become the fifth member of this coterie in place of the fallen Brianna Dusk.'

The Mother then looked up and away, her face going distant for a moment. 'Now I must leave you to attend to another matter of importance. Attend to each other and mend the rift that has previously kept you weak and soon we can be together,' she said and then simply melted back into the tree as Ishmael called after her.

'What about the gods? Why do they have to die?' he shouted, but she was already gone.

Selene turned to Ishmael. 'What is this about the gods, Ishmael?'

'Most of them still live, but not as they were. Now they are as mortal as we are but still have the divine spark within them, and that spark will be the energy that helps to form the new world that the Mother is ushering into place.'

'So while we are locked away in cells and starved of food and the outside world, you have been in the austere company of gods,' said Raul, looking amazed.

'Well, yes, but it is not as great as it sounds, Raul. I have the task of helping them escape the children of Tamul, who are known as the Life Quenchers, who strive to consume them before the Mother can access the spark within them. If they can be victorious in this then the new world will never happen and that will be the start of the end of everything, including our world.'

'Does anybody know who the original children are?' asked Jona from where she had been sitting quietly.

'I thought they were the gods,' said Selene.

'It is said that the original children were created along with the lands of our world as the sacred protectors, and this would mean they are the Ancients,' replied Raul as everyone once again looked to him.

'What? I never pretended to be stupid, and I was trained in the scholarly arts even if I wished to have nothing to do with them,' he said, looking to each of them.

'Raul, you are full of surprises at the moment,' Ishmael commented with a hint of disbelief still in his voice. 'We could have done with your help earlier you knowl,' Ishmael added.

'Truth be told, Ishmael, I never wanted this damn magic at all and have always rebelled against it whenever possible. I never knew my father, who had it before me, and you all can guess the upheaval that the power brought to my life when I inherited the magic. I was born out of wedlock by a prostitute, mother who sold me to a noble woman so she could get back to work for the scum that controlled her. Fortunately the family that I became a part of were very kind to me and I was treated better than I could ever have expected, even though then I had no idea I was not their legitimate child from birth until when I was fifteen. At that time my sentinel made herself known to me, following an incident that scared my new family so much they locked me in a room alone to rot. It was my sentinel that bought my freedom from them, and I will never forget the hurt and loss in my adopted mother's face when I left. She was the only one who truly loved me, but her husband and three sons wanted nothing more than to see me gone or worse.'

'That's terrible, Raul,' Jona said, 'but what I don't understand is how you didn't know that this Katerina was actually an enemy when she took the old sentinel's place.'

'I feel myself becoming tired so it's better if I just show you,' said Raul. 'Here, come near and link hands and see what happened for yourselves.'

They linked hands and saw from Raul's perspective.

Raul swirled and dipped, sweat flying from his long hair as his eyes locked with those of the dancer on the dais above him. He smiled knowingly as his insistent stares and wolf whistles bought out a deep blush to her face, deeper than the flush of exertion caused by her spinning dance. He knew he would have her tonight, and that thought was intoxicating. She had been more of a challenge than most, and he had been forced to frequent the Reluctant Desires tavern for many nights before even managing to win a smile from the exotic Katerina.

A voice shrill with anxiety and fear cut through his thoughts.

'Run before it's too late, they will be coming for you too!'

Raul knew the voice. It belonged to Ishmael, one of the other coterie members who he had been speaking to earlier that night in the dream chamber while he meditated.

The deafening bangs of mugs on tables snapped Raul out of his reverie, and he looked up to find Katerina's eyes on him, her golden skin glistening with perspiration, breasts rising and falling with each gulping breath. The jilting music had stopped, and the musicians and dancers waved away cries for more as they headed to the bar to slake their thirst.

Katerina accepted Raul's hand down from the dais and deftly slapped away his other hand that sought to grope her bottom. She leant close, whispering. 'Meet me in my room and take the back stairs so no one sees you.' Then with a hand on his chest she pushed him away, turned, and disappeared into the crowd.

Raul turned and strutted back to his friends who laughed at him and did ridiculous imitations of his dancing. Ignoring them, he smugly announced he was off to deflower Katerina, swilled down the remains of a decanter of mulled wine, and headed for the back stairs. Raul had no trouble locating Katerina's room; he had followed her here often enough since she started dancing in the tavern a month ago.

'Run, we are weak. They will come for you too.'

What the heck? He held his hands against his temples, feeling a headache coming on. Maybe Caitlin would know what was happening. Come to think of it, where was she? Caitlin was responsible for ensuring he stayed out of trouble and the secret he carried within him stayed safe. Raul cast his mind back over the last few days: he hadn't see Caitlin for three days now, which was highly unusual for the woman who delighted in foiling his plans to lure many women to his bed.

Raul shook his head as if that would get rid of Brianna's voice and the wine fog that addled his thinking. This was not a good time for such distractions. He made sure there was no one around before slipping into Katerina's room, which was a jumble of clothes and travel cases. The room smelled of lilies, and along a window frame sat a collection of perfume bottles. Curiously, below them was a pile of unopened gifts. Katerina was a good dancer, but it was hardly an occupation that promised wealth. Why had she not opened the gifts?

He dragged the cases off the bed and unlaced his shirt, which he threw atop the chest at the foot of the bed. Finally Raul lay back, arms folded behind his head with one knee raised slightly turned out to display his crotch and waited.

He didn't have to wait for long. A ripple of desire thrilled through his body when the door opened. The woman that entered was the same Katerina that he lusted after, but now there were changes. Gone was the teasing smile, pouting lips, and batting lashes. They had been replaced with a steely gaze, furrowed brow, and hands on hips.

'Stay there and listen, we don't have much time.'

He started to make a smart comment but she talked over him.

'I am not who you think I am. There's a choice to make so make it fast. You can come willingly with me or I can take you by force.'

Raul nimbly rolled off the bed and onto his feet. 'I like it rough,' he said and grabbed at Katerina's waist, but she wasn't there anymore, and he felt himself shoved head first into the wall. Tasting blood,

Raul smiled; this was going to be fun. He quickly turned only to find a knife at his throat. Katerina's face was close to his, and there was a pleading look on her face.

'What danger is so great that we must flee without time for a little bed games?' Raul asked as he traced a finger down Katerina's cleavage.

'There are those close by that would hurt you, Raul, for the secrets you carry.' She put a finger to his lips to stop the questions.

'I know about the magic within you and have been trained to keep you safe.'

'But Caitlin, where is she?'

'Ahhh, yes, Caitlin. Raul, you won't see her again. She was told to report back to our master, and I am here to replace her.'

'Why wouldn't she tell me this herself then?'

'To avoid any distraction on your part, we thought it better she just go.'

'I see. You just thought but neglected to care about my thoughts or how my sentinel leaving affects me?'

'This magic you carry within you must be protected long enough for you to meet the other members of the coterie.'

Even with the blade against his throat Raul pushed Katerina away from him. He had suddenly sobered up and his stomach felt knotted with a cocktail of confusion and suspicion.

'How do you know about them?'

'Raul, I know it all, otherwise how am I to protect you? The fact that I do know must be enough for you to trust me in this,' she replied.

'So you will take me to the safe house then?'

'Safe house… yes, the safe house. We will head there as soon as the other sentinels share with me the location.'

Before she could finish talking there was a loud hammering at the door. Raul looked into the pleading eyes of Katerina. The drink he had so recklessly downed now seemed to hit him all at once, leaving his senses addled. He had so many questions.

'Raul, we must go now! Quickly climb out the window and I will follow. I promise you all your questions will be answered, just not here.'

The door bulged as a great weight crashed into it over and over again. Whoever was on the other side was someone he did not want to meet.

Raul climbed out the window and onto the slate tiling. The boots he wore were not made for this sneaking about and he slipped, striking the tiles and landing on his side only to roll off the roof to crash in a heap in the stable yard. His breath whooshed out of him, and straining to regain his composure he managed to pull himself to his knees. Looking up he saw Katerina framed in the window. As he watched she slid down the tiled roof, jumped to the street, and came to her feet in a neat forward roll.

'Let's go,' she whispered in his ear as she hauled him up. 'We can steal some horses and get out of here.'

'Go where?'

'Just away from here for now so you're safe, then we can lie low and decide our next move.'

Even with the adrenalin coursing through his body, he felt his loins stir at the thought of lying low with her, and he followed her into the darkness. She sure was prettier than Caitlin.

'I know now of course that Katerina was always working for the enemy. I just didn't have any time then to attempt to find out the truth of things. Katerina made sure we were constantly moving, and ever so slowly won my trust, and I hate to say it from between the sheets by appealing to my unchecked desires,' Raul added as they broke the link between the four of them.

They were silent now as Ishmael, Jona, and Selene pondered on this insight into the mysterious Raul.

When Ishmael looked up at the other three he could see their forms beginning to dissolve. 'What's happening?' Ishmael blurted out.

'Something is breaking our link with you and this chamber,' he heard Selene say just before the three of them disappeared, leaving him alone.

Ishmael was about to let himself be drawn back to his body when his gaze fixed on the chair of Brianna Dusk, and without knowing why he approached it and lay his hands on the cool stone and found himself in a stone floor chamber with what appeared like prison cells down to his right side disappearing down a torch lit corridor. In front of him was a messy chamber strewn with papers, and a sleeping pallet from where an elderly figure with white hair was just pushing themselves to a sitting position. As he watched, the figure who looked to be male, knelt then used the wall to help him stand. Ishmael could see the man's hands shaking as if from the shaking sickness that often came upon the elderly. Ishmael heard boots on stone and turned to see two warriors enter the chamber wearing white tabards emblazoned with the red flames that he knew so well. Flame warriors! And then he knew who the old man was and turned back to confirm it. Dalwyn Trevlon stood before him, and as he watched, the two warriors knelt before Dalwyn.

'Enough of that,' Dalwyn grunted with a pained expression on his face, 'rise and tell me what you have found from my instructions.'

'Lord Dalwyn, we have found the door and even now your men are assembling, ready for the attack.'

'Good, that is good. Now help me put my boots on, will you. My back still pains me.'

At that moment Ishmael could feel himself dissipating, and he tried everything to stay and watch, but it failed and he found himself returning to his sleeping body.

Chapter 20

The twin brothers Dre and Lim sat cross-legged around the small fire opposite to Haakon, who sat beside Nina's prone form. As Haakon packed a pipe with tobacco, the twins listened to the tale of Latasha's capture and the loss of the stronghold.

'I looked for the both of you when we were all celebrating, and even Latasha commented that she had not seen either of you,' he said as he lit the pipe and the sweet smell of elder leaf settled around them.

Both Dre and Lim looked at each other before Dre, whom Haakon could only identify from the regular twitching at the corner of his left eye, spoke. 'It has been hard enough for me and my brother to be around your kind once more, Haakon. When you brought us here to your kin and clansmen we freaked out, and while you greeted each other we melted away to hide among the fields, intending to join back up with you both at a quieter time. Now we must suffer our selfishness knowing Latasha may well die because of it, like many of your friends and kin have done, and for this we are both eternally sorry. By the time the attack came it was too late for us to warn you, and since then we have waited to see how you fared. In truth, Haakon, we had decided to leave and would have if it hadn't been for your appearance each night looking for us. Your world is alien to us. We are scared but have no wish to lose Latasha so soon after finding the salvation of our race. We are yours to command,' he said, and the two brothers bowed low with their heads to the stone before Haakon.

Haakon almost felt embarrassed at their complete trust in him, especially since it was his fault that Latasha as well as the coterie had fallen into Dalwyn's hands. Without Latasha the Ancients race would die off. She was the last surviving female, and if she died before magic returned to this world then the Ancients were doomed.

The three of them sat smoking tobacco and drinking tea past the first chime of the new day, when Lim, who had been looking at Nina through half-closed eyes caught Haakon's attention with his sudden change in demeanour. 'How did this girl become injured?'

'She was beset on by an astral entity last night while learning the extent of her astral cord. Dalwyn Trevlon, the one who captured this place, knew she would attempt to enter the astral, and he bound an entity to himself to attack her.'

'Due shae lamoire,' exclaimed the two brothers in union and leapt to their feet.

'What is wrong?' asked Haakon as he also rose to his feet in alarm.

'Her astral body is shining. Even though she is still in the physical body, her astral form has disengaged from all its vortices except the eighth one, which hovers in the energy field above the body, as you probably know. Nina's astral body has been attacked at two of the most vital vortices: the heart and the third eye, which has damaged those two in such a way that it leaves the physical body open to further attack of nefarious nature.'

'Like what?' asked Haakon as he began to pace.

'Due shae lamoire which means possession,' replied the twins simultaneously.

'At the time of death, the eighth vortex's energy expands and encases the other vortices in a vessel of light, and then when the being dies the vortices leave the body with its astral form and fade into pure energy or return to source that is within all matter.'

'You mean Nina is dying while we have been sitting here?'

'No, Haakon. Her eighth vortex is damaged but only partially, and I suspect it has been done on purpose because when it is in such a state the victims find themselves only partially in their bodies. They are dissociated and disconnected or caught between worlds, which leaves them open for entities to take over.'

'What can we do to protect her then?' Haakon asked as he felt the tension through his jaw and neck. 'I was damaged during a similar attack when I found Latasha at her home, and since then I cannot even enter the astral otherwise I would have been able to see this happening to the poor child. I should have been able to help her.' Haakon banged his fists against the wall in frustration.

'Haakon, all that matters is that we are now aware of the danger and now we can defend against it, now calm down, it serves nobody for you to be lost in anger, okay?'

Haakon could feel the blood pumping through him, his hands clenched by his sides, jaw tensed painfully, and yet he managed to breathe deeply through his nostrils, turn away from Nina. He paced to the other end of the chamber, where he sank to his knees before the clan symbol and clan ledger book finding release in the familiar position favoured from cycles of meditation. He was losing himself to the stress of the situation with Latasha, the clan and now Nina. He was falling into the traps of emotion he had constantly rebuked his students for when training them for a future in his clan. He needed to relocate his composure again or else risk making mistakes that would end up in more deaths of those he cared for.

Nina knew something was really wrong with her once she had fallen asleep. It was more than the bruising that had coloured her skin, making her wince when she moved. This wrongness was with her energy body and had only been visible to her now she was asleep and her astral body had risen up above her real one. She was stuck now, and something that should have come loose had stayed connected to her body that now lay beneath her. It had to be one of her vortices that had failed to disconnect her and free the energy or astral body.

As the panic began to suffocate her and she saw her real body begin to heave in the air from its sudden urgent need to awaken, Nina became scared. Looking around she saw the chamber was empty; there was no auric colouring of Haakon's body in the chamber, which meant she was alone. Her mind turned to Zacriel, both her tormentor and her guardian even her friend she realized as she remembered what he had done for her on that long flight from Illume to Acclaro, the capital of the Thantos empire.

Nina felt like she was flying now while in that trapped state hovering or floating above herself in this chamber which made her remember the flight she had shared with Zacriel after leaving Illume. Zacriel had shown her a side that he would never have wanted others to see. After the events in Acclaro with the death of the king and Ishmael's escape, Zacriel had been much, much nicer towards her than he had before. It had made her feel better to know he had been scared just like her and she wasn't alone, except now she was.

When Haakon returned to the chamber, his aura a mirage of colours, he wasn't alone. The two who accompanied him were curious indeed to Nina, especially their auras, which were pure green, interrupted with flashes of white or blue that cut through the green. In this state between bodies, sound was mere dissonant echoes, which made understanding the speech of Haakon or his two strange guests whom she now saw were Ancients difficult to understand. Nina shivered with a feeling of joy knowing that Haakon had found the twins.

Nina felt herself return to her body then, and it was only later when once again she found herself hovering above her prone body that she realized what had happened. This time the two Ancients were staring straight at her. They could see her, and as Nina watched they communicated with Haakon in strange echo voices. Haakon became agitated and began his usual pacing like he did when worried. The urgent conversation reflected by the movements of the three only caused more anxiety in Nina. Haakon didn't deserve to be caused more problems with her, and wherever she went it caused problems. Maybe they would all be better off without her, she thought.

Nina watched as the Ancients retrieved coal from the fire and marked out a large circle that encompassed her body, the fire, and enough room for the three of them to stand within. They had also gotten salt, most likely from the kitchen to form a second circle within the first, and between these two circles marked out words in a strange language with their blood, which was gross.

Then one of the brothers took Haakon's pipe, refilled it, then lit it and blew thick puffs of smoke over her body. It made her feel sick in the stomach area, and she was dragged back into her body again. This happened two more times, and by the third only one brother was awake, and Nina realized many chimes had passed. Haakon lay on his side asleep as did the other Ancient while the one awake bathed her skin with water and every so often blew smoke over her body that seemed relaxed her as it dragged her back to her normal body.

The fourth time Nina floated out of her body it was the other Ancient with the strange tick to his eye that was blowing smoke at her. From the side of the chamber near the exit was Nina noticed something strange that seemed to blend in with the wall there, but as she focused on it more turned out to be something very different, and then the wall came alive.

There was an echoed shout from the Ancient that caused Haakon and the other brother to erupt out of their sleep. Haakon's foot struck some logs in the fire pit, sending up sparks that hurt her eyes, and the creature from the night before with its terrible lips and razor teeth snapped at her body.

The monster hit the coal circle then reared back on its thick legs almost in a squatting position, its tongue lolling down over its saliva-coated chin. It launched forward again, this time through the coal line and bloody writing into the salt that caused it to scream in a voice scarily like a lady.

Now Haakon had the smoke and was covering the circle with its billowing clouds while the two brothers had seated themselves. As Nina watched they literally flew from their bodies in blinding flashes of light just as, for the third time, the monster threw itself at Nina. Again this time it grasped her astral form with claws that burnt her and attempted to drag her towards it.

When the Ancients struck they did so with javelins of light; one struck the monster in the shoulder, making it snarl and snap at the weapon imbedded in its dark red pulsing form, while the other one leapt forward then buried his javelin down through its back. The monster shrugged its body, shaking the Ancient and his javelin free, then took flight from the chamber leaving only a trail of silver, ochre-coloured ichor behind.

Haakon blew more smoke onto Nina's form as the brothers recreated the circles, and by then Nina was falling back into her physical body. Had it been a dream? was her final thought.

As it turned out, it wasn't a dream, and when Nina awoke next she could once again feel the heat of the flames from the fire as well as hear voices normally. She looked at Haakon's face wrought with worry and deep hollows beneath his eyes and the solemn faces of the twins and burst into tears.

Chapter 21

Zahra sat beside Ishmael, who instantly fell asleep, and she wondered what had happened between him and Shail of Illume. She felt someone watching her and turned to see a figure at the bottom of the winding staircase that Ishmael had descended. It had the mask of the Jester on and wore dark robes, and she knew she was looking upon the Death Jester himself. As Zahra watched, the god of death slowly turned and made its way up the stairs, and she knew the god was giving her an opportunity to approach him or was it her? but Zahra was unsure she really wanted to do that. She sat thinking a moment then rose and hurried towards the stairs. She had questions and this time they would be answered. Zahra took the stairs two at a time and found her god waiting for her at the top, hands by its side.

The Death Jester reached up as if to remove its mask, but Zahra stopped it with a hand on the arm.

'Please don't. Just leave it on,' she pleaded and the god dropped its hand back down. Then all the regret and guilt came bubbling up and overwhelmed Zahra as tears began to flow down her cheeks.

'Why did you make me yours? You came and took my family away, and I felt that cold touch of yours when you approached me. I could see you, you know, and when you stooped down and touched me it changed my life forever, and then you left me alone with only the dead around me. You could have taken my soul, and that is what I longed for and have since,' Zahra finished and wiped her face with her arm.

'That day I took many souls from your village, and when I got to you, Zahra, it just didn't feel right. It is something I have often pondered but never been able to figure out. All I can say is that it wasn't your time.'

The god put a hand on her shoulder, which turned cold to its touch and the Death Jester tried to usher Zahra over to a seat.

She pulled away from it.

'No! I want to stay here and talk,' she said, wrapping her arms about her shoulders protectively.

'It's all a matter of how you view that day, Zahra. Haakon came and found you, and the experience with me gave you a purpose in this life. It gave you something to go on with.'

'And what about all those I have killed, then?' she interrupted.

'Your victims have never been the innocent or the average person minding their own business. They have been those that have intended harm, and it was this conscience that you have that has led you to this very moment and why Haakon chose you to help him in this very important quest to shape the world into something better. Can't you see that now?'

'That was not my choice. If I refused to go with Haakon I would have died,' Zahra retorted.

'Zahra, your choices are your own, and you have free will. I can tell you now that you would have lived and led a very different life from the one you now have.'

'But Haakon said he recognized me because I had been touched by death.'

'That is true, and yes, Haakon had a similar experience with death when I left him to live, because it simply wasn't his time either. He chose to make that encounter about being touched by death to mean it was his duty to serve me. For an unknown reason people like Haakon and you who have that experience with me seem to be able to recognize each other. Haakon just chose to make that mean I was pointing those ones out to him.'

'So will you be coming with us and the other gods when we leave here?'

'No, Zahra. Unlike the other gods beside Aeon, I have work to do, and until there are no more souls to collect I cannot leave this world,' the god replied.

'How do you put up with what you do? I mean to be the one who witnesses every death, it must take its toll on you.'

'Once long ago it did, until I changed the way I view death. Now it's simply an honour to be there when a soul passes and I send it on its way.'

'Send it on its way? To where?' Zahra asked.

'I cannot tell you that, Zahra, because you simply will not understand.'

Zahra stood there a moment then remembered a curiosity that had always plagued her about the god of death.

'How can you be in many places at once? The deaths of people are always happening and more than one and in different locations, so how do you be there for all of them?'

The Jester laughed beneath his mask before answering.

'I split into as many versions of myself as needed and then merge back to one of myself afterwards,' the god replied simply.

Now go, Zahra. Soon you will be leaving and will need to make preparations, but most of all you need rest. This meeting between us will drain you, and there is nothing that can be changed with that. I have that effect when mortals are around me.'

'So no cryptic comments about my impending death?' Zahra blurted out.

'I have no time for that crap! It is simply that you will die when it is your time and nothing more. I cannot tell the future, Zahra, or the cause of how you die. I will just be there with you when the time comes.' Then the Death Jester turned away from her and walked slowly away.

Zahra went back down the stairs feeling totally exhausted, and when she curled up beside Ishmael sleep found her right away without the shades of her victims disturbing her.

When Ishmael awoke he noticed Zahra beside him. He wondered when she had curled up there. Then so as not to disturb her, he slowly wriggled away from her warm body and rose. The indoor garden around him appeared empty, but voices carried to him fand so he headed that way.

Soon Ishmael came to what seemed a meeting place, and he saw many gods gathered in groups talking animatedly. He sat down to watch what was happening.

Aeon climbed up onto a table and called for quiet as the gods turned their attention to him.

'I have just been informed that the Life Quenchers are at the gates to this sanctuary of ours.' His words caused a ripple of unease through the gods amassed around him.

'The time is upon us all to leave here and go on our journey back to the Mother, and I know that among you there are those who fear this and deny the dreams the Mother has sent us all. It is my role to appeal to you who still feel this way. We are not marching to our deaths, we are simply returning home. Just like everything around us, this world is made of energy; so are we, and it all comes from the Mother.'

The assembly erupted into chaos as angry shouts called out for Aeon to step down and stop talking rubbish, but he stayed on his makeshift pedestal and continued.

'If we stay here, then that is our final death. Our divine spark will be taken from us and used to make Tamul all powerful so he can rival the Mother, and this world will be lost to him instead of being used to shape a new better one. My brothers and sisters our time is over, and we are left with this one last task to return to our creator.' then Aeon fell silent.

A figure climbed up onto another table, and at her stern gaze the gods fell silent. She radiated authority, and her skin was bronzed and unblemished where it showed beneath ochre robes. She brushed her auburn hair out of her eyes and smiled at Aeon, and then Ishmael realized she was Nerith, goddess of abundance and joy

'Aeon speaks wisdom, as he always has done in trying to guide us. Many times have I supported his causes because the issues affected all of us. But today I will not support you, Aeon,' she said, once again looking at Aeon.

'You speak of our return as something we should long for, something to be cherished, and yet in this we are not equal. Let me explain. We are expected to meekly crawl back to the Mother and become a part of her energy while you will live on as god of time. Though none of us can change this role we have all been given as deities, you have no right to stand here offering advice when you cannot fathom the despair our pending return causes in us who are to become nothing. We have learned to love life, and even now when we are mortal I for one will fight to preserve what I have.' When she finished the gods erupted into cheering and resounding applause.

'Then all you have ever done will be for nothing,' replied Aeon. You had the opportunity to stay in the Celestial or Infernal lands, and you all had a hand in the destruction that followed your petty actions that almost destroyed all us gods and this world anyway. Now your creator beckons, and you think you have a choice.' His voice rose higher than the shouts of the crowd.

A large god standing close to Aeon moved forwards awkwardly beneath great rolls of skin that flowed down from a thick neck and shining hairless pate. The movement sent his many necklaces of precious stones clinking against one another as he approached, then reached out and kicked the table out from beneath Aeon's feet, sending him sprawling to the ground, then placed a foot on his chest to prevent him rising.

'You speak against us, old friend instead of for us. You should be fighting for us and swaying the Mother against taking what little we have left.'

Ishmael had seen enough, and his concern for Aeon sent him running over to the crowd around his friend. 'Get away from him,' he shouted as he pushed through the gods, who turned to him in surprise.

The obese figure shoved him with a palm to the chest, and Ishmael fell onto his back, winded. 'You, nothing more than a man, how dare to interfere in the affairs of the gods.' the obese god roared, and spittle flew from his mouth to run down his substantial jowls. 'Seize this fool! What will the Mother do without her precious crystal bearer?'

Hands reached for Ishmael, and he felt the magic stir within him. With a cry Ishmael let it rise and opened his energy vortices, allowing it to burst forth. 'Get away from me,' he shouted, and a wave of power burst into the crowd of gods around him. They flew backwards into each other and fell to the ground. There was silence then, and Ishmael stood and helped Aeon to his feet as the fallen gods stared at him; some in wonder, but most with fear reflected on their features.

Power radiated through Ishmael, and he shook from the force of it all, skin glowing and hair blown back by the force of the expended energy that crackled around the area.

'You speak of death, your deaths, but how do you truly know what will happen when you return to the Mother? She birthed you, gave you everything, and in return you threaten her and her chosen? I doubt that what she has in store for you will be terrible, but do you think you fare any better at the hands of those who hunt you, the Life Quenchers, who now are trying to tear this place down so they can feed on you?'

Ishmael looked from face to face, and when he got to Shail he could see the admiration in her eyes, and it brought a calmness back to him.

'Please, come with me back to the Mother, and then you can give voice to your concerns. If there was one thing I have learnt as one the Chosen it is that our actions can cause change, but you need to trust me, the Mother, and Aeon. We need to work together or all is lost.'

From somewhere in the city a thunderous boom rang out, and outside the temple hundreds of guards ran towards it with weapons drawn.

'We go now,' shouted Ishmael, and he saw Zahra running towards him with Moonbite drawn, the blade glowing brightly.

Chapter 22

Dalwyn used the wraith flower slowly, only refilling the bowl when he seeped back into normal reality. He had been warned of the dangers of using the flower and being stuck in the astral realm while waiting for the effects to wear off. Dalwyn micro-dosed himself twice more before finally Screareed appeared to him again. The entity was close to death, pus-coloured energy leaking from deep wounds. But like a loyal hound it staggered to Dalwyn to collapse at his feet.

'Master, sustenance.'

'You failed me twice, Screareed,' said Dalwyn as he knelt before the entity. 'Now leave until I call you again.'

'I am too weak, master, I will die,' hissed Screareed.

'I know you better than that, entity. You will heal, if only very slowly, which will give you time to think about failing me again.'

Dalwyn was already walking away from the stricken entity. He had noticed the trail of astral energy that Screareed had left behind it and began to follow it down the corridor. Half way down he could feel the effects of the drug wearing off and he quickened his step until he found himself at a wall in an alcove, which was when Dalwyn felt himself recoil as he was dragged back to his physical body.

Dalwyn knew he would be incapacitated for at least a day from the use of the wraith flower while in such a damaged state, except now he had the feeling that he had found the information he needed

to stop the Kenzu pest and Nina, and that was enough for him. He would finally take control of the situation again.

Late the next morning when the sun had almost reached its zenith, Dre roughly awakened Haakon.

'What the damn is it,' he swore as the ancient insistently pulled him up from his pallet.

'You need to see this, Haakon. Lim is waiting for us.'

Haakon quickly dragged on his boots then tottered after Dre; he made his way onto the top of the stronghold, where they stumbled forward to where Lim could be seen staring above the courtyard at a sight that was enough to freeze the blood in Haakon's veins.

Above them was an immense blue creature with tentacles flowing out from the outer margin of bell-shaped body, and below its body four thicker tentacles that seemed to protect a maw of a mouth with rows of circular teeth. The tentacles that swirled around below its body were each connected to large woven baskets that held groups of armoured figures decorated with a symbol Haakon was now very familiar with, a flame. They were flame warriors. Dalwyn's reinforcements had arrived.

As they watched in awe, a ring of muscle in the rim of the bell-like body contracted then relaxed, which shunted the creature lower towards the ground. Its body burst into bright blue light that faded to green as the baskets landed on the ground of the courtyard while its body still hovered in the air, turning slowly. There was something on top of the creature's body that caught Haakon's eye. It was birdlike with dull red and black feathers, and with arms that ended in a shorter version of tentacles of the creature it lay upon. As he watched the bird creature withdrew the tendrils of its arms then leapt from the creature's body to glide down over them with a scream then down into the courtyard.

'They have seen us, we need to move,' said Lim, grabbing Haakon's arm.

They broke into a run, and Haakon couldn't help but look over his shoulder to see the flying creature's body flare a deep red and its tentacles that were free of the baskets flung out towards them. It missed by quite a distance, but the message was clear. Stay and they would die.

Back inside the three of them hurried back to where Nina still rested. With hands that shook from the cold and maybe even the sight of the creature they had encountered. Haakon made tea to warm them while the brothers conferred in their own language.

'What in the world was that thing,' said Haakon, rubbing his arms and stamping his feet to get the blood flowing again.

'They are known as Limpids and were only found in the Veiled land of Auxil,' answered Lim. 'They were slaves to a birdman race known as Monarchs who are a very aggressive, territorial race, the same ones you and Latasha encountered in the Hollow citadel. They had among them those that we referred to as psonics with small tendrils that emerged out of their fingers. The tendrils that could slip inside a victim's ears, nose, or mouth and invade their mind to learn their thoughts, past and present. These few could actually join the awareness of victims to their own and control creatures such as the Limpids, who not only can be formidable enemies but have the advantage of flight. It is the first time I have encountered one outside Auxil, and its appearance with our enemies only speaks of terrible tidings for us all.'

'How do we kill it?'

'The tentacles are the key to killing it. Remove them and the Limpid will just float without direction or sense. The thicker tentacles near the creature's maw will send the Limpid into a frenzy, which usually results in its death, although it is unknown why,' replied Dre as he took a steaming mug of tea. 'The question we should be asking, Haakon, is why the Monarchs are allying themselves with this Dalwyn and his flame warriors.'

'Damn, this changes everything, just when we had Dalwyn where we wanted him. Now we have scarce chance of rescuing Latasha and the coterie,' said Haakon, throwing his mug against the wall, shattering the clay vessel.

'What do we do now, Haakon? Do you have a plan,' asked Lim as he checked on Nina, who still dozed.

'Not for this I don't. We can't move Nina for another day or so, and we can't leave her here either. With what little time we have we need to plan an attack that will confuse and distract Dalwyn and his allies long enough to get Latasha and the coterie free.'

A face appeared above Dalwyn with long hair that dropped down into braids beneath a shiny, shaven crown. Small bloodshot eyes glared down at him from above a remarkably big nose that Dalwyn would never forget. 'Grendel, it's about time you came, brother.'

'I travel half way across the damn Tiriacs to find you sleeping. I swear on our dead mother's grave, Dalwyn, if the letter you sent me is false regarding restoring our family honour, you will never see or hear from me again. It has cost me a small fortune to get the help of the Monarchs and one of their Limpids, which is a debt I expect you to repay me along with the earning I lose by not being able to fulfil the position of Keeper in Shelton's Crag.'

'Yes, yes, brother, I know you are important and usually too busy to help your only brother, however, you need to hear me out this one last time.'

'Well obviously, because if I didn't intend doing that I wouldn't be here. Now get up and tell me what is so important for me to visit this forsaken shit hole.'

'Flint, come here and help me up.'

'Grendel laughed out loud as Dalwyn was helped to his feet.

'You really are getting old, Dalwyn, maybe you should have stayed in Shelton's Crag with the elders in the hall of words.'

Dalwyn sat in a chair then regarded his brother with a grimace. 'Don't even mention those old decrepit bastards, Grendel! I called you all this way not actually expecting you to come, and yet you have surprised me once again. Now before you begin complaining again, the reason is because I know how the magic comes back and we will restore our birthright.'

'So Escindre has finally answered your call then?'

'Well, yes, actually Escindre has. Now not only has it come to light how the magic was hidden from us, but also I know how it will come back. I have in my possession the witch who helped cause the Severing with her infernal powers, as well as the coterie who hold the key to returning it. Brother, soon the Trevlon family will once again rule in Karfael and the tribes will be a thing of the past.'

'I can't pretend to know about that, but what I can tell you is that Infernals have taken over the capital, which is soon to be under siege from the armies of Scuttle, Cavere and troops from Illume have also been seen marching on Acclaro. Even better, brother, is the fact that we may have an alliance with the Monarchs who have all but agreed to give us two troops of their warriors and a score of the Limpids to transport our men for the retaking of Karfael,' said Grendel, slapping Dalwyn on the back hard enough to make him wince.

'Now, by everything I see around me, it seems as if you have been having a torrid time here and need our assistance for more than simple transport, am I right, big brother?'

Dalwyn decided to ignore the sarcastic tone. As much as he hated to say the words, what choice did he have when he was still surprised the little bastard had actually answered his call?'

'I have a few pests who need flushing out is all. The assassin clan who inhabited this place fought us to the death, and most of my men were slain. Now I believe the leader and a child are responsible for putting most of my remaining men out of action, and so your arrival has been auspicious indeed.'

'How so, brother?'

Now that we have what we need to move forward we can reclaim our family heritage together, is that not so?'

There was a pause as Grendel eyed Dalwyn before answering. 'I think it's time I was honest with you. Since we were children you have been obsessed with this returning of magic, our birthright, and so on and on. Well I'm more practical than you, Dalwyn, and not open to flits of fantasy.'

'So what, are you calling me a liar now?'

'No never that, because I truly believe that you think it all to be true, where as I believe with the help of the Monarchs we can retake Karfael, and that is all that I am truly interested in.'

There was an uncomfortable silence as the two ignored each other. Dalwyn reached for the wine bottle and was surprised when Grendel swept it off the table, splashing red across the flagstones. Then they were both on their feet, almost nose to nose, and Dalwyn's hand rested at his belt where his pearl-handled knife was tucked. The sounds of swords being unsheathed around them caused Dalwyn to look around. It was only himself and Flint, the rest were Grendel's men.

'Sit, brother, we must fix this latest mess you have caused without you being addled by wine.'

Dalwyn motioned for Flint to sheath his sword as he sat and forced himself to remember this was his brother and family was important. In the near future he would still need all help he could get.

'Now as I see it we need each other: you want the magic and I want Karfael, which is something we can do together. I have the flames backing me, and you have the connections among the Infernals whom you deal with. I will take you to the capital and even help you fix your pest problem in return for your aid in recovering Karfael. Do we have a deal?' Grendel extended his hand out to Dalwyn.

'On one condition, that I get the temple in Karfael. I will still be answerable to you, but I want it for my own selfish purposes.'

'You can have your god forsaken temple, it's a deal.'

They shook hands and Dalwyn leant in close to Grendel. 'Now as for this problem I have, here is what I propose.'

❧ ❧

Chapter 23

'Are you okay, Aeon?' asked Ishmael, turning to him.

'Yes, I am, thanks to you, Ishmael.' Aeon turned to the gods who milled about in confusion. 'Those of you who wish to live, follow us.' Then grabbing Ishmael's arm he led him away, and Zahra fell in beside them.

They were forced to flee without any supplies or extra guards, which left Ishmael, Zahra, Aeon and those gods who had opted to go with them. Aeon led the way through the labyrinthine tunnels. At times they were so narrow the party was forced to move in single file. When the tunnels opened out again to a cavern they were faced with four different choices of exits, and after much deliberation Aeon led them down one that he said would angle back up towards the surface. This news was gladly received by both Ishmael and Zahra, who were relieved to know that soon their stay beneath ground would be over. He was sick of the claustrophobic world down here and longed for fresh air and sunlight.

They began to traverse a tunnel through which air moved more freely, and the wind began to reach them, causing faint howling sounds as it moved through cracks and crevices as if seeking them out. Aeon told them this area was known as the bellows and was close to the surface. Weary from the fast pace, they stopped briefly when up ahead the tunnel opened and for the first time in a long while they could see the sky; the stars told them it was night. Ishmael went to move forward, but Aeon stopped him with his arm.

'Not so fast, Ishmael. Something doesn't feel right.'

Aeon motioned for them to crouch and wait while he stared at the entrance to the surface. Ishmael and Zahra watched too, trying to see what Aeon was so worried about.

There came the sound of a footfall and some gravel moved and sprinkled down the slope into the tunnel ahead, then Ishmael momentarily saw a shadow pass the entrance before it was gone.

Aeon turned to them. 'Move back slowly through the gods and begin retreating. I will stay at the back and cover us. I don't think we have been seen, but we cannot know that for certain.

Drained of hope due to their near escape, they headed back the way they had come to the junction. Ishmael guessed that they had lost maybe three to four chimes of walking since they were last here.

Aeon moved over to him and Zahra.

'We have no choice but to go deeper and take the long way around. The area we will go through is ruled by one of us gods who long ago left us and has refused contact since, so I know not how we will be welcomed.'

The way onward was soon marked with strange writing on the walls at junctions along with arrows, and the tunnels became clear of debris and well-worn as signs of habitation became more common.

They marched on wearily for another chime and then up ahead saw four figures atop what looked from a distance to be giant grey, hounds. One of the figures, who wore polished silver armour, raised a hand in greeting, and Aeon signalled for everyone to stop. The figures rode towards them at a slow pace before stopping within talking distance. They were all armoured and except the one in silver were wearing chainmail. The one in silver raised its visor.

'That's quite a party you have with you and if I may be so bold, a strange one at that. I see only two or three capable warriors,' he said in a gravelly voice.

'That's because we don't have warriors to protect us. We are fleeing and only by necessity do we come to these lands,' Aeon explained.

'And who are you, sir?'

'I am a brother to your king, and many of my party are also of his kin. You may know me as Aeon, the god of time.'

The warrior in silver turned to his companions and whispered something before turning back to them.

'May we approach your party, sir? We have food, and by the look of you all it would seem either you are poorly equipped for travel or simply have no food. We have some that you and your party may avail themselves if you so wish.'

'Your generosity is most welcome and, yes please, do approach. You will have no trouble from us, in this I give you my word.'

The riders approached, and while the one in silver moved over to Aeon the others pulled strange fruits and bread from saddle packs and dispersed it among the gods, Zahra, and Ishmael. The four riders who had removed their helms were bald, and one Ishmael noticed that was slighter of build than the others was female.

They sat and talked while they ate, and then cool water from canteens that tasted faintly of lime was passed around. 'If it is true that you are gods, then why walk in here on foot instead of using the powers you were blessed with?' asked the leader of the four.

'As you well know, the Severing changed many things, and the gates to the Celestial and Infernal realms have been shut to us. All here but I also lost our powers, and so we come as only we can,' said Aeon with a shrug.

The four looked at one another in confusion and then the leader began to laugh.

'Surely you jest,' he said, shaking his head.

'You accuse us of lying? The Severing happened three hundred cycles ago, but of course you know that,' said Zahra, looking exasperated.

One of the warriors stood and put a hand on his sword hilt and the one in silver barked a word while fixing him with a glare.

'We know nothing of this Severing you speak of, and if you say your powers were lost by this very thing, whatever it is, then why does our king who is kin to you still have his?'

Now it was Aeon's turn to look incredulous, and he shared a glance with Ishmael and Zahra that warned them to be careful here.

'I would be happy if your king Melde does still attain his powers, and I think it would be wise for us to speak with him personally on the matter and that of traversing his lands so we may continue on to our destination.'

'Yes, I believe Melde would indeed be happy to see the ones who cast him away from their jealousy, Aeon,' the leader said mockingly.

'Cast him away? Why, that swine and his hate-filled lies, I will personally…' Then the god of war who had uttered the words fell silent when he looked to Aeon.

'I mean, I would like to hear about this casting out, because it is news to us all here.'

'We don't take threats to our king lightly, and I am of the mind to see you come peacefully under our guard, but know this. If any of you raise complaint against Melde or my people again you will be dealt with harshly, is this understood?'

Yes, we understand, and I apologize for my companion's outburst,' Aeon said rising to his feet.

The journey to Melde, god and king of this strange subterranean realm, was a peculiar one, and soon they were winding their way through cavernous fields of mushrooms that gave off a sickly sweet odour and were tended to by very pale human workers in violet robes whose eyes appeared to be gem stones in the hue of deep red ruby, pale blue sapphires, and the greenest of emeralds. Ishmael exchanged looks with Zahra, who moved to his side.

'Ishmael, I don't like this place or the people. Their eyes are gone and have been replaced by gems, but what does it mean?'

'I am not sure, Zahra, but I don't like it either. It's unnatural.'

As they passed, the field workers would all stop and look in their direction then would sniff the air and cock their heads to the sides.

'The eyes must have been removed so that the others senses become enhanced. Here below the surface sight would be the least important of the senses, so it would make sense that these people value hearing and smell more than their sight, Zahra said to Ishmael, while noticing as she turned to face forward again the last of the four riders had turned and was looking straight at her with those strange eyes. Zahra realized they must now be more discreet than ever when dealing with Melde's people since they would have enhanced hearing many times better than normal humans. The rider who had obviously overheard her and Ishmael sat in his saddle regarding the two with a frown.

Zahra chose to ignore the interest and leant in to Ishmael again. 'So if the eyes have been removed, who is doing it then?'

'I don't know, but I dare say we will find out soon enough,' Ishmael whispered back.

Beyond the fields they came to a new area where the road narrowed to a stone bridge that ended at a plunging crevasse. On the opposite side of the crevasse a huge drawbridge was being lowered as they approached. Zahra could see they had come to a town where every building was round in shape, even what appeared to be a castle that towered over the other structures. All that they could see was covered in moss and lichen that obviously thrived down here out of sunlight, giving the place a distinctly alien feel to it.

They crossed the bridge made from iron and timber and approached the guards beside the portcullis winch, who wore the black chainmail armour and had onyx eyes. The main thoroughfare was crowded as the inhabitants went about their business, and it seemed that the lack of eyes didn't hinder them at all. Most disturbing of all was the noise, a cacophony of sounds that seemed at once distorted and unnerving. The locals bustled around their party as they went, stopping sometimes to sniff the air and call out strange words at these newcomers to their world. At some point Zahra noticed they had acquired a rear escort of the onyx-eyed warriors, who used long spears to keep the crowd from interfering with the group's movement down the road.

The circular castle was something amazing to behold, and the sheer display of precious metals that covered the castle's outer walls where the moss had been cleared away left Zahra breathless and gave the structure the appearance of something out of a dream. Their escorts took them into an area of the castle with interlinking rooms divided by moss curtains.

'Make use of these chambers and we shall have clothing brought for you all so you may be presented to our king, who has asked that you all dine with him in the sky garden. I will send you an escort, and please ensure the members of your group do not stray from this area as we will not be able to guarantee their safety once out of these rooms.'

Chapter 24

Zacriel sat slumped on his throne, totally drained now that the morning's appointments, and petitions were finally finished. He was in the castle hall on his throne circled by torches, while the rest of the chamber sat in darkness. This served two purposes. One being that the torchlight cancelled out the night vision that many Infernals could call on, which allowed Zacriel to keep his guards hidden. The second was that Zacriel preferred to avoid daylight and keep to the night, and the hall offered him solace during the day. When he heard the rustle of cloth, he realized his chance of peace was only a pleasant thought, and not a reality. Zacriel stood ready to give whatever unfortunate lackey it was a piece of his mind. He chose to halt his tongue though when he saw it was the intimidating form of Quail, the Eater of Souls.

Quail's hooked beak clacked, then ground together with a grating sound as the Infernal lords bright, feverish eyes regarded him.

'Quail, you surprised me. I wasn't expecting to see you again.'

The Infernal lord's plume of feathers flared showing its rich colours, and the scales on his body rippled with the movement of vermin. Quail threw back his head and laughed for a long moment, body shuddering with the intensity of it.

'Did I say something funny?' asked Zacriel taking a step away from Quail. It was at this moment Zacriel noticed the bodies of his two guards laying crumpled on the stone at the door to the chamber.

'Excuse me, Bone Lord. I just love that you speak your mind when nobody else has the guts to speak to me that way,' Quail followed Zacriel's glance at the dead guards. 'Get new guards, these two were too easily distracted, and you need to be protected by the best you have.'

'Besides pointing out the uselessness of my guards, why are you here?'

'We have lost Wilhelm's Point. Soarnestia attacked quicker than expected by air while the Brimmerland militia and legions attacked along the Seekers Road. I took the liberty of falling back with my troops since the Point is only a minor strategic target.'

'I disagree with that,' interrupted Zacriel. 'The Point is the best vantage to watch over Brimmerland, Soarnestia, and Trystland. With its loss we have severely been restricted in stopping those nations from attacking us.

'It wasn't as if we were routed, Bone Lord, and we have a gift for you,' replied Quail.

'What kind of gift?'

'A captive for you to use in bargaining, of course.' Quail clapped his hands and two of his winged warriors dragged a body into the throne room, then dumped it at Zacriel's feet.

Whoever it was had suffered at the hands of Quail and his Infernals. A sack that showed a wet bloodstain still covered the persons head, and their hands and feet had been tied too tightly with ropes. The armour the prisoner wore was sleek, black hardened leather with crimson piping, but it was the crest on the armour that caught Zacriel's attention, a raven. This was a Soarnestian raven warrior.

'Why bring me a raven warrior?' Zacriel asked, confused.

One of Quail's Infernals roughly tore the sack off the head of the unfortunate to reveal a man with his lips, nose, and one eye swollen. Somehow the man still managed to appear commanding as his normal eye glared up at both Zacriel and Quail with arrogance and hatred. He struggled against his bonds.

'He is not just any raven warrior, Bone Lord. Before you is Prince Grego, or commonly known as the Prince of Winds.' Zacriel realized Quail was watching him as if expecting a reaction to the man's title, and the Infernal lord was disappointed when he got none. Zacriel turned to face Quail. He couldn't believe that bringing the prince of Soarnestia here would do anything for their cause besides bring down the anger of another nation. He must have kept the look of disbelief on his face because Quail clacked his beak and ruffled his feathers, then stepped forward to stand toe to toe with Zacriel.

'I can tell you are angered by my gift, and take me for a fool. I have been destroying kingdoms and lives for so many cycles I have lost count, while you are a newcomer to these games of power. You look upon me with disdain when I deliver you a hostage of such importance, that it just may allow you to stop a very powerful enemy from joining those who will soon lay siege to this city of yours.' Quail grabbed Zacriel by the shoulders, then used a clawed hand to pull Zacriel forward by the back of the head.

'Don't you even see the leverage we now have over Soarnestia?'

Zacriel brushed away Quail's arm, noting with horror the intense itching that had started where the Eater of Souls had touched him.

'All I see is that the King of Soarnestia will now bring his whole armed might to attack us when they would have been content to stay safe within their own borders. Now, you have given them a reason to leave and fight,' replied Zacriel as his own voice rose to a shout.

Quail tilted his head to look at Zacriel. His eyes widened and he squatted beside the struggling prince at their feet.

'I now understand the reaction you are having, Bone Lord, so let me fill in the blanks of this situation that you obviously are unaware of. Common rumours and propaganda spread by the royal household would have the world believe there are five royal brats of Soarnestia. What only a handful of people know is that Prince Grego is the sole heir to the kingdom of Soarnestia. To make the situation of the royal family even direr is the fact that the queen has been locked away due to being accused as an adulteress. It is whispered through Cabre that the King Luizon, wants to watch her waste away slowly as punishment for her betrayal. Now if that wasn't enough, the old raven king himself has developed a disease where his body is wracked with the shakes, and so the royal family of once formidable Soarnestia is in danger of losing the throne. The raven king will want his son back, and I think if you want leverage then you would be able to target the love King Luizon has for his brat, which may just keep Soarnestia out of the fight.'

'If all this is true, Quail, why risk the heir to the throne in an attack on as you stated earlier a minor military objective?'

'Ahhhh, now you are thinking,' said Quail clapping his hands together with glee. 'There are many who circle the throne of Soarnestia like wolves waiting for the old raven to fall. Due to the internal unrest of the kingdom and royal court, King Luizon believes it is necessary to keep the prince at the head of the war movement as a visible representation that all is well in the nest. This will allow them to avoid the royal family being seen as vulnerable.'

Zacriel nodded his head thoughtfully as he took in all that Quail had relayed to him, and he realized the Eater of Souls was right. The prince was a very valuable hostage.

Quail sketched a flowery bow that Zacriel was sure had been done to mock him.

'My Lord, I request to take my leave now, if that is your will,' rasped Quail.

'Actually, Lord Quail, before you go I have something I need you to do.' The request stopped the Infernal lord who's back stiffened before he turned back to Zacriel.

'I have provided the eastern most tower for you and your bodyguard, and through the upper level is an access point to the sky walk. Since you and your legion are all winged it seems you are the obvious choice to defend the sky walk from aerial attacks. If the call to defend comes, the ballista will be manned by my own warriors while yours are free to defend the sky walk from above and protect the skies over Acclaro.'

'It will be done, Bone Lord. Will that be all?'

'No, it will not be all, Quail. In future you will stick to my plans, any deviation without my consultation will be seen as an act of defiance. Tomorrow evening, the Unseeing lord and Lilith will be arriving to meet and discuss our strategies, and you will join us. Is this clear?'

Quail laughed, a sound not so different to a low squawking of an injured bird. Beside him his two warriors rested hands on their swords, ready to attack at Quail's command.

'I have only tolerated your position, Zacriel, due to respect at what you have achieved, and yet now it appears you are overstepping your boundaries. If you think you can dictate to me, another Infernal lord on how I should act, then maybe I was wrong about you. Only by necessity are we allies, and threats against me will only result in your demise. Quail drew from his feathered body a long Kris knife with its wavy blade covered in runic script, which he levelled at Zacriel and began to approach him.

'Come no closer, Quail,' said Zacriel as he loosened his own sword in its scabbard.

Look around you, Bone Lord, do you think you alone can take the three of us?' rasped Quail and then his two bodyguards surged towards Zacriel. There came a loud twang from the darkness behind the throne as something long and barbed punched through the chest of one feathered warrior, sending it skittering across the stone floor. A blood curdling scream came from the same area, and Rapture, bare chested with his battle axe raised above him erupted into the torch light. Rapture chopped down at the other winged Infernal who barely dodged the vicious downward swing of the axe. Rapture followed up with a head-butt that dropped the Infernal to its knees, the return swing of the axe carved down through one shoulder into its chest lodging there. Quail skittered backward, raising his knife in defence, apparently taken by surprise. There was a long moment of silence, then the grunting of Rapture as he levered the blade of the axe free of the winged Infernals body, and kicked it away from him.

There was noise from the door way. Quail turned to see a score of Zacriel's elite Infernals waiting at the ready. He sheathed his knife then turned back to Zacriel.

Zacriel slouched down onto the throne, one finger tapping his chin thoughtfully.

'Quail, I will only say this once. Underestimate me at your peril. The Lady of Whispers did. If you choose to join her then tell me now, otherwise you will follow my orders while here in Acclaro.'

Quail lowered his head, looked up and met Zacriel's unflinching glare, then turned away and slowly shuffled out of the royal hall. As Zacriel watched him go he knew that this was not the end of the matter.

Chapter 25

In the room Zahra was shown to a basin sat filled with warm water and oils along with a comfortable looking pallet complete with plush cushions. Folded neatly atop thick blankets was a long, red dress that caught her attention. The dress was adorned with chips of ruby that tinkled against one another and gave a distinct sound when she moved about. A servant appeared to help fit the clasps at her back, and this one had the yellow topaz gems for eyes.

'Tell me about your king,' Zahra asked the servant as she rubbed creams into her skin and painted the Zahra's nails.

'It is by his kindness that this place exists at all, and we owe him much for letting us live. There was something I was to warn you of, and that I will share with you now. Do not meet the eyes of our king or it will cause certain death. That is one reason why our eyes are removed at birth so that we live and don't need to look upon his true visage, which would destroy us.'

'And you all just believe this?' Zahra asked.

'Why shouldn't we? Our king has no reason to deceive us, and the mutilation actually helps us live better lives down here. As you might have seen on the way to the castle, our people move freely about just like in other cities of the world. It's just that here they use other senses to do that.'

The sky gardens were at the top most level of the circular castle and closest to the cavern's roof than others structures, which made it the best place to enjoy the glow of the lichen that tinted the subterranean city the softest hue of green. Amongst green moss, a long table had been set for feasting and was loaded with bowls and platters of foods that Zahra had never seen before and by the look of many would never sample.

Zahra was the first to arrive at the table and sat listening to a group of musicians playing large harps as one by one the gods filed in with their escorts leading them. Zahra found herself beside Cinder, the god of war, whose muscles bulged against the flimsy excuse for clothing he had been given, and he grinned, showing a fine set of gleaming teeth. Even his straw-coloured hair had been braided and hung down his back.

Cinder caught her looking and laughed at her.

'It's rude to stare even in this strange place.'

'What would you care? You go to your death anyway,' she said, sampling the strange looking drink in a crystal flute beside her plate. It tasted of rose and melon.

'Do you think so? I mean, do you really expect that we are going to our deaths by returning to the Mother, Zahra?'

The mention of her name made her turn back to him, his intense yellow eyes catching and holding her gaze with a questioning stare.

'To be honest, I really don't know or care. I prefer to live one day at a time, and right now the talk of death should be far from all our minds. I apologize for bringing the subject up,' she replied, finishing the drink.

'The god raised his hand to signal a servant, who refilled Zahra's glass, and then he proposed a toast for the two of them.

'To a night of no pleasures being denied the two of us.'

'A bit presumptuous, don't you think?' Zahra asked as she sipped and clinked glasses.

'Not at all, Zahra. I like what I see of you, and you have done nothing but practically drool over me since I took my seat.'

Zahra smiled to herself. The night was looking better by the moment.

Ishmael felt ridiculous in the long transparent skirt that barely covered his genitals, and wrapped up to coil around his upper body leaving his chest bare. His arms, ears, and chest were all adorned with jewellery that reflected the cavern roof. He took his seat beside Shail, who squeezed his hand and greeted him. He noticed further down the table Zahra sitting beside the muscle bound figure of Cinder, the god of war, and he looked more harmless than the version that the priests had come up with during the festival at the Godhead. They were flirting with each other, and Ishmael smiled at Zahra's coy behaviour and wondered if Cinder truly knew how much trouble he was in.

When Aeon came and took his seat beside Ishmael, his face was dark as a thunder cloud and he tapped the table with his fingers in irritation.

'Something on your mind then, Aeon?' Ishmael asked with a smile.

'We don't have the time to play kings, and this feast is all for show while our enemies close the distance on us by the moment.'

'So why don't you just talk to him alone then?'

Because the damn fool has decided all talk of business shall wait until a feast has been held in our honour, that's why, dammit!'

'Is that so bad? I mean, maybe it's better for you and the gods to be reunited this way with Melde in order to put the past behind you all and find common ground again,' said Ishmael, trying to be helpful.

'If we were talking about a sane person then yes it would be very good to do this. Unfortunately, I believe Melde may just have become too insulated and insane in this little world he has created down here, and the journey to the castle did nothing to dismiss those feelings.'

There came a ripple of exclamation among the gods at the table, and Ishmael saw that their host, Melde, had finally made his appearance.

Six formidable warriors entered in twos with diamonds where their eyes should have been and complete with silver armour and wicked swords at their side. Behind them came Melde in dark, sleek chainmail with boots of gold and a long gold cloak that dragged on the ground behind him. In one hand he carried a huge hammer with precious jewels embedded in its long handle, the weapon looking more like a toy in the god's hands.

Iron, grey eyes regarded the guests arrayed before him as Melde slowly made his way to his seat, thoughtfully stroking the thick beard that hung down to his chest. When Melde arrived at the jewelled chair that was more like a throne than a dining chair, he rested his hammer against its side and then stood silently looking down the table. One of the warriors just to his side banged his blade against his shield.

'You will all rise as lord and god of this realm, Melde, is seated, then you may follow suit.'

Ishmael noticed more than a few annoyed looks from the seated gods at this announcement, but they all stood and waited for Melde to be seated comfortably before doing likewise themselves.

Ishmael expected some sort of welcome speech; however, Melde simply clapped his hands and a small force of servants bustled in with platters of roasted meats and jugs of chilled ale to go with the already heaped dishes on the table.

Aeon was miserable company beside him, practically refusing to enjoy any of the banquet delights on offer, and so Ishmael chose to talk with Shail on his other side.

'Why are all the gods on bad terms with Melde?'

'That is certainly not a short tale to tell, Ishmael. Melde has always seen the gods as the highest powers and for mortals to simply be our tools. Even among us gods we have mostly lived by… a code, I guess you could call it. It was given to us by the Mother, who forbade us to personally interfere in the life of mortals and only give instructions to our followers; however Melde secretly ignored that and moved through the mortal world in person, removing any who could bring opposition to his plans.'

'What plans were they?' Ishmael asked, caught up in the story.

'To unite the gods beneath him and control the races and then eventually usurp the Mother. Melde was banished from the Celestial lands. He chose to come here beneath the ground where the precious metals he covets are in abundance and he was far away from his kin. As you can see for yourself, Melde rules his kingdom with an iron fist and does not allow anyone a say in how he rules.'

'Is that why he removes the eyes of his people and replaces them with gemstones?'

'It is the only reason why that I can even think of, Ishmael, although I don't know for sure.'

Throughout the meal Ishmael noticed Melde staring at him and occasionally would call over one of his people to whisper something to them, or would talk to the gods closest to him, and Ishmael knew by their glances his way they discussed him. The attention made him nervous, and Ishmael knew that soon he would have to face this god who had little or no respect for any mortals, himself included.

There came a lull in the music as Melde signalled for silence to the musicians who stood and filed from the area.

'My lord Aeon, my people have gone to so much trouble to provide this feast and honour you and all our kin, and yet your glass stands full and your plate empty. Is the fare we set so poor to your tastes?'

At the king's words the table fell instantly silent as all turned to see Aeon's reaction.

'There is nothing wrong with the banquet you and your people have prepared for us, Melde, and by the ravenous reactions of all others here I would say it is fine indeed. I however have no stomach for food or ale while more important matters weigh on my mind.'

'Always so serious, Aeon. I'm sure these matters can at least wait another few chimes until we celebrate our reunion. What say you?'

'I say you don't understand the risk not just to us visitors but to you and your people, and I would not bring it up at this time if I didn't think it was so important a matter.'

'Your negativity sours my ale, Aeon. At a time when this could be used to repair our past conflicts, you would ruin it with your pettiness? Now enough with this subject, I have given you my answer that this important matter wait a few more of your precious chimes, and if you refuse to heed me in this matter I will have you removed from our celebrations.'

'Aeon rose and threw his napkin down on his empty plate. 'No need to do that, Melde. I will remove myself so you don't have your meal ruined!'

After Aon exited the dining area Melde stood. 'Come on then, eat and drink! After all, this is a celebration. Now more me more ale,' shouted Melde from the head of the table.

Slowly the sound of chatter rose again, but there were still some worried faces from the gods at the table. From beside Ishmael Shail was one of those. 'I don't like how this situation is growing, and I fear if Melde keeps drinking so heavily things might get out of hand,' she said to Ishmael.

'They will talk after the meal. Melde said he would make time to hear Aeon out.'

'I hope so, but it has become a battle of wills between the two and has always been so,' she replied.

When someone tapped Ishmael on the shoulder, he was surprised to see one of the warriors standing there impassively.

'Melde would talk to you. Please come sit beside him.'

Ishmael looked to Shail for help, but she just lowered her eyes. 'Go, Ishmael; it is not a request.'

Chapter 26

Ishmael nodded and approached Melde, where a servant was placing another chair, place mat, and mug of ale. Not knowing what was expected of him, Ishmael stopped beside the god and bowed low.

'My lord Melde, you asked for me?'

'Of course I asked for you, now sit so we may speak.'

Ishmael did so and then took a large gulp of ale to settle his nerves.

Melde picked at the food before him, his eyes never leaving Ishmael, and Ishmael got the sense that the god was weighing him up. He returned the look, all the while attempting to appear calm and unruffled.

'It appears to me that Aeon dotes on you like you are someone very special and the other gods treat you with respect, a thing I never managed to get from them,' said Melde, chuckling. 'I have sat here trying to figure out why you, Ishmael, are so important, and I was hoping you would be so kind as to illuminate me.' Then Melde became silent and sat back in his chair watching Ishmael again.

'I am known as the conduit for a coterie who have been tasked by the Mother to return magic to our world.'

'Why would you imply that magic has gone?' interrupted Melde.

'The Severing cut the connection to magic just over three hundred cycles ago, and not even the gods were left with their powers,' replied Ishmael.

'Why have I never heard of this Severing, and why do I to this day retain my power then, Ishmael?'

'I can't speak for you Melde. I only know from my time with Aeon and the other gods that this is so. The Mother has shared her visions with me of the Severing since at that time I wasn't even born and when my father died he passed this magic onto me.'

'You just said yourself that magic was taken from our world and in the same sentence added that your father passed it on to you. Ishmael, you speak in riddles.'

'Let me try to explain then,' said Ishmael, taking a long swallow of ale.

'Magic is an inherent part of reality in our world and it cannot be truly removed, otherwise all this world would cease to exist. The magic was stored in five people who were able to hold great power within them, and this would be passed onto their next of kin, or failing that, someone close to them at the time of death. In this way the Mother would be able to heal the world until such time as it was right to bring it back, and now that time has come.'

'An interesting tale, Ishmael, but I have no time for childish things.'

'So you have your powers still then, Melde?'

'I have said so, Ishmael. Would you question my honesty?'

'I am not calling you a liar, Melde. Many times have I seen the truth of what I have told you, and if it is as you say then everyone except you, Aeon the god of time, and the Death Jester, god of death, have suffered the loss of their divine power. Has the Mother not appeared to you in dreams like she has to the other gods and the coterie I am a part of?'

'The Mother and these gods whom you think of so highly cast me out long ago, and since then I have been treated like an outcast from my very own kin,' Melde said. Is it so hard to believe that I would mistrust them when they come crawling into my domain asking for help?'

'This could be the chance for you to extend the hand of peace to Aeon and the other gods, and they are asking only for permission to move through your lands and reach the surface in safety from those who pursue us.'

'Ahhh, yes, of course, why else would you need my help? My people have given no mention of any enemies following behind you to our lands. Why am I only finding out about such dangers to my kingdom now?'

'Aeon has attempted to talk with you, but as we all just saw, my lord, you won't have any dealings with him on the subject of our arrival and so such important dangers to this point have remained unspoken. The Life Quenchers hunt you and all the gods to steal the divine spark that dwells within you still. They would use this to strengthen Tamul's power in rivalling the Mother and his aim in destroying this world,' continued Ishmael, trying his best to appeal to something this god would listen to.

'And, yet, where are they, Ishmael?'

'Your people hardly are equipped to deal with such a threat as the Life Quenchers. They are blinded and these creatures, whom I have seen with my own eyes, move from shadow to shadow silently. They will not announce their arrival, and Aeon fears not just for us but you and your people. Come with us, Melde, and put aside all rivalries before it's too late for us all.'

'I have not sat idle while you have been in my domain, Ishmael, I still have allies among my brethren who inform me they are expected to come quietly to their deaths and return to the Mother who would erase them once and for all.'

'Nobody can know what will happen, but the Mother loves you all as she does all whom she created. You need to trust her.'

Melde slammed his goblet down on the table, sloshing wine over his hand.

'Do not talk to me of trust, mortal. I am the one who has been wronged here. The Mother seemed happy enough to exile me and cast me out, and now you would go so far as to ask me to trust her?'

Ishmael ignored the sudden silence at the table as all turned eyes upon him and Melde.

'If there is nothing else you would do, then just let us move through your land under escort and be on our way.' Ishmael said. 'Let this be a meeting of old friends and put rivalries aside; then we can leave you alone.'

'I tire of this game you play as a pawn of Aeon. I must say he has prepared you well, but I am not fooled and refuse to be drawn into another power play that Aeon has planned. If you are to convince me of the importance of your arrival and demands then you will have to do better than that.' Melde clapped his hands, and more wine was poured by servants who bustled around and also mopped up spilt ale.

As they departed Ishmael was at a loss of what to do to convince Melde to help them. Then he had an idea. He placed his hand on the arm of Melde and held it hard.

'What? You dare to touch me?' Melde began, and then Ishmael allowed his experiences to wash through him and into the god as the magic washed over him and up Melde's arm. He showed the moment his father's power transferred into his own body, the attack on the monastery, and his visions from the Mother herself when the Severing was unleashed. He allowed his meeting with the Harlequin, when he was gifted the earth crystal, to wash over the god and followed it with the fall of Acclaro and the deception of the Godhead with the lies that had been fed to the masses of people who yet believed the gods still had their powers. Finally he showed the meeting with the Sulk, who had remained behind to fight the Life Quenchers who pursued their retreat to this place, and then he let the god go.

Melde stood and fell back, knocking himself from his chair and falling to the ground screaming. 'Arrest him, he has assaulted me,' he screamed, spittle flying from his mouth, his eyes blazing with anger.

His guards swarmed over Ishmael, dragging him down under them where they restrained him, and the gathering erupted into chaos.

Chapter 27

Zahra was busy exploring the delights at the feast, but not so much as enjoying Cinder who was quick mouthed and humorous. A dalliance this night with Cinder was looking, and she was just trailing the fingers of one hand along his muscled thigh when she heard Melde scream. She turned to see Melde order Ishmael arrested, then the diamond eyes soldiers piled on Ishmael, dragging him to the ground. She was on her feet in a moment, and as she skirted the table she cannoned into two of the warriors, using her body weight to knock them over and away from Ishmael.

'Guards, guards, to me,' Melde was screaming, and then Cinder was there alongside Zahra, reaching down and tearing off soldiers then tossing them away.

As more guards ran into the area and surrounded their god, Cinder and Zahra pulled Ishmael to his feet. He looked shaken but unhurt, much to Zahra's relief, and she pressed herself in front of him defensively, silently regretting not grabbing a knife or any such weapon from the table.

'Melde, have you gone mad? Attacking one under our protection is unacceptable even for you,' Cinder growled.

'He attacked me! Am I supposed to let that just happen?' Melde replied.

'Is this true?' Cinder asked turning to Ishmael.

'No, it's not true I merely showed him through the magic all that has happened to me and his reaction was this. He feels threatened because he knows just like with all you gods here that his magic is gone and he is mortal,' Ishmael said, his tone cold and hard.

'You mean you haven't told your people about the loss of magic?' asked Irdalar goddess of water, from the side of the table, and when Melde said nothing her expression grew to one of outrage. 'You cannot do this, Melde. They rely on you, and you can only protect them from the world for so long before they know the truth of what you have wrought here.'

'These are my people, this is my land, and I do as I wish as its ruler. What would have been achieved by telling them,' Melde screamed back and as if aware only now of the words he just said he fell silent.

One of the warriors near him turned to his god. 'Is this true, my lord, that your power is gone?'

Kane, the god of justice walked over to Melde. 'I believe that a simple demonstration of this magic you say you still have will settle the whole argument,' he said stopping in front of Melde.

'I will not do this, Kane, and nothing you all say can make me. I don't have to prove anything, to you gods or my people. They owe me everything.'

'It is the only to settle it, Melde. I think if you refuse then that in itself speaks the truth of the situation. Now begin!'

Melde looked trapped now. His warriors had backed away in confusion and were speaking amongst themselves. Melde glanced at them then turned murderous eyes on Kane and lurched forward. They saw the knife just before he buried it in Kane's throat and the god of justice collapsed, choking on his own blood.

The strange warriors scattered and made for the exits, and Melde dropped the bloody knife to the ground in horror, staring at the bright blood on his hands.

Cinder tore off his shirt and attempted to staunch the wound; to Kane's eyes were fixed on Melde and then they closed and his head drooped to the side. There was an eerie silence now as the gods looked on in horror at their fallen brother.

'Maybe now we can talk before any more of our kin die,' Aeon said from behind them at the open door.

Haakon made sure they kept a guard all the next day as the others slept. He found he only really dozed while his mind raced trying to find a plan that would get the coterie and Latasha out of the cells and away from Dalwyn.

When he awoke it was to laughter, and he realized in that moment how much he had truly missed that sound. He pretended to still sleep as he listened.

'Don't be silly, I know you are not Haakon's brothers, you don't even look alike and you both have long pointed ears and he doesn't.'

'That, my dear child, is because he is the ugly child and we are the handsome ones.'

'What about the ears?'

'We cut them off so nobody will know he is our brother because we only want handsome brothers.'

Nina laughed again. 'You're too silly.'

'Dre, can you remember what happened to the last child who called us silly?'

'Of course, they met the most terrible death of being planted in the ground up to their neck and force fed turnips until they exploded,' explained Lim gravely.

After Nina's laughter subsided, she regarded them both thoughtfully as Haakon watched on, the swivel of the twins' eyes betraying their knowledge he was awake.

'You are Ancients aren't you?'

'Yes we are, Nina. Have you ever seen one of us before?'

'Only in picture books, but they said you were all dead and yet here you are. Were you hiding from everyone?'

'There are only three of us left now that we know of. Latasha, whom Haakon travelled with, is the other ancient. She is like our queen, which is why we need to save her again.'

'Is she pretty? I bet she is.'

'Very pretty and sometimes grumpy because she has a terrible temper.'

'Stop lying. I bet she is the sweetest person ever.'

'Nope, you are the sweetest person ever, Nina,' said Haakon, sitting up.

The smile she flashed Haakon when Nina turned momentarily banished all his worries.

'The twins were just making tea and I have some bread but it's a little stale now, oh and I saved you the best apple I could find except they are soft and not crunchy which is how I like them best.'

'Thank you, Nina. We eat, then I need you to help us plan what we are going to do. Can you do that?'

'I'm not so good at planning, but I can help you. It won't mean going into the astral again, will it?'

'No, we will stay out of that realm for now. You have had enough adventures there for a time.

They spent the afternoon readying their weapons and joking about as dusk approached. Then they readied themselves by going over the plan one final time before Haakon decided to sleep, and after nightfall they would leave this hideout for somewhere else close by. There was a still a chance, no matter how small, that they could still rescue Latasha and the other coterie members.

Latasha had first taken Haakon to this pace that few knew even existed. She had told him it was sacred to the shamans whom the ancients trained, and this place became for them a place of power where they could go in the flesh or in astral form or reflect on their journey through power, a true place of sanctuary.

With the shamans of the ancients now gone, this place was his and Latasha's, and from here he had witnessed marvels, had secrets of power revealed to him, and like Latasha had promised, it had become a place where his power was stored. He had stood on the perfectly circular flat rock that extended out from the cliff edge, a lake far below, the sunlight sending diamond reflections off the water. An eagle screeched far above him, and he looked up to track its movements through the clear sky as the sun burnt bright and fierce, and yet its glow didn't burn him and a mellow wind softly ruffled his hair. The ground rumbled and the rock shook below him, but he wasn't afraid, for it was a sign he had waited for all his life.

Haakon began to slowly dance the steps of power he had learnt from primordial spirits in the astral, on the many astral trips that Latasha had taken him on into the past where he sat and learnt firsthand with the shamans of antiquity. As he turned slowly through a series of steps, he saw his witness there behind him at the edge of the stone watching and didn't need to know who it was. It had been with him from birth, waiting for him, but in this moment the witness could not touch him, and the power and precision of this sacred dance would buy him enough of a reprieve to see that things were complete.

The dance stretched on for a long time, grandiose and filled with pure intent, recalling the story of his life thus far and recalling the power that he had built through stupendous hardships, the battles he had won and lost and of marvels witnessed. Then when he was finally finished and his body thrummed with his personal power, he turned to the witness who simply pointed to the south and the vastness that awaited Haakon, then he woke up.

He listened intently for a time, trying to hear any sound of disturbance over the beating of his heart, but all that came to his straining ears was the low talking of Nina with the twins. He felt refreshed, and the clarity of his mind was for once unstuck with worry and tension as he reflected on the dream he just had although deep inside he knew without doubt it hadn't been a dream.

Lighting a candle, Haakon pulled out the clan ledger and began to write. When he had finished he pulled the loose stone in the back wall of the sacred chamber out and stashed the book within, then he went out to join Nina and the twins. They were sitting talking softly of the nearby granary where they would continue to hide when Lim stood suddenly.

'Someone is coming, just one, his footfalls are soft and practiced, but my ears are better,' he said to them and picked up his bow. They gathered their own weapons and pack just in case they needed to flee and then waited.

Dre peered out into the corridor, and then the sounds of running steps could be heard. With one fluid movement the ancient let fly with two arrows, and the footfalls fell silent. Out in the corridor they found a flame warrior, but how did he know about the secret passage?

'We must leave now, they have found us out,' said Haakon, kneeling and tying Nina's pack on her back and hugging her tight. 'Keep running if something happens to us, little one,' he said and kissed her forehead. Then the four of them headed towards the rear door and ladder that went to the roof. Shouts of exclamation carried to them as their pursuers took up the chase.

Chapter 28

The night sky was riddled with stars as Haakon lifted Nina onto the ladder and she began scrambling upwards with Haakon close behind. When she got up to the top and pulled her body over the edge, Nina was quickly on her feet and running. She saw the figure before her only as he snatched for her; she ducked away from the flame warrior, who cursed, and then she sprinted for the ladder up ahead that would lead to the ground far below and would have made it too if not for the immense, blue creature that descended to hover near the ladder with tentacles undulating from below a mouth of horrible, stained teeth.

A bird man with red-and-black feathers who sat atop the creature snapped out a guttural word, and faster than Nina could react a tentacle wrapped about her waist and lifted her into the air with her arms trapped by her sides. Nina would have screamed if she hadn't been so afraid. She managed to twist around to see what was happening below and saw the twins and Haakon fighting against a throng of flame warriors. Dre took a hit to the head from behind and crumpled to the ground while Lim roared in fury and lay about him with his blade, but they overpowered him and held him down. This left Haakon standing in the centre of a circle of warriors who kept their distance warily due to the many dead that the clan lord had already dispatched.

For the first time from behind the battle Nina saw Dalwyn. The old man looked weak but was smiling as he watched the fight before him, and beside him stood another man of the same likeness but younger. The third person Nina recognized only by description, Latasha, with long, silver hair flowing past her shoulders, who wept as a flame warrior held her chin forcing her to watch what was happening.

Haakon swirled from one stance to the next as warriors darted in to fall before his blade, only to be replaced by more. His blade became trapped in one enemy's chest, and he rolled away then snatched up a fallen blade to continue dealing out death, ignoring the ever-increasing small cuts he had suffered in the fight.

A slash tore the throat from a flame warrior, then the backswing almost decapitated the next just as another of the strange, flying creatures descended from above in a darting motion. One thick tentacle wrapped around Haakon's free arm while another circled his neck. He slashed down at the one on his arm, separating it from its host as the one around his neck tightened, and Nina could hear the sounds of Haakon gasping. Haakon dropped the sword he was holding and drew a dagger, which he used to begin sawing at the tentacle that still held him.

The Limpid, which the twins had called it, dropped Haakon, splashing ichor from the tentacle as it waved about. Haakon hit the stone hard, but slowly he rose to his knees, head bowed, then looked up and screamed with fury at the beast above him. He was unarmed now, and the next tentacle whipped down, grasping his ankle, tearing him away from the safety of the ground. Then it slammed him down, again and again, and Nina looked away as the thuds continued amidst Latasha's high, keening wail.

Nina saw one of the twins roll towards the edge; he wasn't dead as she had thought and, he simply let himself fall over and away into the darkness. The bird creature atop the Limpid that held Nina moved over to Haakon and let Nina fall onto the stone before Dalwyn's feet.

The old man grasped Nina's chin in his hand, forcing her to look at him. She tried to squirm away, but he was too strong.

'Did you think I wouldn't catch you, Nina?'

'I hate you,' Nina screamed at Dalwyn.

Dalwyn slapped her hard, and she fell back, dazed, watching him laugh through blurry eyes. Then someone was on top of her, not pressing down on her but shielding her body from Dalwyn's rage.

'Leave her alone, she is only a damn child. You have made your point, Dalwyn, but if you want my cooperation at all then leave the child alone!'

Dalwyn spoke to his soldiers and ignored Latasha. 'Get them out of my sight and leave the fools body for the carrion to pick at.'

'And the one that got away, my lord?'

'Let him go, but be on watch for his return. We can leave tomorrow with the coterie for Acclaro now we have dealt with that little annoyance,' said Dalwyn, and then he walked away looking more sprightly than he had earlier.

Nina's vision had cleared now, though the side of her face still smarted from the hit Dalwyn had given her. The silver-haired Latasha lifted Nina to her feet, then holding her close, let the soldiers herd them after Dalwyn.

'Come on, Nina, come with me now. I will make sure Dalwyn doesn't touch you again.'

'Thank you. They killed Haakon,' said Nina, feeling her lips tremble and her chest go tight. Haakon was dead, and if she had killed Dalwyn back in Acclaro when she had the chance this would not have happened. She looked up at Latasha and noticed that she also wept, though silently as tears streaked down over her high cheek bones.

The flame warriors pushed both Nina and Latasha roughly into one of the cells, where three other people rushed over and crowded around Latasha and Nina. Latasha began to weep aloud then, and a tall lady with bronzed skin and piercing eyes held her close while she wept. Another shorter lady knelt down beside Nina. 'Hello, child, are you okay?'

'Nina shook her head no, and the lady wrapped warm arms around her and rocked her like a babe. 'There, there, child, no need to talk. Just rest now, and we can talk later.'

Nina just nodded but she knew things could never be the same. Haakon had made her feel safe again, strong even, and now he was gone and she was a prisoner to Dalwyn again. Nina didn't sleep that night, just lay in the arms of the woman whom she now knew was called Jona. Latasha retold the fall of Haakon and watched the dismay grow on these three new people she shared the cell with. The only man, Raul he was called paced, jaw clenched and shoulders bunched, looked how they all felt, which did little to console Nina.

Chapter 29

Melde was put into a holding cell with four of the gods standing guard over him. The body of Kane lay washed and robed on a bench in the apothecary chambers. They all watched on as Aeon stopped and placed his hand on the dead god's chest and closed his eyes. Ishmael felt it when the power came, and it seemed that Aeon blazed with light that was painful to look at and made Ishmael turn away.

There came gasps of astonishment from the gods present, and Ishmael turned back just in time to see something pass from Kane's chest into the god of time; it was like a flow of stars, thought Ishmael as the chamber which had dimmed returned back to its normal light. Aeon stepped back and stumbled into the reaching hands of those closest, steadying him.

'It is done. I have taken back Kane's divine spark and will return him to the Mother,' he said simply, then he fell unconscious.

Later that night Ishmael was still beside the prone Aeon watching over him and thinking on the events of the feast. He had managed to get Melde to admit the magic was gone, but at what cost? Now Melde looked a shadow of his confident self as he sat in the adjoining room under the guard of his brother and sister gods.

Aeon sat up, startling Ishmael. 'They are here, the Life Quenchers are here,' he said and made to rise from the bed.

'Are you sure?' Ishmael asked.

'Yes, I was in communion with the Mother and she showed me.'

Ishmael ran to the window of the castle and looked down into the city, where he could just see beyond it to the fields they had passed through that day. As he watched he saw the lanterns and the strange lights of the fields begin to go dark as if shadows washed over them. Slowly the darkness moved towards the city, and screaming began far below them.

'Where is Melde?'

'In the next room, why?' asked Ishmael.

'We need to know if they have enough light to hold back the Life Quenchers for at least a time.'

When they entered the adjoining room Melde was on his feet and trying to reason with his guards.

'Something is happening to my people out there, can't you hear the screams? At least let me see what going on,' he has pleaded with them. When he saw Aeon he moved towards him but once again was stopped by his guards.

'Aeon, something is happening out in the city. I know you can hear the screaming.'

'Yes, Melde. The Life Quenchers that Ishmael spoke of have come to your little haven here. They are hunting us and we have waited too long, which has put us all in danger.'

'I must go to them, fight beside them, and you all will help me. Together we can defeat them, Aeon…' He trailed off as Aeon shook his head.

They are too strong and we cannot suffer any more losses as it will weaken the Mother and hinder the return of magic.'

'Then what can we do? Aeon, please, we must do something.'

'The lighting for the city, where does it come from?'

'We use great crystals that are charged with sunlight from the nearest surface tunnel where it meets the Jewelled lands,' Melde replied.

'The ones that are being used now, how long will they continue to supply light to the city?'

'Until morning, which is when new ones are hung. We keep some in reserve, maybe enough for another five days until the latest caravan returns with fresh ones.'

'Is it possible to get all the spare ones and light the walls of the city to keep the Life Quenchers at bay? They abhor the light and cannot function well within it. If we can deny them the shadows we may just have time to escape.'

Zahra lay breathing hard and let a smile creep over her face. Beside her Cinder looked at her. 'Why are you looking so pleased with yourself?' he asked.

'It's not every day that you can mark down one of the gods as a sexual conquest,' she said, smiling.

'Is that all I am then, a conquest? A last chance to sleep with a deity before they leave forever?'

'Stop goading me, Cinder, I was just making fun of you that is all. It wasn't like that, and you know it.'

They had found a room at an inn away from the castle and the other gods for privacy, and the strange people here were at first drawn to them with curiosity, but had become sullen as word spread among the city inhabitants of the events at the feast and the lie that Melde had held over his people. When they had tried to pay for the room they were told that being honoured guests here meant they would be given free stay. The sex had been frantic, just the way Zahra loved it, and Cinder had been an accomplished lover with endurance to match her own.

Zahra was just about to entice Cinder into another round when the lighting outside dimmed and went out. She went to the window naked and looked down to the front gates of the city where a crowd of citizens had gathered. The inn was beside the great wall around the city and globes of light had been positioned on the wall at equidistant locations. As she watched one farther up dimmed and went dark, and something made of darkness barely able to be seen emerged from it towards the next globe. An axe shot out from the darkness and struck the next globe, and where the arm that had thrown it entered the light it burst into flames and an inhuman cry carried to where she stood.

'Come on, Zahra, back to bed, or is the endurance of the great god of war too much for a mortal woman?'

'Cinder, the Life Quenchers are here and destroying the light atop the walls,' she said, turning to him then running about frantically looking for her clothes.

There was a flicker of fear on Cinder's face and then it was gone and he too began to dress. When they finished and collected their weapons, Zahra also grabbed the globe that had lit the room. 'If you see any globes, bring them with you,' she told him, and he nodded as he stalked after her.

'Time to see if these are as tough as we have been told,' he growled. 'I am sick of running.'

'We need to get word to Aeon and the others to make sure they are safe,' Zahra called back to Cinder as they ran out of the inn where people milled about in confusion.

'Get what globes you can, the attackers hate the light,' Cinder yelled at them. He repeated it until he saw they began to follow his instructions then turned to Zahra.

'Go to the castle and get whoever is willing to fight, then stay with Ishmael. I will do what I can to organize the people here and the defence.' Then he ran towards the gate, calling for the people to come to him.

Zahra set off at a run. They should never have wasted time here with Melde, and now it had cost them what precious advantage they had over the Life Quenchers. Zahra got to the castle in time to see a procession of Melde's warriors marching down into the city holding globes and lit torches. Among them were the gods, and she spotted Aeon with Ishmael and gave a sigh of relief. At their head was Melde, and the god looked wild and angry. He carried a large pick axe in one hand and a burning torch in the other as he led his warriors.

'Cinder is at the gate organizing what defence he can, the globes on the walls are being destroyed,' she called out to Melde as she passed, and he acknowledged her with a nod and set off at a run.

Within a chime the wave of darkness descending on the gates to the city had been halted with a wall of fire and crystal. At various locations where buildings sat close to the wall they were also well lit and guarded by groups of the city folk. Zahra couldn't help but be impressed with Melde's people. They may have been blind, but even then they were well drilled and ready to fight for their home. They coordinated well and followed orders to the letter, which in Zahra's experience was rare.

It was difficult to get a sense of these Life Quenchers. They literally hovered at the edge of the darkness and occasionally would strike at the barrier of light where it was the weakest. Luckily there were many defenders to man the whole city wall, and the gates were defended with a heavy force should they attempt to attack there.

Melde seemed to be everywhere, giving words of praise and advice to his people who seemed to have forgotten the lie of his loss of powers, and it had not seemed to damage his leadership of them. One thing was obvious, they would die for him and their home. The complete and well-organized defence then was caught off guard when the next attack came at the least defended location, the side gates that led to the fields.

As Zahra returned to help Cinder a warning call rang out, and from where Zahra saw a wedge of darkness break away from the shadows and storm forwards into the light. The front ranks of shadowy, man-like figures with tendrils of ropey darkness snaking out from their robes caught fire, and the keening that came from them was deafening.

The defenders braced themselves with lit torches and prepared flaming missiles and flasks of oil, but the attackers had one thing in mind, to destroy the light. They threw themselves forward in a frenzy and swarmed onto the gates, pulling themselves up with tendrils of darkness then hurling their bodies down over globes or on top of the fires to quench them. The problem with the gates as the defenders found out was that they were heavily draped with animal hides to repel any fire attacks, and this only helped the attackers as flames died quickly from the defenders lit oil flaks.

Soon the gates were breached and the darkness was swarming towards the defenders. Moonbite glowed brightly, and Zahra met the darkness with vicious slashes as beside her Cinder began singing while wielding two burning staves. Zahra sliced away a tendril of darkness that reached for her and her foe shrank back. Her next strike split the creature in two as beside her one of the diamond-eyed warriors crumpled to a smoking husk as a dark warrior simply embraced him. Zahra cut the killer down and noticed the attacks of these dark warriors drained the life from the victims and made themselves stronger.

At the call from Melde the front line defenders, of which Zahra was a part retreated quickly, and the line behind them threw down a line of flaming oil, giving themselves a momentary reprieve as the next line walked forward, all pushing flaming carts and wagons that drove the enemy back and over the gates. The first assault had been repelled, but though the defenders had counted minimal losses in men they had lost three score of globes. How long would the supply of the valuable lights last if these attacks kept coming?

Zahra could see Melde was in urgent council with Aeon and Cinder and moved closer to listen.

'We need to plan our escape, Melde. Your defences are admirable, but without an extensive supply of globes we can only hold out for another three or four days at the most, and we cannot ascertain how large a force the LIfe Quenchers have since they appear only as a wave of darkness,' Aeon said, waving his arms around.

'You would have me abandon my people and our home?'

'Aeon is right, Melde, if we stay we all die. If we fight an organized retreat then your people and you can go with us,' pleaded Cinder.

'My home is here in this city, and it is where I always wanted to end my days. I have no wish to go to the surface and return to the Mother, who I fear will never forgive me for the death of Kane.'

'The Mother will forgive all who return to her, Melde, you are still one of her children, 'Aeon said. 'The rest of us gods and Ishmael must leave this place before we become trapped here. You mentioned a route into the Jewelled Lands.'

'You go with the other gods and Ishmael to get them to safety, but I must stay here and defend your retreat. This is what I must to do fix my transgressions against you all. I know that now.'

'This is madness. You don't have to die for us Melde, we need you with us.'

'No, Aeon all I have brought my kin is trouble, and who better to see the retreat than me. I know this world down here and have planned for the event of escape through the Jewelled Lands with traps which I can set off to ensure you get to safety, but that can only happen if someone stays to see that done, and that someone must be me. Allow me this final request, old friend,' Melde said, putting a hand on Aeon's shoulder.

Chapter 30

Zacriel rubbed his throbbing temples, withdrew the large iron key from his belt and locked the doors to his royal bed chamber. He usually left it unlocked, but Rapture insisted that he needed to be able to protect his lord, otherwise what use was it having a bodyguard at all.

The headache had been raging form the better part of the day, and the meeting with the other three Infernal lords hadn't gone as well as Zacriel would have liked. Thanks to Lilith and the Unseeing lord, Zacriel now had another two hostages to worry about along with Prince Grego. He realized now he had been duped not just by Quail, but also the other two lords who without his consent or agreement had taken it upon themselves to all return to Acclaro, each with a valuable hostage. The Unseeing lord had returned with the wife of the king of Scuttle, while Lilith had arrived with the youngest and yet most influential of the five council members of Culchar.

It now seemed also probable to Zacriel that Quail had abandoned Wilhelm's Point before the combined forces of the southern nations even attacked it. This would mean Quail had actually sent a force to capture the prince of Soarnestia. Was this deception planned? Or maybe he was just becoming more paranoid now he was caught up in the other three Infernal lords machinations.

Now it was not one, but two nations, and the council member of arguably the most powerful merchant city that wanted his head on a pike. Zacriel would have been content to let the nations lay siege to Acclaro, and hold out until such time as he had the coterie in his grasp, or that magic had been returned.

Zacriel lay back on the ridiculously large royal bed and chuckled to himself. Without any work from himself his reputation as one of the most feared beings on this world was growing. He had been shocked at how the Lady of Whispers had died so easily and hadn't thought too hard about the consequences of taking her place at the time. Now things were spiralling out of control and the other Infernal lords who, curse their blackened souls, were intent on causing as much destruction as possible while dragging him down with them. Zacriel knew it. He was marked for death and it would be only a matter of time before his enemies would strike to attempt to remove him from power. Zacriel wasn't sure who to fear most, his allies in the Infernal lords or the nations whom would be seeking vengeance for the wrongs he had caused them. Zacriel began to doze. He would rest and tackle the problem of these hostages once his mind was clear.

Even the possibility of a restful sleep seemed denied Zacriel, as he found himself caught in a dream that he had played out many times in his life. It was a dream that had only ever ended up with him awakening as a screaming mess that left him sobbing for a loss he could never remember. This time the dream felt different. He was aware of his sleeping body as well as that of his dreaming body. As the dream coalesced into reality around him, Zacriel found himself once again in that valley amongst the tents of the enemy Celestials.

It was just days before the Severing had changed the world forever, and like so many times before Zacriel crouched in the long shadows of the twisted trees, as all around him the war bands of the Celestial forces celebrated their latest victory over the Infernals.

He waited there in the cold, wet leaves that gathered at the feet of the twisted trees, motionless while lumo ants the size of apples scurried around him. The stripes of luminescent white on their thoraxes made Zacriel dizzy as he concentrated on them in order to pass the time while he waited for the opportunity to strike. He had chosen his location well, and was only a leap away from the tent where the Celestial leader was debriefing her officers and complimenting them on their bravery. From where he lay Zacriel had seen the doubling of the guards around the large camp and smiled grimly at his decision to infiltrate the enemy camp while they were out fighting. He had easily moved past the few guards left to protect it. Let them think they were smarter, let them think they had won. Soon they would know how wrong they had been with their premature celebrations.

Zacriel felt the stirring awareness of his dreaming body as footsteps came closer. A Celestial moved to the edge of the undergrowth, mere steps away from Zacriel's position. The guard's bright eyes looked over him, then away again as he drank a long swallow of wine. The guard stoppered the wine then placed it by his feet, before unlacing his trousers and beginning to piss, right on the spot where Zacriel lay. Zacriel surged upwards, exploding from the leaves and into the Celestial who fell back in surprise.

The strike of Zacriel's hand axe struck the Celestial in the side of the head and he crumpled at Zacriel's feet. Zacriel rolled the Celestial over, momentarily admiring the white, feathered wings. He grasped one in his hand and raised the axe, preparing to rip it from the host when a shadow from within the tent distracted him as the tent interior filled with light. He could make out the war leader's form as she unfurled her great wings and her clothing fell away from her form. He released the wing from his grip, and ignoring the unconscious Celestial at his feet, Zacriel stepped towards the tent.

He was so fixated on the scene unfolding within the tent that he let the axe slip from his hands. The axe fell onto his unprotected foot, breaking the bewitching magic of the Celestial war leader. Forcing down his cry of pain, Zacriel inspected his foot. It wasn't broken, only bruised. He allowed his natural power to rise up through him, knowing that the camouflage it gave him would allow him to appear as a part of the tent to any who watched. Then he moved silently around the circumference of the tent weaving in and out of the ropes and wooden stakes until he stood by the door where a second Celestial sat eating. It noticed Zacriel a moment too late. Zacriel reached down, cupped its head with his hands and began twisting the life from it until with a dry crack its neck broke. He caught the body before it fell, and pulled it with him into the tents interior, allowing the tent opening to fall shut behind him.

'Raheem, did you bring the scented water? I feel the need to wash the death from my skin, and long to be freed from the ghosts of this horrific battle before I take my rest.'

Zacriel lay the dead guards body on the woven carpet and drew his knife. Before him with her back to him was, Alysia, the Celestial leader. She had one long wing with azure and white feathers pulled back to one side while she examined the bloodied feathers there. The other wing was fully extended to the side showing long, braided copper hair spilling down over golden-brown skin down to curved buttocks that rested on her heels. Zacriel shook his head refusing to be bewitched by the beauty of his enemy. He had come here to kill her and tear the heart out of the Celestial force, and in his mind he heard the clamouring of devilish voices promising him his reward should he succeed in this most unholy task they had set him.

Caught in the dream, Zacriel stepped forward to begin the slaughter, and found Nina standing between him and his target staring up at him defiantly. Her kind eyes called to him to put down the axe, and deny the evil flowing through him that wished to destroy this fantastic being before him. He shook his head as Nina's words rang through his mind. 'Don't do this. You are better than this and you have a choice. Remember that.'

Zacriel felt the anger in him as he attempted to push Nina aside. He had to finish this otherwise he would never ascend to his destiny.

'Halt. Go no further!' Nina's words stopped him where he stood. He screamed at her to move, but his words had no effect on Nina as slowly behind her, Alysia turned sea-blue eyes upon him. Zacriel knew he had failed. He fell to the ground and wept as small arms wrapped around him.

The voices within him rallied, turning poisonous as they whispered the terrors they would unleash on his soul now he had failed them, like he had everyone of importance in his life. Zacriel howled and struck out, and as suddenly as they had begun the voices vanished. When Zacriel opened his eyes, Nina lay broken at his feet, and the Celestial leader stood wings extended triumphantly looking back at him in judgement.

With a cry, Zacriel awoke to his real body and the darkness of the royal chamber. It had been a chime afternoon when he lay down, and now he could see the sun setting from the open window to his side. Open window? The thought had him on his feet in a moment, he couldn't recall opening it. Zacriel slammed it shut then slid down the wall with his head on his hands, and that's as when he felt Nina's presence again. He looked around, bewildered at how this could be, and finally he sat back relaxing into the calm that had come over him. Somehow, Nina had helped him.

Chapter 31

The next morning, tired and afraid Nina shrank away as the cell was unlocked by flame warriors who removed them one at a time with no trouble. There was no use fighting while so outnumbered. They were marched out to the front of the fortress where three of the fearsome Limpids hung floating just off the ground with large baskets held tightly in their tentacles. They were loaded into one of the baskets and had their arms tied to metal rings built into the tough wicker. Three guards climbed in beside the prisoners, and they were made to wait for a long time until Dalwyn finally emerged from the stronghold looking smug and in high spirits. Nina now knew that the man with him was his brother who had come to his aid with these terrifying creatures. Soon they were rising slowly high up above the stronghold where two bodies still lay motionless on the unfinished roof top.

As they rose higher and higher, Nina thought ahead with dread at returning to Acclaro and what waited there. Zacriel was there, which was okay, she thought, but what evil plans did Dalwyn still have in store for them all was something that made her tremble with fear and dig in tightly to the side of Latasha, who stood staring down at the stronghold long after it had dwindled away.

They shared the skies with the birds for close to a day before Nina realized they were descending. She had fallen asleep behind the legs of Latasha, and as she looked up Latasha smiled and lifted Nina to her feet.

'Where are we?' Nina asked.

'It looks like we are heading to that castle, called the Witness,' Latasha replied in a low voice as one of the flame warriors glared at her.

'I thought Dalwyn said we were going to Acclaro,' replied Nina over a yawn.

'Even the Limpids must rest, Nina, and I imagine the soldiers will also need rest before they go to the capital, which is under siege now by the other nations.'

'Do you think that when you help bring magic back that the war will end? I don't understand it because nearly everyone I know, even Dalwyn, wants magic to come back, but they still all want to kill each other. Why is it like this, Latasha?'

Latasha stroked Nina's hair. 'You are wise beyond your cycles, Nina, but not everyone is as clever as you. Sometimes people want to be the ones in charge and have the power over others. People get greedy or jealous of what others have and they make their decisions based on fear, not love.'

'Will things change once the magic comes back?'

'I sure hope so, Nina. This why we are doing this, so the world can once again be in harmony and all can flourish, not just the few who would take it for themselves.'

They descended down past huge stone towers though not as big as Acclaro castle Nina noticed, and the figures far below in a courtyard slowly transformed from ants to people. A flag with a red moon from which a teardrop fell fluttered in the wind from one of the towers, and Nina knew that flag to be one of the red moon Tamul.

As they were unloaded from the baskets, Nina saw Dalwyn walk over and embrace a man of his own age who was bald and had a short, trimmed snowy beard.

'Virgil, it is a good thing you made it and took the Witness,' he said after the embrace.

'Well I could hardly stay in Culchar after you set it to the torch, Dalwyn. You ruined my inn,' the other man accused but was smiling as he said it.

'All for a good cause, my friend. Tamul will reward you for your loss with eternal life, and that time grows near.'

'That is good, Dalwyn, because the Jester watches my every move, I swear I fear if that day doesn't come soon I will not be here to witness the new age.'

'Well, are yoi going to keep us waiting here in the wind much longer, Virgil? I would welcome hot food and wine, as would my men.'

'Yes, of course, come along then. Are these the coterie then?' Virgil asked, nodding at Nina and the other prisoners.

'Three of them are, and the Ancient is one of the sorcerers who created the Severing. It is imperative that they are kept under heavy guard at all times and my men will see to that once they are in the dungeons.'

'And the child, who is she?'

'A tool, to keep in check a reluctant ally in Acclaro. Now lead on, I tire of conversation.'

Warriors wearing the symbol of Tamul placed Nina and the others in the dungeon, which was cold and of course stone like every dungeon she had ever seen. The stone was damp in places, and more than once Nina was startled by rats who maybe were annoyed at these people who now invaded their home. The only good thing that happened was that they were given real meat to eat with a cold broth and stale bread, but Nina tucked into it and even licked the plate clean. She shared a jug of water with the others and then leaned against Latasha as she tried to fall asleep.

After tossing and turning for ages she gave up on sleep and sat up. Jona, Selene, and Raul had been more successful than she had and lay quietly. Only Latasha was awake, and her eyes shone in the darkness like a cat's sometimes did.

'How long have you been travelling the astral?' Latasha asked Nina as she grasped Nina's hands lightly.

'Maybe two or three months while I was a prisoner in Acclaro. Dalwyn was studying the astral and I tricked him into believing I couldn't read, then I would sneak a book away and study it.'

'It's a dangerous thing, the astral world, and you could have been seriously hurt or killed,' chided Latasha.

'I know, but I had so much time, and being trapped in a prison is so boring even if it's really nice there. It was a way for me to escape. I was even attacked by an astral entity that Dalwyn sent to kill me, but the twins protected me and scared it away,' Nina said. She stopped when she saw Latasha's smile fade away. 'Sorry, I didn't mean to make you sad.'

'It's okay, child.'

'Do you think Haakon or the twins survived?'

'Haakon is dead and one of the twins for sure, though I know not which one. The other may have escaped but died of his wounds, I can't be sure.' Latasha changed the subject.

'How many of the vortices did you manage to travel through?'

'The first two usually, although once I had the golden astral river in sight but then was sent back to my body. I also learned to use the astral in the real world and move around the castle, but Raul who I didn't know then, saw me and trapped me in a room then Dalwyn came and got me and took me away with him.'

Latasha looked surprised at Nina's words. 'Almost getting to the river without any formal training is a great feat, Nina, well done.'

'Do you use the astral as well, Latasha?'

'Yes, I have used the astral for many cycles' It was one of my duties to access the memories of times past and record important events to help my people but that was before the Severing.

Would you like to travel with me?' Latasha asked.

'What? Now, you and me?'

Yes, child, we can go together, and I will help you. Can you meditate?'

'Oh yes, I can, and it's easy too.'

'Well, begin meditating and allow yourself to enter the astral. I will be waiting for you there.'

'Nina lay down with the thoughts of adventure in her mind, and for a while the deaths of the twins and Haakon were gone as well as the seriousness of their situation.

When she entered the astral she looked at the three friends sleeping and their auras lit their forms, then she turned to see Latasha standing there glowing brightly like an angel; she looked beautiful. Latasha approached her and slapped Nina on the back just below the neck not on the flesh but the energy field that surrounded Nina. The slap made Nina's vision waver, and then she looked over her shoulder and could see an area that bled amber light. A stream of light flowed from Latasha's navel, and when it touched the amber hole it seemed to merge and Nina felt different, stronger and clearer than she had ever felt in the astral world.

'What did you just do?' she asked Latasha.

'That point over your shoulder is called the assemblage point, and it is that which allows us to travel to times far in the past. Are you ready?'

Nina nodded. She felt excited and also nervous, but she trusted Latasha. If Haakon had trusted these people, then she knew it was okay to do so as well.

They shot through the first two vortices at high speed, which took Nina's breath away, and soon the golden river beckoned before them. They dived right into the river that washed over them in streams of gold. Latasha wrapped her arms around Nina and laughed aloud at Nina's screams of delight.

All knowledge of time disappeared, and then they emerged into a world tinted by soft purple and began floating down towards a beach and an ocean on the coast. They softly landed on the sand, which showed no footprints when the two of them walked.

Latasha took Nina by the hand and walked close to the water where small boats could be seen casting fishing nets, the sound of singing carried to them as the fishermen sang to the god Auril for a good catch. Up ahead a woman in long skirts stood walking through the rocks near the water's edge with a basket, the wind tossing her long, auburn hair into a mess about her head. She knelt and retrieved something from a shallow pool and placed it in her basket. *They must be clams*, Nina thought as they got closer. Nina could see where the water had wet the woman's skirts and how she shivered as she searched. Nina caught a glance at the pretty face of the woman, and her nose was red from the cold but she was smiling.

A cry came from the water and the woman looked up at the disturbance. Nina followed her gaze to a fishing boat that rocked violently, and then the man standing at the front of the small vessel fell with his arms pin-wheeling into the water. As he fell he hit his head on the boat edge. The woman gasped and put down the basket then hurriedly began to untie her skirts, which fell to the rocks, then she hurried into the water and swam towards the boat. She was a strong swimmer and moved through the water with ease. Nina glanced up at Latasha, who indicated she should keep watching.

The swimmer got to the floundering man who, kept dipping under the surface as shouts of alarm came from other fishermen. Then he was in the arms of the swimmer, who held an arm around his chest and began slowly dragging the man back to shore. She was strong and pulled the man from the water as he coughed up sea water, then she collapsed beside him, chest heaving with exertion, and Nina was full of admiration for her.

After the man finished choking up water and sat up, he looked at his rescuer and laughed then fell to coughing again.

'What is so funny, you fool? You nearly died and killed me too!' she exclaimed angrily.

'I'm sorry, and I'm very grateful for your help, but you seem to have lost your pants,' he replied as water dripped down his face from dark hair.

The woman squealed and covered herself with her hands, then looking about she spied her basket and skirts and clambered over to them, quickly pulling them on. From behind her the man called out, 'Nice ass by the way,' and she shot him a venomous look.

'I save your life and all you can do is look at my ass?'

'Sorry, I truly am, but I couldn't help but notice. I am Darun by the way. What is your name?'

The woman ignored this question, gathered her basket and began making her way back over the rocks towards the city there. Then she turned and shouted back, 'I am Jeanne.' With a fleeting smile then hurried off.

Nina's mouth fell open as she realized she knew these two names, they were those of her parents. She looked up at Latasha in wonder, and then the two of them were being pulled back up towards the golden river and once again it washed over them.

The next time they exited the river they floated down into a city where it was night and lanterns lit the city with glowing points like stars. In a garden below where trees were adorned with crystals and lanterns, children danced, men and women mingled, and a feast was under way. Nina saw her mother, dressed in a gown of green and gold, her favorite colours, surrounded by women talking excitedly and shooting glances at a group of men who gathered around her father, who wore a smart suit, looking handsome as a prince. A new, slower song began playing from the musicians, and Nina's mother and father were pushed into the middle of a circle of onlookers who clapped their hands and cheered. Her parents danced, and the loving looks they gave each other brought tears to Nina's eyes. They were both so beautiful.

They watched the celebrations for a while and then Latasha took Nina's hand and they sped back to the river once more. 'One more place to go, then we return to our bodies,' she told Nina in a voice that was only heard in Nina's mind.

They floated down into a house where Nina's father paced up and down a hallway looking anxious. He stopped and drank from a mug, spilling ruby contents down his chin, and wiped it away with his sleeve. A cry came from the top of a staircase, and he stopped at the bottom, staring up.

'What's happening up there?' Nina turned and asked Latasha.

'Go and look, Nina. You can just walk through walls and doors in this realm.'

Nina started up the long staircase, stepping past her father who didn't even notice her, and then stood before the door at the top, and then she stepped through.

Her mother was on a bed, one woman behind her supporting her upper body and another wiping her sweat lathered forehead with a cloth. A lady knelt between her mother's legs, and Nina could see blood on her hands and staining the blankets beneath her mother's backside. Her mother was breathing hard, gulping at air, and she gritted her teeth and snarled out a growl like scream.

'Nearly there, Jeanne, just one more push, I can see the head,' the woman who knelt between her mother's legs said.

Her mother strained and screamed, then the woman before her laughed and held aloft a baby, which was turned and slapped a few times on the back, which made it start wailing as it was wrapped in a blanket. Her mother lay back panting, but her face was alive with wonder, and she began calling her father's name.

He came through the door at a rush.

'Is it done?' Then he saw the child and began crying. A lady used a knife to cut something that still held it connected with her mother, and then the baby was passed to the father.

'Oh, Jeanne she is beautiful.'

'Do you have a name prepared for the little one?' asked one of the ladies as she wiped blood from her hands.

From the bed a weak voice said, 'her name is to be Nina, after Ninaretus the star watcher.'

Nina was so caught up in the moment that she only just then realized the baby was her and she had seen her own birth. Nina watched her parents embrace and giggle over the child and felt the happiness of them radiate through her.

Latasha took her hand and spoke into her mind. 'It's time to go, Nina.' and then soft warm arms wrapped around Nina from behind and they both floated up slowly through the roof and sky towards the shimmering river and their resting bodies.

Chapter 32

Zacriel looked on in disbelief. Twelve days ago he had flown with Rapture and seen for the first time the march of the Harlequin. The strange race had turned to liquid crystal and flowed down the Winding River then down Jingtalla falls before reverting to their own forms on land and marching towards Acclaro. Now Zacriel stood less than a day's ride to the capital watching the mass of Harlequin marching in perfect unison. They moved slowly and relentlessly onwards without the need for food, water, or sleep. The last thing Zacriel wished to do was approach the Harlequin, but in less than a day they would come upon the first encampments of Zacriel's army, and he intended there to be no blood shed before finding out the motives of these enigmatic creatures.

Zacriel kicked the side of his cular mount and its head whipped to the side to regard him with a large eye, then it hissed and started forward towards the Harlequin force. From behind him came a questioning call from Rapture which Zacriel ignored. Rapture would follow him, he could count on that at least. He wheeled the giant lizard mount and came in alongside one of the Harlequin near the front of their force causing the nearest of the strange warriors to fall into combat stances with their crystal weapons readily aimed at this intruder. Once again, against the advice of Rapture, Zacriel dismounted, then he approached the darkest of the Harlequin near him. The deep purple warrior followed Zacriel's every move intently.

As a show of peace Zacriel kept his hands in the air to show he was unarmed, then he stepped forward and closed the gap between him and the purple Harlequin. Even more swiftly than he had expected he was intercepted by two warriors whose blades were at his throat before he could utter a word or make a move towards his own weapons.

'I have come to speak with your leader,' said Zacriel, noticing his voice communicated his uncertainty in this matter.

'The purple warrior regarded him through eyes dark enough to be obsidian, and just when he had decided the Harlequin would refuse to answer his question it spoke to him.

'Any attempt to interfere with our march will be met with force. We owe you no explanation for our actions,' said the Harlequin in a toneless voice.

'This is true, and yet in less than a day's march you will encounter my forces camped around the city of Acclaro. We are not your enemy. I wish to merely avoid any conflict by ascertaining the reason for your foray through Thantosian lands.

'You talk as if you are king of these lands and yet before me all I see is one of the cursed. Our destination is close to this city of yours, but no closer. We have our purpose to fulfil for the Mother, that is all. Leave us to do what we must without interference.'

'You will be among the site of the siege of the city if you continue onwards. Already forces of Cavere, Scuttle and from Culchar are gathering at their borders ready to march this way,' replied Zacriel trying to dissuade the Harlequin from their destination.

The Harlequin regarded Zacriel silently while its brethren stood motionless, ready to act and chop him to pieces if he made a wrong movement.

'We have no interest in the petty squabbles of your nations, and aim only to fulfil our purpose given to us from the Mother.'

'Yes okay you have said that already, but what is this purpose?' asked Zacriel growing impatient.

'That is something I cannot tell you. If you value the lives of yourself and this army you talk of then it is imperative that you leave us to our task.'

Zacriel rubbed at the stiffness of his neck and swatted away an irritating fly that kept landing where his nose once was. 'I want answers, not threats. If you can't tell me the reason for…,' before he could continue he was being dragged back away from the bristling Harlequin warriors by Rapture.

'Let go of me, you swine, is this how you treat your lord?' shrieked Zacriel as he tore himself out of Rapture's grasp once they were a safe distance away.

'I am your general, Zacriel, my duty is to keep you alive. If you intend on having a tantrum like some little child as well as threatening Harlequin warriors, then I will be forced to stop you.'

They stayed there watching the Harlequin march past while Zacriel composed himself once again with Rapture standing silently by his side. Zacriel knew he didn't need to apologize or explain himself, and yet he spoke anyway. 'We need to know exactly what they up to and whether we trust them, said Zacriel.

'Nobody can trust the Harlequin, for nobody knows what they are all about. This is the first time in history that they have left the Jewelled Lands, and I fail to see how we can stop them.'

'No, we don't do anything. Whatever they have planned near Acclaro may well buy us some time. Scuttle, Cavere and Culchar, like us will have no idea what the Harlequin are doing here, and we can use that confusion against them to at least buy more time in preparing for the upcoming battle.

At sunset of the following day which was the beginning of the winter month Iktah, Zacriel stood once again alongside Rapture looking on at the Harlequin force now just out of range of the siege catapults within Acclaro. Zacriel knew this because days earlier they had tested the firing distances of the catapults. Was this mere coincidence or did the Harlequin know more than anyone really knew? The Harlequin warriors that had apparently reached their destination set up a circular perimeter facing outwards. They stood silently as those following moved into their center, and so the mass of Harlequin grew. A group of young Infernals broke from the rank to Zacriel's left where a force from The Unseeing Lord was located. They hooted and screamed as they ran towards the Harlequin warriors with their morning stars and slingshots.

'Damn them! Cant the other lord's even control their own fodder?' grunted Rapture as he started forwards after them. Zacriel stopped him before he could go any further. 'Leave them, I want to see what happens when they attack the Harlequin,' he said with a grin. 'This last few days has been sorely lacking any real entertainment.

The Infernals charged the Harlequin and those with slingshots fired their projectiles which struck the crystal warriors before bouncing off. Now the ones with morning stars moved forward, egged on by the assembled Infernal army with war cries and by smashing weapons against their iron shields. The lack of action from the Harlequin goaded the Infernals to close within combat distance, and the retaliation of the Harlequin was brutal, and swift. Harlequin warriors burst into movement and skilfully danced through their opponent's formation, cutting them down like one would grass. Within a few breaths they were dead, and the Harlequin had stepped back into their original positions as insults rang out from the Infernal force.

'Send the word to all officers. Nobody else is to attack, the Harlequin are not here to fight us, and we cannot affords to weaken our armies with senseless slaughter.

Ishmael was eating a well-deserved meal when Melde found him. He began to rise at the god's approach who waved at him to stay where he was.

'I know it's much too late, but I apologize for the way I have treated you here in my home. I just wanted to thank you for showing me the truth of things before you leave.'

'So you haven't changed your mind then?' Ishmael asked, putting down his food.

'No, this is my home I will stay here and die if I must.'

'Then we have failed here. Even if just one of you is left behind it deceases the chances of making the world a better place when the Mother brings back the magic,' he said, trying to smile at the sadness he felt for Melde.

'Someone must stay to activate the traps that will allow you safe passage, and then I and my people will fight for our homes. If I survive, then I will come to find you.' Melde shrugged.

'You won't survive this, Melde. The Life Quenchers are too strong; even though they fear the light, you saw them attack anyway. They grow bold, and for any of us to survive will be a miracle.'

'One that you must make sure happens then, Ishmael,' Melde said grasping Ishmael's shoulders. 'Don't let our sacrifice be for nothing!'

The next attack came soon after as a street of houses parallel to an outside wall suddenly fell into darkness. 'Ishmael, with me,' Melde yelled, and they both set off with a group of warriors. The gods were resting in readiness at the castle, and Ishmael hadn't seen Zahra, who would most likely be in bed with Cinder. Ishmael grinned at the thought despite the tense situation he was in.

From within the dark houses, bloodcurdling screams rang out and husks of bodies lay littered in the street.

Ishmael took five warriors and ran into the first house. He had promised Aeon and Zahra he would stay out of danger, but it was too late for that. The home was two stories and small with a kitchen and entry hall on the bottom and presumably the bedrooms upstairs, which was accessed also from the hall. First they entered the kitchen where a pot of food had been overturned and the smoking body of an adult lay beside it.

Ishmael took a torch from the warrior beside him and held it up for better light. The shadows retreated and something scrambled away from them with a hiss. A tendril of darkness snaked out at his throat, it missed and slapped around at his chest, he held the torch to it, making it retract, but as it went it tore the torch from his hands. If it wasn't for the warrior stepping forward at that moment and swinging his sword, Ishmael knew he might have died then. The warrior fell instead as the Life Quencher grasped him, giving Ishmael scant moments to do something.

Somehow he got the earth crystal out of his side bag at his hip and it flared; its intense light struck the Life Quencher, and it imploded leaving Ishmael alone. With trembling hands he steadied himself and followed the other four warriors upstairs.

The enemy upstairs didn't wait for them to reach the top. One careened into the top warrior, shrieking, and he fell back off balance knocking all four of them back down the stairs. Ishmael was the last on the stairs and was knocked the farthest back as the earth crystal spun out of his hands and landed on the floor four feet away. Two of the warriors collapsed as the darkness claimed them, and the third was partially inside the safety of the light from the crystal beside Ishmael.

Ishmael sprang and snatched the crystal up, raising it above him, but before he could pull the warrior into its glow a mottled brown hand dragged him away into the darkness where Ishmael could hear a brief scuffle, and then it went silent. Ishmael scrabbled backwards and snatched up the crystal, holding it in front of him warily. From the shadows he heard soft voices that promised madness; one whispered. *'It's him, the crystal bearer, he is here.'* Ishmael stood and thrust the globe forward, making the darkness retreat. 'Stay back,' he shouted at the voices still babbling beyond his sight, and then in a moment of madness Ishmael rushed forward.

For a brief moment the light illuminated three of the Life Quenchers where they squatted with dark tendrils waving around their upper bodies, and Ishmael saw the tendrils actually were part of the cloaks themselves. Beneath the cloaks the Life Quenchers skin was pale with spiral primitive tattoos and necklaces of dark stone hung around their necks. As Ishmael rushed forward their mouths opened to reveal multiple rows of teeth before they burst into flame and writhed around on the floor.

The upstairs was still unsearched, but Ishmael swivelled to the entrance as he heard a noise from above. He crept upstairs as slowly as possible, moving the crystal in an arc before his body to be sure the whole area was illuminated. There were three pallets on the floor and storage areas filled with clothes and household items. Something moved where the clothes were, which were heaped in a corner, and Ishmael spotted what looked like a leg.

'Hello? It's okay to come out now, they are gone and I can take you to Melde so you are safe.'

There came a whimper from the clothes as Ishmael approached and set down the crystal then he slowly pushed some of the clothes away. A woman and small child shrank away from him.

'Easy, I am a friend, one of the guests that arrived yesterday,' Ishmael explained in a calm voice, and slowly the woman sat up, clutching the child to her chest protectively.

'My husband was downstairs,' she began then trailed off.

'I am sorry, but he is dead. We must go and get you both to safety. Is there anything you need from here?'

The woman shook her head no and Ishmael led the two of them out of the house while bathed in the crystal's light. Outside, warriors were placing many globes around the houses, and the wall that stood behind them was now safely bathed in light again. The mother and child were whisked away to the safety of the castle, and Ishmael went with the warriors farther down the street, which still stood silent and foreboding.

The darkness came to them as Life Quenchers flowed out of it, erupting into flames but advancing rapidly and gaining the element of surprise on the advancing soldiers. The wall of darkness before Ishmael was clamouring with enemies as hundreds of the deadly tendrils snaked out to knock away torches and weapons or drag men back into their roiling depths.

The call went out for reinforcements and Melde's people began to arrive with fresh torches, forming a wall of light. The attack continued, however, and was aimed at the centre of the defenders where Ishmael stood with the earth crystal. As the enemy died in waves, more clambered over their burning bodies, relentlessly pushing on. Many defenders fell in that attack. They were targeting him, realized Ishmael. The Life Quenchers in the house had seemed surprised to know he was there, and that meant they had been aware of him all along. The crystal simply made him a target.

He removed the sky crystal and stood there, slowly turning with both crystals raised above his head. The sky crystal began to pulse, and the crackling of energy was all around Ishmael. A wave of blue energy rolled out from them and burst upon the wall of darkness with a concussive blast that dispelled the shadows and left anything in its wake suffused with light. The whole street was now blazing brightly.

They had stopped it. Ishmael was thankful and also surprised at what he had done. He had never seen the crystals as weapons, but tonight they had become just that. He made his way back to the castle aware that being out and involved in the skirmishes breaking out around the city was too dangerous now that he had practically hung a target on himself.

Back at the castle he made his way through the crowd where most civilians had gathered until he found Aeon.

'How is it down in the city?' the god asked as he moved around, replacing nearly burnt out torches with fresh ones and coughing from the oily fumes they sent whirling around him.

'The Life Quenchers grow more desperate, and in one of the attacks I heard them whispering about me when I used the crystals to help us. The next attack seemed coordinated directly at me, as if they know my importance, and so I came back to rest and stay safe.'

'They will know about all the coterie, and it would be so much easier for them to make their plans come to fruition if you fell and the two crystals you have were lost. From now on you go nowhere alone. Now get some rest.'

Chapter 34

Nina awoke the next morning well rested and excited. She had so many questions for Latasha, and seeing those precious moments from her parent's lives had touched her deeply and given her something that nobody could ever take away. Nina resolved right then to learn how to do what Latasha had done, and she rose hurriedly and rushed over to Latasha who was sitting in a circle with Raul, Jona, and Selene.

"Latasha,' she said, tugging on the ancients robe impatiently.

'Latasha turned to her, smiling, and put a finger to her lips. 'Hush now, Nina, I am discussing an important matter and then you can have me to myself for a time, okay?'

Nina felt hurt, which made her feel even sillier because there was no reason to feel that way. She nodded and went over to the bars of the cell they were in, and one of the guards looked up from eating food to stare at her so she poked out her tongue at him and then she sat down and tried to remember every little thing that she had seen in the astral last night while she waited for Latasha.

Finally Latasha finished and turned her attention to Nina.

'Why did you take me and show me those things, Latasha?'

'To give you hope, Nina, and let you learn that our memories live on especially in the astral realm, where they wait to be experienced or accessed for information if you know how to get to them.'

'So I can learn how to do that too then?'

'Yes, you can. It's not easy though, and you need to master the first four vortices otherwise it's too dangerous. You are a very special girl, Nina, and have something very important to do in the future. The astral world will have a big part in that life if you so choose it,' Latasha said, looking very serious.

'What do I have to do?' Nina asked excitedly.

'You need to make yourself strong, Nina, like you have done already. There are a series of practices that will allow you more control in the astral and reinforce your energy vortices. And you must meet the Mother, who is very important, but you know of her already.'

'Will you be there with me?'

'This meeting between the two of alone not for me.'

Nina nodded and must have looked scared, because Latasha laughed and ruffled her hair. 'You have nothing to fear from the, Mother, Nina. Now come on stand up I have a dance to show you.'

'Really?' said Nina getting up and smiling even more as Jona hurried over and joined in while Selene and Raul watched smiling.

'These movements are the basic ones for the vortices, and you must do them in the morning and before sleep every day, whenever possible, Nina,' Latasha explained. They stepped through the dance slowly at first, and then faster as Nina began to learn the movements.

Later they all dozed except Raul, who was feeling restless, and he placed himself in the corner closest to the guards in the hope of hearing something that they could use to gain a better sense of their situation.

When the guards brought them food consisting of pears and buttered bread, Raul shared what he had learned.

'We are staying in the Witness for another day while scouts return. The armies down on the Glyph have encircled the capital, and the siege is under way. A great tower is being built close to Acclaro by the Harlequin, but nobody is sure what it's for since they attack anyone who goes to close. Virgil, the leader of those who wear the red

Tamul insignia, is worried that Soarnestian raven warriors will attack them when the Limpids attempt to land in Acclaro. There is another rumour that the Bone Lord, who I presume is Zacriel, has captured the prince of Soarnestia, which has the militant nation in an uproar.'

Latasha put down her food and motioned for them all to gather close. 'Since we are here another night, then we will use that to see for ourselves what is going on down on the Glyph. Rest as much as you can today, then we will link and I will take you there. I will care for Nina once in the astral, and if anything happens then the rest of you know what to do.'

'What about you Latasha? You are still too weak for the astral,' stated Raul.

'It is necessary that I put my fear and injuries aside now, Raul. We will need every advantage we can find.'

That night once the guards had changed over and the new ones were lost in a raucous game of cards, they lay down to meditate. Nina did everything like she had learnt, but when she went to float out of her body she went nowhere and could only hover just above, nothing more. Once she gave up in frustration and worry that she would miss out on the excitement, she woke herself up and the others were talking quietly.

'What happened? I couldn't leave my body,' Nina said.

'That is because somewhere there is a protective symbol that blocks our travelling. We went into the astral last night so it must have been put here while we all slept, and I suspect it was Dalwyn. He is relatively new to the use of symbols, so it should be easy to bypass, but first we need to find it. Nobody had entered the cell except when the guards brought food, so it couldn't be in the cell,' Latasha told them.

'It may have been placed on something brought into the cell,' Raul added, and they looked at the bottom of the platter, bowls, and the jug of water they had been given. At the bottom of the jug they found the first symbol. They drank the water so not to waste it, and then Latasha cut herself on the arm and drew a new symbol over it with her blood.

'There will be more, so let's search the walls and bars,' Latasha said. They began to look everywhere. Raul used the platter, which was lacquered and had a shiny surface which he used to look at the outside of the bars. With a fist pump he turned to the rest of them smiling. 'I found it. It's on this bar here.'

Latasha hugged him then once again she smeared her own blood over the symbol in the hope it would cancel out its power since it was too difficult to complete her own.

They lay down and tried again.

'This time Nina rose effortlessly from her sleeping body to find the others waiting for her. Latasha bound Nina to her once again by the assemblage point behind her left shoulder, then they left but not the usual way to the dungeon past the guards. 'They will have further wards to stop us escaping, so we go this way through the wall.'

'There is nothing but the mountainside there, Latasha. I'm not used to this sort of travelling like the rest of you,' Jona said, and her words sounded strange and elongated as they stood there.

'I will be right beside you Jona, simply keep me in sight, and we will all make sure to watch you.'

Moving through so much stone was like moving through water but slower, and then they were out of the castle and floating away slowly down out above the mountainside. In the amber world Acclaro stood out as a red pulsing aberration in the distance surrounded by the lights of campfires, and Nina noticed in three places pulsed with white light.

'What are the white, pulsing lights?' she asked Latasha as they continued their descent.

'They are powerful beings who have considerable power in this world and are ones we may yet meet though I have masked us as best I can to keep others away lest in draw attention from the enemy.'

'Why do I hardly ever see Infernals in the astral, Latasha?'

'Their energy is unstable and draws the astral winds and other denizens, and that makes it more dangerous in this world for them. The Infernal lords will watching over the astral from Acclaro to stop any attacks from this realm. We cannot expect to walk into the capital without being seen. We are here to watch and learn what is happening. Now hush; we must form a pentacle as we get closer.'

Up until that moment Nina thought it was only herself and Latasha who were able to communicate with each other, but at her words Raul, Jona, and Selene took up position with Latasha at the point of the star and Nina to her left. To the right of them as they drifted down, a large force moved slowly through the night in complete darkness, and they angled down low enough to see banners of savage tribesmen dressed in furs. Many rode louts and covered the flanks of the force. At their head sat a large handsome man upon a real horse.

'These are tribes from Tunoka, who have also mountain tribes of the Tiriacs with them. This type of union from the tribes hasn't been seen since the Severing, and with their distrust of magic it will be interesting to see what they plan to do,' Latasha told the rest of them.

From here they could see the forces arrayed below them as the five of them slowly did a circuit. To the west a force in the yellow and blue of Culchar had placed themselves beside another enormous force of cavalry from Cavere with their fine steeds and tents. Flanking them were he arrayed armies of Scuttle, and even a force from Illume. It was once they were aiming back towards Acclaro that a great structure with five tall towers suddenly lit up the astral world around it.

'Ah, there it is,' said Latasha, and they hovered as she spoke. 'This will be where the crystals and the coterie must end up. It is Goetz the Elemental temple and will be the centre of the new world if we achieve our goal.'

'It is crystal,' Raul remarked from behind them.

'Yes, pure crystal of the Harlequin. who have melded together to form the structure and will protect it and the crystals once they are safely inside. We must continue,' Latasha warned them. 'Our remaining time is short.'

They moved off south, with Acclaro looming ahead of them. They skirted out over the edge of the Jewelled Lands where Arrowhead Lake pulsed a sickly yellow that was slowly spreading out along the adjoining rivers. To the north east, Brimmerland and Soarnestia had a combined force that stretched along the Glyph grasslands and completed the circling allied forces around the capital.

It was then that Selene on the right point of the star formation was suddenly dragged backwards screaming towards the castle of the Witness where their bodies lay.

'What's happening?' shouted Jona, and Nina felt afraid as Raul then also was dragged away at a terrifying speed.

'Go with it,' boomed Latasha's voice in Nina's head. They must have realized what we are doing and are waking us up.'

Jona shot back past Latasha and Nina, and then Nina felt herself disengage from Latasha's connection and Latasha was torn away from her, leaving Nina hovering there alone with the others fading into the distance.

'You know what to do, Nina, trust in yourself and come back to us,' were Latasha's final words as she disappeared from sight.

Chapter 35

It was two chimes of constant eating before Dalwyn even attempted to tear himself away from Virgil's gluttonous feast. 'Oh, Dalwyn, don't go,' fawned one noble's daughter who had fled the burning of Culchar with Virgil. 'We were just getting to know one another,' she added, running a finger down his chest.

'It has been a long day, my dear, and I have much to prepare before I retire for rest,' Dalwyn explained as if to a child, and by the look of this girl she could easily have been his granddaughter.

As Dalwyn ambled towards the door on unsteady feet, the girl's friend, a petite red- haired woman of considerable assets, ran over and grasping one arm each the two young women led Dalwyn back to the table and pushed him into the seat.

Opposite him Virgil was just lighting his pipe and chuckling at Dalwyn.

'These girls don't like to hear no, and are very persuasive,' Virgil said, stroking his moustaches down at the side of his mouth.

'I really shouldn't be here with so much to do and the coterie and that sorcerous ancient to watch over,' Dalwyn began but was cut off by Virgil.

'Shut up and enjoy yourself, Dalwyn. We are no longer young, so how many more times can you expect to have old friends, pretty women, and great food available together all at once? My men are very capable as are yours, so I'm very sure they will not fail us by letting the prisoners escape.' Virgil smoked his bowl and refilled it using two different blends, one a dark, black tobacco and the other a white bone colour. This he passed to the red-head who took it and sat on Virgil's knee while she inhaled it and then blew a considerable cloud of thick smoke down her body. The pipe came to the girl beside Dalwyn next after Virgil packed it tightly with only the dark tobacco.

'What is the white mix that you and red have smoked while you only offer me the other tobacco?' asked Dalwyn holding the pipe and sniffing the mixture.

Virgil raised his eyes and smiled. 'So you did notice that then? Well, the pipe has normal tobacco packed now, and the white stuff is from wraith trees, which allows...'

'Yes, yes, I know what it does. I am just curious at why you wouldn't offer any to me, your oldest friend.'

'Your brother, Grendel, bid me not to allow you any more intoxicants that would weaken your already considerably damaged health,' Virgil shrugged apologetically, ' and I quite agree, Dalwyn.'

'But you are happy to offer me wine and ale, which last time I checked were considered intoxicants?'

'Bah, don't get this all twisted about, Dalwyn, I'm just invested in you living for at least a few more cycles just like your dear brother is, that is all.'

Dalwyn could feel himself getting angry. How dare Virgil and Grendel discuss his health and then make decisions based on what they thought he should be doing. Not many men half his age could have survived what he had lived through. It had only been two days since he had last used the damn wraith powder himself back in the stronghold, and then it had been while he was already weak. Now he felt stronger and found himself keen to enter the astral world again.

The wraith would allow him whatever experience he wanted depending on the dose he decided to take. Just a pinch of the wraith on the tobacco wouldn't allow him much of a stay but enough to keep him satisfied. Nobody warned him of the addictive quality that the astral world could have over its travellers, how the wondrous voyages left you wanting more. Sure, they warned of the dangers of astral denizens or the astral storms that could come upon you suddenly, but not of how the normal world felt faded, becoming drab and devoid of life leaving you craving that next voyage. Dalwyn looked over at Virgil. 'I have used this wraith powder before, Virgil, and know my limits, now pass me some to add to the tobacco or unfortunately these two beautiful nymphs are going to be forced to witness two old men fight, and we couldn't have that, could we, old friend?'

The tobacco had been soaked in rum at some point of its cycle and the taste was to Dalwyn's liking. It cancelled out the sharp, acrid wraith powder taste that always seemed to stick in the back of his throat.

He leaned back in the comfortable chair and exhaled then opened his eyes. The wraith must have been from a mature tree, because Dalwyn's vision wavered and sparkles began to appear then pop out of existence again as he looked across at Virgil, who raised his glass of brandy in salute as he in turn watched Dalwyn.

Dalwyn began laughing. It seemed that at that moment he couldn't find any sense in anything he had been doing or planned to do. Nothing really mattered, he thought, and that simple thought caused relief and panic simultaneously to thread itself through his thoughts. Beside him the young woman draped herself over his front, and together they lay back and let the wraith roll over them.

The amount he had smoked was never going to give Dalwyn a full experience in the astral but would allow him for a brief time to enjoy the strange world. Dalwyn linked hands with his young companion and together they meandered through the castle that now had become infused with soft pulsating light that reminded Dalwyn of a great heartbeat. They raced each other up the seventy two levels of stairs fuelled by the wraith root that leant them the strength to do in moments what would take the fittest person half a chime or more to complete.

The great door that opened up to the eye that gave the Witness its name was locked and guarded as it should be, and so they floated up through it to stand within what Dalwyn had always regarded as something special. When the Witness had originally been built this crystal chamber shaped like an eye was placed at its zenith to allow sight of any danger approaching Acclaro, the capital of Thantos. Manned by someone with power, it could be used to zoom in or out in any direction and allowed the user to warn Acclaro that danger approached. With the Severing the eye became useless and would stay that way until magic returned.

Dalwyn stood at the centre, where two vertical rods of crystal slowly descended from above him. At both the rod's base was a circle of crystal that pulsed like the rest of the structure. He had never heard of this happening, although how would he since this was just the third time he had ever entered this chamber in his life and the first time while in astral form.

'I think it wants us to put them on like crowns,' the woman said, and when he looked at her she was the most beautiful thing he had ever laid eyes on, bursting with energy, vigour, and life and burning with passion that drew Dalwyn to her like the lunars to the moon.

'Put the circlet on and let's see what this is all about,' he said and they both placed their heads into the circlets so they sat like crowns on their skulls. The structure began moving about from side to side in half turns, then their sight shot forwards or back over varying distances that made Dalwyn feel disoriented and ill. He had already seen the woman with him remove her circlet, and so he did the same.

'That was scary and weird,' she said to Dalwyn. 'Let's go and find the others. Have you ever had relations when in astral form?'

Dalwyn shook his head. He now thought he knew what to do and couldn't shake the feeling he had stumbled on the answer to a question that had long ago been lost in history.

'You go and I will come find you right after I have another look through the eye. Then you can teach me all the parlour bed tricks you like, my young flower,' he crooned and happily watched her leave.

With her departure one of the circlets merged again with the structure, and Dalwyn placed the remaining circlet on. This time he focused his vision forwards, which was south at this moment, and the military town of Whitman's Point swam into view. Then Dalwyn drew the sight back out again to where he currently was and turned to face Acclaro. Zooming in was an incredible experience, and he could go close to the city and actually see down inside it at some places.

It was then by accident that Dalwyn learnt how to switch his view so he was looking back in his direction, and he wasn't really sure how he had done it. Slowly he moved the vision back towards himself in the eye, and a glowing shape caught his attention before disappearing again only to reappear moments later. His heart raced with excitement. Astral travellers or a great entity was possible. Dalwyn zoomed in carefully and was met with five familiar figures of Latasha, Nina, and the coterie. He watched their synchronized movements as they traversed the astral with ease, and Dalwyn knew he was at a disadvantage. They had a real life ancient mage who had lived hundreds of cycles and held more power in her hands than anyone since. A ghostly band of energy connected Latasha to a point in Nina's energy field. Dalwyn had read of this technique to help new travellers adjust to the astral world.

He began to feel the wraith powder wearing off, not that it mattered since he had seen quite enough. Removing the circlet, Dalwyn used the remains of the drug to return to his body, where Virgil and the two women cavorted in a tangle of limbs. While the other three were still returning to full awareness he rose and left the chamber. The time in the astral had not exhausted him as usual, and he wondered whether it was because of the wraith powder or the use of the eye that had galvanised him into action.

⚜

Chapter 36

Heading for the dungeons, Dalwyn passed startled guards who followed him wondering what the hell he was up to. When he reached the dungeon, Dalwyn had to stop and regain his breath before demanding entry. Taking a torch from a sconce, Dalwyn examined the place on the outside of the cell bars where he had placed the warding symbol, and he found it had been smeared with blood. Inside the cell he spied the clay jug in which he had added a second symbol, and this had been shattered on the stone. So this is how they had travelled.

Dalwyn snatched the cell keys from a yawning guard and opened the lock. Pick up Nina but be gentle, I don't want her to wake from the trance she is in.' They did as he told them and relocated Nina to the adjoining cell. With this done Dalwyn turned his attentions to the resting bodies before him that were totally vulnerable and at his mercy. He ached to cause them all pain, but reason overcame his lust and Dalwyn simply shook them all hard to wake them and had cold buckets of water tossed over their resting forms, which sent them sitting upright with shock.

Latasha turned a dripping face to him. 'Where is Nina? You cannot leave her alone in the astral, it's too dangerous!'

'I set the wards to stop you travelling the astral, and yet you still disobey my will, Latasha? You gave me your word to cooperate if I left Nina in your care, and this is how you repay my trust? I guess now we shall see how much Nina has learnt from her own studies,

then, won't we,' he replied slowly and slammed cell door shut behind him.

As Latasha's form vanished, Nina felt it begin. An overwhelming sense of dread fell upon her with the realization of the danger she now faced being stranded alone without a guide deep in the astral realm through a vortex that she had not mastered or even entered before.

The blood pounded in her ears, her heart thudded in her chest, and her hands shook. Nina's vision shrank as darkness closed in from the sides, but instead of succumbing to panic, Nina allowed herself to float while focusing only on her first vortices that connected Nina to the Mother. Without this connection it would be impossible for Nina to even be here. The first vortex was spinning clearly and evenly like they all were meant to, so Nina followed that link upwards through her centre to the next vortex known as the home of the self, which was coloured orange, and once again found a strong connection and a free spinning vortex. Nina continued up to the next vortex, the yellow one, which was spinning but lopsided and slower than the first two. There was no energy flow to this vortex and thus Nina now knew she was connected only to the first two vortices which created an unusual problem for her to solve.

If she had enough energy to connect to the first three vortices she could have accessed the astral river, and if she could have connected to the fourth then she could have used it direct herself within that realm where she wanted to go. But since Latasha had carried her from the second vortex without using the astral river at all, Nina had no connection to follow back to her body.

Nina could recall the warnings in some of the tomes on the astral that she had read, and one had mentioned that if stranded within the amber realm without the recommended connections to the vortices then the unlucky traveller must do as little as possible while finding a solution. To panic or waste energy thrusting about without focus would not only attract attention from astral entities but also leave Nina exhausted and stranded. Nina allowed herself to spin around slowly to get a sense of what lay in each direction. If she failed to find a way back to her body she would slowly die and become an empty shell, lost, floating on the astral plane.

It was not as easy as returning to the Witness, and the astral mirrored location of where her body was on the material plane. She needed to find a way back to the real world and then her body, which would be dangerous unless somebody from where her body lay came and pulled her out or woke her up. As the moments passed without any sign of Latasha or the coterie returning, her chances of survival were more than halved. There was another way that Nina had read about from a forbidden text that she had found in a book at Acclaro and not shown Dalwyn. It involved binding an astral denizen to herself and then forcing it to do her bidding.

Nina floated for a while longer watching around her as she continued to spin and ponder on what the book had said. From the direction of Acclaro with the pulsating red mass, a light shot across the astral that broke into five smaller ones that left a trail of sparks behind them. Infernals were the only beings to leave sparks in their wake as they moved through the astral world, although Nina didn't know why that was. Her breath caught in her throat as she feared they were coming for her, but then when they sped off in other directions she relaxed again. Turning herself back towards the Witness and the mountains, Nina focused on the edge of the Glyph plains and shot forward. The ease with which she managed that almost convinced her to enter the castle to return to her normal body, and the only reason she chose against it was that Dalwyn would hurt them all if she did that. Dalwyn hated her, Nina knew, and he would be expecting Nina to try returning and would have some sort of trap waiting. She would try this and might gain a friend doing it, and then if nothing worked she would try the castle.

Nina focused and let energy roll down into the first vortex until it stopped spinning and formed an anchor to her real body; this also held her in one position as protection from the winds or drifting away. Her low energy would only keep her stationary for a short time before the vortex began spinning again. Taking just a trickle of that energy, Nina projected it just out in front of her body where it formed a red, circular barrier.

From the second vortex Nina did the same, and soon another circular barrier, this time orange, appeared above the red. A soft clapping of her hands joined both points together, and the energy flowed into a perfect red circle with a burning orange outline that expanded as she wished it to until it was taller and three times as wide as she was.

Looking closer at what she had done, Nina could see the fibres of the energy trap and remembered what to do next. She reached in and strummed the fibres first in one direction and then another, sending ripples through the trap, which then began to vibrate and give off a low humming noise. *One more thing to do,* she thought and then moved up to stand before the trap, which wrapped around her as she drew both her hands together.

Now encased in a globe of red and orange energy, Nina waited. She wanted to laugh and jump around while congratulating herself on her skill but this was just the beginning and she needed all the energy she could save. In the back of her mind was the recent encounter with Dalwyn's astral entity, but Nina quickly withdrew from pondering on that to focus on the task at hand.

Sitting there silently floating in the ocean, amber world, Nina saw the similarities to the fishing she had done on numerous occasions with her father down at the docks, except this time the prey wasn't some fish for the dinner table. It would be just as easy to use the remaining energy she had by travelling to a distant place or even try to enter Acclaro, but each of these had their own dangers, especially Acclaro. since it was sure to have many enemies who were stronger and more experienced than she. Nina wouldn't just give up and wait for death because Haakon had not done that. He had fought to the end even though he must have known he couldn't kill all the warriors who pushed in on him relentlessly. He had fought until his very last breath, and she would do the same.

Chapter 37

When Nina began moving she realized the connection holding her in place had run out of energy, and now she was helpless to stop herself just floating wherever the astral took her. The movement of the energy trap increased the vibration giving out a faint whistling sound as she floated out over the Glyph plains and away from the mountains. Up higher and to Nina's left something hit the energy trap, knocking it and Nina over and over until they finally slowed again. Nina's eyes darted about trying to spot whatever had hit the trap and alighted on a strange cloud hovering there from which slim bolts of lightning shot out.

As Nina stared at the strange cloud, three figures toppled, from it somersaulting down towards her. They looked delicate, with thin bodies the size of young children, and their stark alabaster skin had swirls of blue markings that pulsed across their skin. Nina had seen the three creatures while studying books, and they were called sylphs, or air spirits. They hovered before Nina's trap, their long hair waving about their heads from a wind that only seemed to affect them. Nina heard them talking in soft words and sighs that she couldn't understand, but the body language of the three made it plain that one was arguing with the other two. As the third one moved closer to Nina's trap, the other two gesticulated wildly, and Nina felt a pang of guilt wash over her but knew she still had no other choice. The sylph hovered before the trap, and Nina could see its unearthly beauty in great detail. It reached forward experimentally to touch the energy shimmering before it, and with a snap the trap was sprung and the fey creature was encircled in red energy. The sylph shrieked and fluttered like a bird in a cage throwing itself against the energy barrier as its two companions outside screamed and hovered outside, unwilling to touch the trap themselves. For what seemed an eternity the sylph fought against its imprisonment and then just slumped panting to its knees, head bent.

Nina looked at it with sadness. 'Don't worry, I won't hurt you,' she said, barely louder than a whisper.

The sylph's head jerked up and its eyes blazed with blue light that widened as she most likely saw Nina.

'And yet you have trapped me,' came the sardonic reply.

'Only to help me, and then I promise to let you go,' Nina said quickly, while outside the trap the other two sylphs were now striking the energy trap with some type of sword, but they weren't having any effect and couldn't pierce the energy of the trap.

'You don't mean that! There are right ways to get help here, but you have chosen the bad way, the nasty way.'

'No, I didn't. You see, I am not strong enough to be here. I was trapped here when my friends were woken in the real world. If you don't help me, I will die!'

'Let me out and I promise I will help you,' said the sylph.

'I know you are tricky creatures so no, I won't let you out without a binding. Put your arm through the middle of the orange barrier, and that will bind us once I grasp it.'

From outside two distinct voices were calling for the sylph not to do it. The sylph stared at Nina, neither of them flinching away from the gaze of the other. In its eyes Nina saw fear and distrust as well as pain, and yet something gentle and playful stirred behind those things. When they broke that look, the sylph smiled tentatively.

'Help you do what, exactly?'

'Return to my body in the real world. I cannot use the vortices because we are deeper in the astral than the first two, and so I am trapped here,' Nina explained.

'That takes great energy for us to materialise in your world. What are you willing to do for me?' the sylph asked.

'It doesn't work like that and you know it. Now tell me your name and let's get on with it so I can go home and you can do whatever you want,' Nina said, getting annoyed.

'Keeya is my name,' the sylph said, and then it stopped and its ears flicked back. 'They have left me,' Keeya said, looking alarmed.

'Why would they do that?' Nina asked.

The sylph looked back at her as if it knew something she didn't.

A shadow fell over the trap and both of them, and then a being was there looking from Nina to the sylph with glee. Energy crackled over its body on which small mouths opened and closed silently as if craving sustenance. Both Nina and the sylph were frozen in place by the horror of it. Nina could only watch as energy from its base vortex pushed out of its body, and where it struck her barrier it cut through, opening a hole through which the entity thrust a wickedly taloned claw and grabbed the sylph by the neck.

Keeya didn't struggle, just sat there accepting her fate, and then she was torn out of the trap into jaws that extended out wide before snapping down on the sylph with a spray of blood and white energy.

Still dripping the life fluids of the sylph, the being turned to Nina.

'You are not from here. Never mind I will help you return to this body you spoke to the sylph of, but first I will feast on your life and then you will take me to it.'

Yellow energy swarmed out of the beings midsection, encasing Nina within it as her trap fell away. Now connected to this being, she watched it turn away from her and drift in a direction she thought might be south because of the position of Acclaro to her right. She felt for a weakness in the energy field around her and probed it with her energy of the two vortices, which earnt her a mocking smile from her captor.

They shot forward then, and Nina saw their destination, a metallic silver city stained with red that reminded Nina of bloodstained blades. Something vast and black lay above that terrible city, and as they got closer Nina saw it was a vast pestilence of flies.

Cries of torment carried on the astral winds to her ears that sent her heart thumping and mind quailing at the madness she heard within, and Nina screamed with every last shred of energy she had, throwing open her vortices in a last cry for help, hoping they would hear it and come for her. Nina's primal scream rocketed away from her, and now her energy spent, Nina fell back and watched her captor glide down through gates that writhed with living bodies bound together and crying out their hopeless torment. They moved down a street of vendors from which many creatures of the races hung from hooks or sat chained to stone plinths. Gutters flanking the road sluiced a syrupy liquid that sloshed over its edges. Nina saw creatures like the one that had caught her dip goblets into the gutter and then force the liquid down the throats of those chained.

They stopped at a small home of the main street of horror in an alleyway that smelt of decay and vomit. The energy trap around Nina suddenly fell away, then she was hauled up by the throat and her captor sniffed at her hair then looked at her with eyes that unfocused, scanning her vortices with its astral sight. It looked at her in frustration. 'So much available energy for one so young, but fortunately for you your body needs rest before I can feed from your strength. I will bring you sustenance.' Yellow bands of energy once again flowed from its abdomen that snapped around her body, holding Nina immobile.

Chapter 38

According to a weary Melde, it was dawn, but you would never know that down here. The gods had gathered outside near the escape tunnel and in turn solemnly said their farewells to their brother Melde. Once they were safely in the tunnels away from this entrance, Melde would activate the first defence, a collapse that had been rigged to close the tunnel off from this end. It would take them half a day to reach the Jewelled Lands, where any pursuing Life Quenchers would hopefully be seriously depleted of power due to the ever present crystal glow that the strange forest provided.

Half a chime after entering the tunnel they still hadn't any sign of th tunnel collapsing, and Ishmael turned to Aeon. 'If Melde was going to block the way after us wouldn't have he done it by now?

Ishmael caught the brief look of concern before Aeon could hide it. 'there is nothing we can do about what is happening back at the city, we must press on with haste,' he replied then set off again. Now there was only the way forward and they moved quickly and quietly with the sacrifice Melde and his people had provided for them fresh in their minds.

The tunnel slowly widened, and lichen poles that had been placed at regular intervals lit the road that Melde's people had carved out for the recharging of their crystals. Rather than breaking to rest, it was decided to push on and make the Jewelled Lands as soon as possible. When the cry came up that the end of the tunnel was in sight Ishmael estimated they had been moving for two to three chimes, their fear of pursuit driving them on relentlessly. He felt the heaviness and fear he had been plagued with beneath the earth fall away and ran forward to see what all the commotion and excitement up at the front of the party was all about.

There stood a cart that had been partially loaded with crystal globes, but no sign of Melde's people except blood spatters on the stone.

'Is it possible they could have beaten us here or another group of Life Quenchers had entered from the forest?' Nina asked Aeon from beside Ishmael.

'If they have, Nina, then we are in serious trouble.' From their high vantage point the Jewelled Lands were spread below in all their splendour. The crystal here looked as thick as snow, where it crusted the thick trees below in deep purples, mauve, and blue in places through which a river wound clear and sparkling. An uneven stone staircase twisted and turned down all the way to the ground way below and a faint, constant, roaring noise carried on the wind

The trip down was treacherous now that they were at the mercy of both a biting wind and the slippery stone steps from a recent rain shower. They cautiously descended, the path which wound back towards the towering mountain behind them, revealing the roaring noise to be made by a magnificent horsetail waterfall that plunged down the mountain face into a great pool far below. As they drew closer the noise became deafening which made any talk impossible. The path descended through a great hole in the surrounding thick forest canopy that allowed the sun to enter this fantastical place. It took another chime for them all to reach the base of the steps where a plume of spray mist turned the area around them into a ghost land that glittered with the vibrant hues of the forest. Around them the lush forest teemed with life. The rich, dark soil was thick with worms and insects that buzzed around. Ishmael saw a man sized reptile sunning itself on a rock, and it seemed totally disinterested in them. By the bank of the pool which trickled off into a narrow river,

Ishmael found stacked piles of crystals that had been placed directly below the sun's rays. There was still no sign of Melde's people, beside the crystals and Ishmael returned to the clearing nearby where Aeon and the gods had been setting up camp and were busy passing around food.

'Can we expect the Harlequin in this area?' he asked Aeon.

'The Harlequin have left the Jewelled Lands and work with purpose to see the Mother's plans come to fruition just as we do.'

'I thought they would die if away from these lands too long. When I was gifted the earth crystal, one of their kind told me they are like a hive and aware of each thing the individual learns. If they have left, then where did they go?'

'You will meet them again, Ishmael. They have formed what the Mother calls the Elemental tower, which is where the coterie and the gods will be taken. Now I need to speak with the gods, Ishmael, and for this you must leave us alone,' Aeon said and moved away.

Ishmael looked about and spied Zahra down by the water. She had stripped her clothes off and now was sliding into the clear water. He made his way through the foliage and down to the river bank just as Zahra resurfaced from a dive.

'Can I join you?' he asked, reminded of a time not so long ago like this. He had changed since then, grown into a man with responsibilities and been forced to make choices, and through all that Zahra had attempted to guide him and keep him safe. He owed her a lot.

'Of course you can, Ishmael, the water is delightful,' replied Zahra.

Ishmael dived in and swam over to where Zahra floated on her back. The canopy above them was light purple and Ishmael felt almost instantly relaxed in the beautiful surroundings. They swam together for a time not needing to speak, just comfortable in each other's presence, which made Ishmael think that maybe Zahra had begun to forgive him for leaving her behind back on the Glyph grasslands.

'Ishmael, with the danger we are going into, I need to know I have your complete confidence. If I am to protect you, then you must be totally open and honest with me. We have come so far and to fail now is unthinkable. I cannot let that happen.'

'I know what I must do now, Zahra, and before we get to the tower and Acclaro I will meet with the coterie so I know their whereabouts. You have my trust, and I give you my word that I won't betray it again.'

When they finished dressing and then returned to the camp, the gods had finished their secretive discussion and were getting ready to leave.

'So soon, Aeon?' Ishmael asked.

'We cannot rest until we are sure of the god's and your safety.' Aeon shrugged then set off at a walk heading north. The other gods fell in behind Aeon along with Ishmael, leaving Zahra and Cinder to take the rear position. Ishmael had counted the gods to number forty-two. He knew maybe half of them, but as he walked he realized he had not once seen Escindre the god of all things evil. He hurried up to Aeon's side.

'I just noticed that Escindre has not been with us,' he said to the god of time.

'Yes, he has shunned us, no doubt up to one of his nefarious deeds. His absence can only be something bad, Ishmael, but what it is I can only guess.'

'I had always thought it was the Harlequin that made the Jewelled Land, with all the amazing colors from the crystal that forms here. If the Harlequin have gone then it can't be true,' Ishmael mused out loud.

'Usually it's hard to get a word out of you, Ishmael, but lately you won't shut up,' Aeon said smiling.

'I guess it just takes my mind of everything else that's happening. There is so much still to do, and so much can go wrong. What happens if we fail somehow?'

'Then our world will become a true reflection of the Infernal lands ruled by Tamul and will slowly die.'

They walked in silence after that, Ishmael turning his attention to the amazing surroundings as the path they forged caused the thick, mossy ground to light up. Flocks of coloured birds threaded their through the canopy high above them, screeching as they went, and once Aeon paused to point out three white deer speckled with purplish crystals along their snouts who stared at the party intently. At a river crossing they stopped to refill canteens from the pure water.

'If the gods have been mortal since the Severing, then who was there to collect the divine spark left in the bodies like when you took the one from Kane?' Ishmael asked Aeon.

'Any of us gods can take back the divine spark of our fallen; however with it comes the burden of knowledge of what was lost, and most of my kin have passed the spark of the fallen onto me. For some reason it doesn't create a sense of morose depression in me like it does my brothers and sisters.'

'So you carry the divine spark of more than one god?' Ishmael asked in awe.

'Yes. It makes sense for me to carry them because I will not be absorbed into the Mother like the other gods.'

'But you can still die, or worse be captured then held prisoner, then you would be unable to help the Mother.'

'Which is why I'm in such a hurry.'

They walked until Ishmael and the gods began to trail behind Aeon's loping gait and disappeared from sight. When they caught up to him, he had lit a small, covered fire next to which lay a deer carcass.

'About time you got here,' he said as he began skinning and gutting the animal for cooking.

Zahra and Cinder arrived half a chime later with the last of the gods who had been struggling to catch up. Ishmael found a mossy bed then lay down to rest. He would need his energy to contact the coterie soon since he was the only connection to them.

From what Zahra could tell night had fallen on the strange, faerie-like forest. It was different to the area where Ramon had let them stay with him, more wild and untouched. From her vantage point on a branch she looked down over the camp where Ishmael and many of the gods slept. They looked so vulnerable.

Over head the canopy of purple shuddered as if from something of great weight, causing her to look upwards in alarm. With her gaze scanning above and around them, Zahra couldn't see what had caused the movement, which left her feeling uneasy.

There came a short whistle below her, and Zahra saw Cinder's straw hair as he climbed up beside her. He passed her some meat wrapped in leaves, which she took thankfully.

'I sense something in the canopy but cannot see anything,' Zahra said between mouthfuls of the meat.

'You too then. Whatever it is seems to have other things on its mind, otherwise it would have already attacked us while we are vulnerable.'

'By the look of the mist rising it looks like we may need to rest here a while,' Zahra said, wiping the grease of the meat on her trousers.

'You should get some sleep, Zahra.'

'I'm too wired to sleep even if I wanted too,' she said, regarding his blue eyes.

'We could just sneak off and do something to take your mind off whatever is keeping you awake,' Cinder replied, grinning.

'Yes, that would be great when we return to find Ishmael and the other gods dead because they were killed while we fornicated in the bushes,' Zahra scowled.

'You can't tell me it didn't cross your mind, though,' said Cinder, widening his eyes in mock exasperation.

Zahra did sleep there, leaning on Cinder's shoulder, and when he woke her he had his hand placed over her mouth. 'It's okay, it's me. Look!'

Zahra followed Cinder's nod and stared out where the trees fell away into a gully they had circled around where the canopy was thin and the stars peeked through. A thick flock of crimson birds flew in circles, squawking as they rose, and dove through the mist that shrouded the forest.

'What, they are only birds. We have seen many flocks on the way here,' she replied quietly.

'Yes, that is true, but this is different. Since nightfall the only sounds we have had about us were the calipo frogs by the water's edge.'

'Do you think we are being pursued?'

'Maybe and maybe not, but we cannot take the risk of not investigating,' Cinder answered then shimmied down the trunk.

They entered the camp first to notify Aeon and found him sleeping beside Ishmael. Ishmael sat up suddenly with his sword angled towards them, only relaxing when he saw who it was.

'What's wrong?' Ishmael asked, suddenly alert.

A disturbance back behind us a ways. We need to check it out,' Zahra told him after a long drink of water. Wake the others and have them ready to move, and if we don't return within a chime then go without us. If there is danger we will lead it away from you.'

'Take care out there, and make sure you look after Zahra, I need her,' Ishmael added, looking at Cinder who nodded, all seriousness now.

Chapter 39

After locking the royal chamber Zacriel had scaled the outside of his tower then moved around the tower to the balcony he favoured during the day. With his personal guard still outside his chamber, Zacriel pulled the whistle from his tunic and called out to Midnight, then waited. It didn't take long before a slice of darkness detached itself and glided onto the balcony. He was used to riding Midnight now, and the beast also seemed to share an affinity with him from the bond of mount and rider.

Once up in the sky, Zacriel ached to scream with joy, but to do so would alert his own forces below, and since he wasn't meant to be anywhere except safe in his chambers he fought down the urge.

Zacriel flew high above the Harlequin trying to garner any information as to what they were up to. They were building something, but not from the earth or any resources other than their very own people. It seemed to Zacriel as he flew that the Harlequin were being slowly absorbed into some type of structure, but what, and why? Not knowing really unnerved him.

Zacriel turned and directed Midnight, north, west of Acclaro where the Stained River that was the natural border of Scuttle met the hills south of Culchar. Zacriel sped over this area making sure to stay high enough above any potential arrowshot as he passed over the encampment of Scuttle forces at the Stained River. When he moved east he noticed that where the Lonely Woods were, an army was on the move through the trees and it took a few passes by to recognize the yellow and blue uniforms of Culchar warriors. So it has begun, thought Zacriel as he turned and made another pass over the woods. His enemies were gathering.

Zacriel flew further to the east over the Glyph grasslands, and there he saw a force to rival his own. They flew the banners of barbarian tribes. Zacriel estimated that within three days they would be in shouting distance of Acclaro. He turned Midnight and angled back towards Acclaro, tomorrow he would take council with the other Infernal lords and his officers. It was when he was high above the skywalk of castle Acclaro that the attack came.

There was no warning, or battle cry. One moment he was flying and lost in the distraction of what he had witnessed, and the next, large talons were snatching at him. Somehow he evaded them, and they speared instead into the soft flesh of Midnight behind its head. The creature above him was a raven, and as he realized this its head jerked down as it sought to tear out his eyes with its beak. The attack narrowly missed the precious orbs and instead struck his cheek, tearing flesh. Zacriel swatted away the next attack as above him he heard a command. 'Rise Steele, take them to the thermals.'

He had forgotten the Raven warrior and cursed under his breath at his own foolishness in leaving without an escort. Midnight was keening loudly, helpless in the ravens grasp as it beat powerful wings and took them higher. Zacriel, now at least free from further attacks from the raven's wicked beak pulled his only weapon on him, his knife. The vulnerable underbelly of the giant raven was armoured with hard leather plates, and so he decided to target the muscles of the legs only to find them similarly armoured. Using the knife he dug into the strapping that protected the tendons of the talons that held Midnight. Zacriel plunged the blade through the leather over and over again with all his strength, managing to work a cut into the worn armour. When he struck the tendon the Raven screeched and they all fell for about twenty feet before the bird stabilized. It still had Midnight in its clutches, and now the raven warrior was attempting to lean down to see what Zacriel was doing to his bird. Zacriel kept sawing away, and when one of the tendons snapped causing the Ravens talon to release its catch, they hung lopsidedly with the night air rushing by. A sword swept past Zacriel's head, but missed. The body of the raven was proving to be a valuable shield from the warrior's attacks. He began on the other leg of the raven as they fell in a rush of feathers as the raven attempted once more to tear him apart with its beak. Zacriel curled in around the one good leg of the raven as he sawed at the muscle and tendons, while the screams of the raven and curses of its rider grew ever more desperate.

Below them and coming closer was Acclaro castle, if he could just get the raven to let go of Midnight they could manage to reach the sky walk. He stabbed at the leg in a frenzy and was rewarded with another lurch as Midnight was released, sending them into a freefall away from their enemies. Midnight righted herself, antennae whirling madly and Zacriel guided her as best he could down to the sky walk near one of the corner towers.

Midnight struck the tower close to the walkway with a cry. Zacriel was momentarily stunned by the collision, then searched above him for their enemy as he released the catches of his saddle. The raven was circling above and he could see the warrior peering down at them. With a screech the raven dived towards them for the kill. Zacriel staggered free and stood unarmed as Midnight flopped on the walk nearby. The raven struck midnight and careened into Zacriel which knocked him onto his back. The frenzied beast attempted to stand on its talons, but Zacriel's knife had done its damage well, and it collapsed on Midnight with its iron covered beak tearing over and over into the flesh of the lunar. The raven warrior was cursing and trying desperately to free himself so he could fight Zacriel, but the jerky movement of the raven made that nearly impossible.

The tower door opened then, and Rapture followed by other Infernals ran out onto the sky walk. Rapture tore into the raven with his axe, and it fell upon him and the other Infernals tearing with its beak as it flapped while trying to stand on damaged legs. Rapture became trapped beneath the creature and the Infernals with him were being torn to shreds by the raven as its rider finally jumped free onto the skywalk.

Zacriel charged him as the warrior frantically tried to release his sword from the scabbard. He was too slow, and Zacriel slammed his shoulder into the warrior who fell back against the protective fence of the walkway. Zacriel followed up with a punch that would have taken the man's head off if he hadn't managed to step forward and smother most of the force of the blow. Zacriel tore at the man's face and throat, and gained purchase by grabbing the riders long hair, pulling it down savagely and smashing his elbow into his face. The rider collapsed to the walk, and behind him Zacriel could see Rapture finishing off the raven with his axe. He turned back to the warrior and noticed the man had a deep wound to his chest from the fall and collision. He straddled the man and slapped him back to consciousness.

'What do you want?'

'Prince Grego, is he alive,' replied the man, then he choked up blood that spilled down his chin.

Zacriel leant in close.

'You will never know the horrors we have visited on prince Grego. That is the only knowledge you will take to the grave!'

He watched until the light of the man's eyes dimmed, and then he rose painfully as all the fresh wounds sang out with their pain, and staggered over to Midnight. The lunar was a shredded mess, and its death only showed Zacriel how foolish he truly was. When Rapture approached, Zacriel expected to be lectured for his foolishness, but the formidable Infernal just met his gaze, nodded and led his lord back into the safety of the castle.

Chapter 40

With a flick of his scarred fingers, Zacriel sent the bone flying down into the city and chased it down with the blood wine that the Unseeing lord had seen added to his every meal. The meat that Rapture had sent Infernals far from the capital, risking their lives to find for the bone lord, had been exquisite.

Zacriel burped then stood and stretched. He knew his power and the loyalty of his troops was beginning to annoy all the other three Infernal lords, not just Lilith, who had seemed quite deflated and petulant after Rapture returned Zacriel safely to within the castle walls following his battle with the raven warrior. Quail had been strangely subdued since Zacriel had outsmarted him in the throne room. The three had been cooperative since the raven attack, which left Zacriel more wary than ever.

As he approached the door, Rapture stepped forward to close and bolt them behind Zacriel.

'You will be going to your bed chamber then, Bone Lord?'

'Well I wasn't going to just yet, Rapture. Is there something I'm forgetting?'

'Just a matter of the truce meeting and exchange of hostages, nothing important,' drawled the powerful Infernal.

'Mind yourself, Rapture, or I may just replace you with another Infernal that doesn't know what sarcasm is.'

'That won't be easy, Zacriel, as nobody wants to work for you, the most hated creature in the known world right now,' Rapture quipped. He shut Zacriel's bed chamber door in his face.

Zacriel lay back on the bed that once kings had slept in and pondered the truce meeting. He had been fought by the Infernal lords every step of the way against this, and when he expected them to turn against him they had given way instead taking the suggestion on board. The thing that Zacriel couldn't work out was why they would suddenly change their minds and accept what Zacriel had wanted. He blew the candles out and was soon dozing.

Zacriel awoke and sat up feeling disoriented. With a look at the window shutters they flung open, revealing the stars outside from behind the barred windows, and he realized he was lucid dreaming. He allowed himself to float up from the bed and over to the window where a storm brewed in dark, foreboding clouds. Something was coming, he was sure of it, his body strangely charged with energy, but for what?

The thunderclap of an image of Nina being dragged toward a steel city in the astral tore into Zacriel's vision just before Nina's plea crashed around him, making him cover the remains of his ears instinctively. Around him stone collapsed leaving a gaping hole in the wall before him and flinging Zacriel back against the opposite wall. He then realized why Nina had done it this way when the energy of her plea flowed back over him like a wave dragging him back out with it into the astral world.

Nina was in danger. Zacriel automatically rose up through the vortices, connecting the first three easily. His form gave off a shower aura of sparks as he moved on the wave of pure energy like all his kind did, and he knew this would attract unwanted attention from those who lay siege to his city.

Only now did Zacriel have a moment to stake stock of the situation. Nina was in danger in the astral world, which was no place for a damn child anyway, and she somehow managed to send out all her energy reserves to not ask for his aid but bring him to her. The image he had first seen was of a place so terrible even most Infernals didn't dare go there lest they become slaves for eternity to the race that ruled the Veiled Land.

Nina was inside the Broken City.

Chapter 41

As Zacriel rose the crest of the energy wave he recounted what he knew of this place. The true forms of the Incubi lay sleeping in the real world, protected in their towns obfuscated by the terrible storms that ravaged the nation. Since the Severing, these Incubi had only been able to function in the astral world and sought human travellers, preferably females to enslave as sources of energy. The unlucky victims would have their energy syphoned off until they died or reached breeding age, where their victim, impregnated with the child of the fell creature, would be returned to its body and the changes would begin, thus creating a sub race of human and Incubi called Macubis. The Macubis could function in the day and often journeyed in packs to reclaim the bodies of those victims caught in the astral then take them to the Veiled land. If Nina was left here, she would eventually have her mind torn into and the location of her body revealed, and Zacriel would not allow that to happen.

The bronze gates stood ahead. Zacriel looked for a way past, but the glowing runes that covered the walls and crenellations of the city would cause him too much damage should he attempt to bypass them and enter the city that way.

Two figures by the gates grew as he approached until they stood at least ten feet tall, and as the wave of energy hit the city it dissipated to nothing. Zacriel halted his sudden fall and floated down before the two bronze warriors who blocked the way.

'Infernals, even one such as you, are not welcome to our city,' one figure said as the other took up a defensive stance with its spear aimed down at Zacriel.

'Then return what is mine and no harm shall come to any who dwell here,' Zacriel replied.

'You have no ownership of the souls brought to this place, Infernal.'

'And yet there is one who I have placed under my protection, guardian, and I have no hesitation in razing the Broken City to the ground to get her if I must,' Zacriel snarled back.

Zacriel felt a burning coming from his chest and yet he hesitated to look away from these two guardians. He began to approach, and a sword materialized in his clawed hand as he formed it with the energy that boiled within him.

The spear of the second guardian snaked down at Zacriel and a curious thing happened. His chest felt torn apart as a black growth exploded out from it to form a protective shield around him, when the spear struck the shield, it and its user were thrown back against the gates and the fallen guardian shrank back to normal size.

The other guardian leapt forward to wraps its bronze arms around Zacriel, but it as it attempted to lift him Zacriel could see where the strange shield had developed dark tendrils that delved down into the stone, holding him immobile. The guardian flexed and battered at the shield and managed to breach it in one place. As it tried to remove the arm to strike again, the metal closed around it and deep thorns bit into its body.

It thrashed, frantically attempting to remove itself as the shield reformed around its trapped arm. Thorned vines grew and snaked over the guardian's body, penetrating the metal. They grew and grew until the guardian was covered in the black tendrils, which then tore outwards, pulling the bronze warrior apart as its death cry reverberated and faded away.

Zacriel looked down at the rose of spite from which the shield had formed. The roiling mass of branch-like tentacles retracted then covered his body, forming spiked, jet-black armour. He had no idea the rose could do any of this, but he did know that any Infernal object of power always took something from the user and he wondered what the cost would be.

Putting that to the back of his mind, Zacriel approached the gates, which swung open before him.

Zacriel watched the gates swing open as he waited to see what would dare try to stop him getting to Nina. Ahead a wide roadway stretched away around a corner. Gutters ran with blood, and corpses hung from hooks and chains attached to the eaves of houses or shops along with those who still thrashed about, dying.

Blocking the road ahead stood a figure with a grotesquely long face with elongated eyes and lips standing with soldiers crowding around behind him. The man stood still, arms folded, regarding Zacriel with a cautious amusement. With the rose of spite still activated Zacriel could see the waves of psychic energy that sizzled around his form. This was one of the older Incubi, which meant they were taking him as a serious threat. With his astral sight Zacriel scanned the Incubus and saw the energy that cracked over him was due to thralls like the ones on the roadside who were connected to its vortices allowing him to siphon energy directly from them.

'Explain yourself, Infernal lord!'

'I have come for the child named Nina. One of your hunters brought her astral body here, and she called me to her. She is under my protection and purchasing her is not an option, no matter the offer,' Zacriel said.

'Do you truly think that you could come to the Broken City and demand something for nothing? The girl is young and has a life of power ahead of her. She practically oozes it. Her life force could keep one such as myself alive another century or so easily. So what will you offer for such a valuable commodity, yourself?'

'A promise!'

'You would speak nonsense while bartering with me?'

Zacriel ignored him and went on. 'A promise that if you bring the girl to me, alive, right now, I will not only let you Incubi live but I will also stay away from the Broken City.'

'You cannot harm any of the Incubi permanently. If you even manage to escape us here we will regenerate and hunt you down, Infernal lord. Best turn yourself around and leave our city before I lose my temper.'

They are stalling me, Zacriel realized. 'I know your secrets and where your true forms lie. Should I need to I can call on a force of Infernals that this world has never seen and we will tear the Veiled land apart until all your race are dead.'

'An empty threat, Infernal lord.'

'Not empty, Incubus. I know that the ones whose bodies your fell children recover breed and protect you from danger while you sleep in the mausoleums there. You may be a match for me, but these offspring cannot hope to stop my army of infernals!'

Zacriel projected himself forward, and the warriors flowed around the Incubus protectively. Zacriel had no plans of attacking it; instead he moved to the first of the bodies that hung with their faces contorted in soundless screams and slashed two down, killing them. The incubus hissed, flesh flared up like a hood behind its head, gleaming eyes all fastened on him.

Zacriel guessed by the fumes of whatever filled the gutters that it was flammable and he willed his blade to catch fire then touched it to the gutter. It burst into flames and flared up, igniting a row of precious victims. A howl of anger almost deafened Zacriel, and he looked up just as the Incubus attacked.

He batted away a sword that slashed at him but was too slow to stop the hand that struck the shield and the armour from the rose of spite. The touch drained the roses energy and flowed back into itself leaving him vulnerable. Warriors flowed around him holding Zacriel immobile and the Incubus grabbed him by the head where his astral eye was. Zacriel's eyes dimmed and he could only see shadows now, tendrils shot out hitting his vortices and connecting to him. Zacriel thrashed in the iron grip of the Incubus and its warriors, he was growing desperate now, realizing he had was totally unprepared for this type of encounter with a powerful astral creature.

Nina was resting since there was nothing else to do. The bands that held her had no give and only tightened if she struggled. The one that had captured her had not returned yet, and she dreaded what would happen when it did. A scream of rage awoke her from her rest, where she had almost slipped into a deep sleep. When the bands that held her fell away, she fell hard, hitting the stone below her.

Still weak, Nina dragged herself out of the room she was in and into the alley then around a corner to the street which she had been led past. The opposite side of the road was ablaze, and the gutter and the bodies suspended above it burned, giving off psychic screams as the captives died. There was a commotion to her left towards the gate, and Nina saw a press of bodies holding someone immobile while a figure wreathed in energy attacked someone with its vortices.

It was Zacriel. He had come after all.

Nina struggled to her feet and staggered towards Zacriel. Beside those involved in the fight the street was now empty, its denizens fled. Zacriel's attackers were so focused on him that Nina moved unseen, and as she neared them she caught sight of what looked like an urn. She grabbed it and discovered it was filled with the viscous liquid in the gutter. The fumes of it burned her senses, and she gathered herself and ran forward, throwing the liquid over the creature attacking Zacriel. Then she used her second vortex to flare her hands with fire and touched it. The creature turned in surprise to regard her, a flare of skin rising up like a hood behind its skull. Then it began screaming and Nina fell to her knees and covered her ears as the psychic screams pounded inside her head.

As it thrashed around in the flames, warriors around it caught alight as well and others fled. The creature also tried to flee but was still connected to Zacriel and couldn't until it had detached its vortices. Now open and vulnerable, it failed to protect itself, and Nina saw the reverse in energy flow as Zacriel literally drained the remaining life from it. It fell, still burning, now only a husk.

Nina knelt by Zacriel, who had collapsed, and he smiled at her. 'I'm sorry, Nina, I came too late to prevent this,' he said, looking past her.

She turned to see three more of the creatures that had attacked Zacriel floating down the street towards them. Nina slumped down beside Zacriel and wrapped her arms about him. 'At least you came,' she said and burst into tears.

The three fearsome creatures floated closer then stopped and Nina wondered why. She looked around back at the gates and saw a naked woman walking towards them. Her skin was bronzed yet tinted green in areas, moss and leaves covered her lower sexual organs and wreathed her forearms, and her long hair was a wreath of coloured butterflies that swarmed around behind her head. She surged forward to Nina's side and, looking at Zacriel, touched his forehead and he disappeared. Then she turned eyes of the bluest sky to Nina and scooped her up from the ground. 'You are safe now,' she said, and Nina felt herself slipping away into sleep.

Chapter 42

As Zahra and Cinder were leaving the camp another figure fell in beside them dressed in light-brown garb with a greyish cloak, quiver on his back and long bow in hand. It was Kudra, god of hunting. 'I can track as well as cover your asses out there,' he growled then moved off without looking back.

They raced back through the indigo crystal light using the gap of thin foliage they had spotted as a reference, then when they got closer moved off the path into the thickest of the foliage and belly-crawled to the lip of the gully. Here the crystal to the sides of the thin canopy above was a darker purple, even a swollen red, in places. Beneath an overhang of rock, the entrance to a small cave lay, and from it they heard mewling.

A den,' Latasha whispered though she not have bothered since the cries of the birds who still flew above covered any noise.

As they watched a lynx crept out of the den, its white, tufted ears pinned back, fangs showing as it hissed at something they couldn't yet see. It braced itself, ready to defend the young it must have in the den.

Something flashed in the bruised light slamming into the lynx, an arrow that hit the beast in the chest, knocking it down. It growled and tried to rise as another feathered shaft took it in the throat, but it was still breathing.

Cinder put a hand on Zahra's shoulder to keep her in place as a cowled figure crept from the purple shade. It was hunched yet moved with grace on legs that were bent in a strange way. When it moved the soft sounds of metal chinking together could be heard. Tendrils of dark swished about from its cloak as it inched closer, still holding a bow in blackened almost human hands. The tendrils snaked down, gripping the still-alive lynx and dragging it to its body, forcing out a squeal from its victim, which appeared to shrivel in its grasp.

The birds above the gulley went wild, more breaking from the canopy overhead and scattering in all directions. The Life Quencher looked up, and Zahra could see its features for the first time; dark skin with amber-colored spirals on its cheeks, a glittering ring that hung from its nose, a ring maybe, slivers of jade decorated the outside of stretched ears. So they weren't just shadow creatures. There was some substance to them, Zahra noted. Kudra tapped Zahra's shoulder, and then Cinder signalled them to edge back away from the gulley.

They found some shelter beneath a high tree with low, sweeping violet-lit branches and long grass around its base.

The grave faces of the three told what they had already realized. Zahra spoke their concern in a low voice. 'We saw only one of the Life Quenchers but we all know there will be more, maybe many more.'

'We never heard the collapse of the tunnel so they must have got to Melde and his people before they could collapse it. Now they must have our scent since we are upwind of the bastards,' growled Kudra.

'For all we know there may be more who have gotten behind us and are approaching our camp. We can ill afford to dally now,' Cinder said.

'So lead them away from the others or return to them ourselves?' Zahra asked urgently, feeling the need to move and get back to Ishmael.

'Safety in numbers, so we return to camp or, if Ishmael has them moving, then we catch up as fast as possible. In the event of us being attacked or flanked, then we must lead them away. Let's move. I have the bow so will take the rear,' Kudra said, nocking an arrow.

They moved swiftly through the undergrowth. Zahra glanced repeatedly to her side, scanning for any of the fey creatures. One big way they had underestimated the Life Quenchers, she realized was that once they entered the Jewelled Lands they had assumed that their enemy was defeated since they had always clung to the shadows or darkness. The light here was still a dark purple or lighter violet, which did not affect them since the thick canopy shut out much of the daylight. The ornaments the Life Quencher they had witnessed had worn indicated a tribal aspect to their enemy, but Zahra knew they needed more than simple observations. They needed to find a weakness since they couldn't prune the canopy overhead or find many open areas where the sun's rays would give them respite from their pursuers.

Zahra forced herself to breathe evenly now she had her rhythm running over the uneven ground. Her fitness had suffered recently from lack of sleep and rest, and it was the fear of the danger they found themselves in that spurred her onwards. They were close to the camp when a sharp challenge rang out ahead.

'Name yourself or die,' came the cry, and ahead Cinder slowed to a walk with his arms above his head.

'It's us, Sledge, at ease. Zahra and Kudra are behind me.'

Zahra joined Cinder, who stood opposite the god of smiths and iron. Sledge was shirtless, his oversize muscles straining as he stood ready for trouble with both hands on his great hammer. The rest of the gods and Ishmael stood up from where they had stayed hidden from sight in long grass and the camp had been cleared away.

'What did you find?' Aeon asked, the strain evident in his eyes.

'The Life Quenchers are behind us, and the dappled light has done nothing to stop them following us. We saw only one, which is enough to say there will be more,' Cinder reported.

A murmur of panic spread through the throng of gods.

'How can we stop them then?' Shail exclaimed

Kudra jogged in to join them all, he hadn't even broken a sweat. 'Let's move while we can, we can discuss possible tactics as we go.'

Zahra noted with satisfaction that most of the gods had armed themselves with their own weapons or with sharpened staves. Someone had been thinking, which was good since if it came to a fight they would need everyone to play their part.

They had been fleeing for the better part of a chime when the hooting started. It came first from far behind, a long wailing, that ended with an owl-like hoot. When another came from far to the left of them Zahra felt the fear prickle along her arms along with the thrill of possible violence.

The Devouring River which ran parallel to their left, had now branched with one route cutting back towards them from up ahead and a natural island lay in the middle of the river free of trees. The hooting now rang out all around them, even to their front. The Life Quenchers had them surrounded.

'The island! Head to it now! We have the best chance of defence there and they must approach through the water to get to us,' Cinder ordered them as his authority took over. They angled to the river's edge, throwing themselves into the water which came to waist or shoulder height for many of them. The first onto the island pulled their kin from the water up beside them.

'Get your breath back,' roared Cinder. We make our stand now. Those of you that have flint or tinder attempt to make a fire for the spears, we know they hate the flames.'

Zahra saw Ishmael kneel and remove the white earth crystal from his pack, its bright light a beacon in the purple light. Two of the gods were fumbling with a flint and steel. They had a small pile of grass and leaves as well as paper to use for the sparks to light, but by just watching Zahra knew the flint stick was wet, as was the steel, which would make it very difficult if not impossible to use.

The sound of vomiting came from behind Zahra. She turned to see Alyshea, goddess of beauty, wiping her mouth and trying to look brave. Zahra gave the goddess a smile and nod of encouragement then turned back to watch for the arrival of their foes.

They came in ones and twos to stand on the banks either side of the island, and it was their total silence that was more unnerving than their cowled figures with tendrils of darkness questing out from their upper bodies. The only noise was the movements of the defenders and the scratching noise of the flint stick on the steel as the holder continued to attempt to make a fire.

The Life Quenchers continued to grow in numbers on the two banks, now standing two or more ranks thick. How many were there of the damn creatures, Zahra silently wondered. The waiting was the worst, and why they hadn't attacked yet she couldn't say. A tall figure standing at least eight feet tall emerged from the forest cover and made its way down to the river bank. The other Life Quenchers parting before it.

'That's their leader.' Zahra pointed as he approached. Kill it and maybe they will falter.'

Kudra, quicker than the eye could see, fired three arrows at the figure as it stepped forward to the water's edge. Its tendrils whipped up, protecting its face and chest as two arrows were batted away, the third took it in the shoulder, which didn't seem to bother it at all as it tugged the arrow free and threw it in the water.

There was no signal for the attack. The Life Quenchers closest to each bank entered the water, interlocking their arms about each other's shoulders as their tendrils swirled around protecting their heads. Then they slowly moved forward until the distance from the nearest was just out of the longest weapons range and crouched. forming a living bridge over which the ones behind began to flow over at speed, coming at the defenders from both sides. Spears lunged out, knocking the first ones back into the water only to be replaced by more.

Cinder began slashing at the nearest foe while Kudra and two other gods who had bows fired almost point blank into the faces of the oncoming Life Quenchers. Beside Zahra, Ishmael thrust the crystal forward, which blazed with power, making the enemy shriek and the closest fall away, their skin and robes smoking.

Zahra waited until the first enemy to come at her was almost reaching for her before she drew Moonbite and slashed the head from its body with a cry of triumph. She devoted the death to the Death Jester who would be awaiting souls for its collection. Incoming arrows began to fall on the defenders, where a number of the Life Quenchers had produce their own bows and began picking their targets while those knocked into the water thrust tendrils out to tug at the legs of defenders.

Beside Zahra, Alyshea was torn away into the water, disappearing beneath the surface. Sledge had his impressive hammer torn away and wrestled with two of the enemy whose tendrils attempted to strangle the life from him.

Aeon went to his rescue, jabbing his spear into both unprotected faces of the creatures, one fell back into the water while the other slammed a clawed hand into Aeon's head, knocking him back before Sledge picked up a spear and repeatedly stabbed in into the hood of his enemy.

Light burst from Ishmael's crystal in waves as he hurried about attempting to ward off the enemies where they threatened to overrun the embattled defenders. In order to defend against the enemy archers, Kudra now stood at the center with the other two bowmen, firing on their opposites who fired from the safety of the banks. Maybe it was the Mother who aided them, thought Zahra as she saw fire in her peripheral vision. A flask of oil was broken and its contents flung onto a group of the Life Quenchers then set alight with a spear also dipped with oil. Thick smoke came off the burning enemies as they ignited. This could turn the tide of the fight and the hopes of the defenders were raised by this small success.

Then a figure leapt onto the island, the leader, with a savage blade hacking down and almost cutting one of the gods in half. Ishmael thrust the crystal at it, which flared weakly, as its power had dimmed from constant use, and the back swing of the blade's pommel clipped his jaw, spinning him to the ground.

Cinder engaged the enemy leader, both their blades a whir that sent sparks flying at the fury of the blows. Zahra wanted to aid Cinder, but two enemies were simultaneously attacking her. Something grabbed her hair, ripping it from the roots and pulling her off balance as tendrils wrapped one of her ankles; which she slashed them away but fell as she did so. The second Life Quencher threw itself at her, forcing her to abandon Moonbite so as to protect herself from being smothered. The momentum of her enemy aided her as she grasped its waist then tossed it over her where it landed on the small fire and began to burn while it screamed.

Ishmael grabbed Zahra, pulling her to her feet. He had blood running down his chin and his eyes were wide in terror. Aiding her left him open to attack, and an enemy charged him with its tendrils and arms outstretched; its hood had fallen back and a face almost human except for segmented, large eyes like a spiders focused on him.

Shail got there first, throwing herself in front of Ishmael and shoving both him and Zahra out of the way. The Life Quencher covered her and she simply deflated with a scream.

Zahra tried to rise but was caught beneath Ishmael. She saw a huge form fall from the canopy above and land half on the island and half on top of the Life Quenchers in the water sending, a torrent of water over the battle. Light of all colours flared, and the Life Quenchers around them burst apart. The brightly lit creature scuttled up onto the island, standing over them all on thick, hairy legs that ended in sharp claws. Its great head descended and pedi-palp claws latched onto the leader's abdomen, holding it immobile as the Life Quencher stood above the fallen body of Cinder.

The Life Quencher stabbed up with its sword, impaling the brightly lit creature's swollen abdomen as the jaws closed on the leader's head, causing a geyser of viscous, dark blood to fountain upwards.

The battle site fell silent as the remaining defenders stared in shock at the huge, multi-coloured glowing being above them. As they watched it crept back off the island into the water then leapt to the river bank where it scuttled away and up trees into the foliage, leaving behind a trail of ichor and the native flora shaking from its passage.

'What was that?' Cinder asked as he rose from the ground, covered in gore.

'A Jewelled One,' replied Aeon from where he sat. 'Maybe the very last of them.'

The cost of the battle soon became apparent. Out of forty-two gods they now numbered only twenty-seven still alive. Shail, Alyshea, and Sledge were among the fallen. Ishmael wept over Shail's remains as the other gods began to collect their dead so Aeon could take back their divine spark into himself. Aeon bled from wounds of his own and refused any help binding his own wounds until he had finished with the fallen.

Zahra went and found Ishmael where he sat alone on the river bank. He gave no sign of acknowledging her as she sat beside him.

'Shail died bravely, Ishmael, saving you so you could finish what you need to do with the coterie,' she said, trying to relieve him of some of the loss he would be feeling.

'Shail died because of me, like so many others have. If I fail them it will have all been for nothing, Zahra.'

'So let's not fail them then. Let's finish this, Ishmael, so all the sacrifices have meaning and they died making this world a better place.'

When Aeon had finished doing what he must, they moved down stream away from the blood-tainted island, where they stayed until morning.

Chapter 43

Nina opened her eyes to see taking an amber plain that spread out before her. In the distance flashes of lightning lit the strange landscape. She was still in the astral, floating, and what looked like a thin branch was embedded into her second vortex connecting her to the biggest tree she had ever seen. The tree omitted strange sighs and rustling noises around her that when she focused on seemed more like a voices. Nina turned and faced the tree's mammoth trunk, from branches stretched in all directions, the smaller branches questing as if searching for something unseen. As she floated there trying to piece together all that had happened since the Witness, her connection began to reel her in towards the tree. It didn't worry her at all, and she felt no danger around her, just her own curiosity at what would happen next.

As Nina reached the trunk she raised her hands to avoid collision, and was surprised when she simply was absorbed by the tree. She found herself in a chamber sitting in a stone chair and before her another tree whose branches crowded the roof high above. Alongside her sat four more chairs, and the woman who had saved her in the astral stood before her looking just as she had at the Broken City. She sat beside Nina on one of the chair arms next to her, smiling. Nina was mesmerized by the woman's hair that by all appearances was a mass of butterflies. When Nina reached for them the butterflies began fluttering erratically around the woman's head, making Nina laugh in delight.

The woman laughed too and placed a hand on Nina's shoulder.

'It is good to see you happy, Nina.'

'Who are you? I mean, thank you for saving me, but I don't know you or where I am now.'

'I am the Mother, and you are dreaming, Nina. Your astral body is now reconnected to the real body and healing as we speak.'

'Oh, you're the Mother. Latasha told me about you and how I was meant to meet you,' Nina said, watching as little coloured blossoms opened along the skin of one of the Mother's arms.

'That's correct. You are a very important person, Nina, with a purpose to fulfil that will help the whole world should you choose to do it,' the woman said.

'I'm not sure about that. Since my mother and father died I have just been trying to stay alive and have been so many people's prisoner that I thought I would never have a long life. Maybe there is someone better for this. Maybe you got the wrong person,' Nina replied.

'All you have been through makes you special, child. You never gave up even when a prisoner of Zacriel and then Dalwyn. You stayed strong, and there are few who could have survived what you have.'

Tears welled up in Nina's eyes. 'But people keep dying when they are with me. My parents along with my brother, and Haakon. How can I do something so important if I couldn't even save them?'

'Sometimes in life things are out of our control, Nina. You cannot be blamed for what happened to them. You will be the fifth of the coterie of the heart, of which you already know three. They will help you, as will Latasha,' the Mother said shaking her hair and sending the butterflies swarming around Nina.'

'It will be dangerous, won't it?'

'Yes, it will. That chair you sit upon has a name of Brianna Dusk on it, and she is the one you will replace. Your determination and spirit will be of great help to the coterie, and as the fifth you will be of the element of spirit, which binds the other four elements together.'

'Will I be able to come and see you whenever I want?'

'Yes you will, Nina, this chamber is for that exact purpose and to also allow undisturbed communication between the coterie.'

'Then I will do it,' Nina said, clapping her hands together in excitement. 'Latasha says the magic coming back will help the world and save many people, so if it will do that then I will do it.'

The Mother extended her arms out to Nina. 'Come and hug me, child, and when you awaken you will be back at the Witness.'

Nina enfolded herself in the Mother's hug and felt peace wash over her.

Dalwyn was surrounded by thick forest. It was night and the red moon, Tamul dominated the sky above, drowning out the white moon, Aspre. As Dalwyn moved the plants worked against him, holding him back from his destination, a hill up ahead that appeared a focus for the moonlight provided fromTamul.

Branches hooked on his robe and slapped against his face as the wind tore at him, but he kept on trying to fight his way free of the undergrowth fuelled by the knowledge that greatness awaited him if he could just get out of the forest. Behind him he heard his name whispered in the wind and turned to look. A woman stood there with arms out reaching for him, her eyes pleading for him to turn back. Dalwyn paused, taking in the figure who was lithe and beautiful with small blossoms that opened as he watched along her arms, and her hair was a cloud of butterflies.

He knew she was the Mother and knew she would have him turn away from his path and back to her to be free and forgiven and live in peace during the twilight of his life. Dalwyn turned away from her and heard the sigh of her disappointment in the wail of the wind. He had a destiny and would follow the path of his ancestors to power, and that meant embracing his god Escindre, and the red moon Tamul.

As if his decision had decided his future, the grip of the thick foliage fell away, and he stumbled the rest of the way to the hillside as with one final attempt to stop him his robe snagged on the last of the trees. His robe tore away from him leaving his pale emaciated form naked in Tamul's red light. Thin cuts from the branches striped crimson lines across his arms, which he ignored, and Dalwyn began stumbling up the hillside, finding more strength with each step until he stood at its zenith with Tamul appearing close enough to touch.

Beneath Tamul the age began to fall away from Dalwyn. His aching limbs were no more, his vision cleared, and his back straightened, leaving him feeling twenty cycles younger and full of vigour. Ahead of him the rays of Tamul seemed concentrated on one place creating almost a cylinder of light that formed a red circle in the grass to which he moved and found himself in Tamul's presence. The red moon bathed Dalwyn in its light, and he felt his energy vortices opening, connecting to it, and then the visions washed over him.

Dalwyn saw the rise and fall of his family when they had ruled Karfael, relived the many cycles of his life as he searched for meaning and attempted to follow the path of power that his feet had long ago been set upon, and then Tamul showed him why he had been chosen and what he must do to fulfil his destiny. He saw the final battle and what must happen if he would finally have all he had wished for. Tamul also showed him the cost of failure, leaving him old, decrepit and awaiting execution. He had been chosen, and there was no room for excuses. Live and prosper or die in failure, he knew what he would choose.

Then he found himself back in the Witness, in bed. The dying light of candles threw strange shadows about him, and from these shadows he could see a tall form.

'Hello?' he said, ignoring the breaking of his hoarse voice from lack of fluids.

The figure stepped to the foot of the bed, revealing a tall, muscular man with dark, blue-black skin and a thick, greying beard that encased his chin and chest area. Dark, cold eyes met Dalwyn's and he knew this was Escindre, the god of all things evil, the deity he had dedicated his life to.

Escindre held something that glittered and looked like blood. The god held it out to Dalwyn who took it and saw it was a crystal, not unlike the ones he had taken from two of the coterie of the heart. 'When the time comes you will know how to use it,' Escindre said in a grating voice. 'Dalwyn, you have proven yourself, and to you I entrust this, the crystal of Tamul. Don't fail us now when we are so close.'

Then Escindre simply walked back into the shadows and was gone just as the final glow of the candles failed and plunged the chamber into darkness. Dalwyn was so exhausted and fought against sleep as it came for him, but he lost and was carried away.

⚯

Chapter 44

Trumpets blared in the early dawn light announcing the arrival of the four Infernal lords to the Phoenix gates of Acclaro that opened out to the Glyph grasslands. The gate was rarely used except in times of war, and this was one of those times. Outside the gate a large, white pavilion had been erected a shouts-distance away between the city and the gathered forces of the nations that lay siege to the capital of Thantos.

Zacriel teetered on the back of his trull. The oversize hound had been muzzled to stop the fierce creatures snapping at each other or their riders. They were hard to control, especially once blood was spilled and so Zacriel didn't approve of the choice of mounts that The Unseeing Lord had chosen for them all. 'They lend us another edge of terror and will shake the bones of those we meet with fear,' he had drawled from beneath that plain, unsmiling mask he wore.

After the encounter with the Incubus who sought to enslave Nina within the Broken City, Zacriel was left weak from the exertion and energy loss. He would have likeed more time to ponder the miraculous escape with the help of whom he suspected was the Mother herself, otherwise it was likely he would never had returned to his body and neither would have Nina.

Meeting the leaders of Cavere, Scuttle, Culchar, and even Soarnestia if the rumours were true would have been bad enough with a full night's rest let alone none, and yet here he was shaking from fatigue along with the company of the other three Infernal lords, whom he knew he couldn't trust. Trailing behind Quail, who wore splendid green-tinted scale armour, came the hostages. Prince Grego, the sole heir of Soarnestia, Trailee the pretty young wife of King Scuttle and old enough to be his daughter, whose long, curled hair had been roughly cut off leaving her looking like a wild eyes peasant girl. The third hostage was Nizar, a highly influential spice trader who had risen to prominence from his business and now occupied the lofty position as the third breath of Culchar.

Across the field of battle waited the leaders of the other nations, King Otto Kelson of Scuttle, King Jurian Bleak of Soarnestia, and King Rhys Martinez of Cavere. They each stood proudly with a banner man and six guardsmen as was agreed on. The morning was cold with a chill wind that tore at the hair and garments of those present.

'They look so regal and smart, I'm really going to enjoy this,' said Lilith. She wore a striking gown of fawn that hugged her body tightly and had even impressed Zacriel until he had learned it was created from the skin of dead people. Lilith's grey hair was braided, adorned with the skulls of children that clunked as she moved and hung down past her knees.

As if sensing his eyes on her she turned and met Zacriel's gaze with her own eyes that blazed red. Lilith licked her lips suggestively then blew Zacriel a kiss. The obese form of the Unseeing Lord stood beside her in black leather wearing a sad mask, a huge blade across his back, and the many mouths on his arms laughed continuously.

Zacriel found himself nervous and wished it was over already. They would meet and exchange unpleasantries and then the hostages would be handed over as a sign of goodwill before they discussed the subject of the coterie and return of magic, something they all wished to happen. Zacriel hoped it would be enough to seal the badly needed peace to halt the epic slaughter that awaited if this should fail.

'Raise the gates,' shouted Zacriel, and his guards began to turn the huge winches.

The infernals within the city and bordering the outside of the sprawling town to their left that hugged the city began banging shields, screaming, and taunting the enemy forces, who also began shouting their king's and nation's names in retaliation as not to be outdone. Both groups began moving slowly towards the pavilion and stopped twenty feet apart alongside the pavilion to the cheers of their armies.

As the sun peeked over the horizon, its newly born rays hit the eldritch tower of quartz crystal that the Harlequin had formed, reflecting off the uneven surfaces a sparkling glare that forced all to turn away from it. At the field of battle, armies and Acclaro stood bathed in that brilliance until the sun finished rising, and then the tower changed colour to a blue that gave the surroundings a cold, bleak feel to them. If this was an omen he was sure it was not a good one. The whole spectacle had quieted the two forces, and the silence was strange after so much clamouring.

'Since it was you, Bone Lord who erected the pavilion we would first check this to be sure there is not devilry planned,' called out Jurian Bleak. Zacriel knew the king of Soarnestia was at least eighty cycles old, and yet his voice was strong and carried to them effortlessly.

'If my word is not enough then do so, King Jurien, we will wait,' replied Zacriel as behind him he could hear Prince Grego attempt to call out but the gag made his words unintelligible.

The six Soarnestian warriors in obsidian armour and armed with long falchion swords did just that. Taking their time, they inspected first the pavilion from the outside and then from within. They exited the pavilion and hurried back to their king, where they spoke quietly.

'It appears that the pavilion is in order, Bone Lord. You enter with your… ahh…, party, and then we shall follow.' Zacriel nodded and gave the order to move. The trull were tied to a picket, and a single Infernal left to see they stayed that way while the rest of them entered the pavilion where two half-circle tables sat facing one another. The pavilion was lit with sun-blazer globes, and its table had been set almost for a cheerier event with the best of royal dinnerware and diamond encrusted goblets. Food sat heaped on platters, and pitchers stood full of wine or water even though Zacriel doubted any of it would be consumed for fear poisons.

The four Infernal lords sat with the guards placed behind them along with the three hostages. The opposing party entered soon after, warriors first with hands on hilts in defensive positions on their side of the pavilion closest to the exit. Then the lords entered and sat, exchanging hard stares with the Infernal lords.

When all was done and Zacriel was preparing to speak, King Otto with his considerable gut looking uncomfortable beneath heavy chainmail spoke first.

'Now hand over the hostages. I would see my wife to safety before we broker any deal between us,' Otto said, wiping sweat from his forehead even in the cold morning chill.

'That won't be happening, King Otto. We will not part with our trump cards before business is concluded. As you can see, the hostages are well and you will be able to force your heavy girth upon your young wife soon enough,' Lilith said, smiling.

Otto bristled at the insult and only a hand on his shoulder by King Rhys stopped him from rising.

Zacriel rose and all eyes turned to him. 'We find ourselves in an unlikely situation of wanting the same outcome and seeing magic returned to this world. By now we all know of the coterie, who aim to return magic and work at the Mother's behest. The tower that the Harlequin have formed is for that very purpose. Since the Severing our kind have been trapped here without choice, and we would like nothing more than to return to the Infernal lands. By all means stay with your armies around Acclaro to give witness of this momentous event, and when the gates open we can withdraw with our forces to our home and leave you to this world. Only together can our forces see this outcome happen peacefully.

'You speak clever and reasonable words, Bone Lord, and yet, we know that none of the Infernal lords are to be trusted since again and again our trust has been torn away and thrown back in our faces.' snarled Rhys from his seat.

'You act like you have some choice in this, King Rhys. Never have the walls of Acclaro been breached even in times of magic. Do you think you will take the city if you attack while our forces outnumber you at least three to one?' Quail said in his strange, clipped voice through his beaked mouth.

'We purged the capital of you murderous scum once, or do you forget that, Quail,' shot back Nizar.'

'Or so you all believed, and yet our late sister the Lady of lies stayed hidden from within, poisoning the people and taking over the royal family. A hollow victory if ever there was one, Nizar. You have only yourselves to blame for deserting Thantos and leaving them vulnerable,' Zacriel said.

'But let's not talk of past transgressions, let them stay in the past while we create history between us with a peaceful outcome.'

'To business then, and let's put aside this unnecessary bickering that serves none of us,' King Otto, said throwing his hands up in exasperation.

The ironing out of details and demands turned out to be a laborious event that left everyone in the pavilion nervous as they argued back and forth until finally Zacriel realized they were nearing the end of the necessary discussions. A treaty had been penned by one of Otto's men as they went outlining what each side would agree on. No attack would come to Acclaro while they awaited the arrival of the coterie, who would be given leave to enter the crystal tower unharmed to complete the necessary ritual and return the magic. Food and supplies would be allowed into the city by the main gates as long as they didn't include humans for consumption and the allied nations' forces would stay in their positions around the city while the Infernal host would stay in place and stop taunting their enemy. The treaty had merit if both forces could abide by it until the unknown time of the coterie's arrival.

'Now I believe you must show this faith you would have us believe in by handing over what is ours,' Otto said, eyes on his wife. 'Unbind them and let them come to us and we shall take our leave.'

The Infernals guarding the hostages moved them to the area between the two tables, which was when Zacriel noticed something he hadn't earlier. The three Infernals were dressed in the armour of his warriors but were Lilith's Infernals, and he knew by the glance they gave to her after he gave the order to free the hostages. He turned to Lilith, who met his glance and turned away.

The Infernals drew long knives to cut the rope bindings, and as one they stretched the hostage's necks back and drove in the blades. Blood spurted and yells of horror came from the assembled lords, who came to their feet instantly, swords hissing from sheaths.

Guards surrounded their kings protectively while half the Infernals charged forward with only Zacriel's warriors staying where they stood at his shouted command. The Unseeing lord smashed down the table he was behind and reached over grabbing Trailee and tossing the bloodied woman through the air at the king of Scuttle.

'Here's your bitch, dog king!'

Quail was amongst the fight now, his vicious blade cutting down a soldier who threw himself in front of King Rhys as the three kings rallied with blades drawn behind their men. Zacriel pushed out of his chair and stood back with his warriors, who were visibly struggling not to join in the attack now blood had been spilt.

Jurien Bleak, king of Soarnestia, was singing with his warriors, who charged the Unseeing lord, and at the last moment the men parted for Jurien. He ducked the wild swing of the obese lord and then with a roar slashed with a backhanded blow of his own, taking the left side of the Infernal lord's head clean off along with the mask.

Then the ground trembled violently and soil and grass heaved up from the middle of the pavilion. Otto attempted to flee out the exit just as the three trull burst into the pavilion. One locked its jaw on Otto's shoulder and dragged him to the ground, where it began to tear at him.

The ground heaved again, and a long hooked appendage broke through, then another, and then a creature Zacriel had never seen before burst forth with six long legs on a segmented body of chitinous, ochre exoskeleton. Black compound eyes glanced down at the combatants and mandibles snapped open and closed as its long antennae sprang to attention, then it set upon the kings and their troops. Its height was such that the pavilion was torn free and the wind outside lifted it like a sail whipping it away to the side.

From around the battlefield a huge roar went up as the armies realized the betrayal and the allied forces charged in towards Acclaro while a lesser force manoeuvred into an arrow formation heading towards the stricken leaders.

'To me!' roared Zacriel, and his warriors surrounded him. 'Fight our way back to the city. We are finished here and the demon will kill us all!'

As they went, Quail and Lilith fell into their force along with their Infernals that still lived. The demon snapped down and tore through Otto's abdomen with its mandibles cutting him in half as Jurien managed to break free with his wedge of warriors attempting to flee, ran into Zacriel's Infernals. The king was a fierce warrior even at his advanced age, cutting down two infernals and would have been free to attack Zacriel if he hadn't acted. Zacriel slid his blade free and stabbed the king where his leg greaves met the groin area, causing Juriel to fall to one knee, and then Quail strode up, grasped the king's helmet, and literally tore his head from his body with a shout of glee. From outside came a resounding crash as the opposing armies met and the battle began in earnest.

Arrows began to rain down around Zacriel and the Infernal lords as they fled. Most missed their mark and others clattered off armour.

'Interlock shields,' Zacriel cried out, and his Infernals linked together to protect their master from the rain of steel.

Zacriel took in the carnage as they moved. Whatever the creature was that had risen in the pavilion was laying waste to the small force who fought to get to their leaders and bodies flew from a sweep of its long legs. In the skies the raven warriors had arrived and dived down into the battle to tear at the Infernals. Others darted around the monstrous beast, attacking from different directions at once to confuse it. A ballista bolt the size of two men tore a bloody hole through the Infernal ranks not far to the left of Zacriel, who led his warriors into the gap and more safety where they became trapped by the press of Infernals trying to reach the frontline of the battle.

'Hack down whoever gets in our way and get us out of this madness,' screamed Zacriel to his warriors. With a thunderous clanging Zacriel saw the chain wall released around Acclaro as protection against the swarms of raven warriors. The gate was in sight now, and on the back of a huge trull Zacriel spotted Rapture with his fell axe scything through those who got too close to him and making a bee line towards Zacriel. Great stones were flying through the air now and striking the walls of Acclaro before toppling down to crush ranks of Infernals below.

'Bone Lord, fall in and follow me,' yelled Rapture as his warriors on trulls formed an outer perimeter around the infernal lords and began ushering them back towards the Phoenix gate.

Finally they made it to the gate.

'Help get me up theses bloody stairs, Rapture, I would see what happening on the field,' Zacriel said between gasps as his head swam from weariness.

Rapture assisted him to the top of the gate and the wall there just in time for Zacriel to see the monstrous creature topple as a wayward stone the size of a cart slammed into its head. Warriors of Cavere swarmed over it, and it didn't rise again.

They stayed and watched the slaughter as the battle tipped in the favour of the allied nations until another force of Infernals burst from the city to the east main gates in the thousands.

As the day wore on the corpses mounted, making it hard for the enemies to reach each other, and sometime around noon the allied forces retreated to their side of the field. The Infernal forces bellowed their victory cries as the enemy regrouped, and soon the day was rent with the cries of the injured and dying.

'I have seen enough, Rapture. I need rest and then I would meet with the other lords. Triple the guards to my chambers as I know not if we are still allies.'

Rapture helped Zacriel out of his bloodied armour and then left him alone. Zacriel fell onto the bed, and as the realization of the betrayal settled upon him he covered his face with his trembling hands. He had failed.

❧

Chapter 45

Nina wished she were still in the astral safe with the Mother. Since returning to her body she had also returned to the torment of her jailers, who kept the five prisoners from entering the astral with food that contained considerable amounts of char. It kept them awake and too jittery to focus enough for entering the astral realm. When Latasha told them to avoid eating then the guards had begun drenching them all with cold water at least once a chime or made a racket by running their blades across the metal bars of the cell making sleep impossible.

'They can't do this forever,' insisted Raul, shaking his head and sending droplets of water flying after the latest drenching. 'We will be so exhausted that even these tactics won't be able to keep us awake.'

'Dalwyn is no fool. He knows we will have to sleep soon and that we will be too fatigued to travel the astral realm,' Latasha answered after a long yawn.

From within their dark prison, Nina had lost all sense of time, not knowing if it was night or day.

The laughter and gaming of the guards became muffled, and it would take her a long moment to realize if Latasha or one of the coterie had spoken. Though she wasn't able to sleep, she found herself missing chunks of time and suddenly becoming aware of the cell and her friends again. Latasha would begin singing softly and held Nina close. Latasha explained that they would begin experiencing fragile moments of sleep regardless of their treatment because it was the only way their bodies could keep going. Nina noticed the others staring off with glazed eyes, and then suddenly they would be back and aware of themselves again, but each time their eyes would go wild and they would seem confused.

In one of her more wakeful moments one of the guards slid two trays of food into the cell, he beckoned Nina forwards. She looked at Latasha, who nodded that it was okay, and then crept over to the trays.

'You already know we have been putting char in the food, but I put none in this meal. I have a little girl maybe your age back home in the city of dreams, and I would be appalled if she were treated as bad as you and your friends are. All of you need to eat this, Nina. It has some herbs in it that will make you sleep even through the noise and buckets of water. If you don't sleep very soon you will start going crazy, but Dalwyn doesn't care about that.'

'Jonas, what's taking so long?' a voice from the guardroom called out.

'Coming now, I was just inspecting the prisoners, that's all,' he yelled back.

'Eat, your friends too. I don't know when, but we will be leaving soon.' Then he was up and hurrying back to the other guards.

Latasha was smiling weakly when Nina carried the two trays back to them.

'See, not everyone is against us, Nina. There are unexpected friends around us.'

Nina doled out pieces of sweet, red melon, cracker biscuits, and salty meat. They shared a jug of milk between them, and feeling more content, curled up against each other.

Jona squeezed Nina's hand, and she looked at the kind woman before closing her own eyes. No cold water came that chime and finally Nina, Latasha, and the coterie slept.

When Nina awoke to the whispered conversation between Latasha and Selene, she stretched and yawned.

'What's happening?' Nina asked.

'The same guard came earlier and told us we will be leaving. He said it was night and the limpids are being loaded with supplies,' Selene told Nina.

'Lucky we have you here, Nina, and he could show compassion since you are his daughter's age, otherwise by now we would all be like zombies,' Selene continued, miming a zombie with wide eyes and outstretched arms, making Nina giggle.

When the guards did come, they led them out into a courtyard. It was night, and Nina took in a large breath of the fresh air that was free from body odour and dampness.

They were forced to strip naked and they huddled together in shared humiliation as they were drenched with cold water before being given fresh clothes to put on. Then they were manacled and taken to another courtyard where the five limpids floated just above the ground.

Nina saw Dalwyn talking with the other old man called Virgil, who was shouting out instructions to the warriors who hurried around loading the Limpids. A warrior led the prisoners over to one limpid, and tentacles snaked down and plucked the five of them up, placing them within the basket below its body. Their basket held the five of them and was not too crowded.

Dalwyn watched his and Virgil's men finish loading the limpids. He felt the thrill of excitement at their impending departure from the Witness. He checked that the crystals were still in the pack slung over his shoulder and began to walk toward the limpid he would ride in when a shadow told him there was something above him. Raising his arms as if to shield himself, Dalwyn cringed as one of the monarchs landed beside him. He stood and glared at the creature, which flared its neck feathers and stared back in defiance.

'I didn't mean to scare you, old one,' the monarch, said regarding him with unblinking eyes.

Trying hard to hide his distaste for the bird monarch, Dalwyn broke eye contact with it. They were known to be a highly volatile race that wouldn't back down when challenged.

'We are ready to leave now,' Dalwyn said.

'You must gag the prisoners,' the monarch replied and flared its feathers.

'Gag them, why?'

'If they cry out it will give away our position, and we can't risk that, old one.'

'I will see it done,' Dalwyn replied and headed over to the limpid in which his prisoners waited. He spoke to one of his flame warriors. 'Gag the prisoners so they can't cry out. Watch them closely; they are up to something, I'm sure of it,' Dalwyn added as he climbed into the basket. The warrior cut loose the rope holding the basket and the limpid immobile then jumped into the basket and began to do as he was told. With a screech the monarch flapped back to its position behind the limpids head. As it connected to the limpid the large creature came alive, its skin turning from white and blue to black and blue as it adapted its camouflage for the night.

This was it, Dalwyn thought. Reach Acclaro and safety, then he could plan his next step. Ishmael, the final member of the Coterie of the Heart, would eventually come to him. He had to because Dalwyn had his precious coterie and their crystals.

The limpids shunted away from the Witness and floated down towards the Glyph grasslands. The journey down along the mountain side was painfully slow, but they needed to keep as low as they could and away from the deadly patrols of Soarnestian raven warriors who could easily tear the limpids apart.

In the distance Acclaro was a cluster of flames. Scouts had since informed Dalwyn and Virgil that the city was relatively undamaged so far and it was the town that clung to its walls that burned along with the surrounding grasslands. Much of the glow from Aspre and Tamul was cut out by thick cloud cover, which would aid their movement above the open grasslands. Grendel had made it clear that they should cross from a south easterly direction where the troop formations and camps were the least dense.

For half the night they moved above the Glyph grasslands and the unsuspecting forces, and Dalwyn was surprised at the endurance and speed that the limpids managed to maintain as they made their way across the grasslands. When the limpids began to slow they were only miles from the walls of Acclaro. The flames and sounds of battle agitated the great beasts, so the monarch handlers took the limpids up away from danger and detection.

Below them Dalwyn thought he could sometimes recognize encampments, but he couldn't be sure due to the many fires below. From Acclaro a series of loud whooshing noises could be heard as the city catapults launched something.

Moments later a barrage of projectiles that Dalwyn realized were oil flasks when he batted away one coming straight for him with his sword. The reason for the flasks became apparent when soon after volleys of fiery arrows cut through the night some striking the airborne targets and setting the sky alight with falling flames, other arrows hit the ground igniting the areas where they struck. Dalwyn had been in Acclaro long enough to see the crates of oil stacked for just this purpose. He grit his teeth and clung onto the edge of the basket.

Beside him Nina and Latasha gazed about, their eyes were wide with fear but they didn't say a thing as they all silently hoped to survive this. The ground below them had become an inferno, and cries of the dying were terrifying. The limpids began to rise and move faster towards the city and safety, and then came that whooshing again; the catapults had fired once again.

Dalwyn saw something strike the limpid slightly ahead of him, and the creature began thrashing just as the second wave of fiery arrows shot out, some striking the limpid and igniting the oil that had broken on its body.

With an unearthly wail it floundered around, making the basket below swing wildly. Warriors flew from its safety to a fiery death below, and the flaming limpid smashed sideways, striking the one that carried Dalwyn and his prisoners. Then missiles began to strike the other limpids and also set them alight. They whirled in a panic, mindless of the other limpids or their passengers.

As Dalwyn looked on with a prayer to Escindre on his lip he saw another limpid rush past falling down towards the ground as it burned, and he caught sight of Virgil as he fell with it, then his old friend was gone from sight. Dalwyn was thrown forward, colliding with Latasha and Raul then they fell away from each other again. Nina was hugging Latasha and screaming. As the limpid turned sharply to one side Dalwyn was thrown forward again towards Raul, who grabbed Dalwyn by the robe. Maybe he thought he was saving him, Dalwyn thought, just before Raul smiled and smashed his head down into Dalwyn's face. His nose broke with a crunch, splattering blood.

Before Dalwyn could react to the attack, Raul pushed him up against the edge of the basket then twisted, and Dalwyn was thrown clear of the safety of the basket. As he fell he could see a cluster of figures below, then a flaming limpid smashed Dalwyn sideways and he collided with something below him before losing consciousness.

Chapter 46

They had been in the basket so long that Nina thought they would never get to Acclaro. As they did though she could see the soldiers from all the armies who were fighting against the infernals in the city. There was fire too, lots of it, and with that came the horrible cries of the people caught in the flames.

As they began the very last part of the journey, now angling up towards the top of the walls of Acclaro, the limpids were caught in the wave of fire arrows and began to panic. Nina grabbed Latasha by the legs and held on as hard as she could. Everyone was shouting or screaming as the basket rocked from side to side, throwing them all one way and then the other. Next to her Nina saw Dalwyn get hit by Raul, and then Raul pushed him up against the baskets edge. Selene leant in and helped push Dalwyn too, and suddenly Dalwyn who had tormented Nina for so long fell over the edge and disappeared below.

The limpid was almost level with the warriors who stood defending the wall now, whose bows sent arrow after arrow into the limpids body.

'Get down,' shouted Raul, and he pushed Nina and Latasha down so they weren't such easy targets. The wounds inflicted by the arrows had a maddening effect on the limpid as it smashed away Infernals with its tentacles then lifted away up away again. The chain wall that Zacriel had ordered built to defend the city had barbed links. They tore gaping wounds in the limpid from which oozed a clear ichor, but it pushed through and then up onto the sky walk where it hovered and the basket touched down.

The limpid released the basket and began to rise again, however, its injuries were too severe and Nina watched it fall from the sky and hit one of the castle towers as it whirled down into the city.

Nina noticed the back pack that Dalwyn had brought with him from the Witness. She snatched it up and peered inside. There lay the three crystals of spirit, fire, and water. 'Selene, Dalwyn forgot the crystals,' Nina said, handing them to Selene who hugged her and kissed her on the head. 'See, Nina, our luck is changing.'

Their descent had not gone unnoticed, and as they climbed from the basket Zacriel's elite warriors approached from two directions. They were still prisoners, but Nina would rather be a prisoner to Zacriel than Dalwyn. She saw the first running towards them in heavy armour, cloven hoofs and wielding a fearsome axe; it was Rapture.

'Rapture, it's me, Nina, don't hurt us. These are my friends and are the Coterie of the Heart,' she called as Rapture slowed to a striding walk.

Shouting came from the sky walk on the other side of the basket where warriors in blue were also approaching.

'Take them quickly up to Zacriel's tower, place guards at the balcony and the door and await the Bone Lord, the rest of you to me,' Rapture said, shouting orders to some of his warriors. A group of his Infernals quickly surrounded Nina and the others and began leading them away.

'Quail holds command of the sky walk, the prisoners should go to him,' said an Infernal whose face was half covered with feathers.

'Your lord's orders were from the Bone Lord who holds control of the city; by that right I claim them as his,' Rapture fired back, hefting his axe in both clawed hands.

'Then we have a problem, Rapture, don't we?' the feathered infernal sneered.

'Yes, we certainly do, you insipid feathered scum. Are you going to wait to die all day like cowards?' laughed Rapture, and that was all Nina heard before the sound of fighting took over as Zacriel's warriors hurried them into the tower and down the steps.

As Dalwyn fell he could see the cold stare of Latasha following him down. A limpid smashed into the side of him as it frantically tried to right itself. Its Monarch handler lay limp behind its head, and the impact jarred every bone in Dalwyn's body.

There came a flash of black wings and a leather armoured figure to his right and for a moment Dalwyn looked into the wide eyes of a raven warrior, then they collided. Somehow Dalwyn managed to hold onto the saddle of the rider, the ravens iron tipped beak imbedded in his upper arm, tearing muscle and skin as it sought to slash him apart. The extra weight dragged the raven down into a dive and thankfully Dalwyn managed to extricate himself from the beak and finish on top of his enemy and its mount before they hit the ground.

In a daze he got to his feet and staggered away from the raven which still flapped about in its death throes. There was fire all about him and the sound of thunder that shook the ground. He realized at the last moment that it wasn't thunder when a score of riders on heavily plated mounts broke through the haze of smoke. With no time to flee Dalwyn was run down, trampled into the mud.

When he regained consciousness something or someone was dragging him by the arms causing great pain in his torn arm muscles. They were talking to him, but the words were alien to him. He was rolled over and a dark skinned face loomed above him, its thick beard tickling Dalwyn's face where it touched.

'Escindre?' he said though it pained him to speak. The face swam closer and appeared to be laughing down at him. Not able to keep his concentration on Escindre, Dalwyn slid down into unconsciousness.

Chapter 47

Zacriel sat in his chamber. Since the betrayal on the Glyph his summons to the other two Infernal lords Quail and Lilith had gone unanswered. Their guards had refused entry to Rapture or any other messengers he sent on his behalf to their towers. For his own safety Zacriel had stayed mainly in the tower unless under a large escort of his own Infernals. Earlier that night he had sent Rapture up to the sky walk to clear it so he could view the battle from up there and now he missed his general. Without any doubt Zacriel knew the other two lords intended to murder him and reinstate one of their own as the new lord. Already he had received news that the rose of spite and rod of Infernals from the dead Unseeing lord had been given to one of Lilith's own commanders, someone they were calling the Butcher.

If Rapture didn't return soon Zacriel knew he would have to take things into his own hands. He had donned his mail and his sword hung at his side. He was like a caged animal, and his lust to take this rage out on someone was increasing by the moment.

Zacriel left his chamber to the main room. The eight warriors there stood as he entered. 'At ease. Has there been any word from Rapture?'

'Not yet, Bone Lord. Do we stay here and wait or go?'

Before he could answer he heard raised voices at the base of the stairs.

'Halt. Name yourself before you approach!' The challenge rang out.

'We are with the Bone Lord and have prisoners with us. Rapture battles Quail's men on the sky walk, and I have sent more warriors up to help him, but be warned the next who approach may not be our friends.'

Zacriel's warriors formed a protective circle around him, moving him back away from the entry of the stairs.

Two of his warriors came into the chamber with the prisoners, and yet Zacriel only focused on one, Nina. Was he really seeing this, or was it some cursed trick of his demented mind?

Then she looked at him and shouted his name as she ran towards him. Zacriel pushed past the circle of guards and knelt, taking Nina in his arms. She was real.

Zacriel held Nina close as feelings overpowered him. He had thought he would never see her again, and the relief at knowing she was alive and safe for the moment was overwhelming.

'Zacriel, you will squash me if you don't stop,' Nina laughed and pulled free of his hug.

Zacriel reluctantly let Nina go and stood. Then he looked at those who were with her. An ancient one who could only be the one he had been told about by Dalwyn.

'Latasha Meldoriel, I presume,' he said, bowing slightly. 'I would say it's good to meet you, though in these dark times those words would mean little.'

'I know little of you, Zacriel. Though I trust Nina's judgement and if she calls you friend, I will too,' Latasha said unsmiling. Her eyes said otherwise, but Zacriel could hardly blame her. He was hardly a pretty sight to look upon. 'This is Selene, maiden of the seas, and Jona, a native to Acclaro. The third is Raul whom I believe you have met though under different circumstances.'

'Yes, we have met. Raul was brought here by Dalwyn and was to betray the coterie. Are you sure you can trust him now?' Then Zacriel laughed wryly. 'Just forget I even uttered those words, Raul. I am hardly the epitome of goodness and just days earlier found my own self betrayed while attempting to bring peace through treaty and returning hostages to the assembled forces that now besiege Acclaro.'

'I was tricked into believing the coterie had turned against me at that time and unknowing to me my true sentinel had been murdered,' Raul said, unflinching. 'It is my sole fault that Selene and Jona were captured, which also led to the situation we find ourselves in.' 'I know now the truth and what I must do to fix the wrongs I have caused.'

'We are all here now, thrown together in this. I know that you have the same aim as we to see magic returned and the coterie free to make this happen. Let's put all else aside and find a way to bring that about,' Latasha said. 'Now if it is to your liking I would hear of this betrayal you speak of. We have been kept prisoners and know nothing of this treaty or hostages.'

Latasha listened to Zacriel retell the story of the failed treaty in horror as she sat with Nina on her lap. Zacriel still had received no word from Rapture, which could only mean more trouble.

'I know of you, Zacriel. You have been fighting against the forces of good since before the Severing. You murdered the leader of the Celestials and worked tirelessly to find out what had happened to the magic of our world. Then you hunted down Ishmael and the coterie alongside that devil Dalwyn Trevlon. I believe you had a hand in the rebellion beneath Illume before coming here to Acclaro and killing the Lady of Whispers to take control of the city. Here now with all the power you hold I find it strange why you would suddenly decide to help us,' Latasha said.

'My father taught me the value of hate at an early age, and when I was offered the chance to escape his abuse and step onto the path of power, I did so with relish.' Zacriel began. 'Apprenticed to a mage of incredible power, I learned all I could under his instruction. He taught me to take what I want and not be a victim anymore. My act of evil made the gods take notice of me, and Escindre promised me ascension to the ranks of the Infernal lands if I could accomplish one last deed, kill the celestial leader who was a dangerous obstacle against the Infernals taking this world. Then the Severing stripped me of my right, leaving me bitter and twisted. When the Infernal lords sent me to Dalwyn, who claimed to know what happened at the Severing and how to right that wrong, I was only too happy to help if it meant I would finally realize my ambition.

'I nearly died beneath Illume while pursuing Ishmael, and there I first met Nina, who reminded so much of myself when I was a child. I intended to show her the ways I had been taught, but she fought against me. When Nina nearly died and the rebellion failed, I fled with her. We hid, and I began to help Nina recover from all she had experienced from the trauma of her attack at the hands of a lord Perdomo. That time alone with Nina made me begin to question myself and motivations. I find it hard to explain, but the two of us formed a bond during that time, and yet craved vengeance at the perceived wrongs delivered upon me from Ishmael and his sentinel.

'In Acclaro I lost control when coming face to face with the celestial Raheem, the personal bodyguard of Alysia whom I had murdered. Then the call of the Infernal Lady of Whispers came to me and unable to resist her, I went. I never wished to be one of the Infernal lords but saw it as the only way to survive. I was in deeper than I could escape, still believing I needed Dalwyn so magic could return and I could go to the infernal lands. When he fled with Nina, what little belief I still had in wanting that dream to become a reality was lost.

'The arrival of the other Infernal lords only deepened that decision, but how would I extricate myself from their machinations? Nina called for my help in the astral, and so I went. Thankfully I was able to help save her, which left me weak. Then the betrayal on the Glyph happened, and my hope of peace between the two armies was destroyed. I know the coterie needs to go to this tower the Harlequin have built and will do all I can to aid you make that happen. The wrongs I have committed in my long life can never be forgiven and I know this, but I can see magic returned and hope it will make a better world, that for me will be enough,' Zacriel was surprised at the tears that had wet his cheeks.

Nina ran over to Zacriel and threw her arms around his neck. 'See, Zacriel, I knew you weren't all bad,' she whispered in his ear, and he hugged her back.

Chapter 48

Ishmael rested, but sleep evaded him and he soon gave up on it. He lay there as the gods and Zahra slumbered around him. Cinder stood guard, though he thought there would be no other Life Quenchers waiting to catch them unaware. They had thrown everything at Ishmael and the gods and nearly succeeded in doing Tamul's work.

He was dozing when he became aware of sunlight on his face. Sitting up, he could see that the crystals that caked the trees were melting away and through the gaps the first sunlight Ishmael had seen for many days now shined down upon him.

They broke camp late morning with Aeon on a stretcher. He babbled incoherently and tremors ran along his body. Cinder said the cost of carrying all the divine sparks of the dead gods was wearing him down now. Without being forced to hurry now, they made camp mid-afternoon so Cinder and Zahra could hunt for them.

Irdalar estimated they would make the edge of the Jewelled Lands sometime the next morning, which left them with a new challenge, getting to the tower and finding the coterie. Ishmael found solace in sleep and once rested he sent out a message to the coterie that they must meet in the dream chamber. Then he waited until the appointed time.

The dream chamber materialized around him the same as always but for two differences: the trees branches swayed as if by the wind, healthy now and radiating power; and the chair that had been Brianna Dusk's now had a new named carved on it, Nina.

The only Nina he knew of was the child that had led himself and Zahra out from the belly of Illume, but what did this all mean?

The coterie didn't keep him waiting for long and began materializing at the same time. Seeing them again was a welcome sight, for without even one of them Ishmael feared the task of returning magic would be too much.

They gathered about him in excitement, and Ishmael could see the difference in their faces, a weariness that he knew must also be recognizable in himself. Nina, the girl, was there too, shyly not meeting Ishmael's stare. She was so small and her legs only just brushed the stone floor.

'Nina, I am Ishmael, which you most likely already know. Don't be scared, he said kneeling before her chair.

'Nina is our fifth and the replacement for Brianna. She is the bearer of spirit,' Selene told Ishmael.

'You look much better than last time I saw you, Ishmael. I really thought you were going to die,' Nina said finally meeting Ishmael's stare.

'And for that we all have you to thank, Nina. Without your help who knows what might have happened.'

Jona placed a hand on Ishmael's arm. 'Ishmael, we only have a little time. Danger is all around us and we are in Acclaro city right now.'

'The city is ruled by the Infernal's,' Ishmael said, 'it is the least safe place for you to be right now.'

'We had little choice in the matter, Ishmael, Jona explained hurriedly. 'Latasha the Ancient is with us, and we have found a strange ally in one of the Infernals who has pledged to get us to the tower safely once you are reunited with us.'

'And the crystals?' Ishmael asked.

'Safe with us. We have three and if you still have the earth and air crystal then they are all accounted for,' Raul replied to Ishmael.

'I am with my sentinel, Zahra, and the remainder of the gods. We were attacked by the children of Tamul in the Jewelled Lands and only survived when a Jewelled one came to our aid. Tomorrow we will reach the Glyph, and then it's on to the tower. Can you get to the tower by nightfall tomorrow? I think it's too dangerous for me to come to Acclaro. What of Dalwyn Trevlon?' Ishmael added as if an afterthought.

'Raul pushed Dalwyn to his death while getting to Acclaro. If he even lives he will have been captured by the armies that now besiege Acclaro. The old fool shouldn't bother us anymore,' Jona said, growing excited. Soon we can all be together and finish this. I long to return to my family whom I dreamt of last night, and I think they still live.'

'Then it's to the tower and our first union,' Ishmael said. 'We can and must do this. Good luck to you all; you are my family now, don't let me lose you too.' He waited until they all winked out of the chamber then let himself fade out too and back to dreams of the peaceful life he had once lived in the monastery of Illume.

The remainder of their time in the Jewelled Land was spent trudging through the slurry created when the crystals began melting. They may as well have been walking through a damn swamp, thought Ishmael.

Ishmael paused to wait for the stretcher that held Aeon, now being carried by Cinder and Zahra.

'I thought you couldn't die?' Ishmael asked Aeon as the stretcher came level with him. Aeon looked terrible, gaunt now with damp, pasty skin and always thirsty.

'That's right, although at this moment I wish I could,' Aeon replied a glitter in his eyes that told Ishmael he hadn't need to worry about him. Aeon was stronger than he looked even while carrying the divine sparks of many of his kin.

The mood of the remaining gods slowly began to brighten. The forest was looking more like any other forest now with clear sight of sky. Ishmael knew the changes had something to do with the Jewelled one, which would have died from the grievous wound it had taken while fighting against the Life Quenchers' leader.

Ishmael knew that soon he would not just be enveloped in change, but at the centre of it once again. This time the cost of failure was too high to even contemplate, and getting to the tower that the Harlequin had created would be the least of his worries.

Just before noon they reached the edge of the Jewelled Land. Trees became more sparse as it turned into the Glyph grasslands. To the east lay Acclaro and Arrowhead Lake. Even from this distance Acclaro couldn't be missed, the capital was shrouded in dark clouds with an inner glow of flames. He had left the city when it was burning, and now even after so long the city still burned on his return. Beyond the city to the north was a tall column of white fire.

Cinder took command of their group now Aeon was still weak and required the stretcher. They moved carefully onwards towards Acclaro, the sky darkening as they drew closer and the sound of the siege no longer a murmur on the wind but now a roar that dipped and soared in volume.

They came to a sudden halt when Cinder paused, his hand held for them to stop. There was a skirmish up ahead. Four men fought side by side against seven Infernals who had surrounded the men and now toyed with them as they darted in and out of range, inflicting small wounds as they did so. Ishmael could hear the laboured breathing of the men fighting, and he realized it would be over soon.

'This way,' Cinder signalled and began moving off towards Arrowhead Lake to the east. With a last glance at the valiant stand, Ishmael followed. It would have been foolish to attempt to save them, he knew, when it was imperative that they stay hidden as long as possible. Attempting to put the sudden screams behind him, Ishmael hurried after the others.

When they made it down close to Arrowhead Lake they stopped in horror

The gently lapping water of Arrowhead Lake had become a grey sludge covered in a layer of pale-yellow oil that gave off a pungent stench not unlike rotting flesh. He pulled his shirt up so it covered his mouth and nose as they ran from a grove of splintered, broken trees to the burnt-out remains of three wagons, where they rested as Cinder decided their next action.

Now closer to the lake, Ishmael could see through the haze of smoke and mist to the monstrosities that slithered from its waters on bellies then stood and lurched into the shanty town created by the influx of Infernals. Ahead of them figures were fighting, but the mist hid any discerning marks of whether they were friend or foe. At least the smoke would help mask their passage to the tower, Ishmael thought as he waited. Beside him Irdalar began weeping into her hands that she had clasped over her face.

'Irdalar, what is wrong?' Ishmael asked.

'We can't just leave the lake like this. The destruction of a beautiful site is bad enough, but if we do nothing then it will begin poisoning all the water ways that flow from it. There must be something we can do,' Irdalar pleaded.

'Unfortunately, there isn't,' Ishmael said.

'What about the second crystal, the blue one? You used the white one to help defend us from the Life Quenchers,' Irdalar insisted, taking hold of Ishmael's hand.

'I will try,' Ishmael replied. The conversation had given him an idea, and he removed his pack then uncovered the second crystal. It was the wrong element, being air, but it was of the Mother herself. Zahra had informed Cinder to wait for a few more moments, and Ishmael crawled to the water's edge while making sure none of the water came into contact with his flesh, then, holding the crystal in two hands, he lowered it down until over half of it was submerged. Nothing happened, and Ishmael began to lift it from the ruined lake.

'No! Keep it in the water, Ishmael, give it more time,' Aeon called out from his stretcher.

'We don't have time for this,' Cinder hissed, but nobody turned to follow him. They stood transfixed as did Ishmael to see what would happen. Slowly the blue of the crystal began to pale and its colour leached out into the water around it until it reached towards the middle. That's was when the water began to bubble as if boiling.

Beneath the surface hundreds of figures encapsulated in cocoons thrashed about, fighting to escape the steaming sludge. Where the water turned blue and touched the cocoons they burst and those creatures that had already escaped the lake milled about in confusion on the far bank. Some of them attempted to return to the water, which had now changed as it purified from the blue crystal. The contact of the water touching the infected creatures sent them scampering away howling in pain. It didn't take long for the blue waters to totally cleanse the lake, which within a short time had returned to normal except for a pulsing blue deep down beneath the surface.

Ishmael smiled and shook his head in amazement. He hadn't expected that to happen and he was nearly knocked into the lake waters from Irdalar, who threw her arms around him. 'You did it, you actually fixed it, Ishmael! I will never forget this, neither will the generations of people who live in Acclaro. Thank you!'

Before he could answer, Cinder was beside him grasping his shoulder. 'Good work, Ishmael, now we must make haste before this brings unwanted attention to us.'

Ishmael packed away the crystal that still was blue but faded. Then they were off again, carefully navigating their way around the outskirts of the shanty town. Luckily most of the fighting was at the walls of Acclaro and they had only to hide from the regular patrols of Infernals that skulked through the haze.

As they edged farther north, they began to glimpse the great crystal tower, which pulsed with a bright light as if a beacon were calling them home. The sight of a camped force of mercenaries and Infernals forced them to trek farther east in order to avoid confrontation, and they somehow managed to walk right into the middle of another force.

'Name yourselves now,' rang out the challenge. Forms in darkened armour and white cloaks raced along their flanks with a clattering of armour.

Zahra and Cinder had taken up battle stances at the front of their group, and from the back came the warning that whoever had confronted them was behind them as well.

Ishmael peered through the haze and recognized the emblem of a sun on the cloaks, Illume.

'Surrender,' he called to Cinder, 'they are Illume blades, they are friendly.'

Cinder looked unconvinced, but Zahra sheathed her sword and he followed her lead as the forms closed in.

Zahra called out to them. 'We are what remains of the gods and we have one of the Coterie of the Heart with us, bound for the crystal tower. We do the work of the Mother and are friends to you.'

'Seize them,' came the call, and armoured men closed around them, removing weapons and force marching them all with haste to the north.

At least they were heading in the right direction, Ishmael noted though the dismay at having his pack and the crystals once again taken from him weighed heavily on him.

Once farther away and out of the darkened haze where sunlight fought valiantly to reclaim the sky from the thick smoke and unearthly mist their captors, hard, grim-faced men bound their hands and blind-folded them. Ishmael lost track of time as they were marched along, and he was relieved when they stopped. Through the gap in the bottom of his blindfold he could just see tent pegs and canvas material. They must be at some sort of camp.

'Who is your leader?' someone asked in front of him.

'Aeon is our leader, the one on the stretcher. Be careful, he is unwell and you will want to speak with the one beside me, Zahra, and her ward, Ishmael,' he heard Cinder reply.

When they had established who those three were, Ishmael had his blindfold removed.

'You are Ishmael?' a gaunt tall man asked, and Ishmael nodded. 'I am going to release your hands and you will carry your friend. There is no room for a stretcher in the tent,' he said cutting Ishmael's hands free.

Zahra helped Ishmael carry Aeon forward, and they were directed into a pavilion tent that had been laid out with furs on the ground. A broad, unshaven man in chainmail armour sat behind a table made of crates regarding them coldly.

'My men captured you close to the Infernal city, and now you are by the laws of war my prisoners. What have you to say for yourselves?'

'I am known as Zahra, a sentinel of the Kenzu clan tasked with protecting Ishmael,' she nodded at him, 'and delivering him and the gods to the crystal tower. Aeon here, is the god of time,' she said simply.

In return the man before them roared out a barking laugh. 'I have no time for foolish lies. Do you truly expect me to believe this nonsense?'

'Zahra speaks only truth,' Ishmael broke in. I was raised in Illume in the monastery of Shae the lady of Illume, and if you hail from that great city them you will know that no monk of Illume will lie regarding their faith,' he finished.

'If that is so then speak the litany of light, the man goaded him.

In times of darkness my light will protect you.
Wash the weariness from your bones.
Scrape the fingers of the dark from your soul.
Brighten your days and return you to the living.
You will shine with all my love.
Banish the evil, bring joy to all you touch.
Celebrate the life you deserve and know you are never alone.'

The tent fell silent.

'Anybody who has visited the monastery of Illume may well know that,' the soldier behind Ishmael stated.

'Enough of this,' Aeon said, pulling free of Zahra and Ishmael.

'You all know the stories of Aeon god of time, don't you?' Ishmael asked.

'We'll say for our sakes we do, so what?' the seated man asked as he scratched at his chin.

'Aeon has strange eyes, one of day and the other of night, do you refute this?'

'Well, so it is spoken of in legends, yes, but what does this have to do with you?'

'I am Aeon, the one and only,' the god of time said in a commanding voice.

'Bring him forward and let's see these eyes of his,' the man answered then ripped a chunk of bread from a loaf and began chewing it.

Aeon moved forward, and the man stood leaning forward to get a better look. His eyes widened when he saw Aeon's eyes for himself. 'A clever trick,' he began before Aeon cut him off.

'Your name is Marcus Tolvene. You were born in Whaleson and moved to Illume when but a babe. Your father was poor and put to work in the glitter camps hoping against hope to make a good find, which was when he caught the fever and died with his dreams unfulfilled. Your mother, a beautiful woman, had no other choice but to marry a noble lord so as to guarantee yours and her safety. A hard life for a step son to a noble, but you proved yourself in the duelling grounds and showed a sharp intelligence for warfare that couldn't be ignored. You were drafted into the Illume blades as the youngest warrior to accomplish it at the age of just sixteen,' Aeon said then fell silent. 'Should I continue?'

'By Illume, how can you know all that?' the man said, food falling from his fingers.

'I told you and so will do so again, I am Aeon, and I and the other surviving gods need to take Ishmael here, of the Coterie of the

Heart, tasked with the return of magic, to the crystal tower that the Harlequin have forged in the name of the Mother. If you still don't believe us, take us there and the truth will be seen.'

'Prepare an escort of thirty men, and await me to ready myself, I will go with them.' Marcus Tolvene said and got to his feet.

'You can't be serious,' the man behind Ishmael said.

'I am deadly serious, Alen. How can he know all that about me unless he is who he says?'

'It is just an attempt to gain time for their rescue. We cannot trust them, you must believe this my lord,' the man petitioned.

'What harm is there in doing this, then? The Harlequin stop anybody approaching the tower, we all know that. If he truly is Aeon and his friends are who he claims them to be, then we only hinder our chances for surviving this fell war. I tire of sitting here guarding the shanty town's flank. Should their claims prove false then they will answer for their lies. Now go and see to the escort,' Marcus ordered and was met with a clank of armour as the soldier saluted him and rushed away.

— ❧ —

Chapter 49

The sight of the tower that Ishmael had only ever been told of was one of the few true spectacles he had ever seen. It towered into the sky pulsing in time with light that blinded him momentarily if he looked upon. Other times it changed colour to green, red, and blue before fading into white again. Ishmael marvelled at it as he realized he couldn't find any fault in its structure, it was just one huge piece of crystal without any adjoining lines as if melted together.

Far to their right lay Acclaro, and the ranks of armies moving ever closer with banners also took Ishmael's breath away; it was as if all the forces of the nations had gathered to remove this evil that had claimed Acclaro.

Beside him Zahra nudged him with an elbow. 'See, Ish, we are not alone, many fight for you and our cause.'

They stopped within throwing distance of the tower's base which curved away at the sides away from them indicating the structure was at least the girth of a castle at ground level. There came movement from the tower and it looked to Ishmael as if the wall ahead simply melted away and formed into Harlequin warriors. They marched forward with their glittering swords angled down at the earth. At twenty feet away from Ishmael's party and one stepped forward from their ranks, coloured a dark blue with black at its joints.

'Let them approach,' Marcus said, and the soldiers around, Ishmael, Zahra, and Aeon parted to allow it.

The three walked slowly forward, and as they came within touching distance of the strange warrior it knelt, suddenly bowing its head as if greeting a king.

'Greetings, Aeon, god of time, we know you. Greetings, earth bearer, we know you. Greetings, warrior of the Kenzu, we know you,' the Harlequin intoned then rose again. As one the Harlequin behind it all fell into a kneeling posture in response to their leader's acceptance of the three.

'Take us home, children of the Earth. I and my companions have travelled far through many perils and are in dire need of sanctuary,' Aeon said, and he stumbled. Ishmael and Zahra barely grabbed him before he collapsed, and then the Harlequin gathered protectively around them.

'Wait!' Ishmael said, 'we have need of our possessions.' He turned to where Marcus still stood in amazement, looking on.

'Our possessions, my lord. We need them if we are to finish this.'

Marcus turned to one of his men, who ran forward with Zahra's sword and Ishmael's pack. He handed them over, then, not knowing what to do, bowed awkwardly and ran back to his lord.

They began moving forward again and the shout, 'May Illume shine upon you!' rang out from behind them, which made Ishmael smile. The sacrifice of Shail and the other gods had not been for nothing. New challenges faced them now, but in this moment they had succeeded in getting the gods and themselves to safety.

The Harlequin formed a line either side of them as they approached the crystal tower. Ishmael could see no doors, but as they stepped within touching distance a door appeared in the structure before them.

From his pack came a voice, and Ishmael knew it was Onyx, the crystal from the God head; he had forgotten it was even there.

'I am home,' Onyx said simply, and the emotion in the voice was filled with such joy it touched Ishmael deeply. Beside him Aeon had started weeping. 'Yes, my friend, we are home.'

They stepped into the tower. The crystal floor lighting below them to show a smooth corridor and the wall slid closed as if none had been there. Ishmael stopped and moved back to the wall before him, wondering if it was like the Jaldurial monastery where he had been raised.

'Show me,' he said out loud as Zahra and Aeon watched on beside the Harlequin warrior. The wall cleared like a window, allowing him to see Marcus and his men moving away with the dark shrouded Acclaro behind them.

'Amazing,' he said, shaking his head, and then he returned to Zahra's side and the three walked onwards into the magnificent structure.

Chapter 50

The tower was like nothing Ishmael had ever seen before. The entrance passage opened out into a gigantic chamber, from each corner four staircases wound upwards out of sight. Above them Ishmael could see balconies stretching up out of sight from the many levels. In the centre of the main chamber and enclosed by clear crystal walls was a lush, thriving garden overflowing with fruits, herbs, and vegetables, even a spring of bubbling water.

Ishmael stood gazing inside with wonder. This must have been the work of the Mother. The amazing sight before them was not lost on Zahra or the gods either, although the latter seemed to Ishmael subdued, and he remembered with a pang of sadness that this was their final destination and many feared what was coming.

Aeon approached Ishmael and hugged him. 'We did it, Ishmael. Enjoy this time of respite as we await the rest of the coterie, and if you don't mind I would take Onyx from you so I can place him where he will become the voice and mind of this great place.'

'I could accompany you, if you wish it,' Ishmael said.

'My thanks, but no. This is something I must do, and I would spend some time alone with my friend,' Aeon said, squeezing Ishmael's shoulder.

Zahra took Ishmael by the arm, a twinkle of excitement in her eyes. 'Let's explore together.'

With all fatigue fallen aside the two of them walked the great chamber noting the lack of any doors. The tower was just the shell, and over time it would need to be filled with the necessary things for whoever was to live here. As they explored on the levels above the first they saw that a great tree that rose five levels from inside the garden and must be the Mother. They didn't discover any place where the crystals would be housed and both agreed it must be in that garden where the Mother's physical manifestation was. Continuing up one corner of the great tower's staircase, the two of them experienced a thing of true wonder. From the main chamber it was apparent the height of the towers was beyond their comprehension, but as they climbed they reached a chamber from which all the walls were clear, and from this vantage point it looked out over the surrounding land dwarfing Acclaro below it.

'It makes no sense, Ishmael. To climb here would have needed to take us many chimes if not a day, and yet here we are,' she said.

Ishmael was about to reply when a voice came from around them, a voice they knew as Onyx.

'I have been placed in the tower to control the structure just as my less fortunate Harlequin spirits who controlled Jaldurial houses. I could hear from your conversation where you wished to go and so shortened the distance to make it possible before you collapsed in exhaustion. You may implore me to do such things as open or close doors, clear the crystal to see out, and lengthen or shorten distances.'

'That is welcome news, Onyx, and a worthy appointment for such a venerable spirit. Can you explain what this tower is for?' Ishmael asked.

'Each of the four towers will represent one of the elements. That is all I know at this time, even my knowledge has limits it seems.'

As the excitement begin to wane and exhaustion crept in, Ishmael and Zahra returned to the main chamber where they found Aeon, Cinder, and the other gods. 'Chambers are provided for our rest, but I wished to wait for you. It is my choice that my final days would be spent with you, Zahra,' Cinder said, taking Zahra's hand in his. Cinder smiled at Ishmael, and then he walked away with Zahra leaving Aeon alone with Ishmael.

'Have you known what this would be like all along?' Ishmael asked the god of time.

'No, the Mother is secretive and only showed me what I needed to know as she wished. Not even I could have imagined such a place, and it is fitting to be the centre of the new world.'

'And where is your place to be in all this, Aeon?' Ishmael asked.

'Here, of course. I have never had a true home, but this is where I will spend my future unless we fail in these final days.'

'For a moment I had forgotten this wasn't over. This miracle of a place has given me maybe too much hope,' Ishmael answered.

'Your coterie are in good hands, Ishmael, and we must trust in all that is good to see this through.'

Chapter 51

With the coming of dawn, Rapture returned. The fierce Infernal was limping badly, one hooved leg raw and bleeding and one arm held close to its body looking broken. The other Infernals with Rapture took up defensive positions on the stairs and balcony as their leader reported to Zacriel.

'Bone Lord forgive me if I don't kneel. Quail's forces hold the sky walk, and we barely escaped them. There were too many of the bastards, and they are fierce warriors. The two towers of Quail and Lilith are also lost to us, and we are in danger the longer we stay here.'

'What of my two legions in the city?' Zacriel asked his general.

'In your absence they had been redirected in battle and Lilith had them defend the main gate, where they were driven out in a sortie to catch the attacking armies by surprise, and every last one of them was slain. The last of your legions is at the phoenix gate ready to defend in your name but cut off from us.'

'We shall flee by the lunars in the hatches then,' Zacriel replied, leaning forward intently.

'Unfortunately the hatches have been burned to the ground in an attack from the raven warriors of Soarnestia. If we are to escape then it will be by foot, Bone Lord.'

Zacriel threw the nearest thing at the wall, a crystal goblet that shattered spectacularly, throwing shards in each direction. He regretted the action straight away since Nina and the coterie were resting in his bed chamber in the next room.

Latasha sat regarding him from a chair alongside him. Her cat-like eyes unnerved him, which was funny since he had spent much time with creatures far more dangerous and fearsome than her. Her eyes seemed to see right through him into his wallowing soul, and though she said nothing they spoke volumes of her distaste and mistrust of him.

'I apologize for my childish behaviour,' he began, but Latasha waved it away as if it was nothing.

'All this time I thought I was clever and two steps ahead of Quail and Lilith, now I am shown to be the fool and find myself trapped in my own city with a weakened force of those who still fight in my name cut off from me,' Zacriel explained.

'We are not done yet, Zacriel. There will be a way; we just need to be clear headed and calm enough to find it.'

The dawn brought another surprise, and it was Rapture that noticed it. He came down from the chamber above them, the third and highest of the tower where he and four Infernals had guarded the windows from aerial attacks.

'You should see this, Bone Lord. it may be nothing but something has changed the lake.'

Zacriel and Latasha followed the limping Infernal up the stairs to the chamber that looked south over Arrowhead Lake. The lake had become a breeding ground of evil and the handiwork of Lilith, from which monstrous infernals had crawled to join the ever growing ranks of her army. Now the morning sun glinted off blue waters. Somehow the lake had returned to its natural state.

'What could have done this?' Zacriel asked aloud to nobody in particular.

'Does it matter?' Latasha replied in a low voice.

'What do you mean?' Zacriel said, turning to the ancient.

'Don't you see, Zacriel? This gives us a means of escape that I never even thought of. The lake is safe again, which means we have our way to escape Acclaro.'

Zacriel turned back to the view of the lake, thinking furiously. The castle did have a dock for boats that the guards would use to patrol that edge of the city.

'We first would need to get to the castle dock and if there are any boats still water worthy then use them to paddle across to land, which would put us out of the shanty town,' Zacriel mused.

'Not impossible then?' Latasha asked.'

'No, not impossible. Lilith and Quail know they have us trapped here, so we would need a lot of luck to escape the castle to the dock and maybe need a decoy to distract them away from us, but not impossible.' He turned to Rapture.

'Who controls the dock and stables area from the main courtyard?

'Quail's Infernals, though they tire from the lack of action and hunger for flesh. Only yesterday they complained to me of their lord neglecting them and asked for food as well as wine to entertain themselves. I made sure to keep a large quantity of food aside for us in one of the tower safe holds, though it may be spoiling by, now or at least the meat will be.'

'That is something we can exploit then,' Zacriel smiled as he and Latasha returned downstairs. Zacriel pawed through the contents on the many shelves that lined one wall and returned with two vials of liquid.

'It's poison,' Zacriel said in answer to Latasha's questioning look.

'If that's all we have then it will have to do,' she replied in a calm voice.

Mid-afternoon came and went and still no attack on the tower came from Quail or Lilith, who seemed content for their fellow Infernal lord to stay trapped up in his tower. The food was salvaged from its hiding place and consisted of dry meat, thick biscuits, ale flagons, and wine. They chose to poison the wine and ale to mask the smell of the poison then a group of Zacriel's Infernals took the food and drink now in sacks and set off with their task.

While they were gone, Latasha turned to Zacriel.

'Why do your warriors still follow you? They know I and the coterie are your enemy and that you plan to bust out of the city with us, which will leave them in more danger. Wouldn't it serve their nature better to just turn us over to this Quail or Lilith?'

'My warriors know my intention is to see magic returned to the world first and foremost. I have allowed them the knowledge of how this is to happen, and they are well aware that under the command of the other lords they are nothing but fodder for slaughter. With me they have a chance to return to their own plane in the Infernal lands. Not all us Infernals wish for the total destruction of the world.'

'So that is where you will go when this is all over and the gates open again?' Latasha asked Zacriel.

'Look at me, Latasha. I am the thing of nightmares, a monster.' Then he shrugged. 'I no longer know what is right for me, nor have I thought much about it of late. Once I revelled in slaughter, but now it simply sickens me. I believe I have Nina to blame for that. '

'Yes, Nina is a very special girl. She won't want you to go, you know.'

'Which is why I must. She may accept me, but others will fear me, and we destroy that which we fear, as you well know, Ancient,' Zacriel replied and turned away from her.

They didn't have to wait long for the return of his warriors, who came in with a great amount of back slapping, grinning terribly.

'Well, what happened?' Zacriel asked impatiently.

'We made it look like we were deserting and when they saw the sacks they attacked. Of course we dropped our loot and ran back here. The bastards will be having their fill as we speak.'

'Good work. You do me great honour with your service,' Zacriel congratulated them.

'I will wake and prepare the others; we must go while we can,' Latasha said and left the chamber.

Chapter 52

A chime later Zacriel along with the coterie, Nina, and Latasha descended down to the throne room with their escort of around thirty one Infernals of his elite guard led by the injured Rapture. Three guards wearing the blue of Quails Infernals lay with a bladder of wine between them. Rapture gave each a kick and got no response. They were dead.

They hurried down a side corridor past an armoury where another guard lay mouth stretched in the act of choking. Many of Zacriel's Infernals took fresh weapons from the armoury, then they moved on, making sure to skirt one of the barracks from which laughing could be heard.

'Wait here,' Zacriel told them, 'we cannot afford to leave those in there alive or sooner than later they will discover their dead comrades and raise the alarm.'

He crept away with a handful of warriors, and once they had seen Quail's warriors numbered only three Zacriel led his warriors into the barracks. Quail's warriors gave little resistance against them and were soon dispatched.

They made it down to the docks, which required a set of thick, iron keys to unlock the entry door from the courtyard. Zacriel fished the keys from a pocket with a grin. 'I'm glad I held onto these,' he said, unlocking the door, which he relocked once they were all through.

The door opened into a storage room with four alcoves to the side that bordered on the lake's edge cloaked in the shadow of the castle. The remains of bones and charred wood showed someone had camped there recently, most likely the guards tasked with defending the lake entrance.

The gate was up which was strange and the castle was much easier to defend when the gate cut off this way in. However, this time the gate being raised aided their cause, and they began to search through many boats that had been pulled up onto the stone. Out of the many boats tied to the dock, four of them were selected to be suitable. They loaded what little supplies they had and sought out decent oars, all the while expecting Quail's or Lilith's Infernals to come smashing down the door or climbing in from the lake to attack them.

The tension running through them all was palpable, keeping them quiet and fearing every sound. The thumping of rocks from great catapults had started up again as the walls were attacked. Soon after that stopped would come the ladders as the gathered nations once again attempted to gain entrance to the city. So it must be a night assault then, which would benefit the raven warriors. The only reason they had not come in from the lake, he surmised, was that it was an infested breeding ground for Lilith's children and too dangerous to assault. They had tried of course, and the still visible remains of some of the craft half sunk out in the middle of the lake attested to that, but how long before one of the enemy forces decided the lake was safe enough to try again?

Finally the day waned as the sun set to the west, although at first Nina wasn't sure if it was getting darker since the city had been covered with great, dark clouds of smoke for days now.

From where she lay huddled against Jona, Nina saw Zacriel conversing with Latasha, who nodded and weaved her way back to the coterie.

'This is it. We go now. Once at the lakes bank where it meets the shanty town we will disembark then find our way through to the

Glyph, which will be closer to the tower so we can make a run for it. If you get separated from us, then head for the tower anyway. Zacriel and his warriors will give us what protection they can. He has been informed that warriors of Illume and Scuttle defend against attack from the town to the west. Come now, let's get in the boats,' Said Latasha to Nina and the coterie.

The four boats loaded with them all soundlessly pushed off from the dock, paddling slowly as they made their way across the now-clean water. As they neared the middle then began turning to the western bank, a thumping sound came from the west, and a moment later something struck the lake, sending up a great wall of water that crashed over the last two of the boats and drenching all within. Nina's boat was the second out of the four, and they remained dry.

'Catapults,' Latasha said, standing at the front of the row boat trying to see ahead.

'Have we been spotted?' Raul asked.

'It's hard to tell. They could be just finding their range so they can hit the lake gate,' Latasha began before her voice was made inaudible as more lumps of stone began raining down.

One struck the first boat, sending bodies flying as it smashed through the timber. Zacriel and the Infernals within momentarily disappeared, then bodies floated to the surface around the coterie's boat. Raul spotted Zacriel, and as Selene and Latasha held his legs he stretched out with his oar so Zacriel could grasp it, then they pulled him in. He seemed uninjured, just wet, but behind him on the water Nina saw Rapture hadn't been so lucky and now floated face down, blood flowing about his body in a crimson cape.

With all thoughts of silence forgotten, the three remaining boats hurriedly made for shore as the missiles continued to fall, not closer to the three easy targets but moving away towards the lake gate, which must have been the target all along. The unexpected missiles had forced them to beach within the town limits only a third of the way across the lake, and they scampered up the bank to the first row of crude houses for cover. Zacriel sent scouts out who returned with dire news regarding their situation. Lilith's Infernals had the western area of the town under their control and seemed to be massing for an attack while another force, this time of Scuttle infantry men, gathered west of them, which meant that their party could be caught in the middle of a battle between the two forces.

'What do we do now?' Latasha asked Zacriel, who was cursing silently.

'We either run for it now or wait and hope the attack passes us by,' was his reply as he drew his darkened blade, resting it across his legs.

From somewhere the sound of banging started up. Raul moved in a crouch to the window opening farther back in the hut to see what was going on as the racket grew louder.

He passed news back to them that warriors with large, oval shields were advancing through the town in their direction, beating weapons on their shields and singing.

'Why are they doing that?' Nina asked, feeling frightened.

'To scare their enemies, and the singing will raise their spirits, it's a war song,' Selene answered Nina.

Bloodcurdling screams came from the east mixing with the sounds of rattling armour and booted feet; then the sound of battle enveloped the huts they hid within. Nina covered her ears, trying to be brave. She hated those sounds of screaming and dying men mixed in with howls of some hellish creatures she could only imagine. They cowered there as the battle raged.

'Infernals are hiding within the huts, torch them,' came a cry close by.

'We must get ready to move,' Zacriel said, now on his knees. The door of the wooden hut burst inwards as a figure rushed in, a man, and there was a moment where everything paused as his eyes widened at the sight of them all. Before he could scream out the alarm, one of the Infernals covered his mouth and pulled him down to the ground.

'Don't kill him,' Latasha hissed.

The Infernal glared at her then struck the back of the man's head, and he fell limp. From outside came a low, menacing growl; something had been pursuing the man and now sat hunched outside the entrance. Selene pushed herself in front of Nina.

The growling continued and through the shadows Nina could see the hulking beast inching forwards into the hut, gleaming green eyes and saliva coated fangs dripped fluid onto the sand as it moved forward. Two of the Infernals moved between it and their Bone Lord giving the coterie even more shelter, and Nina squeezed her eyes shut trying to make the creature go away simply by wishing it. Through her hands she watched it move forwards now crouching over the fallen man's body just inside the doorway. Its growl deepened as it focused on the mass of bodies within. One of the Infernals hissed then lunged at the beast with its sword, making the beast hesitate.

'They are mine,' the Infernal growled as it prepared to fight and the beast growled again then sniffed the air, then its head snapped down, grabbing the unconscious soldier and dragging it away out of the hut. Nina covered her ears as the crunching of bones and ripping of flesh could be heard outside before thankfully the sounds stopped.

'They have fired the houses behind us,' Ishmael said from the other window. 'We cannot stay here much longer.'

'Let's go then! Stay close and be ready to defend yourselves,' Zacriel said, pushing them past him and out into the night again. Nina held Selene's hand now as they moved. The sight of the battle was disorienting as figures clashed in the light of the burning huts. The fire was spreading faster now, consuming the wooden homes and the large amounts of strewn garbage around them.

With no wish to be here in the middle of the battle, they moved fast as Zacriel and his Infernals cut down any who strayed too close. Somehow the group managed to avoid the thickest areas of fighting and found themselves on trampled grass at the end of the town where it met the Glyph grasslands. Ahead of them rose the crystal tower that reached high into the sky bathing the area with its glow, allowing them full sight for a short time. Of to their left warriors in crimson armour were marching into the village. A shout of alarm went up, and just before the towers light faded Nina saw the figure at the head of the crimson warriors, a woman in bone-coloured armour with grey hair streaming out behind her. She stopped and stared in their direction then pointed with the two swords she wielded.

'To me! The Bone Lord is here with the coterie, take them,' came the scream that cut through the sound of battle around them.

'Form up for a fighting retreat, Lilith has spotted us,' Zacriel roared, and his Infernals fell into formation around Latasha, Nina, and the coterie. The first rank of crimson warriors rushed in to be cut down easily by Zacriel's elite, but more jumped over the fallen, pressing the defenders.

Nina had never felt this frightened as they ran trying to escape. She felt numb, and the sounds around her faded together as Nina concentrated on just staying with Selene, who was practically dragging her along. In front was Latasha running awkwardly and somehow appearing calm as she urged them to keep going.

Thunderous noise descended around them, making the ground shake which made Nina panic more. She needed to get away from here.

Fast moving animals carrying warriors burst out of the smoke around them to the side, smashing into the crimson warriors and some of Zacriel's as well. Swords cut into the Infernals sending them spinning away, and then the strange riders were gone again into the darkness and smoke.

Nina fell, breaking her grip on Selene's hand. She tasted grass and earth then looked up as Zacriel's face swam into view. He snatched her up in one movement and kept running.

Nina glanced over their shoulder as Zacriel carried her away. Behind them the grey haired woman snarled and burst into a run, bloodied swords still in hand. They locked eyes, and the woman began to laugh. Even from here Nina could see the pale, blood-speckled skin of her face twisted into a look of utter hatred, and Nina felt her bladder go but she didn't care she just wanted to get away from the terrifying woman and her warriors.

The thunder returned, which Nina now realized was the striking of the hooved feet of the beasts that carried men upon them. One passed close, and a man hugging his steed's neck raised a blade to cut her and Zacriel down. At the last moment his eyes widened as he saw Nina was a child; the blade didn't fall, and then he was past them.

The tower burst into light again, it was close now. Strange warriors marched towards them in a perfect line, they looked made of crystal and formed a half circle as Latasha and the coterie reached them. Nina could see that Jona, Selene, and Raul held their crystals and she wished she had one. The strange crystal warriors attacked as Zacriel carried Nina past them.

The woman chasing them with the crimson Infernals slammed into the crystal warriors, and the fighting was graceful as Nina watched them weave around the foe, slicing many of the enemy down. The woman was of a different level of skill, however. She impaled a blue glittering warrior through the chest and it burst apart, sending blue shards spraying away before kicking another away then impaling a second. More Infernals entered into the fray from the side, and crystal warriors fell to their spears and swords, then darkness enveloped them all again.

Zacriel stopped and lowered Nina to the ground. 'Go, see there?' He pointed to where Latasha stood with the coterie, whose crystals were glowing now, then he turned his back on her. Nina looked towards Latasha standing between lines of the colourful crystal warriors defending against infernals who attacked from both sides.

She wouldn't leave Zacriel to die! Nina turned and grabbed Zacriel's waist, trying to tug him along with her.

'Nina, go, I can't protect you anymore. Go!' he screamed at her.

'No, I won't leave you, Zacriel, I won't let you die, just like my parents did,' she yelled back, though she was sure Zacriel couldn't even hear her.

He slashed a crimson warrior down then fixed a fierce scowl at her, but Nina refused to leave. Then as the world began to shake from the approaching riders again, Zacriel grabbed Nina and sprinted towards Latasha and the coterie, who were almost at the gigantic tower. Nina closed her eyes and did the only thing she could think of, she prayed to her parents to keep them alive.

Chapter 53

Ishmael and Zahra watched the latest battle begin as the sun dropped from sight. He was amazed at what Onyx could do. They had inserted Onyx onto a pedestal at the pinnacle of the great tower, and through Onyx Ishmael could get the outer wall of the chamber to clear and enable sight outside the tower and even focus on something in particular by zooming in or out.

They watched as the armies on the Glyph managed to get great siege engines on wheels to the phoenix gate and begin to smash at the gates. Thousands of ladders were raised against the walls as defenders dropped stones, oil, and other projectiles on the enemy below. The skies were filled with battle between squads of raven warriors, who hunted down winged Infernals as they dove down into the city to escape.

The scanning of the battlefield around the capital brought them to the shanty town that had formed around the great main gates all the way to the lake where Ishmael and the gods themselves had passed. A large force of crimson Infernals marched out the gates into the shanty town and Ishmael focused the crystal wall on the end of the town, where a second force had gathered and now moved forwards with torches and began setting fire to the town.

'It will become an inferno,' Zahra said beside him. 'That area cannot survive the flames.'

They watched the two forces clash as they scanned slowly over the area.

'What was that?' Zahra suddenly exclaimed.

'Where? I didn't see anything,' Ishmael replied.

'Move back a bit then zoom down more,' Zahra said excitedly.

Ishmael gave Onyx the instructions, and then he saw a wedge of Infernals break away in pursuit of another, smaller group.

'Onyx, move in closer!'

'That is the limit of my vision,' came the monotone voice of the sentient crystal.

'Who are they pursuing?' Ishmael said out loud.

'I can't see who they follow, but the other group is heading right for the tower.'

Ishmael and Zahra were now totally immersed in the action unfolding outside the tower. The fleeing force made it to the grassland, and then Harlequin began marching towards them.

'The Harlequin go to their aid, Ishmael, they must be friends,' Zahra said, pointing. Then two points of light formed, one the red of fire and the other the green-blue of water. Beside Ishmael the two crystals began to glow from inside his pack.

It's them,' Ishmael exclaimed. 'It's the coterie! We must get them inside to safety.' Ishmael turned to Zahra, but she was already moving and had drawn Moonbite as she ran. Ishmael sped after her. There was no sign of Aeon or the other gods and it felt as if they were alone in this great tower as their eerie footsteps echoed around them.

'Onyx, open the wall where that group will reach the tower and guide us there,' Ishmael called out. He reached for his pack and the crystals before realizing he had left them behind. It was too late to go back for them now, so he ran onwards.

'Clear the wall for viewing,' Ishmael shouted when they could go no farther. The wall cleared, and the scene outside coalesced before the two of them. Harlequin were fighting a desperate battle with crimson-armoured infernals led by a demonic woman who carved death into any enemy who dare step before her as she strived to get to the coterie.

Another woman was almost at the tower with three figures close behind them and Ishmael recognized Jona, Selene, and Raul running close behind a hobbling Ancient. He didn't have time to wonder who she was. His coterie were finally here but not safe yet.

'Onyx, open so they can enter the tower!' he shouted.

As the crystal of the wall pulled back into itself the smoke of the battlefield and the overwhelming sounds of fighting and the screams of the dying crashed over the two of them.

'Here, over here,' Ishmael screamed and waved his arms above his head.

The Ancient who led them spun around to face him. Infernals were closing in from the sides as the remaining Harlequin fighting began to falter. The coterie and the Ancient made it to the entrance and ran inside to the corridor, the infernals close behind them, and burst inside only with a handful of Harlequin to protect them.

Zahra leapt to their aid, danced beneath a blade then slashed across the face of an Infernal before spinning away and sending another crashing into the wall.

Outside the demonic woman was striding towards the entrance. She could not be allowed to make it, Ishmael knew or it would be all over. He could see it in those eyes that bled utter hatred and evil.

'Onyx close the damn door, now!'

The wall began to reform and closed just before the woman reached it. Ishmael saw a girl among the fighting cowering on the ground, and he moved to help her then stopped as he caught sight of a figure that had continued to cause him nightmares.

He stood facing a tall Infernal in ripped finery, its shirt had been torn from its back, revealing the nubs of tissue that could only be the remains of wings. The flesh of its body was a pale pink mottled with shades of red, taut tissue, and when it turned to face Ishmael he saw its nose was gone, leaving two jagged holes, mangled flesh twisting it's that into a hideous image of terror.

Ishmael knew that face, though it had been beautiful then, but still he realized this was the Infernal that had hunted him and Zahra through Illume and under the mountain and then had come for him again at his sister's house where Manu the celestial had fought it to ensure Zahra and he escaped.

Time stopped as they regarded each other. Then a burnt, bloody hand reached towards him as it said something he couldn't hear. Ishmael screamed and tried to run, but his feet wouldn't move; he was paralysed with fear.

Chapter 54

Zahra felt the Infernals sword slice down her arm, bringing sharp pain with it. She riposted its next attack and knocked the Infernals blade from its grip then punched her blade through her attacker's side, which was when she heard Ishmael scream.

Ishmael stood facing a gruesome Infernal which seemed to be trying to say something as it stood with one arm outstretched. Strangely the action of the Infernal seemed to be that of trying to calm Ishmael, she thought as she leapt towards it with Moonbite raised above her.

The infernals peripheral vison or just pure luck warned it of her attack, and it managed to get its curved blade up in time to deflect her sword.

Zahra pressed her advantage of surprise, but the infernal was good and matched her blow for blow, though she pressed it slowly back towards the wall. This gave her time to study her foe, and Zahra was almost caught off guard as she realised it was the Infernal that had attacked them not once but twice and had killed Manu. This was the one they called Zacriel the Bone Lord, and that realization gave her the energy to rain down blows on her foe.

Zahra scored two hits, one to Zacriel's shoulder and the second across his chest where the flesh parted easily, but she was not the only one to strike true. Zacriel struck her with the flat of his blade across the side of her face, making her ears ring, and then on the thigh, which almost took her legs out from underneath her. Why was it withholding its attacks? She pressed in again, this time smashing her pommel into Zacriel's chin, which sent him crashing against the wall.

'Zahra could hear two voices through the battle fury. 'Please stop hurting him!' The voice of a child, and then, 'Onyx, open the wall.

As Zacriel straightened himself, his chest heaving with effort and blood dripping from his wounds, the wall retracted behind him. Zahra smashed a boot into his sternum, sending the infernal flying backwards out of the tower to land in the dirt and corpses there.

'Onyx close the wall, but leave it clear!' came Ishmael's next command, and the wall slid closed, leaving them safe from Zacriel the Bone Lord.

As they watched Zacriel yelling something towards them, a figure came into view behind him. It was the woman who had pursued the coterie and she now wielded a long, glistening whip. They couldn't hear what she said but saw Zacriel slump, and then he rose to his knees and looked behind him.

The whip shot out and coiled around Zacriel's throat. He fought to pry it away with his hands, but she tugged it and he fell forward. Then the woman began kicking him savagely to the head and back. When she had exhausted herself she stalked away, and the corded muscles of her arm flexed as she dragged Zacriel away with her. The momentum of his attacker rolled Zacriel over so that he once again faced the tower, and he stretched out an arm then shouted something that even safe inside the tower they all heard. 'Nina! I'm sorry for everything.'

Nina stayed there with one palm against the wall, staring after Zacriel long after he had disappeared from view. When an arm went around Nina's shoulders, she glanced up, and when she saw it was Latasha, burst into tears.

Latasha didn't say a word, and there was none that would have consoled Nina then. Nina didn't expect anyone to understand why she wept for Zacriel. They might even think it was just the behaviour of a child, but Nina didn't care about any of that. Zacriel had saved her, but when it truly mattered she had been unable to save him in return. Now he was gone just like Haakon and her family.

Ishmael found himself overwhelmed with emotion. He had seen the rest of the coterie many times through visions and the dream chamber, but this was the first time he had met them.

Raul engulfed Ishmael in a bear hug. 'It is good to see you, finally,' Raul said clapping Ishmael on the back.

'You too, my friend. It seemed like it would never happen, and yet here we are. Are you ready to finish this, Raul?' Ishmael asked, looking the man in the eyes. '

'Yes, I believe we all are, Ishmael. I for one am tired of having to deal with this magic and will be truly happy to be rid of it.'

They were joined by Selene and Jona and for the first time the coterie were together.

Zahra watched the girl, Nina, break down, and Latasha go to her. She didn't understand what that was about. Looking around Zahra realized she hadn't seen Haakon. Where was he? Ishmael was laughing, and Zahra saw the four coterie members were gathered together, she and turned and made her way over to Latasha and Nina.

When Nina saw Zahra she ran over and hugged her too. 'Looks like Nina knows you already Zahra. Well met to you, and you deserve the highest honours for getting Ishmael here alive,' Latasha said.

'Nina saved me and Ishmael from staying lost beneath Illume. If it wasn't for her we would have been rat food,' Zahra said, mimicking a rat with fangs.

'Nina, come here so we can go explore. There is a beautiful garden here where the Mother is,' Jona called out, and Nina wandered over to join her.

'Latasha, why isn't Haakon here?' Zahra asked now Nina had gone.

'He died a worthy death, Zahra, one befitting a legend. When he fell he was surrounded by the corpses of his attackers. You were one of his favourite people and he often marvelled at the strength and determination you had been blessed with. The Kenzu need a new leader now, and you have fair claim to that if you should choose to pursue it.'

'Are you okay, Latasha?' Zahra asked, hugging the Ancient.

'I have had time to come to terms with his loss, but as you know the pain never truly goes away, it just fades. Haakon had a great part in making sure all this could even happen and I will see this through to the end.'

Chapter 55

That afternoon as the battle for Acclaro raged, inside the crystal tower a celebration was in progress in the name of the Mother. Marcus Tolvene had been summoned to the tower and had seen over the arrival of necessities like a camp stove, cutlery, and even the butchered meat of a doe. In return for his help he was given a personal invitation to attend the celebration.

The fare was simple but delicious. There was the sweet water of the spring, ripe fruits from the trees, and root vegetables to go along with the grilled meat. As they ate, Fade, the god of music, sang songs from through the ages, uplifting the group with his immaculate skill that spoke to all their hearts.

They dined within the garden beneath the drooping branches of the great tree, which Zahra had been told by Aeon was the Mother in her true form. Zahra gazed up from her reclining position against a mossy rock, gazing into its magnificent branches that swayed softly, and when she tried to listen she thought that she could detect a faint whispering but wasn't sure. That was how Cinder found her.

Cinder lay back against the rock beside Zahra. His hand found hers and squeezed it tight.

'She is truly beautiful, isn't she?' Zahra said, pointing up at the tree that dominated the great garden.

'Not as beautiful as you, Zahra, Cinder replied, turning to her and moving an errant strand of hair from over one of her eyes.

'Are you afraid of what's coming, Cinder?' Zahra said, tracing the line of his chin with a finger.

'Since we have arrived, much time has been spent in communion with the Mother, and our return to her has and always would be unavoidable since she is the source of everything in this world. Without the energy she needed to create us gods this new world is doomed to fail and fall into the grasp of Tamul. Already there is talk of my missing brother, Escindre been seen in the war camps outside but his intent is unknown.'

'You could just stay and be with me until I die,' Zahra said.

'I think not. I would prefer to have the sight of how you are now stuck in my mind when I go rather that a wrinkled prune of a grumpy old fish wife,' he replied then burst out laughing at her scowl.

'Zahra, come with me. I have found the perfect place for us to spend time together while we still have it.'

'How did you find it? she asked letting Cinder pull her up.

'With a little help from Onyx, but that is all I'm saying. Oh, and you have to be blindfolded,' Cinder added as they walked out of the garden towards one of the corner staircases Cinder stopped at its base.

'Hmmm, you are a brute, even savage that lives for war, and you would have me blindfolded while taking me to an unknown location? I'm not sure if I can trust you,' Zahra murmured as Cinder tied a blindfold over her eyes.

'You always have had strong instincts and once again they are correct, you can't trust me at all, but since now you have become a victim to my immense charm I knew you would be a willing quarry, now hush and soon all will be revealed.' Cinder led Zahra up the stairs.

'Onyx you know where I want to go, my friend.'

Zahra felt a tremble in the stomach region similar to what she would feel when she jumped from cliff ledges into the ocean when at Whaleson City.

A short walk later they stopped, and Cinder kissed her deeply.

'Are you ready for the most amazing sight of your life, sweet Zahra?'

'If you keep me waiting any longer, that life will be over,' she replied as the blindfold fell away. They were up higher than the four towers, which Zahra could see below her, above her a thick spire was the only area of the tower higher than where Zahra stood now and was where the crystal Onyx now sat.

The floor, walls, and roof were all clear crystal that allowed the complete view of the land from their vantage point. The sight was breathtaking.

Cinder produced a wine flagon, fruit, and a blanket, then he settled down and beckoned Zahra to him.

They stayed in each other's arms for the afternoon, sharing stories and enjoying food until the sky darkened and the stars revealed themselves along with the white moon Aspre beside the red Tamul. From their position it seemed like they were amongst the stars themselves, and it was a sight Zahra knew she would never let fade along with this man who had once been a god beside her.

Thank you, Cinder, for making this so special,' Zahra said then pulled him down onto the blanket, and they made love among the stars.

Chapter 56

The casualties kept coming in, and before noon Dalwyn was given some water and stale bread then asked to leave since others needed his bed more. Being evicted didn't bother him though, he was impatient to get going. During his brief stay in the pavilion Dalwyn had overheard someone mention Lord Trey Urvile, the husband of Tia. Lord Urvile could be of some use in hiding Dalwyn's identity and give him some free movement through the forces that attacked Acclaro. The area around all the pavilions were only loosely guarded, while apothecary's and their aids as well as volunteers hurried about. Dalwyn spotted a line of men waiting to see two officers who sat at a table. The men were placing black arm bands on some of those who waited while others were directed to another table close by.

'What are you all waiting for?' Dalwyn asked one of the men.

'Allocated duties. Those who are free to do so are needed running supplies or messages to the various camps. This line is for supply runners, but you, my friend, will be found to be too old, so I suggest you line up at the next table and run messages.'

'The answer riled Dalwyn. He forced a smile and refrained from striking the man for daring to say he was too old, then he calmly walked to the next line, which was disappearing quickly as those already there were pressed into service. When it was his turn, Dalwyn stepped up to the table.

An officer looked him up and down, clicking his tongue as he did so.

'You look half dead,' he said.

'Just released from the medical tents, my lord, for minor injuries, but I can move fine.'

'Can you read?'

'Yes, and quite well, sir. I just want to do my bit and help.'

'Well you have come to the right place then. Now place this on your arm and report to that tent there,' the man said and moved on to the next man.

Dalwyn walked to the nearby tent, showing his armband to the two soldiers who stood there wearily, and they waved him through.

Through a haze of pipe smoke he saw tables where men rapidly scribbled down notes, and he approached one.

'How can I help?' Dalwyn said appearing attentive.

'Take this scroll to the command tent west of here. It's marked with a golden eagle flag, and hurry.'

Dalwyn took the scroll then left. Heading west through a supply train of carts, he grabbed an apple from a box as one cart rolled by and was rewarded with a string of abuse for doing so. Dalwyn ducked behind another cart and opened the scroll, but he was disappointed to find it written in some sort of code. For half a chime he wandered west, taking note of the different forces, and finally he spotted a golden eagle flag flapping in the wind and made his way towards it.

As he did so he saw another man exit a tent close by wearing the Urvile family crest. His jet-black hair was greying at the temples and he had a thin moustache, it could only be Trey Urvile. Tamul must surely be smiling down on him.

Trey Urvile marched past Dalwyn, who followed at a distance and watched as the lord stopped where a group of women sat beneath the shade of umbrellas. Trey talked a while, then one woman took his arm and they both angled off to a smaller, grey tent.

The women were camp followers, Dalwyn realized with a grin, and Lord bloody Urvile was about to be caught dipping his prick into some whore. Tia deserved better than this runt of a man, and even though Tia was no longer his, Dalwyn was not about to stand by and let her honour be tainted.

He waited at the tent until he heard the groans of pleasure, then looking about to be sure he wasn't being observed, slipped inside. Trey Urvile had the whore bent over in front of him as he thrust away. Dalwyn spotted the lord's sabre on the ground near the entrance and slid it out of its sheath.

'Hey, what do you think you're doing? You can have her after me,' Urvile began. Then the sabre punctured through his side and with a squeal Trey fell off the woman to the ground. The second strike sheared half of Trey Urvile's face off.

The whore turned and looked in shock, clasping her gown to her bosom, then collapsed as the sabre slashed across her throat. She fell back gurgling, and Dalwyn watched her die before rifling through Trey's pockets, finding nothing useful.

He examined himself, happy to see there was no blood on him, then spat on Trey's body. 'Oh, Tia, if only you knew what I still did for you,' Dalwyn said then left the tent and hurried towards the golden eagle flag with a spring in his step. It had felt good to kill Trey and destroy yet another enemy of his. Handing over the scroll to an officer by the entrance, Dalwyn was directed to another table for another task.

'I have a message to get to one of the Tunoka leaders,' the officer said, not looking up. 'It's a way away. Can you do it?' he asked.

'Yes sir, it's no trouble.' he took the scroll and left with no intention whatsoever of going near any Tunoka warriors. The confusion and throngs of people made it easy to blend in, and Dalwyn knew that if he just had a scroll he would be overlooked by most people. Dalwyn confidently headed farther west towards the tower past fresh, untried warriors whose faces were white with fear as they waited for their chance to dice with the death jester. As he walked past siege rams and great catapults he contemplated setting fire to the siege weapons but now was not the time for distraction, each step brought Dalwyn closer to his destiny, closer to immortality and returning to his home city the fabled Karfael, where he would rule. Grendel's death was a shame and left him alone to carry on the Trevlon legacy. Grendel had been an accomplished leader, a true reflection of the greatness that had filtered down through their family, but also a damn nuisance who had taken to mocking Dalwyn's age as well as questioning Dalwyn's sanity. It was just one less problem he would have had to deal with later.

Chapter 57

With the tower firmly in his sights and his attention so focused on it Dalwyn failed to realize he had strayed across a picket line into a new area of the camps until his path was barred by two warriors with spears.

'Halt, where you are! You may go no farther this is the Scuttle camp,' one of them said, staring at Dalwyn suspiciously.

'My apologies, sir, I seemed to have wandered,' Dalwyn replied not needing to feign genuine surprise. He showed the two men the scroll he held, and one took it.

'It's in code, Jess. Keep the old man here while I fetch someone who can read it.'

As the warrior stalked away Dalwyn studied the other man, whom he could see was young and nervous.

'You are one of the lucky ones, eh?' Dalwyn said, sitting down and attempting to put the man at ease.

'What do you mean by that?' answered the warrior with a puzzled expression.

'Safe back here guarding the camp while others are out there dying. Maybe you have friends in high places or a brother or father who is reluctant to send you to your death?'

'I just follow orders. It is not for me to say what role I play, that's for the officers, and I don't need to be questioned by a doddering old fool the likes of you, so shut your trap and be silent!'

Dalwyn did just that, enjoying that he had riled the man so easily.

When the other warrior returned he had an officer with him who now held the scroll.

'This is him, sir, he was just wandering along in a world of his own.'

The officer stared at Dalwyn; they were of the same age. 'You do realize that these messages are for the Tunoka and not the Scuttle forces, messenger?'

'Don't really know, my lord. All the messages are meant to be coded, so I just go where I'm told to go. It's been a long morning and I may simply have misheard my instructions. Now I know, I can take them where they should be and be on my way,' Dalwyn said, extending his hand for the scroll, but the officer didn't hand it over.

'Get some rest, friend I will have one of my men deliver it so I can ensure it actually gets there. Maybe you would be better off at one of the food tents ladling out soup instead of messing up important business!'

Dalwyn clasped his hands in front of his chest. 'I'm truly sorry, sir I didn't mean to mess up. I will do as you say and return to the Culchar lines where I came from,' Dalwyn apologized then turned to leave. He would need to find another way to bypass the Scuttle camp to get to the tower. He knew the three warriors were watching him as he left, and every step away from his desired destination seemed a chimes worth of effort.

Purposefully he angled between tents and carts so he would be out of sight and then stopped to evaluate his options.

Nearby a cart of supplies was winding its way behind two cular lizards with three men slouching inside.

'Where are you headed?' Dalwyn asked, walking beside it.

'The front lines with these weapons and shields. Now let us rest we haven't slept in days,' a man growled.

'Mind if I catch a ride? I have to take a message that way myself and my hip is giving me pain.'

All he got in return was a shrug, so Dalwyn pulled himself up over the edge and leaned against the cart back where he tucked his cloak up about his neck trying to blend in.

The cart rocked along towards Acclaro and the front line, then turned west, Dalwyn smiled. He was heading in the right direction again. His excitement was short lived though as up ahead he spotted a checkpoint with Scuttle warriors and Culchar warriors, checking carts and questioning anyone who accompanied them. He needed to find a way through the checkpoint, and fast.

The cart stopped by the checkpoint, and the warriors ushered Dalwyn and the three other men out of it as they checked the contents of the crates and questioned the driver. There was no lethargic behaviour here like farther back behind the lines, only calm, ordered control and very thorough men. Dalwyn was searched along with the others.

'What's this then?' one warrior asked Dalwyn as he found the red crystal.

A keepsake found on the battlefield. I was ordered to take it to my superiors after delivering these supplies,' Dalwyn replied. Beside him one of the men who was in the cart looked at him incredulously.

'That's not the truth, he just hitched a ride with us, complaining of his hip,' the man told the warrior. 'We don't even know him.'

'I know him,' came a voice from behind the checkpoint, and Dalwyn turned to see the officer that had sent him on his way to ladle soup. His shoulders drooped in dismay.

'You two take this man to my tent and stay beside him. He tried to bypass the Scuttle lines earlier, and I will question him.'

'He had this on him, sir,' one of the warriors said, passing the officer the crystal. Then the two warriors pushed him before them roughly, nearly causing Dalwyn to pitch over onto the ground.

The tent stank of body odour and old food. Papers littered a table and crumpled clothes lay strewn about a pallet in the corner. Dalwyn was made to sit on the ground as they waited.

'Is an old man really that dangerous that you must stand with your weapons ready to kill me?' he asked them attempting to strike up a conversation and lower their guard but, these were stout soldiers.

'Open that mouth of yours one more time and you will regret it,' said one, and Dalwyn decided to take his advice.

When the officer entered the tent he cleaned away the papers on the desk, stacking them as he went, then pulled a crate up opposite it.

'Sit there,' he told Dalwyn then took a crate for himself as the two warriors took up positions either side of Dalwyn.

'Who are you really?'

'A messenger, like I told you,' Dalwyn replied.

'Do you still expect me to believe that nonsense after disobeying my instructions and attempting to sneak through the checkpoint?' sighed the officer.

'I'm sorry, sir, the truth of it is that I am searching for my son who may be dead out there on the Glyph or in the action. Are you a father?'

'That has nought to do with this, now what is your name?'

'It's Jed. Sir.'

'How do you come to be here, Jed?' the officer continued.

I came with the men of Culchar from whence I hail. I promised my wife I would find our son. You see he is not fit to be a soldier even though he would tell you differently, and he is our only child.'

'Enough of the crap!' roared the officer and he struck the makeshift table, knocking a goblet over. Papers fell to the ground and wine pooled on the table top.

'Who are you spying for? If you come clean and give me the truth we will show you mercy, otherwise you are set for the gallows.'

'I'm no spy, and I want no part in this war. I am just trying to get through the camps near Scuttle where my son is supposed to be right now. With you delaying me he may have already gone into battle, for all I know he could be dead!' screamed Dalwyn.

The officer began to clap his hands slowly. 'Rarely have I seen a better actor than you. The lies just flow off your tongue, don't they?'

Dalwyn didn't react to the officer's question but sat following the man's movement.

'Who are you spying for?'

'I'm not a spy,' Dalwyn began, and an arm wrapped around his throat choking him. As he began to weaken they let him go. He gasped for breath and from his bent position saw the officer's boots as he stepped in front of Dalwyn.

'I consider myself a man of honour. Even in warfare I am fair to the enemy and so having to resort to the behaviour you have just had a taste of makes me sick to the stomach. Truth be told, Jed, I never have had the stomach for blood and guts, which is how I rose up through the ranks. It's much easier to avoid this from behind the lines and your men, don't you think?

Dalwyn glared at him.

No answer? Never mind, Jed, I have more to say. When you are in the thick of close combat, you never forget the gruesome sights that it brings. They are scarred into your very soul.'

'Just make your damn point!' Dalwyn said.

'My point being, Jed, is that though I dislike torture I will use it to find out if you are a spy or not because we cannot afford to have someone moving through our lines and murdering anybody be they officers, lords, or peasants!'

The light in the tent appeared to dim, or was it just that the murder he had committed had just stained his soul a shade darker?

'It couldn't have been him. He is my man,' came a voice from behind Dalwyn.

The two guards sheathed their weapons and saluted. The man walked into the tent and light flooded back in around him. It was this man that had caused the darkening of the tents interior from his tall, broad body coloured a shade of darkness tinged with bruising and a thick, greying beard to his waist. Dalwyn grinned; Escindre had come for him.

The officer took in this newcomer and stepped back, obviously feeling intimidated. 'Who are you?' the officer managed.

'I am Duke Reeve and next in line for the throne of Scuttle should our new king fall before he is even ordained. This man is a precious friend, no longer himself and not sound of mind, and he played a big part in my upbringing, so you cease this assault on his person this very moment. Come, Jed, you are safe now,' Escindre said, offering Dalwyn his hand.

'Hold on a moment, you can't just march in here and take my prisoner. I am proving he is a spy, and you,' the officer said, pointing his finger at the duke, 'have no authority here. This is still Cavere lines.'

'Do we have a problem?' asked Escindre stepping forward towards the officer and flicking open his jacket to show the blade strapped to a hip.

The officer looked furious and his men terrified as Dalwyn was escorted from the tent.

Dalwyn stared at Escindre as the two of them hurried away.

'Don't stare at me, it will only look strange,' Escindre growled.

'How did you know where I was?' Dalwyn asked.

'You are my representative in this. I always know where you are,' Escindre replied and when Dalwyn just looked back blankly he continued. 'You are one of the coterie, the sixth one, unlike the others and so despised and mistrusted. You are the antithesis of the others,' Escindre said as they walked.

It took a moment for those words to sink into Dalwyn's mind.

'One of the coterie? How can that be since I carry no magic within me?' replied Dalwyn, stopping.

'You were the only one without it, but like the others you can hold magic within you. There is a balance between good and evil that always has been and always will be. This is just one of the reasons you are their opposite. I have guided you with the help of my most loyal followers.'

'And yet you kept me in the dark and let me stumble through my life into my wisdom cycles as if it were nothing? snarled Dalwyn in confusion.

'Nobody knew what had become of the magic, Dalwyn. All I knew was that you were the latest to inherit the dark mantle of coterie. It was always up to me to guide you in the search, and we succeeded. You found out what had happened to the magic and made all this possible. Now our goal is in sight and we can change the world in the name of Tamul and your dream of immortality will become realized,' Escindre said in a low voice.

'You left me to struggle alone, letting me believe I had nobody to turn to for guidance,' Dalwyn accused.

'That is not our way. You already had the spirit and ambition, and my belief in you was total. Looking at our situation now I would say this belief was not unfounded, wouldn't you?'

They had reached the Scuttle lines now. Warriors guarding the perimeter snapped to attention as Escindre approached.

'Have two extra men placed by my tent and bring food for two then don't disturb us under any circumstances, do you understand?' Escindre told one of the men.

The tent was lavish compared to any Dalwyn had seen, furs lining the ground along with cushions and a table set for meals.

'Now sit and let me explain what we must do.'

As Dalwyn listened he began to smile at the plan that was unfolding

Chapter 58

Somehow Ishmael slept that night. This was the day when the ritual would be held to the return the gods to the bosom of the Mother. Aeon had spent time to make sure the gods and the coterie knew their roles. Zahra had not been idle. She had searched the area around the garden where the ritual would take place looking for any defensive weaknesses, but due to the nature of the place and the fact that the walls were clear crystal it would make any planned attack almost impossible to succeed. Through Onyx Zahra had found that she could request warriors, and for the coming important rituals that's what Zahra did. Now fifteen Harlequin warriors stood unmoving at each of the two entrances to the Mother's garden.

Ishmael had dressed in white trousers and jacket with a deep green doublet beneath it. Around his neck he wore the necklace he had received when he became a fully-fledged monk of Illume, a spire of gold flaring out with an orange carnelian at its centre. Ishmael made his way down to the garden. There was still more than two chimes until dawn that could have been spent getting more rest however Ishmael preferred to spend this magical time of the morning reflecting on his life in silence that hinted at hidden knowledge, and allowed one to feel connected to the world around them. He sat with his back to the Mother and closed his eyes. They no longer shared the connection that had been in place, but Ishmael could sense and feel her power without it now. In time, figures began emerging to gather outside the garden.

The gods would gather at one end and the coterie the other then meet in the middle. Latasha wore a gown of flowers and moss that left her many scars for all to see. They only added to her fae beauty, and it pleased Ishmael that she was able to wear them as a testament of her devotion rather than as the markings of a victim.

There was Selene clothed in layers of different blue silks and grasping the water crystal while beside her stood Jona in a white gown with blue ruffles showing beneath them. He greeted them both and moved along to the others. Nina stood wreathed in a silver dress with a matching circlet on her head and gleaming shoes that reminded Ishmael of the stars. She was giggling at Raul, who danced a silly jig around her. Raul wore high leather boots, black leather trousers, and a blood red shirt; the whole outfit only enhanced his wolfish looks. They all talked while waiting for the appointed time when Latasha would lead the coterie through the garden to the Mother, where they would witness the return of the gods and then place the crystals.

As the beginning of the day replaced the night, Latasha turned to them. 'This is the moment everything has led to, now let's complete what we have come to do and know I am proud of you all, and if Haakon were here he would be too.' Latasha's voice cracked with emotion, then she turned and began walking ever so slowly into the garden towards the centre.

Ishmael noticed Zahra following behind the coterie, scanning about though there was no sign of any threat whatsoever. The Harlequin silently followed her and spaced themselves out through the garden as they moved forward. The dawn light bronzed the Mother's branches and lightened the leaves to an emerald sheen.

The coterie gathered in a half circle around a circular rock that had not been there yesterday when they had feasted here. In the rock sat five natural depressions, and Ishmael concluded that was where the crystals would be placed. Opposite them the procession of gods approached, wearing long robes with deep hoods that hid their identities. The god at their front stepped forward to meet

Latasha then removed its hood. It was Aeon, and he looked better than Ishmael had ever seen him. His worry lines had faded and his energy seemed returned, but most noticeably were his eyes, they shone.

Latasha began to sing, and her words carried through the garden to rise through the corridors and chambers of the tower. It was beautiful and sad at the same time, leading one's emotions to uplifting hope then down to disheartening sadness, which to Ishmael mirrored the highs and lows of one's life.

The song finished. Latasha and Aeon both placed hands on the stone before them, and at first Ishmael thought it was a trick of the light as someone stepped forward out of the tree to stand before Latasha, Meldoriel, and Aeon. The Mother stood with a green tint to otherwise pale, alabaster skin that looked bruised in places. Ishmael noted that some of the leaves that sprouted from her skin had browned and curled up, and as her hair of butterflies swarmed wildly about her head, some fell to writhe in the soil, dying as eyes the green of new leaves cast about her taking in all who were there in the garden.

The Mother turned to Aeon, who stepped forward and embraced her. A tremble shook the ground, the branches of the Mother thrashed then calmed, and what looked like droplets of light began peeling off Aeon and onto the Mother. Aeon gasped through the process, his body shook, but the look upon his face was one of ecstasy. Then it was over and Aeon stumbled then moved to the side with the help of Latasha.

'The first god after Aeon stepped forward and the hood fell back; it was Cinder, god of war and recent beloved of Zahra. Ishmael located Zahra to the side standing with a hand clasped over her mouth. He noticed that Cinder also looked to Zahra, giving her a great smile. 'Don't fear for me or mourn me, my beloved, treasure the memories we shared,' he called to her and then added,' 'I love you.'

Zahra only nodded and Ishmael knew she would have had to struggle mightily to not break down then. Cinder walked forward and took the Mother's hands in his. Cinder's body began to leak light as it broke apart into flakes that were absorbed in the Mother, and then he was simply gone.

The Mother's form glowed, blemishes on her skin lightened as the power regained from the gods healed her. Ishmael was immersed in the scene unfolding before him as the procession of gods continued over the next chime. Only nine remained now and soon it would be the coterie's turn to do their part.

From where the gods lined up Ishmael saw the rear-most one break away and move through the garden to the side towards where Zahra stood. She watched it approach but showed no sign of being alarmed, so Ishmael didn't think much of it until the figure drew back an arm, and it held an iron mace in its hand, and Ishmael could only watch as the hammer slammed into Zahra's shoulder when she turned towards it. She fought to raise her sword from its sheath as the hammer slammed in again, striking Zahra in the upper back and knocking her down with a scream. As Zahra fought to get up the figure kicked her in the face, and she fell down again and this time didn't get up. Her attacker's hood had fallen back during the assault and Ishmael cursed at the sight of Dalwyn Trevlon.

Almost everyone was concentrating on the gods and the Mother, and they didn't see Dalwyn's attack on Zahra until Ishmael cried out. Four more of the robed figures cast back hoods and burst into action. The Harlequin warriors tensed and began to move forwards, then they simply stopped as if confused.

Latasha was grabbed by a robed god with a hacking cough and whose skin was covered in weeping sores, Scourge the goddess of sickness and pestilence. Jona grabbed Nina and turned to run, but standing back behind the coterie were two lithe figures, one dressed like a camp follower in short skirts and a low-cut frock revealing heavy cleavage, and the other dressed as a noble in a gown of purple with a whip curled up in her hand. The sisters of vengeance.

A hulking figure in front of the Mother tore off its hooded robe. Ishmael saw it was Escindre god of evil wearing black leather armour, his beard was braided down his chest, and his head was newly shaven, the light filtering down highlighted his ebony skin. Escindre leapt forward then slammed Aeon against the trunk of the Mother while her female form stood calmly watching what was happening as if it had not been unexpected, but her eyes blazed with anger.

Escindre and Aeon held each other by the throat as they wrestled one another.

'Did you forget your other brothers and sisters, Aeon? I thought you represented us all,' Escindre said.

'Don't play the fool, Escindre, you have always known it would come to this and that there could never be full union of the gods due to observing the balance of good and evil. Our battles to claim this world will continue until you manage to destroy it.'

Escindre overpowered Aeon and stood behind him with one burly arm clamped tight around Aeon's neck.

'The last hooded figure who watched on silently caught fire, its robe burnt, and yet no cries of pain or alarm came from it. As the clothes burnt and fell away, a tall man stood there, flames dancing over his skin. Tamul was here.

'Enough, Escindre, you are a god and yet you behave like a child. Dalwyn search the coterie,' Tamul ordered.

'Come no closer, Dalwyn,' Ishmael warned.

'Why not, Ishmael? After all, we have more in common than you think, did you know we are brothers?'

'What nonsense are you talking about, Dalwyn?' Ishmael snarled, wishing the man would simply die.

'I am of the coterie too, the sixth and final member, always destined to be different from you others but necessary for this great balance we are part of.'

'Don't listen to him, Ishmael,' Nina called out. 'He always lies.'

Dalwyn reached into his robe and withdrew a deep-red crystal with black veins through it.

'I am the sixth and bearer of darkness,' Dalwyn exclaimed.

Though Ishmael reeled in horror at Dalwyn's revelation, it actually made sense to him now, and explained the feeling that something had always been missing. So this was how the forces of darkness would have their chance. They needed to take the coterie into their hands, and it came down to Dalwyn or Ishmael. Whoever out of the two of them was able to either kill the other or connect their crystal, then they would be the one to control the coterie.

Dalwyn moved to Nina.

'Place your crystal in the stone, Nina!' Dalwyn ordered. Nina didn't even look at Dalwyn but instead looked over at Latasha, who still stood in the grasp of Scourge.

'Place your crystal, Nina, then your part is done and you will no longer be a danger to anyone.'

Nina picked up the clear, quartz crystal, hurried forward, and placed the crystal of spirit in its depression before running back to Selene and Jona. Then without saying a word Jona moved forwards with the crystal of air, looked at each member of the coterie before finally glaring at Dalwyn.

'No matter what happens, Dalwyn, you will never have our cooperation and I reject your claim. As far as I see it you are simply an option besides Ishmael, and a poor one at that.' then Jona placed the crystal.

Raul walked up with the fire crystal, placed it, then stepped closer to Dalwyn.

'I see the nose didn't cause you too much trouble. You must be one lucky devil, Dalwyn, for I truly believed you had fallen to your death when we pushed you out of the Limpid,' Raul said.

'Tamul protected me. He is the true power, not the Mother, and when the new world becomes his then you will know that you have chosen the wrong side and I will enjoy seeing that despair settle upon you, Raul,' Dalwyn said, looking as if he was enjoying himself immensely.

'Do it now, Ishmael,' yelled Latasha. 'Place the crystal!'

Scourge clasped a shaking hand over Latasha's mouth, but it was too late. Ishmael leapt forward. Escindre, still holding Aeon by the tunic, grabbed at Ishmael and managed to get hands on his jacket.

Ishmael turned with the attack and the jacket was torn away from him, leaving him free again. Now at the rock he lifted the crystal to place when something struck his right wrist, tugging his arm away and Ishmael with it. It was a whip from Adaya one of the sisters of vengeance. Ishmael dropped the earth crystal to pull against the whip and the sister as Adaya stepped in to strike him with the thick handle.

The movement brought the goddess in near where the Mother still stood, and without warning the Mother grabbed Adaya and held her tight.

'What? What are you doing?' Adaya managed to say before the whip fell from her grasp. Her face relaxed into a visage of pleasure, then she broke apart and was absorbed by the Mother.

Adaya's sister, Hellion, attacked and her own whip caught the Mother across the face, slicing away flesh. Selene and Raul looked at one another then ran at the sister of vengeance, who back handed Selene. Raul knocked Hellion from her feet then held her down as the Mother approached. Soon the second sister's protests were silenced

Ishmael grasped for the crystal again just as Dalwyn stepped past him, pushing him over as he passed. Dalwyn stood and paused with his crystal held up before himself.

'The coterie is mine now, Ishmael!'

The arrow took Dalwyn through the lower arm. He let out a cry and fell back as the red crystal bounced from the stone and off into the sand. Ishmael saw it was Zahra who had fired the arrow. She stumbled closer as she knocked another arrow, and as she did so Escindre growled then charged her. Ishmael thought she would never have time to finish the shot. A moment before his axe descended the power of the bow shot ripped back Escindre's head, which was the thing that saved Zahra's life since the swing of the axe was pulled from its aimed trajectory. Escindre dropped the axe as he clawed at the hole in his face, stumbling back towards Tamul.

'Help me Lord Tamul, I need your help, you owe me that!' Escindre screamed at the red god.

'I owe you nothing,' Tamul replied and threw himself around Escindre's form. The dark god began to fall apart to be absorbed by Tamul whose body was fuller, now of corded muscle.

Zahra's next arrow took Scourge in one eye, and she let go of Latasha as she began shrieking in pain. As she thrashed about Latasha broke away and ran to join the Mother.

Tamul stepped over to Scourge.

'Calm yourself, you are fine now,' the red god simply said then enclosed his arms about her, and she fell silent. Tamul laughed as he absorbed Scourge.

Ishmael was back on his feet now, crystal in hand again. He pulled himself up to the side of the stone as Dalwyn reached him and grabbed his leg. Dalwyn had snapped the arrow that had struck him and pulled it free. Now he had hold of Ishmael's leg, he took the sharp point and dug it into Ishmael's thigh, delighting in the yell of pain. Then he began slamming the jagged arrowhead into wherever he could find flesh.

Ishmael roared with pain as Dalwyn struck his leg. He reached with the crystal to slide it into the depression, but the distance was just too far and the attacks kept coming as Dalwyn found targets for the arrowhead all along Ishmael's leg and in his hip and back. Knowing it would hurt him and maybe cause severe damage to his wounded leg, Ishmael threw himself forward and slammed in the crystal.

Nothing happened. Ishmael had expected something, but all he got was another slash of the arrowhead along his lower spine.

Dalwyn was above him now, and looking up at him as he tried to twist away, Ishmael saw Dalwyn drop the arrowhead and pick up the red crystal then raise it up with both hands. Ishmael raised his own hands in an attempt to defend his face.

Before Dalwyn could drive the crystal down into Ishmael's face, Nina grabbed a knife from Ishmael's boot. She clambered up onto the stone and jammed the knife into Dalwyn's unprotected neck. Dalwyn's arm flung out, knocking Nina off the rock and away, which was when Ishmael shifted his weight and turned, bringing Dalwyn down on to the stone, back first on the five jagged crystals. Dalwyn arched his back in pain and attempted to extract himself from the crystals, but his strength was fading and his vision growing dark.

'No. I don't want to die, please, not like this,' he began, and then the area around Dalwyn erupted into brilliant light as the crystals flared and the whole area pulsed.

The Mother and Tamul continued to face one another. As Dalwyn flopped about in his death throes, Tamul acknowledged the Mother with a nod and a smile. 'There will be another time,' he said and faded away.

'And I will be waiting,' said the Mother in return.

Dalwyn couldn't focus; he was surrounded by light. Maybe he was going to the Celestial realms and had been forgiven for his evil deeds, or maybe they were healing him and he wasn't dying at all. These were his final thoughts as the five crystals that now made up the elemental heart pulsed and five beams of energy shot up through Dalwyn, blowing him apart as they flowed up and into the chamber of their own element then up farther, shooting into the sky.

The coterie crowded around Ishmael and Jona pressed her shawl onto the worst of his wounds to staunch the blood loss. Zahra limped over and flopped down beside him, grinning.

'We did it, Ishmael,' she said.

The coterie and Latasha were laughing with joy; and the Mother who now shone with golden light, moved between them all, hugging them close one by one. When she took Ishmael in her arms, he felt her energy flow through him as pain exploded up and down his legs and spine, making him gasp, and he knew she had healed his worst wounds.

'You have sacrificed everything in service for me. Thank you, Ishmael Shantari, for being so steadfast in your duty,' she told him before taking Zahra in her arms, who looked overcome with emotion. Finally the Mother turned to Latasha. 'My child without your intervention this world was lost. You have suffered and lost everything, but in the coming days you will have a visitor and know it wasn't for nothing.'

'What do you mean?' Latasha asked, genuinely perplexed. Her question went unanswered as the Mother, who was still radiating golden light, stepped back into the tree and was gone.

Down in the battle for Acclaro the ground began to shake violently without warning, toppling men from siege ladders and Infernals from the castle walls. The tremor was quickly followed by another, and the crystal tower began to pulse, then the sky above the tower blazed with colour as beams of red, green, blue, and white shot up from four visible towers, one at each corner of the structure. All sound suddenly ceased, and many thought they had been struck deaf. The shock from the tremors caused so much mayhem among the attacking and defending forces alike that they broke off the battle and began retreating to their own lines.

There was no further battle that day as the two forces kept their distance while trying to ascertain what had happened. As night fell, news began to spread across the Glyph and the forces still amassed there as well as in Acclaro where the Infernal forces stood manning the walls lest another attack came. The coterie had succeeded and magic had returned to the world.

Of the magic there was no physical sign, just an energy that seemed to hang in the air. The four towers of light stood shining into the heavens but the amassed armies didn't leave the Glyph. there was still work to do and clear out Acclaro to regain the capital from the Infernals.

Chapter 59

The earth's shaking woke Zacriel from his prison within the iron cage that Lilith had placed him. The cage hung from the sky walk from long chains and swung violently as the shaking continued, which made the cage also spin. The cage was a form of torture itself, able to be adjusted to fit a person inside then pulled tighter around them until they were squashed in tightly.

Zacriel had spent less than one night in the damn device, and now his muscles began to spasm, once again making him want to scream as the cramps returned. The spin of the cage gave him a chance to look in the direction of the crystal tower where he had been able to get Nina, Latasha, and the coterie to safety. If it hadn't been for the assassin he would have still been safe there among them, but in truth he had been foolish to expect them to welcome the Bone Lord in. After all, he had spent much time trying to kill Ishmael and Zahra. The battle at the door of the tower hadn't given anyone time for them to know he was now a friend not an enemy, but at least the coterie were there now and, more importantly, Nina was safe.

Through the morning sky, Zacriel could see four beams of coloured light that reached up into the heavens from the crystal tower. They had done it. The coterie had successfully united and used the crystals. Zacriel's hearing faded, taking with it the creaking of his chains along with his panting from the excruciating pain that wracked his body. He spat blood that welled in his mouth, and that sent new tremors of pain flooding through him as his tongue touched the exposed nerves of broken teeth from when Lilith kicked them in outside the tower.

Zacriel couldn't say how long the strange silence lasted, but he actually enjoyed the reprieve from the sounds of battle and the cawing of damn ravens as they had circled him waiting for his death so they could peck out his eyes.

Soon the noise of the city returned to assault his ears once more. Throughout the next few chimes he watched as the attackers pulled away from the capital and battle ceased. The turn of the cage now had him facing the castle itself, which was how he was able to notice a sickly-green light from the site of the old castle that had been salted long ago to stop the nest of Infernals that had hidden in the capital from continuing to spawn. That site had also been one of the gates to the Infernal realms. If what he was seeing was real it meant that the gate was open again and the Infernals at last had a way out of this world.

Once not so long ago Zacriel had dreamt of this moment when the gates reopened so he would be able to finally go there for reward for his despicable acts of evil. There was little chance of that now he was caged here to the sky walk.

The afternoon wore on, and he watched as others discovered the gate had opened, but nobody came for him. Night fell as he dozed only to be wakened again and again from the pain of muscles fighting against their cramped positions.

Movement came from the sky walk above him, and the cage was dragged up to smash twice against the railing of the walk where it shook the cage violently. Quail stared down at him.

'Hello, my little bird, I have come to grant you freedom,' the Infernal lord hissed, and the locks to the cage swung open, spilling Zacriel to the walk way.

'Where are you taking me?' he managed to say.

'To see your wish granted, of course, Zacriel. The gates have opened and we return to the Infernal Lands just as you always wanted.

You are mine now, a gift from Lilith herself, and I wouldn't dare leave my prize possession behind when I have endless cycles to torment you ahead, now would I?' said Quail in his broken common speech, then he began laughing as his Infernals dragged Zacriel along behind them.

Chapter 60

Ishmael heard the sounds of laughter outside his chamber. He glanced over to where Zahra lay on a cot beside him. Their wounds had been bad, but with the healing from the Mother as well as the astute care of battle healers, they were on the mend now. Zahra was struggling to sit up. She had a bandage across the forehead where dark bruising still showed, and her left arm was strapped across her chest.

'You look terrible,' Ishmael said, and Zahra laughed then held her ribs with her free hand, grimacing in pain.

'Don't make me laugh,' she scolded him. 'Anyway, I still look better than you with all the holes you let Dalwyn poke into you.'

Nina came skipping around the corner and squealed in delight. 'Finally, you are both awake. I thought you were going to sleep forever.'

'I feel like I want to,' said Ishmael.

'Well I didn't save you so you can laze about, Ishmael,' Nina said, sitting beside him.

'You saved him twice, Nina,' Zahra reminded the girl. 'I'm beginning to wonder who the child is and who the adult is,' Zahra added before laughing again at Ishmael's scowl.

'If this is how it's going to be with you two I think I would have been better off dead,' Ishmael grumbled, and Nina kissed him on the forehead.

'I can't stay long. I am going with Raul into Acclaro to see what can be salvaged from the great library,' Nina said, then at Ishmael's alarmed look added, 'Don't worry, the city has been free of Infernals for two days now since the gates opened and they left to the Infernal lands. Latasha says the coterie must be ready for lessons soon that will teach us our duties and what it means to be the bearers of the different elements.'

Ishmael knew that of course. As he had been recovering, his rest had been filled with dreams from the Mother. Now the magic was returned it was time to learn what this elemental tower was actually for so balance could be restored. As with the Severing, the return of magic would create upheaval across the world, which meant there would be much more to do, and he was determined to be ready for that.

That night they assisted him along with Zahra down to the main hall where long tables had been prepared for a feast. The hall was filled with excited conversation, and Ishmael could see among the throng of people, coterie and Latasha. He didn't recognize many of the other people but was informed by Onyx that they were leaders of the nations among other influential people who would play a large part in turning the tower into a centre of knowledge.

Ishmael ate sparingly as many people engaged him in conversation, congratulating him on his and the coterie's achievement, which left him feeling embarrassed. They had only done what they must, no more, and others had sacrificed more than he or the coterie. But to know he had played his part was satisfying, and looking about at his friends, seeing their happiness after nearly a cycle of hard times, made him happy. For the first time in many cycles he felt like he truly belonged and had a home as well as a family again.

Later that evening after most guests had retired to rest, Ishmael sat with Jona, Selene, and Raul enjoying wine. Close by Latasha and Zahra clapped a beat as Nina danced a whirling series of moves her mother had taught her. A figure came into sight walking slowly into the hall, and Ishmael saw Latasha suddenly go still. Then she screamed and rushed forward to embrace him, another Ancient like herself. He would learn later he was named Drey and had been one of Latasha's people she had helped save along with the Kenzu lord Haakon. His return meant that the continuation of the Ancient race was a reality.

When Ishmael returned to his own bed, Latasha, Drey, and Zahra were still deep in conversation. Nina curled up beside him, and as Ishmael stroked her hair he was overcome with emotion for this amazing young girl. She was one of the true hero's.

Chapter 61

From the top of the elemental tower the golden light of dawn was just glazing the horizon as Ishmael pushed himself through the dance of creation. When he completed it, sweat dripped down his face and soaked his clothes. He was feeling much stronger now. He reached for water then noticed he wasn't alone. Zahra sat watching him.

'I didn't hear you come in,' he said between deep breaths.

'I'm good at staying undetected when I want to be,' Zahra replied with a smile, tweaking the corner of her mouth though she looked solemn.

'What's wrong, Zahra?' Ishmael, asked feeling concerned now.

'There is nothing wrong. I just came to tell you I'm leaving for a while, but not forever.'

'Where will you go? '

'There is the matter of the Kenzu. I am still one of them, and with Haakon's death we must meet to elect a new lord,' Zahra said, moving over beside Ishmael.

'Will it be you?'

Zahra's laugh bubbled up then burst and washed over Ishmael. He loved her laugh.

'What, a woman lead the Kenzu? I think not,' Zahra said.

'They could do much worse than you, Zahra,' Ishmael replied after drinking more water.

Zahra shrugged. 'Maybe they could, though I'm not sure if I will even continue on the path of the Kenzu. With the changes in the world we may not be needed, and Aeon has asked me to stay here to be sentinel of the elemental tower. I have much to think on and need the time and space to sort out what I want. I just came to say goodbye and tell you that you are a rare man, Ishmael. I am happy you have finally found your place. After all we have been through together, I just wanted you to know that.'

Ishmael embraced Zahra and squeezed her tightly.

'When you have finished what you must do, return to me here. There is always a place for you among us, you know that, don't you, Zahra?' Ishmael said feeling his words choke in his throat.

'I will, and that's a promise I can keep,' Zahra replied. Then she walked away, leaving Ishmael to marvel at the beautiful sunrise of a new day with fresh hope and work to do.

THE END.